Miss Bubbles Steals the Show

MAIN

Miss Bubbles
Steals the Show

Melanie Murray

RED
DRESS
INK
™

First edition July 2005

MISS BUBBLES STEALS THE SHOW

A Red Dress Ink novel

ISBN 0-373-89527-5

Author photo by Ron Williams.

www.RedDressInk.com

Printed in U.S.A.

F
mur

b16791010

Acknowledgments

These are the people whose patience, support,
and advice made this acknowledgments page possible:

The members of the Little Red Writing Group, without whom I'd
still be sitting in a four-by-four room moaning to the wall,
"But what am I gonna *do?*": Mari Brown (the mastermind of
our little group), Savannah Conheady and Ingrid Ducmanis,
with a special thanks to Elise Miller for also helping with the
post-writing job of getting published. Also, big thanks to
Rebecca Traister for writing about us in the *New York Observer*
and to Heather Cabot for bringing our story to ABC news.

Of the many wonderful things Kevin Costner has taught us,
my favorite is that if you build it, they will come.
Well, I wrote this, and then a dynamic group of people
entered my life: Tara Mark and Jennifer Unter at RLR Literary,
and Farrin Jacobs and the crew at Red Dress Ink,
who have all supported *Miss Bubbles* without hesitation.

I must thank my amazing mentor, Beth de Guzman,
who has taught me everything I know about the publishing
business. And thanks to Michele Bidelspach, Kristen Weber,
Karen Kosztolnyik and all the other people at Warner who have
made this moonlighting job of mine seem perfectly acceptable.

When I was about twenty, I met a group of people
who, over the years, kept me going, in various small
and large ways. I don't have enough skill to articulate the
debt of gratitude I owe Lindsay Genshaft, Dan Maceyak,
Leila Nelson, Meg Pryor and Courtney Young. And of course,
without Sam "Delphinita" Lawrence and everyone else who spent
even a night at 150 Sullivan, there'd be no basis for *Miss Bubbles*.

Finally, I must thank Chris, who made me write
when I didn't want to, and Ramona, the best bulldog
in all of Brooklyn. She's not a cat and she can't whistle,
but nevertheless, she's my little superstar.

For Christopher

Chapter 1

I peel my eyes open through what feels like layers of dried alcohol, stare at the ceiling and try to ignore two pressing issues.

Issue number one: I'm hungover. My mouth is puckered dry and mossy. My temples are throbbing and my stomach is in knots and I've overslept. But I don't have to be anywhere today, so that's a good thing. I can lounge in my apartment and nurse my aching body. All I need is a glass of water. Yeah, some hydration will really help my situation. Then I can plan the recuperative events of the day. But there's this other, small thing I have to take care of first.

Issue number two: no matter how hard I try to pretend that I *am,* it is becoming increasingly apparent that I am *not* alone in my bed. Nope. Not alone. Not alone at all. Somebody with me. Somebody I don't know, penning me in against the wall, making it impossible to get up without waking him. I hold my breath and remain perfectly still so as to keep him sleeping, as if he's some sort of monster who might gobble me up if he's disturbed. From my rigid position against the wall, I sneak furtive glances at him.

Okay. I definitely don't know him. Not good. Not only that, I have no clue how he ended up here, in my bed, but it's pretty clear that he's not wearing any clothes. I lift my sheet, peek underneath and sure enough, I'm not wearing any clothes, either. This is where panic begins to bubble like a hot spring. Okay, Stella. Think. Ransack that memory of yours for any clue, any inkling of what happened last night.

Let's see, let's see…. I vaguely remember sitting on the sofa in my living room at around eight-thirty last night, commiserating with my cat, Miss Bubbles, over my pathetic existence while watching a recorded episode of *Oprah* and getting down to business with a pint of Ben & Jerry's Phish Food. I remember Steve, my roommate of six years, coming into the apartment with his polite boyfriend Peter, and telling me to stop sulking and to go out and have some fun already. That's it! I knew this was going to be Steve's fault! And Michaela's, too. That's right! I went to Hell's Bar, the favorite haunt of Hell's Kitchen society, and slurped free chocolate martinis courtesy of my good friend and most reliable enabler, Michaela. You're on the right track, Stella! Think, what happened next? I take a deep breath and focus my thoughts. Nothing else is coming to me.

Except the sound of a distant, wailing whimper, coming from underneath my bed. Very carefully, I twist my head around and try to stick my face down between the bed and the wall. A furry white paw pokes up and reaches toward me. "Miss Bubbles." I whisper this loud enough to get my cat's attention but quiet enough to keep the beast snoring. Miss Bubbles peers at me through the darkness and attempts to wedge her nose through the narrow space by the bed frame. "Miss Bubbles, who is this guy?" She mews urgently and bats at my nose with her paw. She doesn't know, either. "Okay. Stay down there, Miss Bubbles. We'll be okay." I push her away from the bed. She yelps in response.

I turn back to my guest and search his body for a clue. He's

got a fairly deep sleep going on—I can tell by the nose whistle, the stomach growlies and the symphonic snoring—so I prop
myself up on my elbow and try desperately to read something
in the freckle pattern on his tanned, slight back. I'm staring and
staring and staring, but nothing is being jogged in my memory. I collapse onto the bed, letting a large mental scream erupt
in my brain.

"STELLA!" In moments of extreme stress, Marlon Brando's
voice always screams in my head. "STELLA." Then my own
voice starts in on a rant. "Stella Aurora Monroe—you have *got*
to stop this. You're twenty-five years old! Good work this time!
You *blacked* out and brought somebody *home* with you. *Nice.*
What is that? The fourth guy in four weeks? Well, Happy New
Year to you, you *slut!*"

I stare at the ceiling, defeated. This is it. This is the rock bottom I've been careening toward since my Christmastime
breakup with Joshua. I wonder if waking up with a naked
stranger is the crown jewel in my failure of a life or if I could
possibly still be on a descent. Let's see. No acting jobs lined up
so I'm forced to cater waiter for meager subsistence wages, I've
been in the same ratty apartment for the past six years, got exactly $74.18 in the old bank account and, if I go by the at-least-
two-date rule, no boyfriend. Yup. Four for four. And now I'm
officially promiscuous. So that's good. And to think I broke up
with Joshua on the moral ground that any boyfriend of mine
couldn't have a pregnant wife. Morals. Ha!

A surge of disgust rises into my throat and I quickly poke
the sleeping monster-slash-stranger in the back.

"Hey!" The shrillness of my own voice is enough to cut
glass. "Hey, wake up. You have to wake up now."

The stranger rolls over, stretches, yawns and tries to kiss me.
"Hey you. How are you?" he says sleepily. His movement causes
the sheet to slip off of his body. He's really naked.

I jerk my head away. "Yeah, not so good. Who are you? Actually, never mind, you have to go home now." Then I jump

out from my corner and sail over him, like an Olympic hurdler, and land on the floor, all the while clutching the sheet to my body. "You have to go." I look at him, get disgusted all over again and then avert my eyes, staring at the dramatic pink stripes on my wall. I desperately grab at the first pile of clothes I see and run for the bathroom.

The door locks behind me and I turn on the faucet. The running water should cool my nerves and maybe the stranger will have the good decency to leave while I'm in here. I let out a deep sigh, my stomach gurgling all the while, and raise my eyes to the mirror, half-afraid of what's awaiting me. It's worse than I feared. My brown eyes look laden with mud, sacks of sleeplessness and smudged mascara bogging them down in black seas of hungover filth. My hair, which on a good day has a natural lilt that frames my face in a pleasing manner, hangs limply, brown and plain and lifeless. There's a dirty, chocolate-brown stain smeared across my right cheek—the remainder of my beauty mark. Who knows why I still apply this to my face every day, it's not like my mother is in town to catch me without it on. But it reminds me of her, reminds me of the mornings when I was a kid getting ready for school in Michigan. She'd curl my hair and pencil in the beauty mark, and tell me that Madonna had one, too.

I dig my pressed four-cloverleaf pendant out of a knotted section of my hair, and make my daily wish.

My pendant is my lucky charm. Every day since I was thirteen, I have held the pendant tightly in my left hand, whispered "Today's the day," three times, held my breath for ten seconds and then kissed it. I don't know what happens when the day finally does come, the day when my Prince Charming plucks me from obscurity and makes me a star. Maybe I'll have to change my mantra? Or retire it? Oh, well, I can cross that bridge when I get there.

I release the clover from my hand, scrub my face so hard it feels like layers of skin are coming off, put on my clothes and press my ear against the bathroom door, listening for any sign that the stranger's left. Unbelievable. He's singing to himself. The gurgle in my stomach churns loud enough to be audible to my outer ear. Pounding my head on the bathroom door, I vow to never drink again and to immediately cease contact with Michaela and Steve and all other bad influences. Excommunicating Steve from my life will be slightly difficult, as he does share the apartment with me, but I'll have to find a way. Immediately after breakfast, I will begin work on a clean new life—as soon as this guy is G-O-N-E gone.

I slowly open the bathroom door and peer around the pink-painted corner to see. There he is, reclining in resplendent glory, taking in the rays of sunshine peeking through the window above the bed, and hardly in any rush to vacate. I tiptoe up to the door frame and poke my head into my bedroom, keeping my body well hidden behind the wall.

"Um, hi. You really have to go."

"I'm going, I'm going." He gets out of bed and I feel a small blush color my face. In other circumstances I might be able to find him cute. His body is pretty nice to look at, actually, tan and thin and completely bare, and as he stretches up toward the low ceiling, his torso looks good enough to lick. Unfortunately the very sight of him reminds me of how low I've sunk and therefore there will be no licking, nor any frivolous, no-strings attached sex. "What's your rush?" He flashes a toothy grin at me.

"I have somewhere to be, an audition in a half hour," I lie easily as I enter the room and search the floor for my bag. "I'll walk out with you."

"Oh, that's right. Michaela said you were some kind of actress."

Aha! I knew this was Michaela's fault! "Yes, I am some kind of actress," I bristle.

"What have you been in? Anything I would know?"

Now, I grimace. At the question. To suffer the humiliation

of being asked the question in my own home is entirely more than I can bear. "Do you know anything about the theater scene?"

"No."

"Then I haven't done anything you would know." By this time the naked stranger has put on his pants and shoes and is buttoning up his shirt. "Hey, your mom called."

"What?"

"Just now. She left a message." His words are barely out of his mouth when the phone rings again. No doubt my mother, who always keeps calling until I answer, the only reason (besides utter lack of funds) I have yet to purchase a cell phone. I spy the cordless nestled in the clothes pile on my overstuffed furry pink bedroom chair, and grab it, "Hello?" I say without enough breath.

"Star Baby." This is her nickname for me.

"Hi, Mommy. I can't really talk right now."

"Okay, I just wanted to let you know that I bought the pattern for Gwyneth Paltrow's Oscar dress. I put it in the mail yesterday."

This stops me dead in my tracks. "Mom, which dress? Not the black one. It's kind of awful, don't you think?"

"No, no, silly—the one she wore when she *won*. Except you'll look much prettier in it. You really have the chest for it."

"Oh, um. Great! But Mom, let me call you later? I really have to go right now."

"No problem, Star Baby. Oh, I also put in clippings of a white pantsuit that Jennifer Garner wore to a charity event in L.A., the address of the store where J-Lo gets all her candles and the vet where Meg Ryan takes her dog. Are you going to an audition today?"

"Yes." Lies. I am going to hell. Not passing go. Just straight to hell.

"Okay. Love you, Stella. Knock 'em dead."

I click off, toss the phone back onto the pile of clothes and turn my attention to the stranger, who by this time is sitting with his legs outstretched on my bed, and thumbing through one of my *Cosmo*s. I snatch it out of his hand and forcefully say, "Let's go."

"Wait." He peers up and languidly asks, "Do you have any orange juice or a muffin maybe? Michaela said you were a really good cook." This guy is totally pushing his luck.

"No. Nothing. Let's go."

"Okay. Well, it was nice meeting you. Maybe I'll see you at Hell's again."

"Um, yeah, maybe you will."

Like a border collie, I herd him out of the bedroom and down the single step that separates my room from the living room and the rest of the apartment. Groggy with sleep, he trips into the clear glass coffee table before I can warn him and steps on Miss Bubbles, who's miraculously made it out from under the bed. She lets out a strangled, bloodcurdling, screechy cat-scream and then whistles at him, a low, mean, clear whistle that scares him out of his skin. He tumbles onto the orange plaid couch and she spits at him before running back underneath my bed.

"What the hell is that?" His face is ashen.

"That's Miss Bubbles. She whistles."

"Fucked up." He nods and nods and makes no move to stand up.

"I don't really have time to discuss my cat's peculiarities, so let's go!" I grab him by the collar of his shirt, yank him to his feet and hustle him out of the apartment door into the hallway, following close on his heels to make sure he leaves. Thank God that I live on the first floor and don't have to contend with getting him down any stairs. Only a few more feet, now, and then I can put this whole sordid episode behind me. But my plans for a quick getaway are ruined in the most cruel, unusually punishing way imaginable.

By Christian.

Christian Porter is my upstairs neighbor and my sworn enemy. First of all, this guy rivals Steve for anal retentiveness but undisputedly wins in the annoying department. Which wouldn't affect me in the least if my apartment building wasn't like two hundred years old with walls as thin as paper. I know his schedule by heart, because I've been listening to it for five years. Five hundred jumping jacks at 7:45 a.m., running at 8:15, vacuum at 9:30, shower at 9:40, than the godforsaken *typing* from 10:15 until I'm driven from my apartment to escape the headache-inducing thud-thud-thud of those "real writers use old-fashioned typewriters" keys. Second, and most importantly, there was the Incident of 2000. The one where I threw a welcome-to-the-neighborhood party for me and Steve, and Christian called the cops and almost got me arrested. Steve claims that he doesn't remember this, but I think he's forcing amnesia because Christian, if the light hits him just right, is kind of good-looking and Steve likes to be friends with anybody who's good-looking.

Right now Christian is walking from the vestibule with his mail. I should have checked the clock because he always gets the mail exactly at noon and is by far the last person I would want to see in a situation like this. He's snooty and condescending and is always making nasty digs about me and alluding to my poor choice in boyfriends. And seeing me corral some skinny stranger out the door in the early afternoon is going to make his day. He doesn't have time to make a crass comment though, because before he sees us coming, the formerly naked stranger, who can't stop fixing the buttons on his shirt long enough to look where he's going, walks right into him. I roll my eyes at his clumsiness. Christian jumps back and looks up, a slow smile crawling onto his face. His blue eyes laugh at me from behind his glasses, and his smile brightens the dimples in his cheeks like Christmas tree lights. I want to punch those dimples off his face.

"Well, well, well. If it isn't Ms. Stella Aurora and one of her, um, friends. How do you do?" He shakes the stranger's hand and continues smiling.

"Christian, cut it out. I'm late."

"No way! You? Late?"

He chortles, mumbles a goodbye and laughs as he makes his way up the stairs. Normally I'd stop to brood, but there's no time. This stranger needs evicting fast. I literally push him outside, follow and turn to close the front door behind us. A blast of late winter air slaps my face as we stand in front of the building and stare at each other awkwardly. We have nothing to say. I nod and he nods before finally turning and walking down the street and hopefully out of my life forever.

I take a deep breath and rest against the door. Everything so normal—a regular afternoon in midtown Manhattan. Cabs idle in the street, mothers push baby carriages, tourists wander around with their chins tilted to the sky and the theater marquees clustered around Ninth Avenue reflect the noontime sunlight. A huge Coca-Cola truck unloads its wares in front of the deli on the corner. All the people walking by don't notice me at all. Yes—a normal day on 47th Street—nobody aware of my transgression. I guess sometimes anonymity is a *good* thing. I let out a deep sigh and turn to face the giant stone angel perched above the entryway to my building. Her face looms serenely overhead.

"Thanks for watching out for me," I whisper, trusting my voice to float up to her ear. I kiss my hand and place it at her feet—another superstitious act I can't stop. For a moment I consider going back inside, but walk the other way and mutter to myself. I mutter about mending my ways all the way to Hell's Bar.

Fifteen minutes later, I'm sitting at a wooden table, stabbing the foam on my latte with a spoon, waiting for Michaela to finish with her customers so I can give her a piece of my mind. People are milling past me, pushing into the red velvet depths of Hell's. Abandon all hope, I think to myself as my anger at Michaela melts into disappointment in myself. How has this happened? Again? How many times am I going to let the party get out of hand, then wake up the next morning feeling nauseous and not quite knowing who slept in my bed with me? How many times am I going to break my resolutions to mend my ways? It's been more than six weeks since my breakup and all I've done since New Year's is carouse in the name of my newfound singlehood. And each time I make myself a promise to behave, I break it faster than you can say "loose woman." Even now, I vowed to go home, clean my apartment, check the chorus call ads and maybe work on getting some auditions, yet here I am sitting in a bar and leisurely enjoying an early afternoon coffee.

"Here's some toast, sweetie." Michaela floats over to my side and rests her head against mine. Her blond hair tumbles into my lap as she wraps her arms around my waist. "Don't feel so good?"

"I feel okay." I want to direct my grumpiness at her but can't. "Just frustrated."

A busboy interrupts us to tell Mic a table needs something, so she releases her grip on my waist and trots off. She looks fantastic, the Hell's regulation black tank top and skirt fit her perfectly, making her legs look longer than they are, if that's possible. She looks like a Viking goddess, standing over her customers' table, beaming that peaceful smile, disarming them with her grace and magnificence. I should be more like her. Nothing ever fazes her—happy, hopeful Michaela. That's actually what attracted me to her when we first met: me an irritable, impatient waitress-in-training, she an unflappable, calming trainer. We hit it off immediately, and she's been talking me down ever since.

I take a bite of toast and stare at my surroundings. Hell's Bar looks so different during the day, almost studious. There are two big, bright windows in the front, windows covered by thick red velvet curtains at night. During the day, though, the sunlight streams in, illuminating noontime conversations and brunches and bound volumes of poetry. During the day the place is crowded with student types: young intellectuals, actors, musicians, self-employed "entrepreneurs." They are all lounging around the oak tables, with their heads bent over their books or laptops, stopping their work to offer passersby a flyer for their upcoming show or gig or party. There's a large corkboard tacked up against the back wall for just such an exchange of information, and more than once I've found my own phone number underneath a caption that says, Monologue Coach, or Cat-sitter, or Need To Talk? written in Michaela's fine hand. Michaela is always trying to help her friends.

Take last night. She seems to think that meeting her boyfriend Carlo's musician friends will make me forget my money woes. Since New Year's there's been a parade of boyfriend possibilities. First there was Jess, the drummer who liked to date men as well as women; then there was Jack, a singer who claimed his mom slept with Jim Morrison; there was Mike the guitar player who on our second date played me eight songs he'd written for his ex-girlfriend; and now there was the nameless naked man who almost broke my cat's paw. Michaela means well but I'm beginning to hate myself for falling into her traps so easily. I know enough to know that one-night stands and short-lived flirtations aren't going to solve my problems. I need to meet a man of influence. A real man of influence, not a guy like Joshua who made promises and dazzled me with fancy trips and gifts but in the end stayed where he was. I need someone with connections who will see that I am special and will introduce me to a world of possibility and wonder. Where the hell is he anyway?

I stop to calculate how many Wall Street bars I've searched for my prince when I remember the ugly truth—I've been in this city for almost, oh my God! For *seven* years. Seven years of schlepping from one restaurant job to the next, seven years of carrying my life around in my bag going from audition to audition, seven years of scrambling for money, seven years of pointless, meandering relationships. Seven years of chocolate martini hangovers. Seven years and nothing to show for it. No love, no money, no career. No faith. Maybe I'm not getting my act together because I don't think it will lead anywhere. I put my head in my hands and wonder if my mother ever felt this way when she was in New York. She mentioned going through some lean times, when she was first trying to get dancing jobs. But never once in all the stories she's told has she ever talked about hopelessness. Christ! She made this town seem like a tower of possibility, or else I never would've moved here in the first place.

"You're paying for that toast, right?" Speaking of a noninfluential man, Michaela's boss, Rodrigo, sidles up to the table and pokes me in the ribs with his forefinger.

"Yes, yes. I'm paying for the toast," I mumble with my mouth full.

He drapes a beefy, muscled arm over the back of Michaela's chair. "So when are you going out with me?"

"When you can get me an agent. Then I'll go out with you." Rod and I have this routine. He asks me out, I say no. He asks me if I'm paying for my orders. I say yes. We both know the truth, but have fun sticking to the script. He clicks his tongue to the roof of his mouth, tousles my hair (which sends my head echoing into spasms) and shuffles off.

"All right, honey," says Michaela as she plops down and zeroes her sea-green eyes on me. "I have five minutes."

"What do you want to know? I went home with him, I woke up not remembering his name—"

"Ned."

"*Ned?*"

"Ned—I knew you guys would get along great. I checked your birth charts. You're compatible, astrologically speaking."

"Michaela! I don't need an astrologically sound one-night stand!" I drop my head to the table and start to moan. "Oh, I'm in trouble. Trouble."

She giggles. "Silly Stella. You're just having fun!"

"Michaela. The time for fun is over. Do you know that I haven't been to one audition in over six months? Six months!"

"Well, why don't you ask Steve if he can help you out?"

I love her but God does she not get the business. "Michaela, Steve cannot help me. Okay? We're not at the same level. He's JV, I'm Little League. Less than Little League. T-Ball. I can't ask him for help. I just have to jump-start things on my own."

"Well there you go, sweetie." She grabs for my latte and takes a sip. "You can just start going out on calls again. You had lots of success before."

Before. Before Joshua made me quit the theater group I was working with. Before I started skipping auditions to meet Joshua at hotel suites. Before I was too busy trying to figure Josh out to care about my career.

An exhale of breath slips from my lungs and I say slowly, more to my latte than to Michaela, "Remember when you met me? Remember what I used to be like? How I'd just hang out at Sardi's hoping to meet Bernadette Peters? Or in the doorway of the Nederlander offices hoping to meet a big producer?"

"Yeah. You'd pretend to smoke."

"What happened to that girl? Huh? When I first moved here I was so sure that somebody would discover me, drop me into a Broadway show and just make all the hardships go away. I was supposed to be bicoastal by now."

"Well, honey. You have to do that for yourself."

My stomach does a samba. She's right. Today is the day. Today is the day that I start changing things. Start going after acting jobs. Start looking for that man who is going to make my career happen. The day I say adios to Michaela's boy-toys and start living my mother's dream.

"I gotta go." I jump off the stool, kiss Michaela's forehead and run out the door.

Chapter 2

When I was little, my mother would lull me off to sleep with her stories of New York. Of being a working dancer, of fancy parties with wealthy men, of beautiful costumes and brilliant light displays. The costumes were my favorite part. In the afternoons after school, I would kneel beside her old trunks and pull out each relic of her former life. I loved to touch the soft fabrics, to catch my reflection in the sequins and to inhale the sweet mingled scent of perspiration and perfume.

Once, when I was six, I stole my favorite treasure from her trunk, a single silver ostrich feather. In my child's imagination the feather was magical, and I thought if I slept with it underneath my pillow, surely my dreams would float up to heaven where a special angel would hear them and make them come true. I slept with that feather every night for three whole years, sure that I'd wake up in a real bedroom in a big house, and that there'd be a father there to take care of me and my mom. I still have that feather taped above my bed.

But my mother didn't only tell *her* stories. She'd tell my story. What was going to happen.

"Stella means star. I named you that for a reason, and someday you'll shine brighter than bright, and be as famous as I've ever dreamed of being."

This particular sentence echoed in my head when I got home from Hell's, and found the clippings she'd sent. I had J-Lo's candle store in one hand and Gwyneth's dress pattern in the other, when Miss Bubbles came limping out from under my bed, mewing her head off. That's when I got the brilliant idea of how to get things rolling.

"I'm here for an eleven o'clock appointment. The name is Miss Bubbles."

The dark-skinned lady behind the counter peers up from a stack of medical folders and stares at me quizzically. I mentally run through my outfit to make sure it's worthy of a rich and famous-pet vet's waiting room: today's power ensemble includes my absolute favorite jacket, red suede with the cowboy fringe, over a blue baby tee and some slim-fitting Jordache jeans, my red snakeskin cowboy boots and long dangly gold earrings that sit neatly in the lilt of my long brown hair. The outfit is topped off with a pair of oversize sunglasses that make me look as if I belong in a seventies after-school special. Steve nodded his approval on my way out the door and said, "Very Jodie Foster à la *Taxi Driver,* without all the emotional baggage. Or the blond hair." And Miss Bubbles, who is nestled comfortably in the red suede bag hanging at my hip, looks good, too. I put her in a faux diamond-studded collar. It makes her long white fur look as if it reflects light. So why am I nervous? Miss Bubbles and I look fantastic! And, might I add, on a budget! (I'm very proud to say that, thanks to the Salvation Army store on 58th Street, nothing I own costs more than twenty dollars. Except for the jacket, which was a present from Joshua and which I refuse to give away on principle. I earned this thing! Believe me.)

Anyway, even in thrift-store duds, Miss Bubbles and I are sure to catch the eye of any important person who happens to be here today. Wait a minute, on second thought; the lady behind the counter must think she recognizes me.

"I said—" I slide my eyeglasses down my nose, like they do in the movies, and lean down to smile at her "—that I have an appointment for Miss Bubbles."

The lady squints and her lip curls into an Elvis-like sneer. "I heard you. Take a seat and the doctor will be right with you."

Hmm. Not as receptive to my charm as I'd like. Perhaps the constant in and out of the famous and their sick pets have dulled this woman's fascination with celebrities. But no matter. There will, no doubt, be bigger fish to fry. I came here with a mission, and a mission I shall accomplish. I hope.

So time to check out the waiting room, this waiting room that has seen the likes of Meg Ryan's dog. I turn from the desk and set my eye on what could quite possibly be the most nicely furnished room I've ever been in. I guess this is what you get in the way of Upper East Side veterinary offices. We've got some leather couches, soft lighting, irises and lilies in clever ceramic flowerpots that seem to sprout from the wall and expressionist paintings of what I assume are animals. Oh, and this whole place smells like the back room of the Magnolia Bakery. Sweet, vanilla, scrumptious. No trace of animal stench. My mother wasn't kidding. This is definitely the place to be.

But my eyes immediately focus on an unfamous, unhandsome man in a brown corduroy suit. His shirt is beige and has a large purple stain on the front. A small Jack Russell terrier is bouncing from his lap to the floor to his lap again. He looks entirely perplexed and keeps cooing, "Chester, please behave." This absolutely won't do. Surely there are better connection candidates than this? Chester the terrier begins to flirt with a miniature poodle, whose equally as miniature owner totally ignores her. She's busy flipping through a script, or something that looks an awful lot like a script. No doubt the blueprint to the next Broadway hit or Hollywood blockbuster. Bull's-eye! I can't believe that I ever, even for a second, doubted my mother's logic and head straight for the empty seat next to the script reader. I push past the Jack Russell, who by this time has begun circling my legs as if I were a tree, yelping up at Miss Bubbles to climb down and play.

"Is this seat taken?" I deepen my voice to sound like an important person.

The woman barely looks up, but manages to communicate with a dismissive wave of her hand that it is not. I plop down next to her; situate Miss Bubbles on my lap, and position myself so that discreetly reading over the lady's shoulder is possible. This woman is impeccably dressed, in clothes that probably cost three times more than my monthly rent. She smells nice, too. I inch over toward her and deeply inhale. Yep, pure, designer, a thousand-dollar-bottle of perfume heaven. Then, as I cast a sidelong glance at the chunky manuscript in her fashionable lap, the gigantic diamond ring on her finger nearly blinds me. Thank God for my sunglasses, that's all I have to say, and thank God for my luck. I think the script is for a play. I couldn't have planned this better if I'd tried.

While I try to read, Miss Bubbles nestles into my lap, holds her limp, bruised paw out in front of her, and begins to aggressively clean it. Every five licks or so, she stops what she's doing to look up at me and mew. "Miss Bubbles!—" I tear my eyes away from the script "—Don't be a baby! It's almost our turn, then everything will be okay." I pet her head and resume my espionage. The oversize sunglasses allow me to take in whole pages of dialogue without drawing attention to the fact that I am blatantly reading the lady's material. I can't figure out the name of the main character, but apparently he's deeply involved in an affair with the wrong woman. Fantastic! Now that's a part I know how to play! This just keeps getting better and better and oh my God! Steve is never going to believe it when I get home and tell him about being cast in a play while Miss Bubbles waited for her checkup. I bet somebody like Matt Damon is going to play the lead. Steve will go bonkers if I meet Matt Damon. Absolutely driven insane with jealousy. Yep, this has to be it. My big break. I'll get cast in this play, I'll fall in love with Matt Damon, I'll be put on *People*'s best-dressed list and I'll become Revlon's spokesperson. I wonder how much money they'll pay me, and where I should buy my first summer home. Malibu? Or South Beach? My mother does love Florida. Or should I just skip the summer home and go straight for the winter retreat in Jackson Hole? I have lots of thinking to do.

Then, all of a sudden, pandemonium breaks out. With a yelp and a growl, the Jack Russell terrier takes a running leap for Miss Bubbles, who launches into a whistling frenzy and claws my thighs, just seconds before bolting for the corner. Before I know it, there is a rabid dog in my lap and a cacophonous sound in my ears as the other animals in the room squawk and mew and bark. The dog leaps toward Miss Bubbles and chases her from chair to chair, as the purple-stained man pointlessly shouts, "Chester! Bad dog! Bad dog!"

Miss Bubbles vaults from the back of one chair to another, bats the air with her claws, hisses, whistles, then leaps vertically onto one of the wall-mounted flower pots. There's a collective gasp from the humans in the room as Miss Bubbles is suspended in midair for a terrifying moment before hauling herself up and trampling the lilies into a dust of crushed flower petals. Chester runs around in circles, howling up at her and Chester's stained owner runs around in circles chasing him. I shriek, "Miss Bubbles, come down from there!" and she continues to unleash her trademark whistle, low and clear and lasting at least three seconds a pop. Then, finally, the man catches the dog up in his arms, and Miss Bubbles, sensing that the war has been won, hisses, spits and rappels down the wall before dashing for cover. The Jack Russell is so excited by the commotion that he breaks free from the man, begins to jump up and down like he's on a trampoline, and pees on the floor.

This was not my plan for the morning.

"Oh, my God! Chester!"

The nurse rushes out with some towels. The purple-stained man apologizes to everyone within earshot and puts a leash on the dog. I want to sit back and laugh at the entire situation, but am too busy trying to coax Miss Bubbles out from under the couch.

"Oh, now Miss B. Don't whistle. It's all over." Miss Bubbles's face is full of anxiety and she gives me the full brunt of her purple-green gaze before springing out of her hiding spot and shooting across the room. "He didn't mean it, come on, come back. Come back." I corner her in between a potted palm and a magazine rack and then scoop her up into my suede arms. "There, there Miss Bubbles, it's all over. There, there."

She starts to whimper and frenetically lick my arm. Ah Jesus. I can't take a guilt trip from my cat. "What do you want from me? We have to have your foot checked. Now just calm down." I pet her hair as we settle back into the chair and I try to get her to relax. What a disaster. I should know better than to bring her to places like this. Goddamned dog, ruining everything! I was just about to strike up a conversation with the script reader, too. Now how am I supposed to meet Matt Damon? And make Steve jealous? All my efforts. For nothing.

But then, like the sound of a thousand angels singing in heaven, an emerald voice lilts across the space of the waiting room:

"That's quite a cat you have there."

I look up, astonished at the sound of the fancy-looking lady, whose poodle has curled up at her feet, apparently totally unaffected by the recent excitement.

"Uh, yes, she definitely has character. And spunk. Spunk and character, like Mary Tyler Moore." Stop talking, Stella, stop talking.

"How did you teach her to whistle?"

"Oh, um, well, she's always whistled, from the moment I found her. Actually, that's *how* I found her. She was huddled against the side of a building, wrapped around herself to keep warm, and just whistling away, begging for someone to take her home."

"So you found her, abandoned?" The script reader leans forward in her chair, folds her hand in the prayer position and nods up and down like a talk-show host. I stare at the rock on her finger as she reaches out and tries to pet Miss Bubbles and wonder how she has the strength to lift her hand. "Wonderful, just wonderful—" Miss Bubbles is way too worked up to allow herself to be petted by a stranger, and tries to climb up my shoulder "—Is she usually well behaved? Can she whistle like that on cue?"

"Miss Bubbles? She's the best! An angel, an absolute angel. And she'll whistle whenever you ask her to." The rapid-fire questions are making me nervous and I start to chew on my upper lip.

"She's a Persian, right?"

Unbelievable. It never would have occurred to me to strike up a conversation about our pets! What a brilliant idea, just the sort of schmoozing that I've never been particularly good at. I have an annoying habit of skipping to the heart of a matter when talking to people of power. Too much aggression, that's what my mother would say, not enough charm. But if she could see me now! Talking with a woman who obviously has connections and money and style, and all about a cat, a cat that my mother hates at that!

"Yes, yes, she's a Persian. And your dog, I love her groom—"

"The reason I ask is that my husband is looking for a white Persian cat."

"He is?" Miss Bubbles's purring warms me through my coat and she rests her head against my neck, still straddled over my shoulder.

"And he won't settle for anything less than remarkable."

I chew my lip vigorously. "I can't give Miss Bubbles away."

The lady throws back her head and laughs like I've just said the funniest thing ever. "Oh, no, no, it is nothing like that. He wants to *hire* a white Persian cat, to be in our next play at the Cherry Lane Theater. He's been looking for weeks and told me to keep my eyes out. Would you be interested in letting your cat do theater?"

My entire body goes numb. I turn my head away from her and stare straight ahead, my gaze finding the receptionist. Breathe. Deep, cleansing breaths, tinged with her gajillion dollar perfume. I came to the famous-people vet to make connections, true. But for *ME,* not for my *CAT!* My mother's voice starts talking in my mind, saying, "Little Star, nothing comes in neat little packages, you know." Right, she's right. Doesn't she always say we have to be fearless and take every opportunity that presents itself? Well, and wait just a minute. I'd get to go to the theater every day. I'd get to be at rehearsals. *I would get to meet the actors and director and producer.* My entire body starts tingling with excitement and an image of me and Matt Damon dancing our first dance as husband and wife, me in Badgley Mischka and him in Ralph Lauren, pops into my mind. *Matt Damon. I will get to meet Matt Damon.* This could be my big break, the big connection, the big thing!

"Yes!" My voice shoots out entirely too loud and Miss Bubbles bats the side of my neck with her paw, annoyed.

"Well, then. I'll let my husband know his search is over." She beams a perfectly even white-toothed smile at me and brings a PalmPilot out of her Fendi bag.

"Your cat is going to be a star!"

As I recite my phone number, a nurse bursts into the waiting room. "Ms. Monroe? We're ready for Miss Bubbles now."

My luck is turning. I can actually feel the *ch-chink* of the gears of my luck grinding to a halt and reversing themselves. My heart is so light that I decide to walk part of the way home. It's a brisk, chilly day, but the February sun is sitting high enough in the sky to lend light to the streets of the Upper East Side. Hot damn, the East Side is so gorgeous! I pull the red oversized handbag from my shoulder to my chest, so that I can show Miss Bubbles, the star to be, the glory of New York City in the daylight. She and I stare down Fifth Avenue. This is a perfect day! A lucky day! I kiss the top of her head.

"Let's walk through the park, Bubbles." She meows.

The lady with the poodle introduced herself as Frances Paine. When she said her name, my heart nearly stopped in my chest. Of course! How hadn't I recognized her? I guess I assumed that people with the fame and good standing of a Frances Paine would never take their own pet into a veterinary office. Wouldn't that be the job of an assistant or something? Well no matter, because there she was. Frances Paine—the poor girl who came from Nothing, Indiana, and ended up marrying into one of the most prominent families in New York. The Paines are society people; they fraternize with the wealthy and flirt with the famous, and basically give every working actor in New York City their paycheck. My mother has kept track of Frances's social exploits since I was a kid, her husband Frederick's, too. Wait until I tell Mom the news!

This is going to seriously make her day. I think she's lost a little faith in me, honestly. I haven't exactly been giving this career of mine the ol' college try in the past few years. And she wasn't what you'd call an avid supporter of my relationship with Joshua, not that she ever said much about it. In the beginning, I thought she would be thrilled to hear that I'd bagged an entertainment lawyer, so I told her all about him, about the elaborate dinners and the moonlight walks and the big expensive presents. But apparently she couldn't get past the "he's married" part. All she would ever say about it was, "Stella Aurora, you were not born to play second fiddle to anyone."

At the time, I just chalked up her lack of enthusiasm to the fact that it made her feel bad, to know that I was living this exciting life while she was stuck in Michigan married to a burly, bumbling plumber and taking care of their stupid baby. Okay, I shouldn't talk trash about my brother. Or my stepfather, for that matter, who is a very nice person and is totally in love with my mom. Though who can blame him? I don't mind saying that my mother is pretty hot for a forty-six-year-old. She may have given up performing when she had me, but she still has a dancer's body and really nice hair. Anyway, a small, petty, obnoxious part of me likes to pretend that my mom's life is exactly the same as when I lived with her.

I clutch at my cloverleaf necklace with my left hand and check to see that Miss Bubbles is doing okay in the bag. Her paw is hanging limply over the side of my purse, (the vet said it would be fine in a few days) and she licks my hand when I pet the top of her head. She's mewing pretty regularly now, begging me to turn toward home, but I'm ignoring her. She's walking through the park and she will like it. She starts batting her paw against my arm. "Oh, come on, Miss B.," I say out loud but low enough so nobody can hear that I'm talking to a cat, "you just got a job today! We have to celebrate!" I continue on the narrow path, taking note of the portrait artists and the pretzel vendors and the street musicians. There's a man by the side of the walkway making balloon animals. A balloon animal will make a serious dent in my $74.18 fortune so I pass him by and promise to come back for a plastic, helium-filled giraffe someday when I have money.

Then it suddenly occurs to me, in a blinding flash, that Miss Bubbles might be paid for her work. Could this be? Can a cat earn a regular salary? My already buoyant good mood springs a notch higher, and I lift Miss Bubbles up and kiss her all over. I begin to dance with her in a circle, letting the music from a busking saxophonist be my soundtrack. I don't care who stops to stare at me. I'm so excited. Connections and money. What a day. Just three days ago I woke up with a stranger in my bed. Now my cat has a job and I have hope. I feel so good, I think about calling Ezra when I get home. Why not?

I haven't spoken with Ezra since ending our professional relationship over a year ago. Ezra Greenblatt, manager, handles burgeoning careers until the people he molds become successful enough to drop him. I met him through Steve, whom he had discovered in an off-off-Broadway musical. He worked with Steve for two whole years, helping him to get two national tours and a commercial. Shortly after the commercial, Steve used his good standing to convince Ezra to meet with me, and then, as soon as I was picked up, Steve dumped him for a high-powered agent. Ezra never complained, though; he knows his place in the food chain.

Signing with Ezra was the best thing that had happened to me since dropping out of school. Getting a manager is an integral step to becoming a professional—without representation, there's virtually no way to audition for film or TV or commercials. And as my mother has said since I was old enough to listen, one good commercial can sustain a theater actress through even the leanest of times. Ezra decided to sign me as soon as he saw one of my old theater company's productions, because he liked my skimpy costumes. He thought my navel would get lots of attention in the industry. One time, when I was complaining about how the business made me feel like a piece of meat, I told this to Joshua. He was so outraged he made me end my relationship with Ezra, even though he was getting me steady auditions and I had just earned enough points to join the Screen Actors Guild.

So the last time I called Ezra, I told him I wasn't interested in working with him anymore. He swore at me and told me I was making a huge mistake; that putting the kibosh on my career for a jealous married boyfriend would not be the wisest decision. I remember being quite indignant with him, I told him it was my life and I could do what I wanted.

But as I'm walking home on this chilly morning, I think that calling him would be the perfect way to officially get my career heated up again. I can tell him that Miss Bubbles is going to be in the new Paine outing and, once his greedy little heart is throbbing to the Paine name, I'll ask if he would consider sending me out on auditions.

By the time I reach my front door, any doubts about the proper course of action have been erased. I let myself into the apartment, empty the grateful cat out of my bag, take off my suede jacket and make a beeline for the phone.

I punch in his number without even having to look it up. It rings just three times, then...

"Ezra Greenblatt." A cottony voice answers the phone. I know it well.

"Hi, Nancy," I say. "Is Ezra around? It's Stella Monroe."

"Stella! Jeez, where have you been? How's Steve doing?"

"He's fine, I'm fine. Listen, is Ezra there? Or can I leave him a message?"

"Hold on." I hold on for what seems like five minutes. What's happening? Is he refusing to talk me? Is he swearing so loudly about me that Nancy can't get away and come back to the phone? Did he hear my name and have a coronary? My resolve starts to melt away, like sizzling butter in a pan. Maybe this isn't such a good idea. Maybe he's going to make this difficult.

But then I hear, on the other line, "Stel-La!" I'd forgotten how annoying his Brando imitation is. "Stel-La! What's up kid?"

I'm a little shocked. I'd prepared to plead my case, but he seems fairly friendly and I didn't come up with a strategy for dealing with nice. I panic for a millisecond before deciding to try a little dose of honesty.

"Well, I'm ready to return to work. Would you be interested in working with me again?"

"You still the same body size?" His voice booms through the phone. I hold it an inch from my ear.

"Yes. Five pounds thinner, in fact."

"Hot. How's your hair?"

"Same color, a little longer."

"Well, okay. Get new headshots and send 'em my way."

"New headshots?" My heart slips into my boots. Pictures can cost nearly a grand. Again, I improvise. "Can you work from my old ones until I can get them taken?"

"Stella."

"No, listen, Ezra, I'm serious about coming back. I'm getting new pictures. They just won't be ready for a couple of weeks and—" again, I think on my feet "—I'm anxious to get started."

"Uh-huh. What about acting classes? Are you working out? Are you ready for auditioning?"

"Yes, yes, I am ready to do it all again, Ezra."

"And what about Mr. Moneybags?"

"Over."

His spiteful chuckle echoes into the phone, filling the one-inch space between the receiver and my ear. "Uh-huh. Okay, kid, I'll send you out if anything good comes in. But it's slow this time of year, so don't expect tons of calls. Come in three weeks with your contact sheet."

I don't argue. I just thank him and tell him how grateful I am and how lucky I feel to have him in my corner and that I'll see him in three weeks time and that I can't wait to go to an audition and make us both some money.

I hang up the phone and stare at it. Miss Bubbles circles back and forth between my legs. I sink onto the couch and she jumps onto my lap, flipping over to her back and exposing her stomach. We sit there while I haphazardly rub her belly and try to organize my thoughts into neat piles. Headshots. Classes. I have money for neither. I look at Miss Bubbles and wonder if she'll be able to afford me. I continue to sit there, with Miss B. purring in my lap, and survey the apartment. I stare at the living room, at the secondhand furniture that doesn't quite match, at the wilting spider plant in the corner and the peeling paint. I can hear the plunking of Christian's typewriter keys. The *clink, clink, clink* underscores the pulsing of my nerves, which crescendo to an aggravation that propels me off the couch. I yank off my boots, one by one, then peel myself out of the Jordache jeans, throwing them to the side as I run for the neon green sweatpants that are lying in a heap on my bed. Steve always gets mad at me when I undress in the living room. He says that just because there is no divider wall between the common area and my bedroom I think the whole thing is my domain. But I can't worry about that right now. I have to get into those sweats. *Tout suite.* I rip off my blue baby tee, unhitch my earrings, shed my entire costume from the morning and replace it with the neon sweatpants (I bought them because they had bright yellow letters down the left leg that say KICK IT) and a Rainbow Brite T-shirt that's a tad too small for me. I sit on my bed trying to escape that annoying *plunk, plunk, plunk.* Miss Bubbles jumps up and sits beside me. She tilts her head to one side and meows. "I know, Kitty. It's obnoxious." I punch the wall three times. Christian responds with three boot kicks to his floor, my ceiling. I shoot up and run into the kitchen, pure reaction. The kitchen is the only place where the sound doesn't trickle down.

I whip open my refrigerator door and see nothing but two packages of butter, a gallon of milk, four eggs, some condiments and three green apples. Hmm. Over to the cupboard where I find a bag of sugar, some vanilla extract and flour. Perfect. And let the afternoon begin….

I've known how to cook since I was kid, hanging out in the kitchen of the hotel where my mom worked as a maid. She didn't like me seeing her clean for a living, so every night before her shift, she'd drop me off in the kitchen. Mom never even put on her maid's outfit in front of me. She would drive us both to the hotel in her street clothes with full makeup on and hair perfectly done up, and wait until I was safely tucked away in the kitchen before changing. When she'd pick me up she was always back to her pretty self. I didn't even know she was a maid, at first, until Thelma the cook told me nobody could clean toilets like my mother. I was only eight at the time, but suddenly understood why there was always a ton of cleaning supplies in the trunk of our car. And even after I knew what her job was, Mom never let me see her in her maid's outfit.

Anyway, I would spend all night with Thelma, helping her prepare all the food for the restaurant: the pastas, the meats, the turnovers and the vegetables. She taught me pretty much everything she knew, even dishes from where she grew up in Mexico. By the time I was ten I could make a perfect turkey—I did all my mother's holiday cooking from then on. My favorite part, though, was the baking of the bread for the next morning. I loved the shapes, the colors, the smells. Thelma would let me knead the dough and shape it on the sheet. I would powder muffins and scones with sugar and dot them with berries. Late at night, after the dinner rush, she would teach me to frost cakes and score pies and decorate other goodies. Eventually I took a job of my own there, and cooked after school to help my mom pay the bills. Those were some relaxing times, just me and the kitchen—nobody to bother you or tell you what to do. Very relaxing. To this day, if I need to calm my nerves, I bake something.

It's a good skill to have, I think. The only drawback to emotional baking is that I end up with more food than people to eat it. That's about the only time when having Christian upstairs is a good thing. He's too wrapped up with his grad school studies to eat decent meals so sometimes if I have extra I'll wrap up a plate for him and leave it on his doorstep. I knock on his door to let him know it's there but leave before he answers so I don't have to talk to him. It may sound nasty, but he does the same thing. When he knows I'm not home he'll come over and have Steve direct him to the leftovers. Or he'll just help himself to any cookies or cupcakes that are out on the counter. It's a mutually beneficial arrangement. I cook without guilt and Christian eats without having to worry where his next meal is coming from. And judging by the mess I'm making right now, Christian could get lucky tonight.

I'm halfway through an apple tart and potpie shell when I hear Steve come through the front door. He hangs up his pea-coat, ever the conscientious roommate, and peers at me. "What are you doing?"

Even though I've known him ever since our first day of college seven years ago, his beauty still gives me pause. He looks so stylish in his jeans and T-shirt, his golden blond hair setting off his brown eyes and bronzed complexion. His tanned skin looks completely natural, but I know how many hours he spends lying underneath sunlamps. He's one of those guys who look like they belong on a *Men's Fitness* magazine cover. Even when he's glowering, like he is right now.

"Oh, don't worry, I'll clean it up. I promise. I just, well, I have a lot to tell you."

He scowls, but I pay it no mind. He's been scowling at me since the day I met him. "*Stella.* You have to be at work at 3:00! It's 2:40!"

I stare at him for two seconds before he holds up his hand and taps the face of his wristwatch. *Agh!* He's right. I've lost track of time. I run into my room, leaving the doughy mixture and the apple slices sitting on the cutting board, the eggshells in the sink and the flour all over the counter. Steve just stands in the middle of the living room floor, arms crossed, scowl still sitting on his face, holding my Jordache jeans in his left clenched fist. "Stella, Stella, Stella. I'm tired of being the only one who knows your work schedule."

I hate when Steve is annoyed with me. Despite his sarcastic comments, which come often, he usually tolerates almost all of my behavior. The dirty dishes, the neurotic forgetfulness, the promiscuity and utter lack of moral judgment when it comes to sleeping with married men... But punctuality, *punctuality,* is a virtue that he never compromises. And right now he's standing in the middle of the room, looking at his watch, and yelling at me, "Don't forget the address, you nutjob!"

I run with an overflowing knapsack slung on my back, grab the piece of paper with the address off the kitchen counter, run for the door, run back for my keys, run back out of the apartment and out the building, stop to kiss my hand and jump up to place the kiss on the foot of the stone angel, then make a right and dash toward the subway. There was no time for me to tell Steve about Frances Paine, Miss Bubbles or my conversation with Ezra.

Chapter 3

I have to say that even though I really need the money and even though I've vowed to stop partying like it's 1999, it really pisses me off that it's a Friday night and, instead of celebrating this amazing day with my two best friends, I'm stuck catering in New Jersey.

It's not the worst thing, catering, but it isn't starring in a movie, either. Basically, I get paid to be a spectator at really nice functions, where rich people eat and drink to their heart's content and show off their designer clothes and soak up the light while the waiters and bus people wither in the shadows. At first, catering seemed like a good way to meet people. I was sure Stephen Spielberg or Anthony Minghella or Susan Stroman would discover me while I served them their food. But I've been doing this for a year, and have never seen a celebrity who rates higher than the C list. And yet, I continue to cater. Why? Because I need to support myself. And because I'm bound to hit pay dirt one of these days.

And, in the meantime, I've learned some truly fascinating stuff. About etiquette. About second forks. And dessert spoons.

And that there's a different technique for pouring red wine and white. But most importantly, I have learned to desperately, desperately covet what I do not have. I have learned to dissociate myself from what I am doing and to totally live in the future. I have learned to resent my present. There is no place in the world where my mood is more irritable than at a catering function.

This particular party might be okay, not only because my entire day has been remarkable, but because it's in New Jersey. Now I am not a person who can claim to know much about New Jersey, but I do know this about fancy parties: The farther away, the more important they are. This party is being held in a banquet hall that's only reachable by boat. To get there you have to take a ferry from 39th Street in Manhattan, which is obviously fantastic, providing as it does an opportunity to frolic aboard a boat and let the wind whip through your hair like a supermodel. But I couldn't even enjoy it. All I could think about was how loud Debra was going to yell at me for being late, unforgivably late to this party.

Debra, who can only be described using language normally reserved for fairy-tale trolls and goblins, is my survival-job nemesis. She hated me instantly when I interviewed for this illustrious job. Now, women instantaneously dislike me all the time, so I'm not that thrown by it. But nobody has ever treated me as shoddily as Debra does. At the interview, when I said I had kitchen experience, she merely laughed and said that the *Company* (she refers to the place where I cater as the *Company,* as if it's a deity whose name cannot be uttered) only hired pedigreed chefs and clearly I was not that. But serving rich people food and drink apparently requires no skills, because she hired me.

Since then she's channeled her hatred for me by being very mean and by never giving me a break. Today was no exception. Because of my tardiness, she threw a bag of clothes at my head and demanded that I wear them. I hate dressing up to coordinate with the theme of the party, and this outfit is especially ridiculous—a German drinking-hall serving-girl number comprised of a short green skirt with a white-flower hem that bares my midthighs, white lacy anklet socks that I'm praying have never been worn before and a puffy white shirt poking out of a formfitting green vest that also has matching white-flower piping. I pinned my hair up in two Princess Leia style buns, hoping to capture the feel of the outfit, but now I'm not so sure that trying to look *more* authentic is such a good idea. And just as I'm thinking I look like an extra from an Oktoberfest extravaganza, two cater girls walk into the bathroom. "Oh my God!" one of them shouts before they both collapse in laughter. "What are you wearing?"

Before I start to get too depressed, I run through the day's events in my head. Frances Paine. The Cherry Lane Theater. Ezra. I give myself a pep talk as I make my way out into the banquet hall, "Stella Aurora Monroe, you are now committed to doing anything, anything to get your career off the ground." And it's true. I've wasted too much time, and now I have to earn the money for headshots so Ezra will send me out on good auditions. So who cares if my ego gets a little bruised along the way? Humiliation's nothing new, and wearing a slightly revealing, slightly slutty outfit is not exactly uncharted territory for me, either. Although usually when I wear such things there's not a mass gathering of rich and semifamous people depending on my outfit to set the tone of their party. Not to mention that tonight could be the night that I meet my Tom Cruise or Leonardo DiCaprio or Harvey Weinstein.

Oh God!! What if tonight *is* the night that I meet him finally? What kind of cruel joke would that be? I try to imagine the scene. I'll be holding a tray of white wine spritzers, looking perfectly odd in my green and white German costume, and the dashing, rich producer who is missing something in his life will see my face across the crowded room and know in his heart that I'm the girl he's meant to be with. But then he'll see my costume and think twice. He'll walk by me just as a sad song swells to maximum volume and the camera pans out into a wide shot of the party.

"*Stella!*" Debra's shrillness snaps me out of my self-pitying reverie. All four foot ten of her is perched right in front of the bathroom door, waiting to pounce on me. "Since you were late, you're going to be greeter." She throws an empty tray at me. "*Now get crackin'!*"

Ugh! That evil little troll! She knows what she's doing. Making me greeter? That's basically sentencing me to a night of hell: of standing outside, in a stupid costume, holding a tray of a dozen wineglasses, freezing my ass off while confused rich people get off of boats and ask where the party is. Where the bathroom is. Where they should hang up their coats. Don't you have any Chianti? Pinot Noir? Why aren't you serving beer? Oh, she's an evil genius, but I say nothing. I take the silver tray, tuck it under my arm and head toward the bar.

I survey the great banquet hall as I go. It's beautiful! The room is so large that it has two bars, one at the north side of the room and one at the south, and is divided in the center by a dance floor. Along the west wall is a stage where a band is setting up. I'm relieved to see that the singers are dressed as I am. I am not relieved when I hear them begin to warm up their voices. They are singing in what I assume is German and what seems to be raucous drinking songs. What exactly is this party for? Am I going to have to listen to this beer polka music all night? I keep walking.

The rest of the decor is just gorgeous. There are paper streamers slung from the ceilings and paper lanterns descending every fifteen feet or so. The colors are in soft pastels, blues, pinks and yellows, and the lanterns lend a sheen of soft whispery quiet to the inside of the room. There are about two hundred and fifty tables, each one with a huge centerpiece of white lilies and pink rosebuds. And on each place setting is a small, gift-wrapped box with a white bow on top. I am dying to know what is inside the boxes. Maybe I can swipe one at the end of the night.

I make my way to the south bar, the one closest to the entrance from the dock, and see my friend Chuck the bartender pouring the wine for my tray.

"Hey."

"Hey Stella." He eyes me up and down and tries to hide his mirth. "Debra out for blood again?"

"Laugh it up, Chuck. She hates me."

"She definitely hates you."

I growl and shake my head. "So what's the party for?"

"I dunno. Some party for a movie or sump-thin. Try this." He slides a shot glass over to where I'm standing. Chuck is one of those guys in his mid-forties who is so *over* catering that he always breaks rules.

"What is it?" I peer at the yellowish drink. Chuck is notorious for the free cocktails, which, though catering drinks are famously weak, is why I try to stay on very friendly terms with him.

"Just try it. I got extra."

Who am I to look a gift horse in the mouth? I down the shot, slam the glass onto the bar out of habit and wipe my mouth with the back of my hand. "Thanks." Three days of sobriety gone, just like that.

"No problem. Judging from the sound of the band, I think we're all going to need some help tonight."

I pick up the full tray and walk out to the dock, where a similarly dressed gay guy is standing and singing "Luck Be a Lady" under his breath. He introduces himself as John and tells me he volunteered to wear the serving girl's outfit when none of the other waitresses would. He also tells me that the spectacle we're about to witness is a party for some World War II spy caper. John says he heard Tobey Maguire and Jake Gyllenhaal might be in attendance, but I doubt it. One thing I know from catering, whoever you think will show up won't.

But my curiosity is piqued—I can't wait to see who's on the boat. When the ferry pulls into the dock and the guests begin to unload, a news reporter from Channel 11 walks backward, trying to get footage of people as they walk ashore. This is promising. Obviously somebody worth filming is on that ferry.

I crane my neck to see, but a middle-aged couple who come to take two glasses of wine blocks my view. They don't look famous to me. Just cold.

"Where's the bathroom, miss?"

"It's inside."

They each down their glasses and place them, empty, back on my tray. I hate that.

A steady stream of thirsty travelers follows, each of them asking where the bathroom is and each putting an empty glass on my tray. Just as my last glass of wine is being drunk, by a fifty-something platinum blonde in a fur coat, John comes over to tell me he's going to get more wine for both of us. He cuts a path through the party guests and comes over to take my empties. I thank him and stretch out my arms, sore from the weight of a dozen full wineglasses.

And then, as I lift my arms to heaven and the wind whips at my skirt, I spot him in the crowd. The most beautiful man I have ever seen in person. He's tall, he must be six-three, and his dirty blond hair catches the sunlight as it dances over the river. I can see, even though he's some feet away from me yet, that his eyes are brownish and that his smile is beaming, bright as a follow spotlight. He wears a white turtleneck sweater and brown suede pants, with a camel hair trench coat to keep him warm in the cool February evening. He glows, just like he does in every picture my mother has ever sent of him. Jasper Hodge. Ascending-to-the-stratosphere actor. He's just simmering on the consciousness of celebrity watchers everywhere, thanks to a little-aired but critically praised drama on Fox, two memorable indie features and one very small role in a summer blockbuster. Not to mention that he's legit by New York standards:

he's been in an Edward Albee revival on Broadway and played Laertes at the Public two summers ago. All around, he's a solid B-lister: a Taye Diggs, Anthony LaPaglia, Liev Schreiber caliber star. I can't take my eyes off him, and quickly promise to devote my life to God if John gets back with the wine before Jasper Hodge passes me by unnoticed.

"Put your tray down. These glasses are heavy." Note to self—tomorrow, devote life to God.

"John, look." The gorgeous one slowly makes his way toward us, grinning and shaking hands with his admiring onlookers.

"What? Aye-yi-yi! That's Jasper Hodge. Good lord. He's yummy."

Jasper Hodge. My heart is pounding. And I can't remember if this is real or just one of my silly fantasies. I knew it! I knew the rest of the day had to be spectacular! I squeal with delight and tilt my chin toward the heavens to thank the angels above, but before I can even think of how to get his attention, he's standing there. In front of me. Jasper Hodge.

"Hmm. Do you have any red wine, my server girl?" I nearly faint. His voice sounds like sweet berries, and his smile, so close up, nearly blinds me. And he has a beauty mark! A real one, right in the same spot as my fake one is! I try to answer but no sound comes out.

"Just white. But Stella would be happy to get you whatever you want." John answers for me. "Wouldn't you, Stella?" He begins transferring all of the white wine from my tray to his so that I can go to the bar.

"Of—of course. Huh-happy to."

"No, no. I can find my way to the bar myself. But it was a pleasure to meet you, Stella. I'll have to remember your name, in case I should need something later." And with another miraculous smile, he makes his way toward the banquet hall. It is then I notice a small blonde trailing him and holding on to his right hand. But it doesn't bother me at all. A trivial matter like a girlfriend is not going to deter destiny from pairing me and Jasper Hodge.

I look at John. He holds up his left hand and extends his fourth finger. "No wedding ring. Up top!" He extends his hand for me to high-five.

I can't answer. I am in a daze, completely caught in fantasies of dancing with Jasper, of sailing with Jasper, of getting married to Jasper, of bearing little Jasper babies, of accompanying him to movie premieres at the Chinese Theater, Sundance and Cannes, of an entire life of riches, love and comfort.

This just has to be it. It's been way too lucky of a day for this chance meeting to be a coincidence. I've just met him. This morning when I made my "Today's the day" wish, the angels finally heard me. They sent me Frances Paine, Ezra Greenblatt and now Jasper Hodge. And all I had to do was let the universe know I was ready. And I did. First by breaking up with Joshua, then by taking Miss Bubbles to the vet.

"I need a camera." I am jerked back to earth by the sound of that voice, that snooty, holier-than-thou voice.

It's Christian. I'm so stunned I can't even think of something rude to say. The level of my annoyance is in direct proportion to how high I have just been feeling. He is standing in front of me, but leaning backward so as to see my entire outfit. He lets out a whistle. An annoying, obnoxious whistle.

"So this is how you're making your money these days. And I thought maybe that scrawny guy I met the other morning was your new sugar daddy." His eyes are dancing with delight, obvious even behind those pretentious wire-rimmed glasses, and the wind blows his hair up in tufts.

"Shut up. Take your wine. What are you doing here anyway? How did a boring bookworm like you get invited to such an upscale party?"

"Claws in, serving wench." I almost throw the tray at him, full glasses and all. "I was invited because the professor I'm assisting acted as historical advisor to the movie that's being released. We made sure they were telling an accurate story."

"How boring. I don't know how you stay awake during the day." I say this as sweetly as I can, seeing as I want to kill him. Christian always seems to catch me in my most embarrassing moments. It's not like I care what he thinks of me or anything, but his judging nature is just so irksome. Like it's some sort of crime to have to do anything possible to pay the rent.

"Well, I should be getting inside. Are you freezing? Do you want to borrow my coat while you're out here?"

I say no, that I'd get in trouble if my boss caught me covering up the costume. He takes one last lingering look at me, and then leaves.

John runs over to me. "Who was *that?*"

"That's just some guy who lives in my building. He's not as nice as he looks."

"Well, aren't you the little guy magnet, just attracting all over the place. Leave some for the other girls, will ya?" And he curtsies and tries to skip back to his spot without spilling any drinks.

It's about another fifteen minutes before John and I head into the banquet hall. There's no way I'm going to find Jasper in this vast sea of designer outfits and snappy shoes, dress suits and laughing happy people—he's probably been sequestered at a VIP table anyway. I scan from right to left and decide to tackle the other side of the room. But I take a wrong turn and barrel into Debra the troll, who snarls at me while I quickly scurry back toward Chuck's bar.

The band is blasting this awful oompah-oompah song and I realize that I'm going to have to wait until after dinner to try to find Jasper. So I get Chuck's attention to let him know I'm there and try to look like I'm at the bar for a reason. A very good thing about being the girl designated to wait outside is that once you're inside, you don't get any tables assigned to you. You become what is known as a floater, meaning you float around and see if anyone needs any help. I generally like to keep out of sight when this is my job, so that nobody asks me to do anything. I have found that hanging around the bar area dupes people into thinking that I am very busy serving drinks or cleaning glasses or stocking whatever beer is needed. So this is my general strategy.

"Long night, huh?" I lean against the bar and watch the rich people dance.

"Oh, yeah. They're all long nights. But I make 'em go by. Here." Chuck casually slides another yellowish shot my way.

"Aren't you going to get in trouble?"

"Not if you hurry up and drink it." Good point. I down the shot and slide the empty glass back toward the other side of the bar. This will be the best way to make the time go by.

"Some famous people here." I say this casually, as if I don't care that the man of my dreams is dining with some blond floozy on the other side of the room.

"Who cares about famous people? Try this one." He passes me another shot, this time it's pinkish in color. I swallow it down and thank him.

"What are you putting in those things?" My esophagus is on fire. He chuckles and waves his hand in the air as if to say, "Don't worry about it!" I turn back around and stare at the table right in front of me. Twelve perfectly easeful, happy, golden people, seated around their table, their complimentary gifts at their feet. And a waiter struggling to place steaming filets onto their plates. And in the background a German-American singer, trying to catapult herself out of the background by inviting people to join her in "Those Were the Days."

"Do you have any more of the pink shots?" Chuck's smile says that he does. I drink it quickly and turn back around, my mouth full of fume and anxiety. Where is Jasper Hodge, anyway? I peer across the great room. Jesus, you need binoculars to see the other side! I think about crossing the hall to the other bar, so that I can search through the faces on the other side, but the risk of being spotted by Debra is too great. My feet are beginning to get sore, and my arms still ache from the wine trays. No, I can't risk being put underneath a full tray of dinner plates.

So I stand there, I'm not sure for how long, just praying for sweet relief from the boredom, the band, the blisters forming on the bottoms of my feet. I pass some minutes shooting mental daggers at the people on the dance floor. Some more time is spent in planning a dramatic liberation of one of the party favors. One whole hour goes by in a mental debate over whether Steve can be my maid of honor, should I be lucky enough to ever get married. Pretty soon there are no more thoughts. Just impatience, annoyance, aggravation. I have to go home. Everybody will understand. I'll just throw a coat on over my outfit and swim home. But then, a voice of berries and now whiskey, whispers: "Stella."

I don't have to turn to see. I know who it is. The band oompahs.

"Jasper Hodge." He is stunning, just stunning. He is leaning against the bar, facing me. He exudes a brand of confidence I've only seen once before, with Joshua. It's this sense of power that must come with knowing that, at any given second, there are about one million people who would give anything to change places with you. But I don't want to change places with him. Right now I am the luckiest person in the world.

"You know me?" He stands there, his smile penetrating the deepest corners of my brain, making me blink, making my insides do a million flips, making my speech slow. But I play it cool, as would any self-respecting heroine who meets the love of her life while wearing Princess Leia buns.

"Do I know you? Do you know *me*? That's the real question." He laughs. Okay, okay. I can handle this. Yes. I. Can.

"I sure wish I did." He leans in. I lose motor functions for a split second, then, "Nice buns." Motor functions permanently deleted from system.

"And here I thought that you came over here for another drink." Good, good. Maintaining ability to flirt.

"Well, now that you mention it. I would like to have another scotch, if I may." Interruption of first banter with drink order—not a good sign. Irritation at marring of "How we first met" story. I shoot back. "Well, the bartender's right there. Why don't you just order it?"

He chuckles at me and, I swear, looks me up and down.

"So what do you do when you aren't working undercover for the Germans?"

"I'm an actress." He lets out an "ah" as he leans over the bar, his sweater stretching over his back muscles like sky over a mountain range.

"Have you been in anything I would know?" Temporary paralysis of heartbeat as I squelch anger.

"Not recently. Just, um, you know. Trying to make it happen."

"Trying to make it happen?" He does not know. His brow crinkles up in the most delicious way as he tries to decode the meaning of what I've just said, for he is far too beautiful and charismatic to ever have been unemployed or without prospect. The next sentence flies out of my mouth before I have a moment to think about what I'm saying.

"I'm actually about to sign on to the new Paine production. Downtown."

"The new Paine production?" he says this slowly, impressed. "Really?"

"Mmm-hmm. I'm just doing this—" I gesture to my costume "—for a little extra cash." Lying to the love of my life. Very bad.

"Uh-huh. The new Paine play? Really? That's an amazing gig, if you can get it."

"Oh, I know, I am totally lucky. It's a great story how I got in, too. I'd love to tell it to you sometime."

"Well, I'd love to hear it. I would *love* to hear it." He smiles at me so intensely that I think Ashton Kutcher might jump out from behind the bar to Punk me. Am I mistaking this? No. He is giving me major signals. There are sparks flying, I can tell. This is fantastic, nothing can ruin it. Nothing.

"You would?" I ask as coyly as I can.

"Absolutely I would." He leans in closer. I can smell him. Regions of my body that I forgot existed begin to tingle. "Why don't you give me your number, Stella." His voice makes this sound like a statement, not a question.

The rest of the conversation takes place without me knowing what is happening. My memory officially stops recording transactions at that line, that marvelous line, "Why don't you give me your number, Stella." I know that I scribble it on a napkin and slide it over to him. I know that he looks at it before slipping it into his pants pocket. I know that he gives me one last grin before carrying his drink back over to the other side of the room.

My senses return with his exit. I follow him with my eyes, sad to see him go but unbelievably excited at the turn of events. I have to steady myself against the bar to avoid collapsing to the floor in a fit of giggles. What an incredible day! I run through the list of amazing things that happened to me over and over, a million times it seems. I just can't believe my luck. I can't wait to call my mother and tell her all about it. She is going to be so happy, so relieved.

Everything and everyone is now lovely. The music, the bartender, hell, I don't even mind when Christian ambles up to me at the bar and tells me I look like a hooker from Vegas. I launch myself at him, throw an arm around his shoulders, and screech, "Christian! It's so good for you to get out of your apartment! I'm really proud of you!"

He throws my arm off him and runs his tongue over his bottom teeth before ordering a Guinness from Chuck.

"No, no. Chuck, make my friend here one of those wonderful drinks."

"I don't think so, Stella." But it's too late for protestations.

Chuck has us set up with three shot glasses and three pastel cocktails before Christian can argue.

I grab a glass and clink the other two. "Here's to fantastic drinkin' music!" I have to scream above the band, which has become increasingly loud and rowdy. A whole crowd of people is gathered around the stage, singing along to the music.

"Jesus, this is the best mood I've ever seen you in," says Christian, in between choking swallows.

"I'm always in a good mood—you're just too busy to notice."

"Really? I'm thinking your good mood has to do with the chummy conversation I saw you and Jasper Hodge having. A guy like that is only talking to a girl like you for one reason. Don't get any ideas."

"Shut up. I knew you'd try to ruin my good time with an obnoxious comment."

"I think you tend to get overly impressed by people who aren't that impressive."

"Christian. Shut. Up. Get my friend another drink, so he'll stop talking. Step on it!" Chuck obliges me again and sets up another round for the three of us.

"To being rich!"

Christian shakes his head at me and he and Chuck down their shots. The band launches into an old Frank Sinatra tune, and the singer pulls one of the party guests up onto the stage with her. The crowd lets out a cheer as this balding, fifty-year-old man shares the mic with the buxom singer. I look at Christian and he's smiling. Fantastic. Even the waitstaff looks to be enjoying the sing-along. This is turning into such a splendid time! And what a splendid party! What a splendid crowd! New Jersey! New Jersey is splendid. To be young and single in the city is splendid! And Christian! How great is he? And lucky, too, because he needs to enjoy his life and not waste his youth studying all the time, and now here's my chance to tell him. And I can give him a lesson about show business, to make him understand. I reach for his hand twice before finding it.

"I have so much to tell you."

He grins at me and leans his head down so he can hear what I have to say. He's going to be my best student ever. And my new best friend!

Midspeech, I see, out of the corner of my eye, a blond sunbeam heading toward the door. A tree-trunk of beauty leaving the building with a perky blond gerbil trailing behind.

"Uh-oh! What's this? Your Prince Charming is going home without you! Oh, no!" I think my new best friend is laughing at me.

"Christian! You understand nothing!"

"Oh, I understand. Chuck? Do you understand?"

"I understand." Chuck downs an entire pint of beer.

"Yeah, well, the two of you can go to hell. Because *I* am going to be getting a phone call in the next day or two." They laugh at me while I talk. "Keep laughing, jerks! You'll see! You'll see!" I point in the air and Chuck puts another drink glass in my hand and the band launches into "Fly Me to the Moon."

"Oh my God! I love this one!" I down my shot and take off toward the stage.

"Stella, no!" Christian tries to hold my skirt, in a fruitless attempt to keep me from entertaining all these rich folk.

"Entertain I must!" I slap his hands and wrench my garment free from his grasp. "I know this one!" I run through the crowds of people, climb the steps and join the only other people besides gay John who are dressed like me. The lead singer hugs me and pushes the mic into my hands.

I turn toward the crowd, raise the mic to my mouth and sing. The band vibrates behind me and the singer warbles the words into the other microphone. The people in the audience grin and laugh and sing along and shout, and my heart hammers away with joy. The lead singer holds my hand and I blow the crowd away with a harmony my mother taught me. The people cheer. They dance. They're happy. I hold that microphone stand in my hands, stroking, up and down, up and down, making sweet, sweet love to the music, making sweet, sweet love to my audience, making sweet, sweet love to my birthright.

But then a disturbance in the crowd catches my attention. The audience parts like the Red Sea as Debra thunders toward the stage. I belt out the last phrases of the song, shout, "Good night, New Jersey!" and spread my arms wide open to welcome the applause. Then I bound down the stage steps, waving all the while, so that the crowd will know how much I love them.

Debra wastes no time. She's upon me like a cop on a gun-toting fugitive.

"Dog house. You are in the dog house, Monroe! Just what in the hell do you think you're doing?!"

I freeze in place, and can't think what to say. What am I doing? I'm living. Entertaining. Performing. Seizing the day, for chris' sake. The look on her face tells me nothing I can say will save me from the inevitable. She settles into her stance for a brief second before inhaling and saying, "You're F—"

"She's what?" We both look over to the strawberry sound. My heart skips a beat. I thought Jasper had left, but here he is. Standing right in front of us, arms folded around that sexy chest. I hope he caught my performance. I hope he's impressed. Maybe he'll tell his agent all about me.

"She's…" Whatever Debra was gearing up to say is lost in her rapture of standing two feet from the sexiest, dreamiest, hunkiest piece of masculinity she's probably ever laid eyes on.

"Because I think she's fairly fantastic." Jasper's eyes meet mine. They lock. I, for the first time in the evening, can't think of anything to say.

"Fantastic? Yes. Fantastic." Debra splutters like a broken faucet, and lands some spray on him. But Jasper, ever the gentleman, flashes that million dollar smile and puts his hand on her shoulder. He turns his gaze to her.

"And I think it's wonderful that you give your employees

the opportunity to display their true talents. It's…" He reaches for the right word. "Delightful. Just…delightful."

I'm awestruck. Usually a display of bullshit this thick, this blatant, this bold is coming out of *my* mouth. I've never actually witnessed it from afar before. Nor have I ever seen anyone lie with such finesse and I've dated a married man! Poor Debra, that little troll, she is knocked out. Completely stupefied. I take the opportunity to dismiss myself.

"Well, I have to get back to work." I want desperately to throw my arms around Jasper, to kiss that tanned golden neck, but not as much as I want to escape the moment with my job intact. He'll come find me later. He has to.

I stagger back to the bar. Literally, I stagger. People keep coming up to me to say how much they like my voice. Flattered but exhausted and dizzy, I make my way back to the bar. Christian just stares at me, then shakes his head, mumbles something about me being drunk and leaves. Chuck is clapping and laughing and has a highball waiting for me, full of the pink stuff. I drink it down in three gulps while searching the throngs for sight of Debra. I am not fool enough to test the waters with her again. It is imperative that she not lay eyes on me until another day.

But I don't want to leave my spot, because I know that Jasper is coming. And I am right. Halfway through my second post-performance cocktail, he finds me at the bar. He takes my hand before I can say anything, pulls me toward him and whispers in my ear, "Scrumptious, pretty Stella." Then he kisses my earlobe, leaves a tip for Chuck and walks out the door without even noticing the pair of women waiting by the exit to catch a close-up glimpse of him.

I don't remember much more of the evening. I barely remember getting my street clothes and leaving. I don't remember the ferry ride, actually, wait, yes. Yes, I do remember the ferry. I remember shouting, "I'm the King of the World" and I remember Christian, right, Christian was there with me, he was telling me to shut up. And then there was a cab ride. Right. I don't remember paying for it—assume Christian took care of it. When did I get into my apartment and my pajamas? God I hope Christian did not take care of that. He'd be the last person I'd want to owe a favor.

Chapter 4

My y seat is vibrating and a mosquito hums in my ears. I turn my head this way and that and don't see any bugs, but swoosh my hand through the air just in case. What is that vibrating? My cell phone? I don't have a cell phone—is it Steve's? I run my hands underneath my pockets, to feel if there's a cell phone. I don't have any pockets. Oh! I am still in this German serving girl outfit! No pockets! No pants!

The vibrating grows, so does the humming. The vibrating is so powerful that I'm being bounced up and down, and I keep leaving my seat. The humming is so loud that I have to cover my ears. I turn around, to ask Miss Bubbles if she is okay.

"Are you strapped in?" I shout over the immense sound of the buzzy hum. She nods. Why is she dressed like that? She's in a leather army jacket, and a flyer's cap with goggles plus a long knit scarf that flows behind her in the air. The scarf sparkles. It might be diamonds, but upon closer inspection they prove to be silver sequins.

She is angry, "Meow. What are you doing? Take off! Take off! Meow!"

Why is she yelling at me? I turn back in my seat and see a propeller in front of me. It must be one and a half times my size, and the speed with which it whirs sends a wind that makes it im-

possible for me to keep my eyes open. To my left and right are large parallel structures—biplane wings.

"Miss Bubbles, I don't know how to fly!" I desperately scream back to her, but she refuses to listen.

"Take off right now!"

And then, without any help from me, the plane starts to taxi forward, gathering speed, until we lift off the ground, about six inches above the earth. Miss Bubbles keeps yelling "Take off!" at me, and I keep telling her that I don't know how to fly, and then she begins to rap the back of my seat with a stick or something. Rap! Rap! Rap!—"Take off!"

My head jerks to the right and I sit up in my bed. Someone is knocking on my front door. Miss Bubbles lies right in front of me, staring up at me, a look of confusion on her face. "Meow?" I rub her head and kiss her. She licks her paws.

The person knocks again.

"Steve?" My voice is shockingly scratchy. No answer.

"Hold on." I try to say this as loudly as I can, but don't achieve much projection. I scramble out of bed and search my floor for a robe. My stomach jerks, like a roller coaster. The only discernible item in all the piles of clutter is the German outfit. "Gotta clean up in here," I mutter under my breath. More knocking. My head pounds. I grab a sweatshirt and throw it over my shoulders.

"I'm coming." I get to the door and throw it open, "Who is it?"

"You're a mess." Christian is leaning against the door frame, looking all the more casual because of his loose-fitting Frank Black T-shirt and khaki shorts. His arm is poised in midknock.

"What? I just woke up—what do you want?" I am *so* annoyed and feeling a little bit dizzy standing there.

"How do you feel today?"

"Awful."

"Well, you certainly were in tip-top shape last night, Kathleen."

I squint at him.

"Kathleen Turner."

I don't get it.

"You sound like Kathleen Turner," he says.

"Steve's not here."

"I came to talk to *you*."

"Huh?" It is way too early for a cryptic exchange with Christian. I loudly blow out a puff of air to convey my annoyance.

"I just wanted to make sure you felt all right. 'Cause I feel lousy. So I thought you must feel lousy, too. You look lousy."

"*Okay.* Gotta go." And then I remember I *do* have to go—to a standing brunch engagement with Steve and Michaela, our ritual weekend meal. "What time is it?!"

"It's just before twelve."

"Ah! Christian, I've got to go—I'm late. Seriously."

"Okay, okay. Can I have my blazer back?"

"What?"

"My blazer."

"Your blazer?"

"My blazer. You wore it last night on the way home and said I could get it back today."

I have no idea what he's talking about and tell him so. He tells me to look for it, and pushes his way inside to make sure I *do* look for it. He follows me into my room and stands in the doorway. Miss Bubbles runs up to his feet and wraps herself around his ankles.

"You're messy."

"Tell me something I don't know. I don't see it, do you see it?" I scoop up piles of clothes and let them fall from my arms.

"Is it in the closet?"

I stare at him for a second, just a second longer than I should. "You look good for someone who did shots all night."

"I got up and ran it out of my system."

I stare again, dumbfounded at the thought of exercising, and then head toward the closet. "Christian, there's nothing in here. I'll look for it later, I'm really late, okay?"

He lets out a deep sigh. "I really need that jacket back—I knew I shouldn't have let you keep it."

"What does that mean?"

"Nothing. Forget it. I'll let myself out." And he turns and leaves.

Normally I would start pacing back and forth, cursing out loud about how rude he is, but honestly, there's no room for pacing in my room just now. And I really don't want to be late for brunch. Michaela, Steve and I used to have brunch religiously, until I started ditching them all the time to see Joshua. But since emerging from my bad-relationship haze, I've been trying to spearhead the revival of our tradition. Michaela is open to the idea and—never one to harbor any grudges or think anything ill of anyone—she acts like it's completely acceptable that I, all of a sudden, make time for the three of us again. Steve isn't such an easy sell, though, and if I miss this meal because of a hangover, that'll be it. I'll never hear the end of it.

So despite not feeling my best, I run around like a tornado trying to get ready. It isn't that easy. Christian is right. Staring at myself in the mirror is a horrifying experience. I have one *Star Wars* bun intact, albeit sitting much lower on the side of my head than it should be. My face looks awful, lipstick smeared up the right side of my cheek and my fake beauty mark oozing from its core into a thin sphere of brown makeup, the size of a dime. I scrub my face and tear my hair out of its bun. I turn the shower on lukewarm and force myself to bathe. My stomach screams, squirms, cries for me to let it out of its misery, but no dice. I am *not* going to sit in this apartment all day and nurse a body that I myself did not take care of. *No.* I am attacking my day, just as I am to attack every day from here after until I accomplish my goal.

I finish the world's shortest shower, dry off and put myself into some respectable clothes. As I grab a wrinkly pink T-shirt that says Not For Sale, I notice a small corner of crumpled fabric jutting out from under the bed. Christian's suit jacket—navy, double-breasted. I pick it up and bring it to my face. Vanilla, and chestnuts, and maybe, alcohol? I crumple it up and throw it toward the wall. I turn my attention to the German outfit. I place it gingerly on my bed, smooth out the wrinkles, and search the pockets, hoping to find Jasper Hodge's phone number even though I know very well he didn't give it to me. But, hey, stranger things have happened.

I throw my hair in a ponytail, grab my Hello Kitty purse and run out the door, ignoring the head and stomach pain that have been steadily increasing since I got out of the shower. I walk briskly and erectly, stopping my pace only to place a bouquet of kisses at the feet of the stone angel. She really knocked herself out yesterday, and proper appreciation is due.

Hustling up 10th Avenue, I get to 49th Street and push my way past the line of people that are milling around the entrance to Hell's Bar. Various line-holders shoot annoyed stares my way as I walk into the restaurant and follow the sound of Michaela's laugh to the best booth in the bar, the cushioned one with the velvet pillows and thick curtains and pasted red-washed pictures of Mae West on the tables. Rod is sitting next to her, and they are having what looks like a conspiratorial conversation.

"Coffee. Thank God." I throw my purse down on the table and reach for the steaming cup that is waiting for me.

"Well, hello Kitty." Rod snarls at me and puckers his lips in my direction. "No free meals today. Unless you wanna go dancing with me tonight."

"Yeah, right. Where's Steve?" I ask Michaela.

"What happened to you? You look awful."

"I think she looks just fine." Rod reaches over and yanks my ponytail. I swat his hand away.

"I only have energy to tell my tale once. But, I have a really weird dream for you."

"Really?" Michaela loves to talk about dreams. "What happened?"

"I was flying an airplane and Miss Bubbles was my co-pilot. And *don't* say anything dirty." Rod swallows whatever brilliant interpretation was on his lips.

"Huh." She takes a bite of bread, chews and mulls over this little Freudian nugget.

"Any guesses?"

"Not a one. You'll have to let me know if you have any more like that."

I sip my coffee and reach for a slice of bread. "I beat Steve to brunch, huh? Maybe he shouldn't spend so many nights at his boyfriend's."

Michaela just looks at me. "Why?" She's so sweet, she probably thinks I have a real reason.

"I don't know. I just never see him anymore, and I don't like that just when I have more time, he gets all involved."

"But he's in love!"

I know that and I don't like it. "You know what, Mic? Pretty soon, he's gonna move out! And then what am I gonna do? I'll have no more friends."

"Hello, ladies. Stella, what are you whining about?" Steve swoops in, slaps hands with Rod and greets us two girls with a kiss on each cheek, four kisses in all. He looks mighty fine for so early in the morning, a sharp contrast to the sorry heap that I am, a pale-faced, pathetic creature trying to mask her pain in jeans and a T-shirt. Steve, on the other hand, looks fresh as spring. He arrives with his sunglasses on, even though the only hint of sunlight in the entire bar is the shade of his bleached hair. It hugs the crown of his head like a blanket of gold.

He squishes himself into the booth seat, the one covered with the red velvet pillows, right next to Michaela. They stare at me and Rod from across the table, two gorgeous people, people who have had plenty of sleep and water before bedtime, framed by a descending, thick red velvet curtain. It's like staring at the new millennial, urban American Gothic.

"Stella was just bitching about you not being home enough for her."

I punch Rod's arm. "Now I'm never going out with you. Ever."

"Uh-huh." Steve likes to ignore my comments sometimes. "So have we ordered yet?" He grabs for the menu.

"I have a big story to tell, Steve."

"Oh! I'm sure you do, darling, why else would you be here on time?" He is an expert at slipping in the casual dig, this one lobbed over the net of the menu, with just a hint of a glance in my direction to catch my reaction.

I'm dying to launch into my story, because Steve's reaction is going to be pure gold. It's not often that I can trump him career-wise, but meeting Frances Paine *and* Jasper Hodge in one day is going to make him green with envy. I can't wait. Steve must sense something big is coming, because he rushes us through our orders and shoos Rod away from the table.

"All right, enough. You got news, huh, big shot? Spill it—start with the part where Frederick Paine's office calls for our cat."

I launch into the whole story, stopping only for sips of coffee—which doesn't help my stomach but does oodles of good for the psyche and for the delivery of the food. From the vet's office to the Ezra phone call to the meeting with Jasper Hodge to the singing—they listen intently, their mouths eventually ending up wide-open.

"What did Debra do?" Steve asks this question with a tone whose subtext reads this way. "You didn't screw up the only job you have, did you?"

I tell them how my new hero and future husband saved the day. Steve crosses his arms, stops eating and leans back into the velvet.

"Where was Christian during all this?"

"Christian? Who cares where he was?"

"I'd like the story better if Christian saved your job."

"Who are you? Ebert? You're criticizing the end of a true story?"

"I'm just saying that I'd like it better if Christian were the hero. He's cuter."

"Oh, Jesus. He is *not* cuter than *Jasper Hodge*."

"Yes he is."

"No he's not."

"Yes he is."

"No he's not." To emphasize my point, I flip a pat of butter in his direction.

"Don't!" He shrieks and jumps back in his seat, brushing it off his lap in one sweeping motion, like you would if you found a spider on your leg. He is absolutely *afraid* of fatty foods. When he really pisses me off, I like to chase him around the apartment with sticks of butter in my hands.

He wipes off his fingers furiously. "So what happened in the cab? Did you guys make out in the back seat?"

"Steve!"

He laughs maniacally and starts chanting, "Stella and Christian sitting in a tree," while I scream over him, *"We did not make out!"*

Michaela, thankfully much more mature than the two of us, ignores our silliness and shushes us by changing the subject. "Wait, so what did Jasper say about your singing?" She holds a single walnut on her fork and gingerly coats it with syrup while looking at me expectantly for an answer.

"He didn't say anything. He whispered, he kissed and then he left."

"Oh my God!"

"That *is* pretty hot," Steve chimes in.

"Well, he's totally going to call you! Oh! Little Stellie—you are going to be a movie-star's wife!" Mic giggles outrageously and leans across the table to rub my head. "Imagine this! You and Steve with such good news in one day!"

I whip my head around to Steve so fast my neck cracks. "What? What good news?"

"It's nothing." He eyes me in such a way that I know it *is* something.

"He got called back for *All My Children,* can you believe it?" Michaela beams at him. A familiar prick of jealousy stabs my insides.

"Isn't that great?" Michaela's enthusiasm is so genuine. She's not an actress, just a person making her way in the city, so news of any audition, callback or read-through gets a big reaction out of her. She's also untainted by competitiveness, something that is exceedingly rare among actors. Normally, competition is the prevailing aspect of any friendship between two actors. In my experience as an almost-working actress, I have found that it is nearly impossible to keep up a friendship/relationship with an actor who is at a different level of his or her career than you. No matter how true of heart the two people in the relationship are, jealousy always, *Always,* gets in the way. This is especially true for people of the same sex who are friends. You cannot be friends with someone who gets a part out from under you. That is why most actresses' friends in the biz are all gay men. There is no chance that the gay friend can a) steal your job, or b) steal your boyfriend/guy you like in the cast (in most cases). It's a miracle that Steve and I have remained friends. But in truth, he has never had any reason to be jealous of me. And today is no different.

Steve, ever the realist, tries to downplay Michaela's ebullience. "It's okay. I made it past the first cut, so that's good. Now Stella, let's talk turkey about Frances Paine. You realize she's lived the life that you want, don't you?"

Of course I do.

"Oh, Stellie! The universe is really opening doors for you. I am going to go home and check the month's transits against your birth chart, and see if the stars predict a happy ending!"

"Hey, check to see what I should do to make money for headshots, okay?"

"Just start charging all the guys you bring home and you'll be able to buy a different headshot for every day of the week!"

I shoot Steve a look, but don't say anything. He catches my eye, and raises his shoulders in an apologetic manner, which doesn't stop him from getting in the next gem. "Mic, when you're looking up her chart, check to see if she's ever actually going to go on an audition. Oh, and find out if she can pay the rent this month. I like having a roof over my head."

It's a good thing Steve and I love each other because I could seriously consider killing him right now. But after we leave Hell's and head for home, he redeems himself by answering every single one of my questions about his phone conversation with the Paine office. I ask him for each detail three times, something that annoys him to no end. He doesn't understand why I can't get the gist of a story in one telling. But I like multiple renditions. It helps me to savor the details.

"Wait, so I have to bring Miss Bubbles to the Cherry Lane on Friday. What else? Did they say to bring outfits for her? Do they want my headshot and résumé?"

"Jesus, Stella. For the last time. Bring the cat to the theater so that the director can meet her. And why would they need *your* headshot?"

I link my arm through Steve's, and mull over what he's said. I am to go to the Cherry Lane Theater on Friday with my cat, to meet the cast and crew of an off-Broadway play and to start making connections that will eventually lead to me winning an Oscar and a handsome Hollywood husband.

I tilt my chin toward the bright blue sky and let the sun warm my face. I don't feel hungover anymore, just happy.

Chapter 5

I sit straight up in bed, the first time I beat my alarm clock in months. Normally on an unemployed Monday morning I would be lazy, rise at say, ten, or eleven even—but in time to watch *The View* while making an elaborate breakfast of eggs, scones and fruit jam. I would shower from twelve to twelve-thirty, then dry my hair to *A Makeover Story* on TLC. At one o'clock I would lift Miss Bubbles onto my lap for some owner/pet bonding over the dog shows on Animal Planet, and then, to treat myself to some luxury, I would relax with some soaps before the emotional roller coaster that is *Oprah* at four. At around five-fifteen I would decide to give the world a little glimpse of myself, and would slowly make my way from the apartment to Hell's Bar to mingle with Michaela until, oh, well that would depend on the adventure awaiting.

But not today.

Today is the first day of the rest of my life. It's a cliché and I embrace it wholeheartedly. *Today is the day.* I sit straight up in my bed and startle the hell out of Miss Bubbles, who is curled up by my hip. She tilts her head at me and I run my hand through her fur before clambering out of bed and running straight to the bathroom without first turning on the television. Miss Bubbles jumps up onto the bathroom counter and looks at our reflection in the mirror as I recite to myself, "Today is the day. Today is the day. Today."

Two things have to happen today.

Must-happen item number one: Jasper Hodge is going to call me. It's been a whole weekend since he rescued me from being fired and not a word. But it's okay. I didn't expect anything until the weekend was over. Why? Well, as best as I can figure, he needed two days to dump that trashy blonde who was with him at the party. Two days is the perfect amount of time to break up and move on. And moving on would begin today.

Must-happen item number two: I have to go to an audition today. Steve's fighting words about me never auditioning landed right on my pride, and there is no way in hell I am going to let him be right. To that end, I bought a copy of *Backstage,* the trade paper that lists auditions for film, television and theater. There's not usually much to choose from: mostly student films or nonunion theater calls. Broadway shows also list chorus calls in *Backstage,* but people rarely get jobs out of them. Really an actor only uses this paper if she doesn't have an agent. Which I don't. Or if she is after experience. Which I am. Also, Michaela says that I have to give the universe a message that I am committed to making my career work.

And let's face it. I can't just rely on Miss Bubbles or Jasper Hodge or Ezra. I have to start going to auditions and trying to get some work on my own. So today I picked a nice and easy chorus call for my coming-out-of-retirement audition. Steve can go to hell.

I'm getting ready to walk out the door when the phone rings. Aha! This can only be one person. I *run* to the phone.

"Hello?" Breathless, but sexy. Remember to be sexy!

"Stel-La! Stel-La!" Ezra's voice booms, like a foghorn. "Stel-Lahhhh!"

"Hi, Ezra." Shit. Not the handsome star calling for a date. Not prepared for this. Actually, I can't believe Ezra's calling. I assumed I'd have to hound him for a couple of weeks before he would take me seriously. I hold the phone away from my ear, a necessity with his booming voice.

"Okay, sweets. Are you awake? Why aren't you at the gym yet?"

"I'm on my way." A big fat lie. I have never been to a gym. Not once. I try not to walk on the same side of the street where there *is* a gym. I don't even talk to guys *named* Jim, in case some sort of fitness mania rubs off on me.

"Good. I can't get a fat actress any jobs, you know."

"I'm on my way." If lies were wishes come true, I'd have no need to daydream ever.

"Good, now listen. Be here two Mondays from today with your new contact sheet. 10:00 a.m."

"When?" Two weeks? Just when rent is due. Even if the Paines give Miss Bubbles an advance, there is no way I can afford to have pictures taken before then. "Um, I don't know if I'm going to be in town then."

"Don't lie to me, sweets. You forget who you're dealing with. If you're serious about coming back, you'll make this happen. See you in two weeks."

After hanging up the phone I sit on the plaid couch and stare at the floor. Miss Bubbles walks a figure eight around my feet, meowing at me. I contemplate calling Debra and begging for some extra shifts, but fear of her reaction outweighs my worry about money.

"Steve?" My shout fills the space of the living room, and disappears into the furniture. I want him to come tell me to suck it up, but there's no answer, just the slight hum of the ceiling fan and the padded footsteps of Miss Bubbles, who jumps up on the sofa to soak up the ray of sunlight seeping in through the gated window. She stares at me, unblinking, steps onto my lap, flips over onto her back and purrs.

"Is this what you want, Bubblicious?" I stick my fingers into the depths of her white fur and begin to rub up and down. She purrs and licks the side of my arm with a sweet sloppy smile on her face and pins me in against the side of the couch. She always takes up as much space as she possibly can. I love that about her—she is a star in her own right.

"Are you a star?"

She sneezes, as daintily as a southern belle.

"Me too, Miss B. I'm a star, too. Aren't I?" I just sit there, rubbing her stomach, feeling her purr on the palm of my hand.

I remain there for a good five minutes, confused at the sensation of being awake so early and knowing that I am going to be late to this audition. Then, the whiz of the vacuum starts up and the chandelier jiggles like a puppet. Nine-thirty. I don't have to check the clock. It's nine-thirty, on the dot. God forbid Christian gets to that dirt a minute later. It's like living in the movie *Mary Poppins,* where the neighbor sets off a cannon every day at six because he's crazy and thinks he's still an admiral on a ship. Except Christian isn't insane. Just an obnoxiously anal jerk who has no consideration for the people who live below him. I run to my room, select a bright yellow Puma sneaker and chuck it at the ceiling. The vacuum stops. I don't know why, but I jump on my bed and burrow under the covers in case he comes downstairs to yell at me. But he doesn't. He stamps on the ceiling with his annoying foot and resumes the all-too-important clean.

And the phone rings again.

Again I run full speed to answer it.

Again it is not Jasper Hodge.

Again I curse my rotten phone luck.

"Star Baby. You left me some messages."

"Mommy." I check my reflection in the mirror above the television. "I have some good news." And I tell her the whole story about Frances and Miss Bubbles, and meeting Jasper Hodge.

After congratulating herself for thinking about sending me

to Meg Ryan's vet and snippily inquiring whether or not Jasper is married, she starts firing questions at me about Frances. "What did she look like? Is she your size? Does she look old or young or in the middle?" She can barely get the questions out fast enough.

"She looks like she does in the papers. Only younger. And a lot thinner."

"Mmm-hmm. Is she very wrinkled?"

"I didn't notice."

"Now, listen, Little Star. Make her your mentor. Write down everything she does, and then follow it to the letter. Ingratiate yourself."

"Okay, Mom."

"Can she put you in the show, too?"

"Mom! You know it doesn't work that way!"

"Oh, I know…I'm grasping at straws, but these are bordering on desperate times. By the time *I* was twenty-five, I already had a couple of Broadway shows under my belt. But, my little star, I *am* very proud of you. You're keeping yourself in the race. Because time doesn't wait for anyone."

"I know, Mom." I have been hearing this from her my whole life. She's always had this thing about wasting time. Like when I left for New York and college immediately after my performance as the Asian gift princess in *The King and I*. Mom made me board the bus a half hour after the last show ended—I was still in full body makeup and everything. But she wanted me to get to New York before noon. "To capture the energy of a New York morning," she said.

"And since you've been out of touch for almost two years now, an opportunity like this cannot be wasted."

"I know, Mom." Guilt invites itself over to the rec room of my chest and starts lying around in my stomach.

"I mean, if we want to get to our goal, we have to start working very, very hard."

"I know, Mommy. Which reminds me. I called Ezra, and he

agreed to manage me again if I get new headshots, but I'll have to pay my rent, too, and I was wondering if maybe you could spot me a little bit of cash, just until Miss Bubbles starts getting paid." What I hear on the other end of the phone is silence. For three whole Mississippis.

Then she lets out a whoop. "Stell, you know very well that I don't have any money to give you. Sal can barely afford to pay for me and Stewart, and you know I'm not working right now."

"I know, I know, I just thought maybe you'd won the lottery or something and didn't tell me about it." My face slowly flushes after making such a lame joke. I'm feeling awkward all of a sudden. Of course she doesn't have any money! She's living on a lousy plumber's salary and feeding that stinkin' half brother of mine to boot! I'm supposed to be making it on my own, just like she did when she was in the city. "Mom, don't worry, I've got some things coming through and I'll pay for them."

"Well, don't be bamboozled, Little Star. Does Ezra even know what he's talking about when it comes to pictures and things?"

"Of course he does!" My stomach feels heavy, like I've eaten two pounds of lead paint, so I try to get off the phone. "Mom, okay, I'm going to go. I've got an audition and I'm totally running late." At least that's not a lie.

"Okay. Knock 'em dead, honey."

"Okay, I love you, 'bye."

I click the phone off and sit on the couch for a second, staring at the *Backstage* and trying to ignore the plunking of Christian's typewriter keys. I can't focus. The words blur into a black and white blob. My mom is a lot of things, supportive and informative and a good source of info about the business. And sometimes I think she wants me to make it more than I do. But I've never once asked her for money, not since I lived in Michigan, and especially not since she got married. She finally doesn't have to scrub floors and make beds, and here I go and put my worries above hers. I'm feeling nauseous.

And why hasn't Jasper called yet? I check the clock. 9:48— a perfectly acceptable hour to make a phone call to the woman you will someday marry. This is no good. Why isn't he pouncing on this opportunity? For crying out loud, *Ezra* has already called. Miss Bubbles jumps on my stomach, tilts her head and tries to communicate something to me telepathically.

"What do you think?"

"Meow."

"Me, too. It'll work out."

"Meow."

"You're right, no sense sitting here and working myself up. Off to my audition."

"Meow."

I'm in the hallway when Christian's door opens. I cannot emphasize enough how fast I sprint to the front door.

"Stella! I need my blazer!" He is halfway down the staircase and gaining on me.

"I can't get it for you now—I'm on my way to an audition." I quickly spit this out while letting just enough space in the door to let myself squeeze through without him following me out. He just stands on the staircase and glares at me through the glass. I wave and then kiss the feet of the angel before skipping down the street— Ha ha! I am Wonder Woman! I just escaped the clutches of the evil anal-retentive grad student! Hee-hee!

Here it is, 3:30 p.m., and there have to be four hundred and twenty-five girls crammed onto the sixth floor of the Harlequin Studios audition space, a nine-by-nine room with one window and floor-length mirrors covering all the walls but one. I was lucky to grab a seat in the actual waiting room. There are girls leaning against every inch of wall space, lying on the floor, spilling out into the hallway and constantly streaming in and out of the room with their coats on, a cup of steaming hot coffee in their hands.

I close my eyes and lean back in my seat. Today is the day. I rub my cloverleaf pendant so hard that the skin on my thumb starts to blister. This actually isn't that bad. So there are a lot of girls here. And so I'd rather be home rolling out pastry dough. One thing I don't want anymore is to be living in the same old apartment, catering, and having no money. So this is good. And who knows? Maybe there will be a call from Jasper when I get home. I wish I had the money to check my phone messages from the pay phone in the hallway, but I don't. So I just sit here and imagine all the wonderful things he is going to say to me, and all the wonderful places he is going to take me, and then I fantasize about Miss Bubbles being the flower girl and ring bearer at our wedding, sashaying down the aisle with our platinum bands snugly fastened around her diamond collar.

I pick up my copy of *Backstage* again and compulsively open to the page with the audition ad.

> *Beauty and the Beast*
> Non-Equity tour, seeking women 5'6" to 5'8".
> Dancing, singing, extra talents please audition,
> 9:00 a.m.

For the thousandth time, I try to figure out what extra talents might be. Does baking a perfect tart count? Because if it does, then I'm *in!* Sleeping around? *In.* Compulsively dreaming about a perfect life? *In!* Drinking your weight to cover up for insecurities around cute semifamous men? *In! In! In!*

The girl next to me peers over my shoulder. I stare her down, just to let her know it's not okay to be hijacking my paper. Though this is my comeback audition, my killer audition instinct has been restored to its heyday levels. I have been sending this girl negative vibes all day, because she is far too pretty. At an audition, it's best to be the prettiest girl in at least

a ten-foot radius, and this supermodel-of-a-girl, sitting practically on my lap, is cramping my style.

"Does it say if they're taking a midday break?" So...she finally works up the nerve to talk to me. She's been wanting to
for the past two hours.

"No, it doesn't say that," I respond, with my fakest, most in-
sincere, actress smile plastered on my face. She sighs, and I can't
help but agree with her sense of hopelessness.

"I haven't been to one of these calls in ages. There are so
many people to get through." She sighs again and I look at her.
She's Michaela-league gorgeous. Almond-shaped brown eyes
with lashes out to the cosmos and perfectly tanned skin with
just the right amount of rouge on her cheeks. And though she
seems innocent enough, I know perfectly well what she is doing.

She's trying to initiate the *actor conversation*. I *hate* the actor
conversation. Whenever one actor/actress wants to scope out
the competition posed by another actor/actress, they invariably
have the same little chat. It goes a little something like this:

Actor #1: "Oh, you're an actor? What have you done?"

Actor #2: Inflated response. "How about you?"

Actor #1: Inflated response with a one-upmanship.

For example, if I had responded, "Oh, I just got in from DC
where I was the ingenue in *Oklahoma!*" then the other actor
would respond, "Oh, really? I just did *Oklahoma!* on Broadway."
This slam-dunk comment would force the second actor to
begin his own line of questioning. Since Actor #1 has proven
to be working in the better venues, Actor #2 can only hope
that he is better connected. Thus begins the "Who do you
know?" routine.

I really don't like these conversations, and this girl is making
me antsy because the only impressive piece of career information I possess right now involves my cat. But the supermodel
must sense my refusal to cooperate in her little reconnaissance
mission, because she leans over and says, "I'm going to go find

the monitor and ask what number they're on. If you save my seat, I'll ask about you, too. What's your name?"

So it comes to this. I have to barter with this girl like a prison inmate. A service for a service. "Stella Monroe."

She smiles and gets up to find the pimply faced monitor. The monitors of these auditions are always about sixteen years old and high on the infinite power they wield, being the ones who control the flow of auditioners into the audition room.

I survey the room once again. There are three girls sitting by my feet, each clad in the same shade of purple bodysuit with matching leggings. They have their legs open in a vee and their feet touching, so that they form a triangle of purple Lycra. They are holding hands and stretching each other out. And the rest of these girls. Sheesh! Why don't they get an issue of *In-Style* or something? I see, without turning my head, about fifteen girls who look like Laura Ingalls Wilder, with long button-down, floral-print dresses, and long, button-down, floral-print curly hair to match. My mother would laugh. In their faces. Hopeless I think, and stare down at my black Armani pantsuit, another gift from Joshua for occasions I had to lunch with him and he wanted to go somewhere "nice," meaning any place where the entrées cost as much as a week's worth of my rent. It's a beautiful suit though, with a sleeveless shirt that criss-crosses in the back. It comes with a jacket too, so that you can keep the skin on your back hidden, for just your date to know about if you want. But I have no modesty, and decide that when the supermodel returns, I will parade my outfit in front of all the Lauras, just so they can see how good I look.

I lean in again, and my mother's voice reverberates through my mind like an echo, "Never go to an audition looking anything less than one hundred and ten percent luscious, stylish and dangerous."

Just then the supermodel returns.

"Well, you're number eighty-five, and I'm one-ten, but they're only up to thirty-eight." She takes a swig from her water bottle.

"That's crushing news. How is that possible?" I lean back and let out a huge exhale.

"I know. I also heard they're only looking to fill one role— one of the girls in the chorus."

"Singer or dancer?"

"Dancer. So who knows why they're having a singing call." Supermodel sighs. "Who knows why we put ourselves through this."

There it is. There's the defeat I remember so well. But I, Stella Aurora Monroe, refuse to give in to the frustration of defeat. Why? Because. Because I was born to be a star and it is time I start acting like it. Hah! Acting! It's time I start acting. Seriously.

The pimply faced monitor begins making an announcement in the hallway. All the girls in this little room surge forward, and I shove my elbow into more than a few sides, willing myself to the front.

"...cause of the number of people, they're going to start typing."

Huge groan from the girls. *Typing.* I can't believe my bad luck. This is the kind of nonsense you hope to avoid at one of these things. Pretty much it means this: You wait around all day, warm up your voice or your body or whatever you need to have prepared to knock their socks off with a good audition. Then the producers decide to "type." They proceed to call in ten girls at a time, line them up against the wall and decide which ones they want to see audition and which ones are too ugly to even make it to the singing stage. This is so not what I wanted for my coming-out-of-retirement audition.

But this is the new Stella. This is the Stella who takes things in stride. This is the Stella who will do anything to start her fabulous new career. This is the Stella who is going to be making money by going to the theater every day. This is the Stella who *makes things happen.*

So *this* Stella will be unfazed. She will march into that typing room with her head held high, and she will be more beautiful, more compelling, more stylish, luscious and dangerous than one thousand Lauras combined. And *then,* when I get the job, and have to go out on tour, Jasper Hodge, my famous movie-star boyfriend (in my fantasies he's a bonafide A plusser), will be heartbroken because we were just getting to know each other. We will have dramatic, crying confrontations where I will insist that my career must come first, and he will try to convince me that *love* must come first. He will be undeterred, and as a show of good faith and intimacy, he will pull strings and get them to cast me in the Broadway company of *Beauty and the Beast.*

My heart leaps into my throat. Man, that will be so *nice* of him! To pull strings to keep me in the city. He totally loves me!

I hope he called.

I wander over to my chair and inspect my items to make sure everything is still there. My copy of *Backstage,* the huge bag that is stuffed full with a leotard, tap shoes, and a huge black book of sheet music, my thirty-two ounce bottle of Aquafina water and my black bubble coat.

The monitor starts screaming, "Forty through forty-nine! Please line up!" A group of ten flower-dressed girls pad up to him and form a loose line. He leads them into the audition room and not ten minutes later they come whooshing out en masse. Some are heading for their bags in silence, and some are talking a mile a minute, "So we get to come back tomorrow? Great! I'll see you there! What are *you* going to wear?" My guts churn as I watch this scenario happen three times before I hear, "Girls eighty to eighty-nine."

I stand up from my chair only after all the other eighties are assembled in line. I toss my hair good and dramaticlike and pick up my old headshot that looks like I'm thirteen and should be auditioning for a commercial for fruit juice or something. I slowly take the few steps over to number eighty-four Laura and number eighty-six Laur—wait! It's the supermodel! She *cut the line!*

"Hey," she says and leans forward to tell me, "I made a swap with number eighty-six. Her place in line for the number of my manager."

I am stunned, upset, jealous, demoralized! She has a *manager?* Of course she does! She's beautiful, she's crafty and she's *represented*. And she may steal my thunder in there.

I look at my shoes and try to take deep breaths. Yes, the supermodel is gorgeous. Yes, she whored herself out to get further up in the line. But there's room enough for both of us in the acting world. Yes? Of course yes. Her presence doesn't change the fact that I am going to get this job, fall madly in love with Jasper Hodge and become the world's next J-Lo. *Today is the day.*

We start filing into the room. I step into the doorway and see that there are three people sitting behind a desk at the far end of the room. Two guys and a girl, all in their midthirties or forties and with stacks of headshots in front of them on their desk. They sit in front of a wall of full-length mirrors, so I can get a good look at the line I'm in.

"Okay," the monitor squeaks out. "Please hand me your headshots." All the girls dutifully and quietly hand him their pictures and he trots them over to the judge-people. They are staring at us, squinting and looking each of us up and down. The woman starts going through the stack of our pictures and every once in a while points something out to one of the guys.

My mother always says that I should use any means necessary to set myself apart from the other auditioners. At dance auditions, she used to add extra spins into her pirouettes just to be noticed. And she'd always get jobs. But I can't do a pirouette turn to save my life, and since we're just standing in a line I take matters into my own hands by smiling really big and flipping my hair over my shoulder every five seconds. Finally, after what seems like an eternity, one of the men clears his throat and says, "Okay, eighty-five and eighty-six? Step forward."

The supermodel and I step forward and I can't believe it. My heartbeat revs up. My whole new life is going to be fantastic! Out of the corner of my eye I can see the disappointed swish of all the floral print and the deflated demeanor of all those Lauras. Those poor things. It's really hard to get cut from these things.

"You two can go. Thank you."

Huh? I stay rooted to my spot as the supermodel grits her teeth and makes her way toward the door.

"I said you can go. Thank you."

I take another moment before I, too, do this walk of utter shame to the door. I check the clock above the door frame—4:15. All day. Wasted.

As I collect my stuff, I hear a voice say in my ear, "I guess they were looking for frumpy. They should have let us know. I would've borrowed my ten-year-old sister's dress." I look up and the amused face of the supermodel is looking at me. "I'll see you around. Have a good rest of the day." She waves and leaves.

She's actually a very nice girl.

I stand in the waiting room, which is not nearly as crowded now, and try to figure out what to do next. I can't believe I got cut! That's not in the new master plan! But it's okay. It's okay. I went to an audition, and that was the goal. So I've actually done a very good thing. And I'll get the next one. Yeah. I'll get the next one. It'll be good.

I button up the top of my coat, step out onto the wind of 43rd Street and 8th Avenue and head toward Hell's Bar. I struggle up the street, weighted down by my bag and all the trappings of my success.

Hell's greets me like a blast from a five hundred degree oven. The late afternoon crowd is in full force. Some guy is reading poetry in the corner and two girls are staring at him groupie-style and a couple is nestled on one of the velvet couches making out to "Smooth Operator" by Sadé. I spot Rod and Michaela bent over the bar together, laughing, arms entwined, and for a second I'm eager to know the joke. But I get close and see that it isn't laughter. Michaela is in tears, and Rod dabs at her eyes with a wet bar towel. "Thank God you're here," he says when he sees me, "I'm not so good at comforting crying women, you know."

I throw all my stuff down like I've just arrived from a twelve-mile trek through the Andes Mountains. Of course, I have no idea where the Andes Mountains are, but that's of no concern at the moment. "What happened!?" I've never seen her like this, and it's disconcerting.

"Carlo's visa was officially denied. He's getting sent back to Venezuela." Her face is covered in tears and snot, and Rod does his best to mop up after her.

"What? When?" I reach out my hand and smooth down her hair.

She starts nodding vigorously as she tears open three sugar packets and pours them onto the surface of the bar. "I don't know when. He just found this out a half hour ago." She dejectedly runs her fingers through the spilled sugar as she cries—she does this often, she calls it a sugar hand massage. Rod grabs another bar towel with his free hand and continues to wipe her up.

"Where is he?"

"At his apartment, making phone calls or something, I don't know." Carlo is a new boyfriend of hers, but she sure seems to like him an awful lot. I guess he's okay, if you're into the Latin, musician, sensitive, muscular type.

"Well, when does he get sent back?" Rod looks over Michaela's bent head and shakes his head back and forth to signal that I should stop talking as Michaela bursts into another bout of tears. "Wait!" I shout. "It's okay, honey, it'll be okay. I mean, maybe it'll be good to have some time apart!"

Rod draws his finger across his throat twice. "Shut up, Stella."

"I'm just saying—"

Michaela takes a deep breath and lifts her head, her sobs quieting into a soft hiccup, "We have to get married. That's the only way."

My internal organs start to play freeze-tag with each other. "Married? You're going to get married?"

"Yes."

"Rod, just give him a job at Hell's." I grab Rod's shirtsleeve and my voice pitches up two octaves.

His face gets all red and he throws his arms up in the air. "I can't do it, Stella. We're already in trouble about breaking the dance regulations." Michaela quietly sniffles and rubs her eyes. A busboy brings me a coffee and a grilled cheese and tomato. "What the hell's this?" Rod gestures madly at the plate of food.

"I'll pay for it, I'll pay for it."

"Ah forget it! Girls! I can't take it." He throws in the towel, literally, and stalks off to the kitchen.

Michaela looks at me and my heart twists into a pretzel. She's not supposed to get upset like this. Not over boys. She's the calm one. She's the one who always lets things roll off her back.

"It'll be okay." My voice sounds small and not at all supportive. She smiles at me and I take a bite out of my sandwich.

She pats my hand. "Let's have some drinks."

When I get home it's after eleven o'clock at night. I spent the whole evening with Michaela and Carlo, who showed up with a five-pound bag of jelly beans, apparently the snack of choice among illegal aliens. We dried Michaela's occasional tears, talked about ways to get married cheaply, planned how to fly Carlo's parents in from South America without letting them pay for it, discussed what kind of music to be played (Carlo wants Cuban big band, Michaela wants an eighties music dj) and about how many people to invite. I sat there shell-shocked most of the time and doing my best to not say anything negative about their plans. I also tried to calm my simmering nerves by reminding myself how impulsive Michaela can be. She'll probably be more clearheaded tomorrow, and realize that marriage isn't the answer.

We also talked about my career plan. It bothered me that I got cut from the audition, but Rome wasn't built in a day. When Steve and I moved into our apartment, just after he graduated and I dropped out of NYU, he went on one hundred auditions in one hundred days just for the practice. I thought he was crazy because he would go to the lamest calls, like for dance videos and stuff like that. But by the end of the hundred days, he started getting offer after offer and turned down each one. It was for the experience, he said, not the jobs. It would pay off later, he said. He was right. Now he can nail an *All My Children* audition without even getting nervous.

When I let myself into the apartment, exhausted, tipsy and expecting only the cat, Steve's in the kitchen.

"Hi!"

"Hi. How's Michaela?"

"Engaged."

"Oh. Good." He doesn't miss a beat—my real-life smooth operator. He glides through the living room and casually sticks out his finger to press the button on the answering machine in midstride.

"Mon-day, Feb-ru-ar-y nine-teenth, nine fifty-three a.m." *Beep!*

"Hi, I'm looking for Princess Leia. This is Jasper Hodge, I met you the other night at the Miramax party. I was reading in a book the other day that some cultures believe if you do someone a favor, that person owes his or her life to you. But why don't we just start with your Friday night and see where that goes? Call me. 917-555-9483." *Beep!*

Chapter 6

The music is blasting in my ears and the water laps over my torso as I stretch out on my back and extend my left leg into the air. My toes point as hard as they can toward the ceiling, then I lift my head up to make sure my mom is watching and to see if any of the men in the stands would make a good father.

Mom's in the stands, surrounded by other mothers, but no dads. I hope she notices that I'm wearing one of her old dancing costumes. She sees me looking at her and starts to wave violently. I lift my arm out of the water and wave back.

A sharp whistle blows. The coach shouts, "Stop!" Me and all the other synchronized swimmers abandon our positions and swim to the edge of the pool to hear the coach's notes.

"Monroe!" That's funny. I didn't know Steve was the coach. "Monroe! You're a beat behind the other swimmers."

"She is not." My mother comes barreling out of the stands and stands chest to chest with Steve. "She is listening to her own headset. It's the music! The music is behind. Not her."

I have butterflies in my stomach. This is going to be a big day.

Miss Bubbles places both paws on the lip of my bag, lifts her head out and licks my face.

"Hey man. She got a *CAT* in there." The homeless crazy man who is looming above my seat, squished in by the dozens of morning rush hour subway passengers, reaches for her. Shocked as everyone always is at her responding whistle, he lets out a sharp, "Whoo-hee. Now that's a cat who knows her mind. Whoo-hee. Strong-willed—just like my Angie. Mmm-hmm."

I gently slide Miss Bubbles back inside the bag, and bend down to whisper, "Stay in the bag, BB." She wrinkles up her nose at me while I tug my leather miniskirt down to hide what I can of my nearly naked legs.

Nothing like rush hour subway traffic. People crammed in like pennies in a jar, one on top of another, some shiny, some dirty, some old-looking, all patiently putting up with the inconvenience and utter immorality of standing so close to strangers before even a morning coffee. I can't think of how many times I've ridden the train with a stranger's hand resting on my rear, or my lower back, or even my breast. But I know that someday I'll be able to take limos to wherever I need to go, and concentrating on these thoughts helps to put distance between myself and the derelicts of the train.

Needless to say, I try to avoid early morning subway rides. I try to avoid trains altogether, really. But here I am on my way to the Cherry Lane Theater, on the outskirts of the West Village and in prime NYU area. I am almost paralyzed by the awesomeness of my task: to bring my cat to meet the Paines so they can clear her to be the lead in their new play. I am half excited and half scared to death. The standard routine of fears is having a dance party in my head: They aren't going to like her, Frances isn't going to remember who I am, we will get to the stage door and they will inform us that they've decided to go with Chester the peeing Jack Russell instead.

This train of thought is going nowhere, and so I mentally

review what I'll wear tonight on my date with Jasper. Jasper. Thinking about him makes my thighs get warm, it makes a lightning bolt of energy course through my body. I hug the cat-bag. I wasn't able to sleep all night. I popped out of bed at six-thirty and had three homemade blueberry walnut muffins on Christian's doorstep by seven-thirty. Then I took everything out of my closet hoping to find that perfect outfit for my date. Thank God Steve wasn't home to hear my racket.

It's been a long time since I've been on a real date. "Dates" with Joshua consisted of clandestine meetings at hotels after 11:00 p.m. and running home by myself at eleven the next morning, long after he'd gotten up and gone to work downtown. Or of me walking to the Upper East Side, hugging buildings like a shadow, hoping not to be recognized by his neighbors as I made my way to the apartment he shared with his wife, who spent her weekends in the country.

Agh! Damn that Joshua, creeping into my thoughts again. I haven't been so good about keeping him out of mind lately. I stare up at the subway walls to distract myself, searching for one of those Poetry in Motion ads that the MTA runs. They have a campaign where they mount famous poems in the trains. It's an odd thing, to bring lyrical, textual beauty to the inside of these trashy train cars, but I find them very educational. Let's face it—I don't read much so it's quite convenient to get a short lesson in literature while making my way downtown. But alas, nothing this morning, not that it's easy to make out anything over the dozens of sweaty, winter-coated bodies. I look down and check to make sure that Miss Bubbles is still breathing. She whimpers at me, as if to say, "Where are we going, Mama?"

"You'll find out pretty soon, missy," I coo to calm her nerves. "Pretty soon."

The subway pulls into the West 4th Street station. "Here we go, Miss Thing."

★ ★ ★

I knock on the heavy red door. A teamster answers. He's about forty-five and wearing black jeans and that navy blue IATSE T-shirt that all stage techs wear, with a utility belt around his waist adorned with a hanging hammer, Maglite and a roll of duct tape. My stomach starts to flutter at the sight of stage tools.

"Yeah?"

"Hi. I'm here, to, um, well, see my cat's right here in my bag." *Goddamn it Stella*—why are you always so tongue-tied? "And, well, I'm supposed to meet the director."

He stares at me. It is clear that I need to turn on my feminine wiles and stop acting like a dork.

I smile and touch his arm. "I'm sorry—let me start over."

He keeps on looking at me. "I'm here at the request of Ms. Frances Paine." I inhale at this point, for dramatic emphasis. "My cat is going to be in the play they're doing."

"What's your name?"

I tell him my name and he pulls down a clipboard that hangs right inside the door. "Monroe, Monroe," he mutters my name over and over as his dirty hand moves down the list. He looks up, "I don't see it."

"What?" Not in my plan. "But I met her the other day! They called my apartment! They told me to be here today!" All my poise—gone.

"Maybe they forgot."

"But they can't forget!"

"Okay, okay…take it easy. Take it easy. What's the cat's name?"

Right—the cat's name. "Bubbles. Miss Bubbles."

"Oh, yeah. Right here. Miss Bubbles!" He says this like I have just given the right answer to a test question. "Come on in."

And he steps aside, like the gatekeeper to Oz, and lets me into this most precious, precious building. The Cherry Lane Theater.

I haven't been in the back of a theater in years. Literally. Two years, since Josh made me quit the theater company I was working with. But *this*. What a way to make a comeback!

I stand inside the doorway, which is just off stage left, and stare across the stage into the stage-right wings. "Check it out, Miss Bubbles." She pops her head up and together we take it all in. Against that back wall are about a dozen sandbags, anchoring a pulley system that keeps the scrims and backdrops in place. The very sight of them makes me smile. There is a flat in that far wing, with part of a set on it—a desk, chair and hat stand. Three men stand diagonal to the set piece and on the stage, one on his knees and the other two behind him—they are drilling a staircase into the stage floor. There is a small boombox on the stage right by where they work, and the sound of Guns N' Roses' "Patience" wafts over to where I stand. One of the techies whistles along. Meanwhile lights come up and down in specific, focused areas of the stage. An intense beam lights the center, then a voice from back behind the audience seats says, "Tighter, more to the left." A tin voice from the ceiling responds, "This light doesn't have much give—all I can do is tighten it about two more inches." Then the light goes off and another comes up on a different area of the stage. Ah! The flurry of the preshow setup! This is the best sight I've seen in my whole life. Well, my whole day.

"Hi, are you Stella?"

A windburst of nervous energy comes barreling at me from behind the stage-left curtain.

"Uh, yeah." His disheveled clothing, the bags under his eyes, the Post-it notes stuck to his chest, the fat folder that is losing papers on three sides and his general air of panic tells me that this is the stage manager.

"Great. I'm Kevin." He pauses to shake my hand. His palm is very sweaty, but he's cute in a downtown, slacker, Sonic Youth lovin', vegetarian kind of way. He is thin to the point of gaunt, and his hair is tight curly brown, eyes blue and skin ivory-white.

"The director is dying to see the cat." And then, taking me in, he promptly begins to melt down. *"You did bring the cat, didn't you?"*

"Oh, she's right here." And, as if she knows where she is and that timing is now everything, Miss Bubbles pops up her gorgeous white head and meows—like a cuckoo bird in a clock. Kevin the stage manager jumps back.

"Oh! Okay, wait here."

"Okay."

He walks away and I look around, one hand underneath my bag and one holding the cloverleaf pendant. To my right is a rickety staircase, leading down to what I imagine are the dressing rooms. Just beyond the stairway entrance is a makeshift area equipped with a mirror and a clumsy clothes rack, on which hang three dress shirts, two pairs of plaid tweed pants and three pairs of the same shoes. I assume this is the quick-change area. To my left is a booth, a stool that sits right in front of the old-style curtain rope and pinup pictures of Playboy models. Love the techies and their sense of beauty. Just then, one of them walks by me. He carries a coil of electric cord and smokes a cigarette. "Watch it there, honey."

"Oh! Sorry!" I jump back, not wanting to be in his way at all.

"No problem. Go take a look at the stage, if you want." He smiles and keeps walking until he disappears down the staircase.

Nobody is in the left wing with me.

I step toward the stage. The men who are drilling the staircase into place don't notice me, their backs remain stooped over their task. Dust plays in the playground of the lights, that are now on as bright as possible for the workers to see by. Glow tape, stuck to the floor to trace the spot where set pieces go, stands silently by, waiting for the darkness to come so it can do its job. I notice a costumer standing in the back of the upstage right wing, lifting pieces of tweed fabric high into the air, shuffling them on her arm. There's someone behind her—I can't see the person's face—but whoever it is, he or she is very upset about something. Voices are discussing the flexibility of a certain pair of clothes, and as they rise in pitch, the costumer begins to violently go through the pile of clothes, as if she's trying to find a cookie to quiet a screaming child.

Then a voice calls from the audience, "Can you bring the cat down here?"

I step out onto the stage, and into the lights. Beads of sweat instantly form on my brow as I say, "What's that?" I can't make out who I am talking to, because the light is so intense. My eyes start to tear, but I don't know that it is necessarily the light. It's just, well, all I can think about is my mom. She would love to know where I'm standing right now. I cover my eyes and try to make out where the voice is coming from. The dust tickles my nostrils, and lifting my head ever so slightly, I can make out the mezzanine seats, waiting patiently above the orchestra, looking down upon the stage to monitor the events.

This time a woman's voice says, "Please bring the cat down to us."

There are some stage steps off to my left, painted black and lined with glow tape. My vision returns as I leave the beam of light, and I can just start to make out the shadowy forms of six bodies, seated halfway up the aisle. All of them are in the middle of a serious discussion, and don't stop arguing even when I stand right in front of them. Kevin motions at me, then says, "Have a seat and just give us one second."

I place myself diagonally across the aisle from them so that I can easily listen to their discussion. There are two women, one of them Frances, who is sitting back in her seat and abstaining from offering her opinion, and the other one a mousy brown-haired girl in corduroy overalls. I decide by the way the mouse scribbles down every word that any of the other people say that she's an intern or the assistant stage manager or something. Of the other four, I decide that the best-dressed man must be Frederick Paine. He wears a crisp blue suit with a white dress shirt that is open at the top button. The sight of his chest poking out from inside that dress shirt makes me start to feel kind of sexy, like when Joshua would loosen his tie after a long workday. Frederick is gesticulating passionately and waving his hands in the air, giving me an opportunity to see the gold ring on his finger. It shines and catches the meager houselights, refracting it back every which way over the seats. The more heated his words become, the faster the mousy little intern writes.

The jobs of the other three men are easy to figure out. Kevin the stage manager looking disappointed and ready to cry, keeps whining, "If you *want* to do that, we can. It's just going to be difficult, that's all." The playwright is easy to peg, he's the one who is really defensive. "But that's not how I wrote it!" he keeps shouting while Frederick is talking. The playwright is such a slob—he keeps pushing his glasses back onto his face, dabbing his sweaty head with a napkin, and nibbling doughnuts, fresh from the steaming box of Krispy Kreme laid out on the makeshift wooden desk in front of them. The director is the exact opposite of the writer—very thin, well kept and soft-spoken. He keeps twiddling his thumbs, shaking his head and saying, "That won't fit into the visual motif as I've designed it."

They finally settle whatever the disagreement is, and by settle I mean the other people agree to do what Frederick tells them to. The power of money…

Then Kevin clears his throat and announces the next item of business. "Well, okay, are you guys ready to audition the cat?"

Audition? I don't like the sound of that word one bit. I thought it was a done deal!

Frederick turns to me and growls, as I notice is his way of talking, "Let's see her!"

I suddenly feel like I'm on display, because six pairs of eyes turn toward me. Frances leans forward. The mouse stops writing. The playwright ceases chewing, his doughnut poised in midair.

Stella: don't trip, don't trip! I get up from my seat, yank my miniskirt toward the ground and step across to them.

I smile at everybody and put my red oversized bag on the wooden desk. I loosen the purse's mouth so Miss Bubbles can come out, and peer in to let her know it's time. But she's cowering toward the back of the purse, quivering like a leaf, moaning a little kitty moan and staring at me with such intensity I don't know what to do.

"Is there a problem?"

It's the first I've heard of Frances's mellifluous voice and I jerk my head up. "No, no. *No* problem. None at all." I lean down into the bag and reach in, but Miss Bubbles bats my hand away with her paw and mews. "Miss Bubbles!" I whisper and pray that nobody can hear me. "Please don't ruin this for me. Come on. You can do it. Come on." She wedges herself as far back as she can and turns her head from me, effectively ignoring my pleas.

"We don't have all day, you know." The six pairs of eyes are still staring and tears start to form in my eyes, because what can I do? But then, immediately, again as if knowing what she has to do, Miss Bubbles springs out of the inside of the bag like a jumping bean and meows, like a kid who's playing hide and seek shouting, "Here I am!"

Well, the six of them are totally blown away by her theatrics. They all jump back in their seats in surprise and let out a delighted gasp. Miss Bubbles keeps mewing at them and they continue to "ooh" and "aah" as she sashays back and forth across the table, strutting like a runway model.

"She's perfect! That's just what I wanted!" The playwright is so excited he puts the doughnut down next to Miss Bubbles, who looks at it, looks back at him and scoffs. She moseys her way down to the other end of the table, closer to where Frederick and Frances are sitting, sits on her hind legs and stares at them. So brazen! So composed! I am proud of her the way my mom must have been proud when I opened as Oliver in the community theater production they did when I was nine. What a smart kitty Miss Bubbles is—settling herself right in front of the people with the money, with the power!

"Frances said she whistles. Can you get her to do it for us?" Frederick looks at me expectantly.

"Sure." I call for her, "Whistle for me, Bubby." And she does, as low and clear as a mountainside pool. And then she does the funniest thing, she turns and looks at the auditioners and lowers her body, like a bow. I swear.

Frances and Frederick and the director and the playwright are beside themselves with joy, clapping, laughing, sounding relieved. Apparently they really need a whistlin' cat.

"Can she do it on cue?" If Kevin is impressed, his all-business demeanor isn't betraying it.

"I bet she can. I mean, you have to ask her to do it, but she'll come through."

"No problem!" the playwright is very eager. "Max can ask her to whistle."

"Max?" My curiosity gets the better of me.

"That's the lead character. Max. He's a writer with a cat who whistles." The playwright takes half a doughnut into his mouth and gulps. "That's how he gets girls."

"Oh, well, I guess if the guy playing Max asks her clear enough, she'll be just fine. I mean, the only other person she'll whistle for is my roommate. And if someone pisses her off." *Why'd you swear?* "I mean, I'm sorry, you know, if somebody makes her angry."

"Don't worry, don't worry, I swear all the time!" and the rest of the doughnut is gone in one vile swallow. I just love it when fat sweaty guys flirt with me.

Frederick, who hasn't taken his eyes off the cat the whole time, finally turns to Frances, who is seated to his right, and beams at her. He leans in and whispers something in her ear, then nuzzles her cheek, sits back up in his chair, claps his hands, and looks at his watch. Frances doesn't even crack a smile. Ice Princess.

"Well, let's introduce the cat to Max. Kevin, take Miss Bubbles down to the dressing room to meet him."

They all rise to their feet as Miss Bubbles flirtatiously struts back to my purse, meows and crawls in. Frederick approaches me and extends his hand, "Well, this has been a wonderful meeting. We've gotten some excellent work done here and I'm very glad to have your cat on board. Will she require a handler?"

"A handler? I don't think so."

"Hmm. We're expecting to have a decent run—you can commit to the duration?"

"Of course! I would love to commit to the duration!" He walks Kevin and me down the aisle, leading me by placing his hand on the small of my back. Again, feeling things that I shouldn't.

"The office will call you to work out the logistics of payment and rehearsal, and Kevin will let you know when we'll need the cat." We stop at the foot of the stage. "And let me say—" he looks deep into my eyes "—welcome aboard *The Happy Ending*."

Then Frederick looks at the cat, who is sitting up in my bag, her paws draped over the side of the red leather, and extends his hand toward her.

"Meow."

Frederick laughs, a throaty chuckle and turns to go back to his seat.

"This way." Kevin the stage manager herds me up the steps. I kind of like his way. He obviously wants to do a good job, because he is very businesslike as we walk up the stairs. He doesn't even turn to make sure that I am still behind him, just keeps walking, all the while giving me info.

"So I'll talk to everyone about the schedule, but this is our final week of rehearsals, so we probably won't want the cat until the final dress next week."

"Um, wait, when does the show open?" By this time we are backstage left and walking toward the rickety staircase.

"Previews start the day after the dress, and the opening is a week after that, so about two and a half weeks from now. We're kind of putting Miss Bubbles into the show at the last minute, but Frederick was holding out for the perfect animal, and it seems like she'll do just fine."

"Yeah, she's a quick study."

Kevin lights our way down the stairs with his Maglite. "Hopefully Max will approve her."

"Max is the lead character's name, right?" I'm intrigued. Getting co-star approval for an actor is quite a feat of negotiation, so whomever I'm about to meet probably has some clout. Hopefully he's cute, too. And single. I silently thank God that I wore such a short skirt.

"Yeah, it's the character. But we have to call the actor by the character's name or he throws a hissy fit. He's one of *those*." Kevin makes a rolling motion perpendicular to his temple, to show me that the actor is crazy. "But what can you do? You have to respect an actor's way of working, you know?"

"Yeah, sure. Is it a large cast?" We snake our way through the labyrinthine underbelly of the Cherry Lane. There are water pipes hanging low on the ceiling and rust stains adorning the walls, which makes the whole hallway look like it was dug out by a prison escapee. There are rooms to the left and right, though, one marked Pepper, one marked Hank, and one marked Closet.

"Well, it's just about this writer Max and the women in his life, and then there's his buddy, too. So five. And they're all okay. Even Max. But we're pretty excited, the cast is really good and some of them are fairly well known, so they should draw some audience. Hey, there's where the cat will stay." He points to a room on his right as we pass by.

I'm shocked. For some reason, I thought that I would sit backstage with Miss Bubbles on my lap during the show, and ready her for her entrance. I didn't think she'd have her own room. That feeling I get whenever Steve talks about his auditions or rehearsals shoots an arrow through my rib cage. I shake it off and try to concentrate on what Kevin is saying.

He mumbles on for about thirty more seconds before finally stopping before a dingy white door with a hand-painted gold star on it and the name Max.

"Well, I hope he likes her. If not, we're really fucked." He taps on the door with his knuckle, and says gently, as if he was talking to a newborn baby, "Max, can you approve the cat now?"

The door swings open. Time freezes. My face burns like an oven. If I had eaten breakfast I would throw up. There, standing behind the dressing room door with the biggest gold star of all, hair perfectly yellow in the dingy basement, height staggeringly high, and chest gleaming tan beneath his unbuttoned shirt, is Jasper Hodge.

Chapter 7

Though I've been sitting at the bar for over an hour, it isn't until I finish my second chocolate martini that Michaela finally realizes how dire the situation is. She leans over from behind the bar, a jade heart pendant dangling from her neck, a brand-new sapphire chip engagement ring on her finger.

"You're overreacting." She takes a big sip of her own drink, Dewar's on the rocks ever since I've known her, and tries to rationalize. Slamming her hands down on the bar, she shouts her conclusion over the din of a Hell's Friday night, "So what? So you were caught in a little lie. So what? You guys are actors! You always lie about where you are in your careers!" Content with her proclamation, she reaches for my paper napkin and starts folding it in a zillion different directions while Rod asks her a question about the schedule.

I grab some cherries out of the fruit case on the bar, pop one into my mouth and put my head in my hands. I know I'm not overreacting. I *had* been overreacting when I ran home from the Cherry Lane Theater, crying and shamed. I *had* been overreacting when I shimmied out of my leather miniskirt, flung myself onto my bed and started moaning. I *had* been overreacting when I begged Steve to take all my clothes to Goodwill, claiming that I would have no more need of my things since I would never again be leaving the apartment.

But now, after an entire afternoon of melodramatic mourning, I have adjusted. I'm in what they call the acceptance phase—I accept that the fabulous future I had envisioned came crashing down around me the minute Jasper revealed himself to be Max.

What the hell was I thinking, anyway? That a man who was a serious player in the New York theater scene would want to spend time with a nobody who waits tables and lies about her career to perfect strangers? Of course he wouldn't! He was probably just horny the night of the party and thought I'd be easy. I certainly *looked* easy! And then he'd throw me away, just like Christian and Steve would probably predict. They're right! He probably takes home a different waitress every night! I try to look at the bright side. At least I'm better off than I was with Ned the naked man. At least I didn't actually sleep with Jasper. Now *that* would be one deep hole to dig myself out of.

My head collapses onto my folded hands and I feel the cool sleek surface of the bar imprint its healing powers into my forehead. My mother's sweet face flashes into my brain, and a fresh rash of guilt sends a wave of goose bumps over my skin.

Ugh! The worst sensation swirls in my stomach, the thought of disappointing my mother. I can't ever let her know what a total loser I am. What a failure I am here in New York. Jesus, I'm so upset that the two chocolate martinis aren't even making a dent in my sobriety. But I keep trying. I slosh the rest of my drink around in its glass. It's cool in my hand, and I stab my pinkie finger in the sticky-sweet chocolate residue on the rim. "Michaela, you should have seen his face. He was *smirking* at me." I lick the last bit off my finger and slide the empty over to her. She shakes her head and slides it back to me.

"Uh-uh. I think you should get out of here. Go home, dress

yourself up and go meet him. There's still time if you hurry." She keeps folding the napkin, which is beginning to look like a flower.

I roll my eyes. "I'm not going anywhere." She shakes her head again.

"I'm serious. He totally looks down on me now." I interrupt her before she has a chance to deny what I'm saying. "And then I just became this idiot! This babbling idiot yammering on and on about how 'my cat was really excited! No, I'm really excited! I mean, well, I hope we have a great time!'" I look her dead in the eye, to convey what a gibberish-spewing moron I had become. "*'I hope we have a great time.'* Michaela, I'm an idiot." I poke a passing bartender with my empty glass, who looks at Mic for the green light. "I'll have another too," she sighs as she leans against the black-bottled bar. "And then what happened? He just said okay to the cat and then that was it?"

"That was it. He didn't even look at me again. He just slammed his door and went back to his actor ways." The bartender sets down our drinks.

"Well, Stellie…"

"*No,* that's it. I blew my shot with him. Now he thinks I'm just some loser animal-sitter who waits tables for a living and dreams of becoming an actress but isn't good enough to get it done."

She starts to laugh at me. "Stellie. People don't think that way!"

"Yuh-huh. I know the score. I know that once you're down you stay down."

She looks at me with those sympathetic green eyes and I think she is about to change my life with wise advice. But instead her gaze drifts up over my head and a smile creeps onto her face, like a curious cat. She grabs my arm and points behind me.

"I think somebody's looking for you." I spin around on the bar stool. Jasper Hodge is standing in the doorway, looking unbelievably fantastic in dark khaki pants and a maroon pullover Henley.

"Holy shit."

Michaela is laughing again. She spins me back around, places the napkin flower behind my ear, taps my forehead with her fingers, and starts waving her hand in the air, shouting coquettishly, "Yoo-hoo!"

I try to push her arm down, to get her to stop waving but it's too late. He has spotted us, and despite my quick prayers to make him disappear, he makes his way toward us, causing more than a few heads to turn. "How'd he find me?"

"How do you think he found you?" she asks with a huge kooky grin on her face.

"Steve." We both say it in unison. I keep facing the bar, because my heart can't take watching him approach. "Michaela, how do I look?" Ever prepared, she whips a tube of lip gloss out from under the bar and shoves it in my hands, then runs her fingers through my hair and pinches my cheeks—hard—but I don't mind. "Lips okay?" I ask once I finish applying. "You're gorgeous!" she says. "And one, two, three…"

"So where's the cat?" That voice. Good lord.

I casually slide around on my bar stool and reply, "She's at dinner." He laughs. Actually it's more of a discriminating chuckle. He hates me and is about to yell at me in front of all my friends and co-drinkers, people who see me every Friday night and expect me to do something foolishly, drunkenly dramatic. But he really looks hot, so at least these people will see me in an embarrassing situation with a really, really sexy guy.

"So I was told I'd find you—" he points at me "—at this bar, with a beautiful blonde, which I'm guessing is you." He smiles at Michaela and I feel a pang of jealousy, like I'm a three-year-old who is watching a bigger piece of cake go to someone else. "I'm Jasper." He extends his arm to Michaela, who giggles and shakes his hand. Curse Michaela for being the most beautiful, feminine, sexy chick in the universe!

Keeping his hand in hers, he leans toward the bar. "I bet you make great martinis." He almost whispers this question, and I wonder if he's practicing for a James Bond movie, using Michaela as an Ursula Andress stand-in. I wonder if I should kick him behind his knees, watch him crumple to the floor and stand over him until he apologizes for making me feel like a moron. I wonder if Michaela is going to notice that, yes, he is still holding her hand. What is going on here?

"She's engaged," I blurt, and only after the two of them stare at me like I have Tourette's syndrome do I realize my mind is getting the best of me.

"Congratulations!" He recovers beautifully. "When's the big day?"

"Oh, we don't know yet. Maybe in a month?" She removes her hand from his, downs the rest of her Dewar's and tells the other bartender to make Jasper a martini. "Stella, I'll be back, okay? I have to take care of something."

She is doing the right thing, leaving me alone with my future husband. But I start to frantically send telepathic messages to her: *Don't go! Don't leave me alone with him! I'm not smart enough or cool enough or drunk enough to deal with this right now!* But her receiving system is shut down, because she turns on her heels and walks toward the back, getting none of my transatmospheric messages. I am left alone, my body completely facing Jasper's as he stares at the back of the bar.

"So." He takes a sip of his drink and then turns to me. I, for a moment, feel the way I did in high school when my mom caught me dancing drunkenly on a bar and shouting, "I'm *out* of this crazy town!" Expecting to be read the riot act, I stare at my red cowboy boots and wait patiently for him to begin ripping into me.

"So." Again with the so. Agonizing. Does he need me to start in for him? Because I have a list all ready to go. He should start by mentioning that I have no right to disappoint somebody like him. Don't I know who he is? Yes, then he should go into what a drunken mess I was the other night. He also might want to let me know that I wasn't that great of a singer anyhow. Then he can get into how ridiculous it is for me to hope that my cat can be my ticket into the Stardom Country Club. I bite the inside of my lip as I wait for him to commence verbal attack. But he doesn't criticize me at all. Instead, he anesthetizes me with his eyes. What the hell color are they anyway? Brown? Gold? Still no sound. Just staring. He drinks again. "You stood me up." Interesting technique. I go into automatic flirt pilot.

"No I didn't," I circle my finger around the rim of my martini glass.

This completely illogical reply pleases him. "Oh, you didn't?" He chuckles again, this time into his drink.

I begin to regain my confidence. Maybe the drinks are taking effect after all. "*No.* As a matter of fact," I pause to bring the martini glass up to my newly glossed lips, "I was beginning to worry that you were going to stand *me* up."

"Oh, really?" he replies, comfortable with the game I've begun. "I was going to stand you up? How do you figure? I was waiting at the hotel for you, just like we planned. No Stella. Please explain." And he flashes that grin, that grin that says, "Okay, you want to play catch? Let's play catch."

I lean in. *"Jasper,"* I drool his name into a long set of scolding sounds, "I changed our plans. I told you to meet me here. At Hell's. And here you are! What could possibly be the problem?" I grab another cherry out of the fruit case, pop it in my mouth and swallow it down leisurely.

He cocks his head and looks me in the eye. "Left me a message, huh?"

"Yes." I look right back into his chocolaty-golden-ambrosial eyes. Not a good idea. I feel myself leaving my body, transporting into a future where his eyes are my own personal, private backyard pool.

"Hmm. Well I didn't get a message. Who'd you leave it with? Do I have to fire my assistant?"

Assistant? I picture a tall, lean girl with a blond ponytail and Madonna-like headset strapped around her tanned head holding a clipboard and striking a pose. "I'm Bambi! How can I help you?" I swig my drink. I don't need to contend with a horny assistant who is trying to bed Jasper down at every turn.

"No. No assistant. I don't go through assistants."

"Hmm. Well this is curious, then, isn't it?"

"Very."

"Well, I found you anyway."

"So you *did* get the message! See? My telepathic skills work great!" I smile at him and stare.

As he smiles he licks his lips, making my thoughts turn to dirty activities that could be performed in my very-close-to-Hell's apartment, but I force myself to keep focused. "That's a good one," he says. "So it was faulty wiring in your telepathic messaging system that caused the trouble. It's not that maybe you were avoiding going out with me because you were embarrassed about the party the other night."

"Or the fact that I lied to your face and then got caught?"

"Or that." He looks at me, not smiling, not drinking, not frowning though, either. "Listen, I don't have a lot of friends, I mean real friends, in the city, you know? I'm only here when I'm working and there's never time to meet people." He turns toward me, so that his body completely faces mine. "And I can tell you like to have a good time, so I thought maybe we can have some fun while I'm here." He puts his drink on the bar and takes my hand. "How does that sound?" He peers at me, expectantly, waiting for my response.

I can't think of anything romantic, witty, or otherwise endearing to say, so this is how I respond: "Um, okay."

"Okay. Let's drink to it." He lets go of my hand, raises his glass and clinks mine.

I recover myself quickly. "Besides I really can't let you get away without finding out what happened with Debra the troll."

He spits out his drink. Excellent. I have made a famous person do a spit take.

"That's a perfect nickname for that little beast."

★ ★ ★

Two hours later, Michaela, Jasper and I are hunched over our cocktails in my favorite corner booth. Jasper is telling us the funniest story about an audition and I am smiling back at him and laughing whenever he pauses, but I don't know what he is talking about because I can't understand English at the moment. I don't know whether my sudden loss of language skills is due to his eyes or the four martinis in my tummy or the fact that I am on guard over Michaela's knee's proximity to Jasper's thigh.

"So I said, 'No *way* am I doing your gardening, lady.'" He smiles, swigs, and I swoon amidst a cloud of puffy laughter that is definitely tinged with vodka.

Rod comes over to ask Michaela if she's still working and eyeballs Jasper before looking at me with a half-raised eyebrow. Michaela checks her watch and says that she took her last table at 2:00 a.m. I can't believe that Jasper has been here this long, and I can't believe that he seems to be having a good time. He is so beautiful. He is clear while everything around him is fuzzy. I can only focus on him, and his lips, those lips that he must inject collagen into on a daily basis. In fact, I think they are rounder than they were when he got to Hell's. As I stare at them, they grow large and his teeth look too white as he smiles and laughs with Michaela.

Water. I think to myself that a nice glass of icy water will still the marching ants in my brain that are making Jasper look like a giant pair of lips and teeth. I get up from my seat too fast and slam the tops of my thighs against the table. Michaela reaches out her hand to steady me and Jasper asks if I'm all right. As much as I don't want to leave the two of them alone, I know that I have to get out of here and get to the bar.

I cruise to the back and nod at the bartender. He hands me a glass of water, icy and tall. Wow, I think to myself. Maybe my telepathic powers are greater than I know.

I swallow it down and hold on to the bar for focus. I lift up my head and count the twenty black rose pictures behind the bottles twice before I venture back to the booth.

"Hey, lady," Steve is at the booth now, with his boyfriend Peter, who stands to kiss my cheek. He is very polite but I still don't like him.

"Hey darlin'," I respond and even *I* can hear the slur to my speech. "What are you doing here?"

He pulls me down onto the seat and says into my ear, "I just thought Pete and I could use a drink. And I wanted to see if you were here."

I stare at him. "You wanted to meet Jasper Hodge."

"Damn right I did," and he cocks his head as if to say, "You go girlfriend."

I look back to the booth of people. Jasper is ordering a round of drinks for everybody. Michaela is on his cell phone calling her boyfriend, um, fiancé, and I can hear her saying, "Baby we are having so much fun. Come over!" Peter is making these annoying moony eyes at Steve, who is staring at Jasper like he is an alien who just walked into our living room. Jasper finishes ordering and asks Steve what he does.

"I'm an actor." This piques Jasper's interest and for a moment the air around the table grows incredibly still, like it's high noon. Jasper and Steve stare at each other for a split second, and I know it's coming. The *actor conversation*. Oh Christ. And poor Steve—this is going to be a slam-dunk victory for Jasper.

Steve sits up a little taller as he starts talking about his recent auditions. I am forced to drown out their talk by swimming in liquor. I peer at Jasper through the bottom of my glass, though, and am surprised to find him leaning in, listening to Steve describe his agent. I lift my head out of the martini. Jasper is asking noncompetitive, interesting questions, not bragging about himself at all, and when they begin to compare notes over who they mutually know, it is without a trace of jealousy. I am shocked, and for some reason the glow of Jasper's golden hair sifts off his head and forms a halo. I shake my head to dislodge this image.

Peter breaks my observations by leaning across the table, and shouting, "So what do *you* think, Stella. Pink or yellow for the bridesmaids?" He is holding Michaela's hand.

I stare at them blankly. "Are there going to be bridesmaids?"

While Michaela silently nods no, Peter goes into gay-fashion-designer mode. "There simply *have* to be bridesmaids! Can you really count it as a wedding without *bridesmaids?* Besides, I want to see Steve in a dress."

Michaela and I start laughing at this. And Steve joins in the fun, "What are you talking about?"

"Whether or not there are going to be bridesmaids at Michaela's wedding."

"Well, I don't want to be a bridesmaid. I just want to wear a Diana Ross wig and sing 'Endless Love' at the back of the bar through the whole ceremony. Do you think Carlo will mind?" Even though Steve and I and Michaela always have outrageous conversations like this, my spine stiffens, because we are being observed by somebody possessing a small pie piece of wealth and national fame, and because I want him to *love* me and therefore don't want to shock him with any infantile behavior. I am preparing to kick Steve under the table, who, at the moment, is singing "Endless Love" almost full voice with Peter crooning the Lionel Richie harmony. But one look at Jasper and my worries melt away like water. He laughs. More than that. He hums the melody for them. Providing accompaniment. What's going on here? Is he drunk or something?

I am shocked at the prospect of him being drunk. What is he, just human? I feel a little disappointed, honestly. But my nerves remain jangled. I look from him to Michaela to Peter to Steve and then stare at a crumpled napkin on the table. Never once in two years did Joshua ever sit at a table with my friends and laugh. I finish my drink and grab the hem of the passing waiter's shirt. "Another," I command and thrust the empty glass into his hand. "Chocolate."

★ ★ ★

After Steve and Peter leave, and I have no idea what time it is, Michaela puts her head on the table and apparently falls asleep. She doesn't stir for a good five minutes, during which time Jasper comes over to my side of the booth and sits next to me.

"You have nice friends. They're funny." He picks up my hand in both of his and turns it over. He traces its lines like a fortune-teller.

"Yeah," I say, rendered ineloquent by the surging sensation in my nether regions, and the static in my brain. "Do you see anything interesting in there?" I nod toward my hand.

"Ah, *yais,*" he says in a funny, phony accent. "I see lots of *good times.* Many good times in *zhee* near future." He sounds like Arnold Schwarzenegger, but I can't help thinking this is the cutest thing ever. Then he kisses me, without letting my hand go. Short and sweet but a kiss nonetheless and before I can worry about what shape my breath is in, he pulls away and kisses the top of my head. "Let's get you home."

He could say, "Let's get your clothes off and have sex on this table right now," and I would do it, for I am completely under his spell. I feel like a rabbit that has just been pulled from a hat. He stands up and reaches for his coat. I look for my bag and gently nudge the back of Michaela's head. "Honey, we're going." She moans without lifting her head and says, "Leave me. Carlo will come." And even though it's probably four in the morning, I believe her. Carlo always comes to get her after work, so that she doesn't have to make the trip home alone. He's a great boyfriend. I turn to Jasper, who is standing alongside the booth, waiting for me to get ready. Maybe he'll be a great boyfriend, too.

"You didn't tell me that Steve is up for a role on *All My Children,*" he says as we start walking toward the door. Fantasy destroyed.

"Sorry," is all I can manage, anything more and my resentment would literally smack him in the face. "He's up for a lot of things."

He just smiles and reaches for my hand. He leads me through what is left of the Hell's patrons—two kissing couples and a pack of guys sitting in the corner, telling dirty jokes. When we get outside, Jasper spins toward me and backs me up against the wall. The coolness of the brick gives me goose bumps. I can't see over his massive frame. "I had a lot of fun tonight. Sorry that I didn't get your message earlier, though. I'll turn on my Stella Telepathic System as soon as I get home." He smirks and kisses my forehead, stares into my eyes, then releases me from his hold, walks toward the street and hails me a cab.

I'm a goner.

Chapter 8

I knock on the heavy red door of the Cherry Lane Theater and nobody answers. I check my watch to make sure I have the time right, and then I notice that the street is still. Funny, my watch says it's 10:00 a.m., that I'm right on time, but judging by the street activity, it seems like it's 5:00 a.m. A white van is crawling from door to door, newspapers hurling out from its back door. A sanitation truck follows close on its heels.

But still I knock again.

And this time I hear Miss Bubbles meowing and feet approaching the door.

The door swings open and Jasper stands behind it, holding the cat and smiling at me. The cat slinks up Jasper's body and swirls herself around his head, forming a kitty turban. She meows at me.

"I thought you'd never get here," he says, and welcomes me inside.

"Hey man, are you here for the audition?" The guy who greets me at the door has on a tie-dye Phish shirt that matches his fuzzy orange afro.

"Uh, yes. Yes I am," I stammer and gulp the fresh air of the hallway before entering into the den of smoke and slack that is waiting on the other side of the door. I step into a kitchen, well, a hallway that is dressed up as a kitchen, and try to not stare at the moldy hunk of bread on the counter. One black lightbulb hangs from the ceiling on a rusty chain to light our way, and truthfully, I am glad to not be able to see.

In the old days, after my semester at NYU and before Joshua, I would never have come to an audition posted by film students, especially not one that called for traveling to the Lower East Side. I'd done so many student films when I was actually a student, I didn't think it was necessary to do more free work in more crappy films with more idiotic juvenile boy directors who wanted to make the next *Mean Streets* and were just looking for the hottest chicks they could find. They would "hire" them (I use this term loosely because, of course, no money is involved in a student film) and then have an excuse to hang out with and flirt with girls who would otherwise never in a million years have anything to say to them. Now that I think about it, I really hated doing these films.

But it's Monday morning, and after a weekend of catering and suffering verbal blows from Debra and after a weekend of *not* hearing from Jasper even though we had a terrific time on Friday and even though he is supposed to be falling in love with me, I have to do something to sustain my career-starting campaign.

Fuzzy orange afro boy, who looks like a young, ugly Harpo Marx, asks me if I want anything to drink. I shake my head vigorously and follow him into the back of his apartment.

"Is there anyone to go before me?"

"Naw, you're one of the first people to show today." Harpo opens a whitewashed wooden door that leads into a large open room, one blessed with three floor-to-ceiling windows but cursed with a sheet of smoke and scent of mold that shrouds the whole place. Sitting cross-legged on a futon against the back wall is an early-twenty-something guy who has purple and orange streaks in his hair and a cigarette dangling out of his mouth. A stack of headshots on the floor in front of him is piled so high he doesn't need to bend down to look at them, and a half-eaten Pop-Tart balances on his knee. He places the Pop-Tart on top of the headshot pile, takes the cigarette out of his mouth and gets up to greet me.

"Hey, man, I'm Booze," he says and shakes my hand.

I start to smile despite myself, but know enough of these self-inventing director types to not question what his real name is.

"Did you bring a headshot and résumé?" he asks, all business. I reach into my bag and pull out my old headshot and hand it over. Meanwhile, Harpo crosses over to the camera that is set up directly across from the futon.

Booze studies my résumé intently.

"Okay, man, cool." He flips it over. "Is this you?" He holds it up alongside my face, to compare. Goddamn that Ezra—he's right. If this drugged out geek can't tell it's me, then I really do need new pictures.

"It's me," I assure him while nearly rubbing a hole into my clover pendant with my thumb. "Can we get started?"

"Sure, dude. Well, Marty here is going to film us, here's the side," he hands me the coffee-stained script that must have served as the audition side all day yesterday, judging from all the pencil marks and tattered edges. I start to wish I was wearing gloves.

"Can I have a minute to read through it first?" Even though I am not digging the Clown Boys' *vibe,* I still want to do a good job. I wish I could take the lines to a coffee shop somewhere, and read through them, to practice, to build my character, but…

"Well, okay, sit on the futon here while you do it, so Martin can focus on you." And he points to a spot for me to sit so that the camera can pick up my face.

"So first, I want you to read the monologue on page three, then we'll get some Polaroids for type and stuff."

"Um, okay." I sit and start to read through it, my stomach sinking as fast as you can say Sundance Film Festival. The script's about a girl who is in love with a guy who slept with her mom.

"Um, did you write this?" I look at Booze and he breaks out into a humble grin.

"I sure did." Unbelievable. But it's okay. Any experience is a good experience. This guy could be the next Tarantino. I'm sure not everything Tarantino wrote early in his career was golden.

After about thirty seconds, Booze asks me if I am ready. I'm not, but more time is not going to make a difference.

"Okay man, just, you know, like say your name for the camera."

I look directly into the lens of the camera and speak, with my best Voice and Speech 101 voice, "Stella Aurora Monroe." Then I smile and tilt my head ever-so-slightly to the side. Marty the afro clown says, "Audition 328. Monologue," and points at me.

"I've been walking around the block and this is what I have decided. I love you. I don't care who you sleep with, and sure, it hurts that you chose my mom over me, but what can I do?" I sigh dramatically to get my forlorn point across, and to also keep from laughing. "I love you. There it is. And if I have to share you with other women, so be it."

"Aaannnddd…cut." Marty is looking into the camera, then lifts his head up to me. He laughs and gives me a thumbs-up. "Good job."

"Okay dude, that rocked." Booze bolts up toward the camera and picks up a Polaroid camera from a side table. He lifts the strap over his head, and lets the camera dangle there, hitting his chest as he rocks back and forth on the balls of his feet. "So I wanna take a few test shots. Can you stand up?"

"Um, okay." I stand, put the dirty script back on the futon, and try to smooth out my black leather pants, a Joshua clothing item. He snaps a photo before I even know what is going on. As the film ejects from the camera, he grabs it and shakes it.

"That won't make it dry, you know."

He laughs and keeps shaking. Just then the buzzer buzzes and Marty runs toward the front of the apartment to answer it. Part of me is glad to not be alone here anymore, and part of me is disappointed to come face-to-face with some competition.

"So what are your plans for the film?" I ask Booze while he shoots another couple of Polaroids.

"Festivals. We want to be represented in as many festivals as possible."

"That's great!" I cock my head to the side and smile big while he takes one last shot. Festivals. That's a good goal. Plenty of nobody actresses have been discovered at film festivals and plucked by famous directors to be in bigger budget movies. "I'd really love to work with you guys." I go for wholesome sweetness. Maybe that'll work.

Booze walks my Polaroids over to a wall and tacks them up in a collage of headshots and snapshots and about a thousand pictures of Nicole Kidman.

"You like Nicole, huh?"

"Yup. I'm not gonna stop auditioning until I find a girl who looks exactly like her."

I blow air out between my lips.

"Would you ever dye your hair strawberry-blond?"

Michaela sees me from the back of the bar and waves me over. She's holding the phone in her left hand. "It's for you," she says as I approach her. I am too puzzled to figure out who could be calling me when I hear that voice on the other end.

"Little Star. *Where* have you been?"

"Mom?"

"I have been calling you *everywhere*. I have news."

Michaela hands me a Diet Coke with a slice of lemon while I pitch the phone under my ear and slip off my bubble coat.

"What news?" I can hardly wait.

"Frances Paine. She's in the paper today." I sip my Diet Coke furiously.

"Really?"

"Yes, yes, Little Star. In the style section. She's wearing sunglasses from Barney's. I'm sending you the clipping. Go get them."

"Okay."

"And make sure you ask where she gets her nails done."

"Yes, Mom."

"And have you been to a rehearsal yet?"

"No, we don't have to go until the final dress."

"Hmm. Well. I think you should get a cell phone. In case Frances needs you."

"Mom, I can't really afford a cell phone right now." She doesn't respond to me. "Mom?" Did I lose her?

"You know what?" There she is. "Some things are more important than other things, right? Of course I'm right. While you are still undiscovered, *nothing* should be as important as getting there. I don't need to tell you this." She works herself into quite a lather. "Do you have headshots yet?"

"I'm working on it."

"*Working* on it! Good lord Stella! Headshots are more important than anything. More than meals. More than your *rent*. I remember one week when I was in the Apple that I went without *food*. Just so I could attend a dance class taught by Fosse."

"Okay, I know, Mom. And I'm trying. I promise. I have some money coming in pretty soon and I'll be able to get the pictures. In fact, I have an appointment next week." My forehead drops to the bar as I clench my fist and hit the surface silently. Why do I lie, and so easily, too?

"Good! See, we're on the same page, aren't we? Well, that's good. Please send me the proofs. I'll expect them in the mail."

"Um…"

"And don't forget to get your eyebrows done. Nothing looks as sloppy as bushy brows."

"Mom, I have to go."

"Okay, Stella."

"I love you, Mom, and don't worry."

"I won't. And Stella?"

"Yes?"

"Don't spend so much time in that bar. I can only imagine what the smoke smell does to your hair. Knock 'em dead."

I hand the phone back to Michaela and fight the urge to ask for a shot.

"Stage mom?"

I shoot her a look. "She's not being a stage mom. She's just looking out for me."

I hop up onto one of the bar stools and change the subject. "I'm here to beg for food."

"I figured." This short sentence is barely out of her mouth when a busboy comes from around the corner holding a plate piled high with French fries and a grilled cheese and tomato.

I look up at her gratefully. *This* is friendship. "Thanks, Mic. I promise when I'm on my feet I'll buy you a car or something."

She giggles. "Don't worry about it. So when are you going to see Jasper again?" She pours some ketchup on my plate and digs into the fries.

"I don't know," I grumble to my beautiful sandwich, the first bit of food to touch my stomach since yesterday's catering gruel. A frown forms in my brain. When *am* I going to see him again? Will I have to wait until the final dress? Uh-oh. A rule was broken. The rule that says that you must always procure a second set of plans before you end the first date.

I hold the grilled cheese in midair. "What if he never calls me again?"

"He'll call. Believe me. He had a good time Friday. I can tell." She has finished her fries and is now pouring sugar straight onto the bar. "You have to get his birthday, though. Then we'll know for sure what your future holds. Have you dreamed about him yet?"

"Um, yeah, I think I did. I don't know. I've been having really weird dreams lately. Like about synchronized swimming and stuff."

"Water in a dream means sex."

"Really?"

"Yup. Sex. Hmm. Synchronized sex?"

I stare at her. She's lovely, but koo-koo. We start to giggle. Oh my God. Between the two of us, we probably don't have enough working brain cells for one whole person.

Then I realize that I've been monopolizing the conversation. "So how's Carlo doing?"

"Good. He has been so cute about this wedding stuff. He keeps calling me his bride-to-be. Oh, hey, just so you know, we're definitely gonna get married here at the bar."

I nearly choke on a thick bite of tomato. "Don't you think that's bad mojo? Getting married in a place referring to Hell?"

She giggles at me and traces figure eights on the top of my head. "No, silly. You're so superstitious."

"All I know is, a relationship begun at a place referring to the kingdom of darkness can't last too long."

"Uh-huh. Well, then, I guess you're doomed, huh?"

"What are you talking about? Jasper and I met in New Jersey, not Hell's."

"Same thing."

Just then Rod comes barreling over to the bar holding a huge bouquet of flowers. "I'm not a doorman." He slides them over to Michaela and me. Michaela grabs the card and screeches. "Oh my God!" Great. Carlo sends her flowers, too. I can't even get a phone call and here she is getting "just because" flowers.

"What's the card say?" I ask halfheartedly as I cut my pickle into two dozen thin slices.

"Seriously, Stella. Either start working here or go out with me. But you don't *live* here, for chris' sake."

Michaela looks up from the card and breaks out into a huge

goofy grin. "They're for *you*." I grab the card out of her hand and stare at these words, "Hope you're having a good day. Keep tomorrow night open. Your new friend, Jasper."

Chapter 9

The Actors' Equity Building stands majestically among the run-down, gnarled brown buildings of West 46th Street, beckoning the lucky actors of New York City out of the murky gray morning into its warm halls. But I'm on the other side of the street, tucked into a small, dirty alleyway between a deli and an apartment complex, spying on the comings and goings of so many union actors. I feel like a high-stakes, superfashionable espionage agent, decked out with my favorite pair of seventies sunglasses (the ones with the lenses so big that they cover half my cheeks) and my hair in pigtails (fastened with Japanese style pink hair ties), covered in my favorite black bubble coat (complemented by a pink feather boa), sipping from my cup of coffee and nibbling at a croissant.

Most New Yorkers *buy* their croissants, but I make 'em. It's no big deal, really, just a slab of butter and a roll of pastry dough. Steve gets really mad when I make them, 'cause he says I get butter all over the kitchen, and that it seeps into his food when he cooks. He's crazy and when I tell him that, he responds by saying that his body is his "instrument" and he must keep it in shape. Whatever. My body is *my* instrument and I must have freshly made croissants.

As I swallow down my last bite, I lean against the inside alley wall and stare. Actors' Equity. The Tiffany's to my Audrey Hepburn. Sometimes, especially in my pre-Joshua days, I would have at least one meal a day here. Today I'm here to keep myself hungry, in the proverbial sense, of course. To remind myself of what the goal is, because, although I've only been to two auditions since my return from retirement, I'm getting kind of discouraged. And also, I have an audition on this block, and I thought this would be a good way to psyche myself up for it.

People just keep on streaming through the big Equity doors, like it's nothing. What is it? Just a doorway, that's all. Steve's allowed in there. Jasper, too. My mom. But not me. Joining Equity is like high school graduation for a stage actor. After you've toiled away in theaters making nonunion wages for a period of time and amassed an impressive enough résumé, you can hope to get cast by a union show that'll pay Equity-eligible wages. Then you get to join. But I've never been cast in an Equity show. So I don't have the little piece of paper that deems me an *actress* and I'm not allowed in that building.

Since I'm persona non grata, I walk across the street to the building next door to Equity: St. Mary's Church. St. Mary's rents basement space out to theater companies: nonunion, no funding, quasi-professional theater companies. My old company used to rehearse here, so I know it well. It's a common thing in New York, rehearsing in a church.

When I get to the gray, stone structure, there's a line of about twenty young girls waiting outside. The flyer that was posted on the Hell's bulletin board is crumpled in my pocket. I pull it out and read one more time:

Columbia Directing Student/Senior Thesis Project
An Original Musical about the victims of Jack the Ripper

Ages 18-24 only. Tuesday the 24th. 10:00 a.m.
We'll be exploring the hopes and dreams of Jack's victims through music. Sing a popular song, a song that might
later be actually used in the show. This will be a collab-
orative effort between the female director and the female
performers. Please only sing a song recorded by a woman
in the past thirty years of pop and rock.
No Britney. Christina okay.

I step behind the last girl in line and tap her shoulder. "Do
we have to sign up?"

She cracks her gum in my face and checks me out. "Nice boa."

"Thanks. Do we have to sign up?"

"Nah. They're taking us in groups. Next group should be
soon." She turns her back to me.

Fifteen minutes later a girl with a black pageboy haircut
comes out of the church and leads the twenty of us inside. We
walk down a flight of stairs and into the spare, black-painted
basement room. I know this room well: I've rehearsed lots of
kissing scenes here. Three girls are standing in the middle of
the floor, all of them wearing black clothes, two with black lipstick, and one with about five piercings through her nose, eyebrows and mouth. The pierced one steps toward us. "Welcome
girls. Today's gonna be a little bit different from most auditions
you've been to."

Oh, great. There's nothing worse than a revolutionary.

"Just put your stuff down anywhere, take off your shoes and
find a spot on the floor."

I know what's coming. I predict rolling around on the floor
and screaming. These kinds of "exercises" were a big part of
the NYU acting curriculum, and the main reason I quit after
only a semester. After three months of acting training in New
York City, something I had looked forward to immensely while
toiling away in the hotel kitchen in Michigan, I was an expert
in group massage, floor-rolling, walking around in a huge cir-

cle at different speeds, moaning on different pitches and pretending to be a variety of different animals, including snakes, birds and big cats.

I thought I'd have a better chance of making it by actually acting and so I quit. Besides, my mom and I couldn't really afford the tuition.

But now, those few months are going to come in handy. The pierced director tells us to lie flat on our backs, and to stretch our legs up to the ceiling.

"Now, grab your ankles and let out a nice hum." A chorus of strangled hums greets this instruction, and I stare at the decrepit ceiling while contorting my body and blowing air out of my mouth. She talks us through several different kinds of stretches: arms, calves, shoulders. I feel like a pretzel.

"Good, good. Now sit up, make eye contact with one of your fellow actresses, and let out a nice 'v' sound."

A girl with long blond hair and ruby-red lips catches my eye and starts revving herself to death.

"Good, good, now gently, gently, lift yourself into a crouching position, and then slowly, slowly, roll up to a standing position. Straighten each vertebra at a time, until you are erect." I follow the instructions dutifully, and chant in my head with each vertebra, "I'm going to be a star. I'm going to be a star."

When we're standing, stretched and hummed, the pierced girl tells us to form a circle. The three other black-haired girls arrange themselves at random intervals in the circle, and one of them starts talking about Jack the Ripper and the havoc he wreaked on working girls, and how it is up to the subsequent generation of working women to celebrate their lives and give voice to their hopes and dreams.

Then she tells us to get our Top 40 hits ready.

"Who wants to go first?" The pierced one looks expectantly from girl to girl, looking for a volunteer. Finally my blond v-ing partner meekly raises her hand.

"Good, good. Go to the center of the circle, and imagine

you're a nineteenth-century hooker about to be mutilated and killed. What would you want to say to the world? The world that looks down on you?"

The blonde looks very, very uncomfortable, but takes a deep breath and starts singing,

"At first I was afraid, I was petrified,
I thought that I could never live without you by my side…"

Hey! *That's my song!* I stare openmouthed at the blonde. She's singing my song! Several girls start looking around wildly, and I can tell that she and I weren't the only ones planning to belt out a little Gloria Gaynor. What the hell am I gonna do?

"Great! Great! Next." The pierced girl cuts the blonde off and gazes around the circle of girls. "Okay, don't be shy, somebody jump in." When nobody makes a move, the director nudges the shoulder of a petite, cute little brunette. The brunette looks really upset, and after another prodding by the director, starts singing "I Will Survive" from where the blonde cut off.

After her, another girl jumps into the center and sings Gloria Gaynor and I am scrambling in my brain, trying to remember the words to any other popular song. Pat Benatar? I could sing "We Are Young." God, what's the name of that song? And now another "I Will Survive"—or is singing in the center— oh dear God, did none of us plan for another song? Okay, okay, not my turn yet—how about "Like a Virgin"? I know the words to that one. Yes. "Like a Virgin." Or "Drrty." Or "Bootylicious" by Destiny's Child? God that would be wrong. How about "What Have You Done For Me Lately?" Oh God, oh God, and the pierced one is looking right at me. She's pointing at me. Oh God. "You're up, the girl in the boa."

A pair of hands pushes me into the center of the circle.

Twenty-three pairs of eyes focus and all English drains away from my brain.

"Go on, sing us what you've got."

I blink and shake my head and open my mouth and hear the chorus from "I Touch Myself" by the Divinyls come out over and over again, like a loop from hell.

And because I don't know any of the other words to that song, I just keep repeating myself until the pierced one mercifully cuts me off with a puzzled look. Girls titter as I take my place back in line. "Nice choice" says one of the black-haired auditioners, crossing her eyes.

After the audition, I make my way home, dragging my heels the whole way. My auditions haven't been going in the best of directions. But it's okay. I'm sure my mother and Steve both survived similar dry spells. And I've just started auditioning again.

The city is particularly smelly this afternoon. Gray and dreary and chilly and smelly. But still I prolong my trip by passing by all the Broadway theaters. The Lunt-Fontanne. The Golden. The Gershwin. The Schubert. The Neil Simon. They seem so inaccessible to me, as inaccessible as the Equity building. I can't even make it through a senior thesis project audition without encountering some humiliation. Or get cast in a student film. Or a stupid tour of *Beauty and the Beast*. Not like I'd want any of those jobs. Would I?

I stare at the marquee of the St. James and think, "Why am I worried?" Why *am* I worried? I have a fantastic new job in an off-Broadway show. Well, as an understudy. Well not an understudy exactly, but the cat needs somebody to look after her. And my new boyfriend-possibility is the star. It's so funny. I get sucked into feeling bad about myself, when really, things are going just great! I have a job or two, a new boyfriend-possibility and a slew of best friends. And a date tonight.

I let myself in the front door and promise to not call Jasper my boyfriend when I see him tonight. Or ever, until he has declared his undying love to me and introduced me to his parents. I wonder where he'll take me. This is his first chance to knock me off my feet with how well he can treat a lady. And I don't even know what time we're meeting yet. I check my machine to see if he's called.

I lean on the kitchen counter and start to peel some apples as I hear the voice of Kevin the stage manager drone, "Um hi. Okay, here's the deal. Like I said at the theater, we won't need the cat until the end of next week for the dress rehearsal. Stacy from the production company is going to overnight you the paperwork and your first check. You'll be paid as of last Friday, when the cat was hired. Good day."

Good day? What a wacko. But that does nothing to dampen my joy. I leap into the air, so happy that Jasper's lack of a phone call barely registers in the back of my mind. A check! Just in time for rent and headshots! "Miss Bubbles? Did you hear that? You're getting paid tomorrow! Yippee!" Miss Bubbles jumps up on the counter and starts nibbling the peelings.

"Not for you Bubby, you have to watch your figure now that you're a big Broadway star!" I swat her nose and swoop her off the counter. She jumps back up immediately, then the vacuum starts. We both look to the ceiling, then back at each other.

"What do you say, Miss B.? I don't think we have to deal with this today. Do you?"

She sneezes in agreement. I drum my fingers on the counter before deciding to take a practical approach. I grab a few croissants and some vanilla sugar that I made two mornings ago. What does Mom say? You attract more flies with sugar. Or is it honey?

When I get to Christian's apartment, I have to bang on the door about three dozen times with my whole fist before he can hear over the din of that dumb vacuum cleaner. When he sees me in the doorway, he doesn't even say hello, just, "Are you bringing me my blazer finally?"

I grit my teeth and try to refrain from throwing the sugar

in his smug face. And why does he vacuum in an outfit like this? A wife-beater T-shirt and cargo pants? Who is he, Stanley Kowalski? I try to peer over his shoulder, because this is probably the closest I'll ever get to seeing the inside of his meticulous haven.

Hmm, even with my blocked view I see a perfectly maintained, well-decorated apartment, with coordination in color and furniture, and a downright fantastic window treatment that looks down onto our yard. Interesting. A girl must have helped him. But I know there is no girl. I'd hear her through the walls. Christian catches me investigating and says again, "Stella. My blazer." I, of course, don't have his stupid coat but try to divert him with the sweetest, sugariest smile I can manage.

"Oh, jeez!" I slap my forehead for extra emphasis. "I completely forgot! I'll have to bring that over later. Croissant?" And I lift the plate up to his nose.

He looks but doesn't bite. "What do you want?"

"Nothing." This smile is hurting my face. "Just thought you might like some breakfast."

"What do you want?" He doesn't blink.

"To be neighborly." Still smiling.

"What do you want?" Why isn't he blinking?

"For you to stop driving me crazy with that stupid vacuum cleaner." I drop my cover for a split second but then replaster my smile. "Please."

He chuckles, grabs two croissants from the plate, says, "Get a job. Then you won't hear the vacuum." He shoves half a croissant in his mouth and shuts the door in my face. I stare at the door for a split second before I retreat in defeat. I can hear the vacuum start back up again as I go.

When I get in the door, I see another message light flashing and try to hold my fluttery heart in check. After the beep, I hear this: "Stel-La. It's Ezra. Where are you, kid? Don't forget we have a hot date next week with some pics of my favorite pinup girl. Don't be a stranger, kid."

Okay, this picture situation is becoming one unavoidable nightmare. I really hope Miss Bubbles is making good money, because there's no way I can put this thing off. I grab my checkbook and check the balance. $168.32. I go to the kitchen cabinets and check my supply level. Half a pound of flour left. About three cups of sugar. Only three more eggs. Ah, Jesus Christ. What the hell am I going to do? I need to go shopping. And the rent. Due next Tuesday. Aye-yi-yi. Okay. No problem. I'll work a couple of jobs for Debra this weekend, I'll get my check for the Jersey disaster and the other parties I catered last weekend and then hopefully Miss Bubbles's share will give me enough to pay for everything.

Keys jangle in the front door and Miss B. goes running for Steve, who looks like a hipster teen idol in his Diesel jeans and Tommy Hilfiger pullover. "Hey. What are you doing awake, princess?"

"What are you doing home?"

"I'm back from my callback for *All My Children*."

My guts tighten. "How'd it go?" I sit on the couch and turn on the television.

He leans in the doorway and gives me a shifty half smile. "What are you doing?"

"Huh? Nothing. How'd it go?"

He takes off his coat and crosses over to his bedroom, "You're quaking in your designer boots aren't you? *How'd it go, Steve?*" He says that last part in a very exaggeratedly breathy voice.

I would get annoyed at him, except he's right. I *am* quaking in my boots. If Steve were to get this, that'd be it. We wouldn't be able to be friends anymore. First of all, he'd be making about eighty times as much as me, he'd be surrounded by gorgeous women who'd make much better straight-girl-best-friends to a gay man than me, and he'd be famous. And I'd be sitting here peeling apples, waiting for my dates to call and watching after my Broadway-bound cat. And with Michaela clinging onto this getting married idea, things are not looking good for my social life.

But I can't let him know this. I pretend that I actually want him to have done well. "Steve, stop being a dick. How'd it go?" Miss Bubbles settles herself on the coffee table, staring at Steve's bedroom door, like she too, can't wait to hear if at least one of her roommates has a better job than she does. He leans in his doorway, with his shirt off and his workout clothes in his arms, "It went pretty well. I think I nailed it, actually. So we'll see what they're looking for."

Why do I feel like my eyes are about to tear up? Why can't I be happy for my best friend? I can. I can act like I'm happy. I'm an actress. "That's great," I say so lamely. He shakes his head at me ever so slightly and goes back into his room to change.

I feel like a jerk. Like a selfish jerk. Well, okay, I am being selfish. But I have to do a better job of not letting Steve know that all I'm thinking about is myself. So I follow him into his room. I knock softly before entering. He looks up at me as he is tying on his sneakers.

"Hey."

"Hey."

"I really am happy for you, and I know you're going to get this. And then I'll be best friends with a famous soap star." My voice oozes sincerity. I even convince myself.

"I know you are, Stell. Don't worry."

"Do you want some lunch? I make a mean 'I-just-nailed-an-audition BLT.'"

He laughs at me. "No thanks, I'm going to the gym." He passes me through the doorway, kisses my cheek and goes out the door. Five minutes later I'm at Hell's.

Any bad mood I was in is gone by the time six o'clock rolls around. I have been sitting at the bar, like usual, listening to Michaela talk about wedding plans. This is all very entertaining. Really. Listening to my best friend describe the party she's throwing to celebrate moving out of the phase of life that I'm firmly embedded in—what could be more fun? I'll admit that planning the dresses and desserts *is* kind of fun but talk of truffles and tarts can't completely get my mind off of my evening's plans. My date with Jasper is supposed to be tonight, so sometime around three I start going home every hour on the hour to check my answering machine. Michaela thinks I'm funny for not just calling from the bar, but I just know I'll somehow erase the messages. Besides, the trips home do me some good. It's healthy to get some fresh air once in a while. That's why people exercise and all. I don't need much, just a three-minute walk on the hour every hour and I'm good as gold.

Six o'clock turns out to be the magic hour, for I have a message from Jasper. Actually, it sounds like Jasper channeling Zeus—spewing forth this thunderous voice, I can hear him banging things in the background. *Bang! bang!* "I've had a rough one, sugar, I won't be able to meet you until later on, like nine-thirty or so." *Knock, knock, knock…* voices lowly talking… "Aw, make that ten or ten-thirty. I'll call you when I'm ready. Ten-ish."

Depending on the rest of the gods, this could either be great for me or awful for me. If he is in a truly bad mood, there's a chance he might forget all about our date, stew in his own juices and never call me again. On the other hand, he could desperately need somebody to cheer him up, to make him forget all of his woes and troubles. Enter Stella. I can cheer up the best of them, all the way to the altar, baby.

Back to Hell's, to recommence the hourly bar-sits. I continue all the way until 9:45 p.m. Please note that I behave myself thoroughly, sipping on Cokes the whole time. Forgoing chocolate martinis.

At nine forty-nine, as I open the door, the flashing light of the machine greets me. Goddamn do I love that flashing light. It's him, saying to meet him at the Upstairs Lounge in the Monsoon Hotel at 48th and Park at ten forty-five. *Fantastic.* An East Side location. *Better yet.* A hotel. *Lots* of innuendo. My flirtation skills are taken to a whole new level when I'm in a hotel. I learned this with Joshua. As a matter of fact, I've been to this particular bar on several occasions, as Josh had a client in that area and would spend lots of time conducting business in the neighborhood restaurants.

I decide to go all out, and paint myself in luscious colors that will scream to Jasper, "This is *marriage* material." I choose pink, because how can a rising star ignore a babe in pink? I dig through the makeup drawer in my bathroom, which is organized according to color. Pink lipstick #5 by Dilettante, Rosy Glow blush and even pink mascara by LIPS. I finish the look by placing sparkle powder on my eyes, oh-so-lightly, not too much so that he thinks I am trying to be younger than I am but just enough to make him wonder where I get that inner glow. I check out the effect. Stunning. The phone rings. I grip the edge of the sink with both hands, praying it isn't a cancellation call. I let the machine pick it up. If it *is* a cancellation call, I don't want him to think that I am home getting ready for our date.

"Little Star? Where are you? Are you at that bar again? I'll try you there." Mom hangs up, I presume to call Hell's. I sit in the bathroom, stare at myself in the mirror and pucker my lips to see what I look like when I kiss somebody for probably three more minutes until the phone rings again.

"*Little Star?* Call me. I was thinking that you should make lunch plans with Frances, if you haven't already. But don't pinch pennies on the location. Impress her with style, my little star-to-be. Okay. Call me. Sal's out bowling and Stewie's sleeping. I have plenty of time to talk."

When I'm sure she has hung up, I venture out of the bathroom to choose my outfit. When I open the closet, Miss Bubbles comes running out and scurries past my feet in a blaze of white fur. I flip through my hangers about twenty dozen times, hopelessly disappointed with each passing shirt and skirt and pair of pants. I sit dejectedly on my bed. I am a cliché. I have nothing to wear.

I settle on a pink knit top, knit so loosely that you have to wear a T-shirt underneath it to avoid flashing people. I match it with a straight black skirt, which might be the plainest piece of clothing I own. But I know from experience that the Monsoon Hotel frowns on both creativity and thrifty dressing, so I choose conservative. Well, conservative for this frugal young dresser.

I check myself out in the full-length mirror before I leave. I've accessorized with eight chunky pink bracelets, all strung with pink plastic dice. And I have four Hello Kitty rings on my left hand. And my fairy necklace choker that accentuates the part of the neck that I want Jasper to kiss. I look at myself and think that I've overdone it. I take off the rings, seven of the dice bracelets, and sweep my hair up into a loose knot on the top of my head. I hold it in place with two mother-of-pearl chopsticks that Joshua gave me after a trip to Beijing. After a swab of lip gloss, I'm ready to go break a heart.

As I am about to reach the front door of the building, I hear a long, slow whistle. I don't have to turn around to know it isn't Miss Bubbles. I am not sure what I've done to piss God off, but I'm getting sick and tired of always running into Christian in the halls.

"Hey, turn around so I can check it out, sparkles." He is sitting on the stairs, with a book open on his knees.

"What are you doing?" I snarl.

"Waiting for somebody. My buzzer's broken." He takes his glasses off and looks at me. I feel an urge to cross my arms over my body so he can't see me, but I don't. I just stare at him back, waiting for the dig.

"You look pretty." He kind of gives two little nods after this, like he is approving his opinion of me. I can't help it, but I feel a momentary thrill rush up my spine and for the life of me I can't figure out why.

"Um. Thanks."

"No problem." He starts to chuckle. He starts to annoy me.

"Have fun, Stella." And he looks back down at his book with a grin on his face. I think the jerk's laughing at me but I can't prove it and don't have the time to try.

I rush out and pass a short blond girl with tight jeans, a hopelessly out-of-fashion T-shirt that has an orange striped *V* on the front, and a pair of bright red glasses. I instantaneously resent the freckles splattered on her nose and her perky attitude. No doubt she is the person Christian is waiting for. "He's waiting for you," I blurt and Perky stares at me, surprised. Before I can help myself, I shoot her the evil eye and let myself out of the vestibule. As the door shuts behind me, I can hear Christian saying, "Hey, lady…glad you found the place." Blech… I kiss the stone angel's feet and say a quick thanks that I won't have to hear the goings-on upstairs tonight.

I cut through Times Square, which, though it's 10:20 on a Tuesday night, is packed with people. Teenagers, tourists, musicians, street artists. There are hundreds of people walking around, shopping, snacking on hot dogs. You're never alone in this city.

I check the clock on the giant Coca-Cola sign. I have plenty of time, so I purposely walk slowly across the avenues to avoid getting all sweaty and gross. Most people would take a cab to get across town, but not me. I silently chant my checking account balance in my head, a mantra of thrift that I must remember at all times.

When I get there, the Upstairs Lounge (which is in the basement) has been completely redecorated. It's dark in here now, with black rugs on the floors and walls, interrupted only by framed picture-sized swatches of different animal prints. The bar is covered in this cheetah and zebra print, and I am surprised when the bartender appears clothed in a plain black vest and white shirt. I was hoping he'd be decked out like a member of the cast of *The Lion King,* maybe a giraffe? No dice.

I scan the front room for Jasper, but no sign. I move slowly toward the little room in the back, the room where I spent many hours groping and being groped by Joshua. This has also been redone since last I was here, which makes avoiding memories all the easier. This room is done wholly in white, with black tinted animal prints on the wall.

I head back to the bar, straining my ear to listen for Jasper's voice. I sit at the bar and surprise myself by ordering a Coke. I swish the stirrer around and follow the tall bald bartender with my eye. Sinatra is playing in the background. I don't think I like this bar anymore. It's sterile.

My stomach flutters. It's ten twenty-eight, and I hate being early to a thing like this because the seconds before whoever it is gets here stretch like bubble gum. I swish my stirrer again and sip. There's a couple in the corner wearing high, expensive fashion (I can tell because of the sheen and the lack of wrinkles). The woman has on a necklace that looks like fusilli strung together. It's huge. I bet it outweighs her head. She's in her fifties and can't weigh more than a hundred pounds. And tan. Probably an East Sider who spends her life dieting and primping. Oh God, she's even wearing a leopard-print coat. Is it real? I can't believe that her outfit matches the bar. Yikes.

There are also three businessmen in suits in the middle of the floor. Maybe they know Joshua. But before I can start wondering where Josh might be tonight, the door opens and in walks Jasper.

It's like he brought in a spotlight with him. Everyone in the room—and I am not making this up—turns toward him. He takes a moment, commanding attention with the stage presence of a honed pro, and looks around the room. I feel the sweep of his head, and suddenly want to make sure there's a spotlight on me, too. Hey, Jasper. Yoo-hoo! Over here!

I wait for him to see me, and when he does, he flashes a million megawatt smile in my direction. He looks fantastic, no trace of a rotten day at work at all. At all! He is wearing a pair of dark camel khakis, that are relaxed but elegant, and an olive pullover sweater that I'm betting is cashmere. He speaks to the maître d', smiles and says something that makes the host laugh: a self-deprecating, thankful giggle. Then they shake hands, and Jasper covers the host's hand with his free one and says something with such a sincere look on his face, that I start to wonder if we're in an episode of *The Sopranos* and Jasper is making some sort of family connection with the seemingly innocuous waitstaff.

He makes his way over to me and I feel the weight of him again. He is really beautiful. And he glows like sunlight. I start a countdown in my head. Ten, nine, eight…

"I'm so glad to see you." He leans in and kisses my cheek. My stomach churns Coca-Cola like lava.

"I'm glad I could meet you." He sits and flags down the bartender. "Hey Sam. How's the night tonight?"

The bartender lights up, obviously this is where Jasper's been staying while he's in the show. "It's good, boss. Very good. The usual?" They slap hands sideways, a gang hello.

"Yup. Thanks. How're the kids?" The bartender answers this question while mixing Jasper's usual. I desperately want to know what that is, but I can't keep track of all the bottles that he uses.

When the drink is set down before him, and they exchange "talk to you laters," I say to him, "Come here often?"

He takes a sip of his usual. "Yeah, I always stay here when I'm in town."

I look around. I look back at Jasper. He fits in here. This is a place dripping with people and things that are worth something. There is a glow around the chairs, the patrons, the bar stools, everything. He is the king. This is his court. I am his courtesan. *Yippee-yo-kai-yay.*

We have a pleasant conversation. He tells me about his rehearsal and how he is the worst actor on the planet. Every actor feels this way at one time or another, and I have to say, hearing him confess such a human emotion, a human worry, makes him all the more luscious to me. I want to throw him down

on the bar and climb on top of him like he's my own private
Everest. Just as I'm imagining what it would look like if I were
to straddle him and start to kiss him on the bar, he interrupts
my fantasy.

"Hey." He looks into my eyes and I am time-warped back
into reality. "Did you hear what I just said?"

"Huh?" I sip my drink and start to giggle. "I'm sorry. What?"

Now he leans back and takes me in with those eyes. I think
he gets turned on when I'm not completely attentive, because
something has changed in his demeanor over the last two seconds—all his predatory instincts have snapped to attention like
a line of marines listening to their drill sergeant.

He leans in and touches my leg with his hand, placing the
drink on the bar with the other. I see out of the corner of my
eye the bartender clear the glass and replace it with a full one,
also one for me. I think for a second that I am prey, lured into
Jasper the Lion's den of lust. The trap has been set and I am
about to be devoured. Awesome.

I stick out my chest. He says, "I said, how long have you been
here in the city?"

I tilt my head, angling my lips toward his, because let's face
it. I really don't want to talk. I want to seal the deal here, so to
speak, so that we can get to the part where he asks me upstairs.
"Does it really matter how long I've been here?" He licks his
lower lip and gives me a look that says I'm not wriggling out
of this conversation so fast.

"Did you grow up here?"

I shake my head. "Michigan." I place my fingers on his upper
arm and rub them back and forth.

He shifts in his seat. "Parents still there?"

"My mom is." I lean a little closer. This time he takes the
bait. His lips find mine, and they are so soft, like feathers. He
pulls my stool toward his and slides his arm around my waist.
The scent of him curls up around my nostrils and I am so
turned on my fantasy is dangerously close to coming true.

He breaks away from me, but keeps his hand to my back. "Isn't it funny that we just happened to meet at that party? And that I noticed you?"

"How could you have not noticed me, in that outfit?"

"True." He laughs lightly and leans in and bites my lower lip. My insides are on fire. A three-alarm, full on *fire*.

"But I wanted to talk to you. And when you sang, you were just so cute." I get embarrassed by this and hide my face in the crook of his neck. Not a good idea. He places his hand on my head and strokes my hair. The smell of him is driving me crazy. I have too many clothes on and I want to take them off. It's good. It's good to feel this way and be sober. My last couple of, um, *relationships* (and I realize how loose, how very loose this term is) have lasted all of one night, and this part, the part where I want the other person all over me, has been diluted in a cloud of alcohol since Joshua.

"Well, I liked you, too. Except for that chintzy girl who you were with. Where is she, anyway?" And I lift up, break our embrace and start looking around the room, as if she might actually be there.

He takes my chin in his hand and brings my face back to his. He kisses me again, a quick kiss, and says, "Let's not worry about other people, okay? Right now there's only you," and he kisses me, "and me." And he kisses me again. I'm done.

We get up without a word and I follow him to his room.

Chapter 10

This is the softest bed ever. The sheets must be like one thousand percent silk or something. Or satin. No! A satin/silk blend. They're white and cloudy, something I'm noticing for the first time even though I've been lying in this bed for about twelve hours now.

I sit up and gather the sheets to my body. My skin feels like a baby's, swaddled and caressed by the sunlight streaming in through the windows. There is a vase full of white and light pink roses on the side table. It's probably the maid's job to put them here, but I can't help smiling as if they were purchased by Jasper just for me.

Jasper. He's in the shower and I can hear him humming to himself. Is that... Oh my God. I think he's singing "Oh, What a Beautiful Mornin'" from *Oklahoma!* I bury myself into the bed in a spasmic fit of joy. He's perfect. He's hot, he's *fantastic* in bed and he loves show tunes. His utter perfection makes me scorn myself for ever, ever thinking that Joshua Davis was the answer to my prayers/problems.

These past couple of weeks have shattered any lingering illusions about Joshua. And last night, *last night,* was the most perfect night of all time. I had sex four times. *Four times.* With an upcoming star, thank you very much. I reach for the bedside phone and punch in Michaela's number.

"Hell's Bar."

"Rod? Put Michaela on."

"Who is this? Stella? Michaela's *working.*"

"Yeah, I'll be quick, Hurry up!" Jasper's reaching the end of the song. I want to be off the phone before he comes out of the shower.

"Stella?"

"Mic! Synchronized *S-E-X!*" I sing the letters into the phone to her before quietly squealing with delight.

"Oh my God!" She shrieks. "Where are you?"

"In the nicest hotel ever. I could use these sheets as collateral for a loan, they're so nice." The shower turns off. "Mic, I gotta go. Love you."

"'Kay. Details later." She clicks off just in time for me to throw the phone back into the cradle and sink down into the sheets.

Jasper comes out of the bathroom in a white terry cloth robe, wiping the water out of his hair with a towel. "Hey gorgeous." He leans down and kisses my forehead. A hundred-thousand-watt jolt of electricity runs through my body and I rise to my knees, letting the sheet fall to the bed. I extend my hand and he takes it, then moves toward me and rubs his thumbs against my belly.

"Will you be late?" I purr.

"I planned ahead. We have plenty of time." He throws the towel to the ground and lets the robe follow.

This is better than my fantasies.

After another mind-blowing forty-five minutes, he gets ready for his eleven-thirty rehearsal call and goes out the door. He tells me to take my time, to take a shower and to order room service if I want. Hell yes, I want. I want this to be my whole entire life. Showers and room service on someone else's tab. I purposely do not ask when we'll see each other again because I am smart enough to know that this question could very well spell the end of everything I am working for. I learned my lessons from Joshua well.

And I'm right, because when he's in the doorway, he turns and looks at me. "I had a great time."

"Me, too."

"Can I call you later?"

"Uh-huh."

He smiles and lets himself out.

Miss Bubbles is crying on the other side of my door when I try to let myself into my apartment a few hours later.

"Well move!" I shout to her. "I can't get the door open!" The door is going to smack her, but still she won't move. She is purposely blocking my entry because I wasn't home all night. She's always snitty when I don't sleep at home, alone. When I was with Joshua, whole days would go by with Miss Bubbles crammed in the back of my closet, moping and refusing to give me any love.

She finally gives me some leeway, and I slip into my home. She cocks her head at me and hisses before running under the couch. That ratty, old couch. In my dingy, mismatched, lovely old home. It won't be long before my home could be on Park Avenue or maybe in Beverly Hills. Not that things don't take time, because of course they do and just because I had an unbelievable evening with one of America's most gorgeous bachelors doesn't mean that this is a done deal. Men need time, the morons, to figure out what their destiny is supposed to be. But I can be patient.

After dumping the flour and eggs I shouldn't have spent the money for on the kitchen counter, I stare into the bathroom mirror and for the first time since the morning with Ned the naked man, try to figure out a new chant. I try a couple of versions. "I am famous and powerful" doesn't seem honest enough.

"Love and money are waiting for me" sounds too New Age-y. So I settle on, "I can have everything I want." I like this. Because I can, right? I can have everything I want. After the third time, the buzzer rings.

It's a FedEx man. It's a package from the Paine Group. Yikes.

I rip open the package and find a contract—my very first off-Broadway contract. Does Christian have a photocopier up there? I want to keep this forever. But then I notice that they sent me a duplicate anyway. Wow. They're awesome. They must realize that actors want to keep these things for mementos. I grab a pen and sign on all the dotted lines, then hear Steve's voice in my head scream to read at least *some* of what it is saying.

Screw you, Steve's voice.

I check the envelope to make sure I didn't miss anything, and sure enough there's a small piece of paper left inside. I pull it out—it's the check. *A check!* I leap into the air and punch and kick with delight.

Then I open it.

Three hundred and fifty dollars.

Three hundred and fifty dollars.

That's not as much as I was hoping for. Miss Bubbles is worth at least five hundred. No?

Three hundred and fifty dollars. The catering checks I picked up on the way home are in my back pocket; I pull them out and add everything up. Okay, Stella, it's okay. It's okay. I have just enough to cover the rent. That's good. And there's a little extra for baking supplies and things like that.

But not enough for headshots. Shit. Okay. I'm not going to worry about this now. There's no reason to worry! Things are great! Three hundred and fifty dollars a week for Miss Bubbles! That's three less catering shifts a week I'm going to have to work.

It's time to celebrate. I'm going to bake Bubbles a cake.

"Bubbles! Bubbles!" I check under the sofa but she's not there. She's not under the bed, in my closet, in Steve's room. I take a breath—she'll show up eventually. I change into my

KICK IT sweats, and head toward the kitchen for a little cake-baking. Miss Bubbles won't be able to resist the rich aroma of baking cakes for too long.

I throw myself into this task with vigor, and the promise of all Miss Bubbles has going for her sparks my creativity. What I come up with is a tower of different colored cake layers, it kind of looks like stacked Neapolitan ice cream. I baked three round cakes: one chocolate, one vanilla and one strawberry. Okay the strawberry isn't really strawberry because I have no fruit. It's vanilla with red food coloring. But nobody has to know. I've cut each cake horizontally into three round pieces so that there are nine layers in the finished cake, and am in the process of mixing a whipped cream and banana filling when there's a knock on the door. I wipe my hands on a towel and go get it. It could be flowers from my new fella.

No dice. It's Christian. "What do you want?" I clip my words, to let him know that there's no welcome mat for him.

"My blazer."

"Get a freakin' life. What is this blazer made of? Gold?"

"Stella. Just get me my coat!" He tries hard not to shout at me, and for some reason I am pleased and decide to play with him. He's just so much fun, and I'm in a great mood.

"It isn't here."

He hangs his head. He is easy. "Where is it?"

"At the cleaners."

"At the cleaners." He repeats, not believing it at all.

"At the cleaners." I lift my shoulders and drop them. Sorry, Charlie.

"When can I get it back?"

I giggle at him. "When it's clean, silly!" I am definitely driving him crazy. Life is so sweet today. "But hey, you don't happen to have any strawberries up in that meticulous apartment, do you?"

I have succeeded in completely baffling him. "I do, actually. Why?"

"I need them." He is so exasperated with me, but I convince him to get them for me in exchange for a piece of the finished product, so in no time flat, I am rinsing and chopping strawberries for my cake filling. Life is too good. Except that Christian's not leaving.

He sits on a stool at the other side of the counter where I'm dicing and asks where I learned to do "all this cooking."

"I don't know. I just picked it up from my mother's job."

"She was a cook?" He gets up and crosses to the cabinet where Steve keeps his wineglasses.

"Naw. She can't boil water. Kind of like you!" And I smile at him. He nods and asks if I have a bottle of wine. I do, but I'm not wasting it on him. He's dead set on drinking wine though, because he goes back up to his place for a second time and returns with a bottle of red.

"Why are you hanging around?"

He looks a little bit, what's the word? Cagey? Wounded? Guarded? Guarded. That's it. He pops the cork, again, seeming to know just where we keep the corkscrew, and pours the wine into the waiting glasses. "I want a piece of cake."

"Fine," I grunt. "Well, tell me if this needs anything." I hold up a spoonful of filling to him.

"Um. It's good."

"Not too sweet?"

"No. It's perfect." Then I realize that he is encroaching on my personal space and so I back up against the wall. "Can you get out of my kitchen now?"

He literally shakes his head at this growl of mine and snarls right back, "Relax yourself. Here's your wine, snippy."

I take the glass and drink half of it down. My stomach is a bit jittery. I drink one more huge gulp and fish around the counter for the bottle, filling myself right back up.

Christian has taken up residency on the stool again and goes right back to firing questions at me.

"So."

"So."

"How's lover boy?"

"Huh? I don't have a lover boy."

"Well, whoever you're sleeping with now. How's he doing?"

I get it. He's toying with me, trying to see if he can piss me off. I refuse to give in.

"I bet he's just as good as the little chippy you had up there last night."

He laughs at me, sips his wine and says, "Touché. Do you know what that means?"

I drop the spoon. "Christian, I know what touché means." I start to stir again with a vigor inspired by my annoyance. "You're such a jerk," I add under my breath.

"You're such a jerk!" Ugh. I hate it when he mocks me like this. He thrusts his voice up into the stratosphere and clucks like a hen. Like I have a squeaky naggy voice like that. "So where's Steve?"

"I don't know." I pretend that I have to concentrate on putting the filling between the layers, even though I could do it in my sleep. Christian thumbs through our mail, and then picks up my contracts. I smack his hand.

"Put those down. They're mine."

"Oh, right, the big job. It must suck having to vicariously live through your pet."

"Not as bad as vicariously living through your downstairs neighbor."

He sucks in a blast of air and then we both say "touché" at the same time; I add that I know what it means. He is so nosy though, and starts reading the contracts.

"I said to put them down."

"It's probably good for at least one person in this building to have read what you signed." It really gets my goat that he assumes that I didn't read it before I signed. Even though I didn't.

"You know what? I'm not a moron. Okay? Just because I

didn't go to the hallowed halls of Columbia doesn't mean I'm a complete idiot."

"Uh-huh." He's too busy reading to respond. "Actually, this looks like a pretty good deal. You don't even have to do anything to cash this check. Dumb luck."

"What do you mean I don't have to do anything?" I grab the contract out of his hands and flip through the pages. "Wait a minute? Drop-off time? Pickup time?"

He leans over the counter for a second, to point something out in the fine print, and my mind is momentarily distracted from the issue at hand by the scent of his cologne. Or is that just his skin?

"What are you wearing?" These words fly out of my mouth before I can stop them.

"What?"

"Um, nothing. It must be the cake." Oh my *God* I don't think I have ever said anything quite so lame in my whole life.

"Uh, okay." He raises his eyebrows at me and goes back to business. "It says right here that all you have to do is make sure the cat's there on time and that you pick her up before the stagehands go home at night." Then he flips to another page. "But you're welcome to wait in the dressing room if you get there early."

I look at him and he's smiling at me. "This is bullshit! I thought I got to be there to make sure she got on stage okay."

"Page three. There will be a handler in charge of that." He's still smiling.

"*Why?* And why are you enjoying this?"

"I don't know, Stella. I don't know. But I really am." His grin is outmatching the Cheshire cat's right now. He finishes his wine and pours some more.

"You're really such a jerk."

"Aw come on. I'm not that bad. Why don't you just admit that you'd built up this fantasy in your mind of being the star of the show? I bet you were fantasizing about taking a bow along with the cat." He snorts at this, extremely pleased with himself.

"Well right now I'm fantasizing about belting you in the mouth. How 'bout that?" He smirks and raises his hands up in a gesture of surrender.

Instead of smacking him, I take the contract into the bedroom and decide to deal with it later.

Christian ends up staying throughout the cake frosting process and when it's done, we have already put a dent in our second bottle of wine, which I tried to unceremoniously produce from the cabinets without him catching my lie. It's not as good as the other bottle was, but tasting better and better with every sip.

"There!" I step back and thrust my arms into a presentation pose. "Miss Bubbles's Fantastic Celebratory Tower of Cake!"

He leans over. "It looks really good. How do you make those frosting flowers?"

"I could tell you but then I'd have to kill you. Actually, maybe I will tell you." I carry the cake out to the living room and place it on the coffee table. Christian follows with the wineglasses and bottle and sets them down. "Should I get plates?"

I get up to help him and we are crammed into the kitchen looking for a cake knife and clean plates. I should really do the dishes more often. He reaches for the forks and the wine must be going to my head because he looks really good, his arm muscles are lean and sculpted and I catch myself staring. He catches me staring, too.

"What?"

"Nothing. I should eat something so this wine doesn't go to my head."

"I like pasta."

He's inviting himself over for a home-cooked meal, that's what. No way, José.

"I don't think so. One piece of cake and then you're outta here."

He tilts his head at me and looks into my eyes for a second longer than I want him to. Then he turns and walks out of the kitchen. "Where's that mangy cat, anyway?"

I tell him she isn't mangy and that he's mangy and that he should just shut up. But he isn't listening. He's found one of my old scrapbooks and is sitting on the floor, thumbing through the pictures.

"Wow. How old are these photos?"

I start to cut the cake. "They're not that old."

"Is that your mother?" I look over my shoulder and put my cake knife down.

"Yeah, that's her."

"She looks just like you." I have heard this my whole life and so make no comment.

I slide over to show him the good pictures. I point out her dance recital photo when she was in high school, and the pictures of her in the ballet corps of *The Nutcracker Suite* in Philadelphia, and in the summer production of *Annie Get Your Gun* the year before I was born. "Look how pretty she is!"

"You're cooing like *you're* the mom."

"Shut up and pay attention or no cake." He resigns, but only after the last of the wine is poured into both our glasses.

"We need another bottle."

While I pick up my glass I hear him shout "Bull's-eye" and turn to find him holding a baby picture of me.

"Oh! Don't look at that!" And I stretch across his body to reclaim it, but his arms are too long and he holds it too far away for me to get it. He's laughing and the glee in his eyes is annoying the crap out of me.

"Look at you. You were so cute. Then." I struggle in vain to grab the picture, and finally clutch a fistful of the skin on his arm and dare him to keep taunting me. He looks down at me then and I start to feel way too uncomfortable. Actually what's making me uncomfortable is that smell, that smell like a warm clean man. Too much wine. I jump back.

"Ha. Ha. Ha. What an original wit you are, Christian."

"Shut up and give me some cake already."

I throw back my glass of wine before getting the cake. "Do you want more wine?"

"I think we're good." Why am I disappointed? And what's going on here? It isn't even seven o'clock yet, and I'm drunk in my apartment with *Christian*.

He starts to put the slices of cake on the plates. "This looks really good."

"Thanks." He's right—the cake looks gorgeous, like a tower of colors, fruit and cream dripping in between the nine layers. I amaze myself.

I take a bite. We really need some more wine. Should I turn on the television? Or put on some music? We're sitting side by side on the floor and eating cake and he's drinking wine and there isn't a sound in my apartment. I'm starting to get itchy. Literally, my skin in starting to crawl around on itself.

But then thankfully he breaks the silence. "So how come you don't have pictures of your dad?"

I nearly drop my fork. Why would he ask that? "Huh?"

"It's just, in my family's picture books, all the pictures are of my father. His military picture, his photos from school and his first day of residency. All kinds of pictures like that."

"None of your mom?"

"Well, she's in the pictures of my brothers and me, holding us and stuff. And there's a wedding album and things like that."

"A perfect, tidy little family for perfect tidy little Christian." He stares at me. I think I hurt his feelings. "Sorry."

"That's okay."

I guess to make him feel better I say, "I don't have a dad."

He chortles. "Test-tube baby?"

"Why are you such a jerk?" I whine and punch him in the arm, but he catches my fist and throws it down to my lap.

"*No.* I just never knew who he was."

He stares at me, and the silence intimidates me into spilling the beans on my life. "It was some actor guy, I don't know. He was married or something, so my mom just up and left her tour in Michigan—where they happened to be playing—and stayed there and had me. She won't tell me who he is."

"Have you asked?"

"Oh!" I slap my hand to my head for emphasis. "Christian! What a great idea! I'll *ask*. Why didn't I ever think of that?"

"All right, all right," he says through mouthfuls of strawberry. "But, there are other ways you could find out, you know."

"I wouldn't know where to start."

"Well, is Monroe his last name?" He's still stuffing cake in his mouth and I'm sorry that this came up, because he's not really a caring enough person to know this about me. But it's too late now.

"Do you think I'm an idiot? Of course it's not his name. It's nobody's name."

"What do you mean?"

"Monroe. It's not a real name. My mother gave it to me, you know, because of Marilyn."

He chokes and has to take three huge gulps of wine to stop coughing.

"Marilyn Monroe? Did your mother realize that wasn't even Marilyn's real last name?"

I can't remember ever feeling so embarrassed. Why did I just tell him all this anyway? Goddamn it. I hate him and want him to leave now, but before I can tell him to get the hell out, the buzzer rings again.

It's a delivery guy, with a huge bouquet of flowers. Pink and white and yellow roses with those little yellow berry flowers interspersed throughout. When I sign for them and bring them in, Christian just stands there looking at me.

"Aren't they amazing?" I gush.

"Yeah. They're nice."

I put them on the counter and start to smell the buds. I read the card. "For the cutest girl in all the Big Apple. Jasper." I start to jump up and down and realize that in the midst of all the conversation and wine, I'd forgotten all about last night.

I'm immediately in a better mood and since Christian is standing in front of me, I lunge forward and hug him. Damn wine.

He kind of tenses up and pulls himself away. Then it's just awkward. Should I apologize? What for?

"Do you want to get something to eat?" Who just said that? Me?! "I mean after all, we did just eat dessert. What better time for dinner?"

He takes a moment and then says, "Naw. I gotta get going. Thanks for the afternoon."

Chapter 11

I am standing outside of a house, and it's made entirely of dough. There are spires alongside the doorway, and Miss Bubbles is trying to eat one of them. I run up to her and tell her not to eat the building, because it might be somebody's home. She wriggles out of my grasp and runs inside the front door. I scream after her that I don't have time to play Alice in Wonderland, but it's too late. The door has shut behind her, she's gone and can't hear me. I look around for somebody to give me a key, but there's nobody on the street.

There's an empty bodega on the corner and I run to it. Christian is there, behind the counter, and when I ask for a key to the building across the street, Jasper comes out of the back room. How do they know each other? They're brothers? Brothers. That's what Jasper says and Christian doesn't deny it. I ask again about the building with the spires. Christian says that if I figure out which spire is the right one, I can enter. How do I tell which one is which? He tells me to take a bite and see.

By now Bubbles has missed dinner and it's getting dark. I head back to the house and stare at both spires until I realize: they're made of chocolate. I stab one with my finger. Not chocolate. Salt. It crumbles

away a bit, leaving only a core of strawberry and banana filling. I choose
the other one and take a bite. It's sweet and chocolatey. So good, like
soft powdered sugar. It crumbles too, leaving a core of steel. Inedible. I
hear the door click itself locked, and know I'm shut out.

Ezra has booked me a commercial audition, so I'm off to read
for a national underwear spot. I wonder if Michael Jordan will
be there, and on my way out, I look up at the stone angel and
kiss her big toe. She's been working overtime on my behalf, really. Jasper called me last night at like 1:43 a.m., and asked if I
could come over to his hotel room. But what did I do? Did I
run out, half-awake and barely pulled together, old-school style
like last year when Joshua would call? *Hell no.* This is the new
me! I said I needed to sleep and would see him another time!
Score one for Stella. Using this self-respect thing to my advan-
tage is new for me, but I'm getting the hang of it. When he
hung up, I could hear the power balance in our relationship
scooting through the phone lines to me. I think it's best for my
longevity that I not make myself available twenty-four/seven.
It helped that I had a wine hangover, too, and could barely move.

So now, I'm signing into the Film & Television Building on
Ninth Avenue, a scant few blocks from somebody's favorite
place to go for a drink. But no cavorting until after business is
taken care of. Seriously, all this self-control. I haven't even seen
Michaela since my night with Jasper.

So, my commercial audition. Underwear. Michael Jordan.
Tyra Banks. Mark Wahlberg. I have to nail this. And then someday my name will be on that list of hallowed undies salespeople.

I've chosen a demure, preteen look, because Ezra said the audition's for an early-twenty-something who'll be cavorting
with her underwear-wearing boyfriend/young husband. I'm
wearing jeans and a short, cropped top that shows just a slice
of midriff. Blue with little silver sparkle flowers sown on—no
red, black or white, because those colors throw off the camera.
Things you learn along the way.

The other great thing about this audition is that Ezra signed me up for a time slot, so I just go in and come right back out. Another reason one must desperately, desperately hold out for commercial and television show auditions. This breaking my back to wait on nonunion theater jobs is really trying my patience.

I sign in and look around for the audition side, the piece of paper with the dialogue. There isn't any. The monitor tells me it's just a visual.

It's my turn already, so I go right into the room and see two executives behind a table and a scrappy-looking, lean, goateed guy behind a camera. He's setting up the shot and points me in the direction of a big, masking-taped *X* on the floor. I hand the execs my headshot and stand patiently on the *X*, waiting for direction. After about thirty seconds of Goatee Man peering through his camera, he looks up and says to the suits, in an exasperated tone, "What am I supposed to do with this?"

Their reaction makes me understand that "this" is *me*. Suit #1 says to me, "Um, why aren't you wearing a skirt?"

"What?"

"A *skirt*." There's no mistaking this tone. The suit is annoyed. "Didn't your agent tell you to wear a skirt?"

"Um, no actually. He didn't." I'm confused, but by this guy's tone, I can tell that I shouldn't let them know I'm confused because they could pounce on me.

"Uh-huh." The execs look at each other and the female one shakes her head in disgust. The other one continues. "Well, how are we supposed to tell what you look like in your underwear if you have those pants on?"

My head starts to buzz like a million bees have landed behind my eyes. I am having strange insights into the future, and I don't like what I see. And because I don't respond right away, sure enough, they pounce.

The cameraman says, irked, "Lady, hurry up and take 'em off. We don't have all day."

And the female exec says, to her coffee, "Where do these people come from? Iowa?"

"Michigan." I respond, before I can help myself. I'm starting to tear up, and visions of Coco from Fame are dancing in my head.

The head exec guy has had it. "Are you taking off your pants or what?"

I unbutton my jeans and start to unzip them and falter. But then I think about my mother and what she would do. She would *definitely* take her pants off if it meant a commercial. I'd be able to get into the Screen Actors Guild if I got this thing. I strip off my bottoms, and then look up hesitantly to make sure I've done right by the judges. They continue to shakes their heads, in perfect unison. "Well?" Suit #1 asks impatiently.

"Well?" I ask, confused.

"Oh Jesus Christ. Top, too. We need to *see* you."

The room grows deathly quiet. Do I take off all my clothes or do I take a stand, like Sarah Jessica Parker, and refuse nudity? Well, let's face it. I'm no Sarah Jessica Parker. I need this job. I need to get headshots. Mom would say that the audition is more important than my dignity. I rip off my top, and stand in my underwear and bra, thanking God that they match. But then I remember that they're *red*. The colors will bleed on camera. Shit.

The judges are still scowling, probably because I've wasted so much of their time. Goatee shakes his head in disgust as he peers back through the camera lens. How bad can I look? I don't have time to worry, though, because he barks, "Well are you gonna slate or what?"

Slate is jargon for telling the camera your name. So I do, I lift up my chin in a pose of pride and say, clear as a bell, "Stella Monroe." Then I stand stock-still. Goatee adjusts the lens of the camera. The lady sips her coffee. I can hear the *tap tap tap* of Suit #1's finger as he drums his annoyance into the table. The walls seem to be closing in on me, and I am standing, frozen, like a deer caught in the headlights. Should I do anything? I don't want to be remembered just as the dolt who didn't bring a skirt. I don't want to be the topic of conversation the next time these jerks get together for a beer. Time is running out. This campaign is slipping from my grasp. It's now or never. And so I adopt a posture like I'm on a surfboard, arms splayed out airplane style and start to chant,

"Love my red underwear. Love my red underwear. Love my red underwear. Oh, yeah."

Then I jump one hundred and eighty degrees to my left and start to surf on the other side.

"Red! Yeah! Underwear! Yeah!"

Goatee slowly lifts his head from behind the camera and stares at me with his mouth open. I'm not positive, but I think the woman spits out her coffee. Suit #1 screams through a strangled throat, *"Thank you."*

I pick up my pants and shirt and slink out the door.

It takes three minutes to get to Hell's and another forty-five seconds before I am on the phone with Ezra, yelling at him.

Well not yelling, but definitely *demanding*. Michaela is leaning over the bar giving her hands a sugar massage and trying to glean information about my audition through my rant to Ezra.

"Ezra?"

"How'd it go kid? Did you nail it?"

"Ezra." I can feel veins popping like bubble gum in my face. "They made me take off my clothes, Ezra. They wanted me naked!"

"For chris' sakes, kiddo, who doesn't?"

This is all I can handle. My voice raises, and Michaela wisely decides to pour me a shot. Jack Daniel's. *"Ezra.* Why didn't you tell me to wear a skirt?" I say these words with too much precision, like I'm talking to a deaf immigrant who speaks no English.

I can hear laughter in the background, and I scream another notch louder, "Am I on speakerphone?!"

"Aw, Monroe." I have to hold the phone out an inch from my ear, the usual position for Ezra phone calls. "What's the big deal? You're hot, who cares if they get a free show?"

I down the shot. "But Ezra." I wince from the burn of the liquor going down my throat. "I don't like doing that kind of stuff. I feel stupid."

"Kid. I'm gonna give you some advice." He inhales, and I picture a fat cigar hanging out the side of his mouth. "Toughen. Up."

"Toughen up?" I repeat, and motion to Mic to keep the shots coming. "Toughen up?"

"That's right, doll-face. You gotta thicken up that sweet-looking skin of yours. There's only one type of girl who gets ahead in this business."

I am now slumping against the bar. Ezra has let all the air out of my tires.

"You know what type that is?"

"Yes." I sigh a blast of hot air into the phone receiver.

"The girl who breaks the most balls, breaks the most rules and turns on the most execs, gets ahead. Now today you learned a valuable lesson, isn't that right? And I'm proud of you. My little girl isn't afraid to roll up her sleeves, or, in this case, rip off her clothes. I'm gonna make you a star!" I hear him clap his hands together in fiendish delight.

My head falls into my hand. "Ezra. I don't like taking off my clothes. Okay?"

"Yeah, yeah, yeah. Okay. Don't you worry your pretty little head about it."

Pretty little head falls to the bar. "Okay."

"Okay. Love ya, sweets. Nice work today. And I'll see you Monday."

"Monday?" This is such a desperate tactic, I know, but maybe he'll reschedule if I pretend that I forgot about our appointment.

Then I can hear him roar as he picks up the receiver, cutting off the free show for all the people in his office enjoying our conversation. "*Monday.* Our date. *Pictures.* Stella. I mean business. No pictures. No deal." And he hangs up. I sit at the bar and hold the phone in my hand for the next five minutes, as Michaela grits her teeth and tries to make me feel better.

"It's bad, honey?"

I moan, then lift up my head and stare into space. "Bad." No other words come to my mind. "Bad. Bad. Bad. I have to come up with some headshots before Monday. Bad. Bad. Bad."

Michaela asks one of the waiters to bring us a piece of carrot cake, then assumes her leaning position, taking my hand in hers, tracing the lines of my palm with her forefinger. "It's gonna be okay. I can take your pictures."

"Really? You'd do that?"

"Of course! Carlo has a camera. How hard can it be? We can do it tomorrow."

I don't know if it's the cake or the shots, but Michaela is beginning to make sense. "You're right! I don't have to worry about headshots! You can take them, right?"

"Sure! We can do it in the backyard." Oh my God. Talk about the light at the end of the tunnel. I inch forward on my bar stool.

"Mic! This is great! Because there'll be at least one shot that's decent, and then I can put Ezra off until I land a job with some real pay! And someday, when I'm famous and rich, I'll buy you a huge house somewhere!"

"I don't need a house. But I do have one favor to ask you. A big one."

"Huh?"

"My wedding. I want you to, you know, cook all the food. And the cake, too."

"Really?"

"Yeah, if it's not too much. Rod said you could use the kitchen here."

I'm shocked. I haven't worked on such a big cooking project for years. But it's Michaela. She's my best friend.

"Of course I'll do it. You have a deal!" And we clasp pinkies, like schoolgirls.

Before we make any more plans, I hear from behind me, "Fantastic. Drinks and dessert, all before two o'clock." Steve swoops down upon us and kisses us both on the cheek. He looks great, his skin is sleek and moist-looking, and I just know he's come from an audition. One where, no doubt, he got to keep all his clothes on.

"What's going on here, ladies? I've missed something juicy."

I tell him about the underwear audition, and when I get to the surfing part, they are both laughing so hard that Steve is crying and Michaela is coughing up chunks of carrot cake.

"It's not funny." But I'm starting to grin despite myself, and Steve puts his hand on my shoulders and says, "Don't sweat it too much. It's just what we do."

I know he's right, but I still have this feeling in my gut that is telling me something I don't want to know. That I *don't* want to do that kind of stuff. "Yeah, well, I'd rather be home making omelets than simulating naked surfing in front of nasty strangers." I lick some frosting off of my finger.

Steve closes his fist and pretends to skim my chin. "Chin up. It gets better."

This is Michaela's opening to ask him what he's doing here, and his response, as I expected, is devastating.

"Just found out that I made it through the callbacks and am going in for another one, this one more intense. I think I'm going to read a bunch of scenes with one of the chicks on the show." Mic squeals and hugs him over the bar, while he tries to shush her and downplay the news. Ever the practical auditioner.

I hold out my shot glass. Mic discards it and produces a regular-size glass full of Jack and Coke while smiling and talking about how exciting Steve's life is. "Yeah, that's great," I muster before taking a deep breath and really trying to sell it. "You're gonna be famous!" And I throw my arms around his neck and kiss him on the cheek sloppily.

He removes my death-grip and shakes his head. "You might want to turn the Jessica Lange down a notch."

I slump back onto my stool and stir my drink lazily. "Sorry."

"Okay, ladies. Off to the gym. I'll see you later." He picks up his bag from the floor and leaves me and Michaela to our afternoon and our plotting. But I've been here long enough and have recovered from my audition tragedy enough to begin the campaign of answering-machine-checking phone calls. Because I'm in control of my life and my relationship, I can check my messages remotely.

And on the first try? Bingo.

"Mic, come listen to this." She puts her ear to the receiver and we listen to the following,

"Pretty Stella… Meet me for dinner tonight…or maybe I'll meet you near your place. Be home at eight. I'll call."

"Ooohhh. He has a sexy phone voice." Michaela's giggles pour out of her mouth, surrounding me with a feeling of peace and calm.

"Another date! Only two days after our last one. Do you think he's my boyfriend yet?" I ask though I know the answer. Mic's eyes go wide and she leans over to where I'm sitting, all important-like, "I think, well, I think… You definitely need to see him in the show."

Lightning bolt. "You're right. The show. I have to see it first. Because, what if he's not any good?"

"Well, there is always that possibility." Thank God Mic is here to talk sense when the sense needs talkin'. I've never seen him in anything, not his movies, not his TV show—what if he stinks? I mean, you hear things on *Access Hollywood,* but how reliable can Billy Bush be? What if Jasper is getting by on his good looks alone?

"You're the best friend I ever had," I say. "Thanks." I look at her and we nod.

Chapter 12

Confirming my suspicions that Jasper is well on his way to of-ficial boyfriend status, he has asked me to dinner. Not just any dinner. But the dinner he is eating on this, his only night off. Monumental. He is choosing to spend his night off with me. Not with some blond chippy or a bevy of theater people. Me. Not going over his lines in preparation for the final dress re-hearsal tomorrow night. With *me*.

Oh, yes.

I am standing in front of the bar at the oh-so-chic, Upper East Side mainstay Café Latrella. There are several attractive women curled over the bar, hugging Cosmos to their lips and possessively clutching onto the pant legs of their husbands/boy-friends/casual dates. I've been here before and am comfortable with the scene. The years with Joshua taught me how to go undercover in this world. I haven't lost any of my skills, and my desire to become a full-fledged card-carrying member of the rich and trouble-free only throbs louder in my ears whenever they're right in front of me. Thinking of Joshua, I glance over to the window table in the corner. The last time we were here together we fought about money and my future. I stare at the canoodling couple sitting at the table now and remember Josh saying I needed to grow up. I stop myself from biting my lip because it took forever to get my mouth looking this luscious and made-up, and I don't want to have to go for a touch-up and miss Jasper's entrance. Instead, my hands involuntarily smooth down the front of the baby-rose-yellow dress that clings to my body in all the right places, courtesy of casa Michaela. It's a good thing Jasper keeps picking places I've been to with Joshua. Knowing what to wear ahead of time really cuts down on my worries.

A focused breeze tingles my left ear, exposed by my upswept hairdo. "Stel-la." I turn and am immediately surrounded by the arms of my dreams. I look up into Jasper's eyes and feel myself blush. He kisses me hello and the blush creeps down into my toes. Kissed by a movie star in a public place. Well, a movie actor. Okay. An off-Broadway star and sometimes movie actor. But who cares? He's hot. I hope at least one of the women at the bar recognizes him and is insanely jealous of me. When he pushes me from his body to take in my dress (which, judging by his lustful stare, is a big hit) I have an opportunity to check out his hunky form, filling out that white dress shirt and gray jacket with muscley biceps that make me want to curl up in his arms forever. I never had this physical reaction with Joshua. No. The excitement there came when he pulled out his credit cards or made all the decisions or looked down at me from his lofty height and told me what to do. He was a man in control. Jasper's just hot. And famous. And good in bed. A triple threat.

"Maybe we should skip dinner," he says with his hands on my hips. His thumb is burning a hole into my hipbone and for a second I want to take him up on it.

But only for a second. I can't indulge all my impulses if I want to keep him around.

"Mr. Hodge," I say coyly, removing my hips from his hands, "I thought you were a gentleman."

He laughs at me and grins. "Who told you that?"

I amuse him. Very good.

We find our table and he pulls out my chair. Very, very good. Mr. & Mrs. Hodge have raised themselves a polite young man.

I tell Jasper to order for us, so I can see him talk to the waiters. Seriously, he is so good with people. Joshua used to dismiss service people like they were some sort of lowly animal, and it used to make me very uncomfortable, because, let's face it. I had more in common with *them* than I did with *him*. But Jasper casts a spell on everyone he meets. It's the smile. He should patent it so that no other person can ever smile again.

Our wine comes and Jasper peers at me from across the table. The crowd behind him, the waiter standing to my left, the music playing softly, all of this fades into the background. He's just sitting there, a working actor, so comfortable in his skin, assured of his future, smiling so dazzlingly as the waiter places the wine bottle in the sweating metal stand. Jasper picks up his wineglass, proposing a toast. If I wasn't so self-assured, I would tear up. Because this is all I need. Just somebody nice who will take care of everything. If I were Jasper's girl, I wouldn't even *need* to go on stupid auditions where I have to take off my clothes, or wait in line, or be cut off before I even get to speak. No, I could just stay home and cook and play with Miss Bubbles. Then at night I'd get all dressed up and go to Jasper's fancy parties, the girl on his arm who charms the socks off of all his theater friends.

"A toast, to a great girl and a great time." That Jasper knows just what to say.

I decide to say, "And to a handsome man who knows how to pick good wine" instead of "And to the man who can solve all my problems."

We clink glasses. "You look beautiful."

"Thank you." The wine burns my throat, cutting a path to my swirling stomach. Why do I feel like crying? I don't know. But I do.

And then, Mr. Hodge proves *again* how perfect he is by picking up on this.

"Are you okay? You look like you're about to cry."

Love him.

"Let me ask you something," I say as I place my glass on the table. "When does auditioning get easy?"

"When you retire."

Really. I love him.

"Be serious!" I say through a huge smile.

"I am serious! Auditioning always sucks, but then you get a great job, and before you know it, you've forgotten all the stuff you hated."

"I don't picture you hating anything about the business."

"Well, everyone hates it."

"I don't think Steve hates it."

Jasper butters a roll. "You just have to know how to put things in perspective." He takes a big bite, and butter sticks to the corner of his mouth. I look away. And then a phone rings. His cell phone. He reaches into his jacket pocket, pulls it out, checks the number, and says to me, "Oh, honey. I have to take this."

I don't know whether to be thrilled that he called me honey or annoyed that he's taking a call during our date.

"Hey. What's up?" He leans an elbow on the table and wipes the butter from his face with a napkin. I fold my hands in my yellow lap and pretend I'm not listening to every word he says.

"I told you not to worry about that." He smirks to the table. "Uh-huh. Uh-huh. It'll be fine." There is a pause and he continues to look amused with what the other person is saying. "Yep. Still a go. Okay. Don't worry. Don't worry. Okay. Bye."

He flips the phone shut and replaces it in his pocket. "Sorry about that. Where were we?" He finishes his wine and fills it back up. I am dying to know who that was. His agent? His mom? Another girlfriend? Why am I so suspicious? It's not like I'm his keeper or anything. I mean, he *is* allowed to talk to people other than me, right? Of course right.

And so I don't ask. Because I am cool. And because I want to continue to be in control of this situation. So I change the topic altogether and ask him if he's nervous about the opening of the show.

He hems and haws but I can tell that he *is* nervous and this makes me want to jump his bones. He's just so *real*. And throughout the rest of the meal, as he tells me about his parents in California, and his sister who writes music in Italy, and about his first job as a singing carrot in a commercial for Campbell's alphabet soup when he was twelve, and how he likes New York, I forget about the uneasiness I felt when that phone rang.

The waiter brings the dessert tray and I am about to decline politely (because I am a girl and know how to behave in social situations) but Jasper the Prince of My Dreams orders a crème brûlée and a chocolate mousse cake before I can demurely pass. He looks up and smiles at me. "I know I shouldn't, but this wouldn't be a date without sharing desserts, right?"

He should write a handbook on how to treat ladies. I'll write the foreword. It'll sell millions of copies and we can just add it to the pile of perfection that will be our lives together.

When the desserts and accompanying cappuccinos arrive, he grabs my cup so that he can "dress it up." I sit back and watch him sprinkle cinnamon and sugar on top of the frothy, bubbly foam, just like I do! He's *perfect*. It's all I can do not to climb up on the table and start singing, "Ain't No Man Like the One I Got."

He slides my cappuccino over to me, winks and digs into the mousse.

"I wanted to ask you a question."

"Yes?" My hopes skyrocket to the stars. Questions are good.

"You're going to be at the final dress tomorrow, right?"

"Of course." I demurely lick some crème brûlée off of my spoon, making sure that he gets a good view of the tip of my tongue. "I have to support my cat."

He laughs. "Well, I was wondering if you'd be my date to

the opening night party. I mean, I guess that you'd be going anyway. But I wanted to ask if you'd go with me, you know, like be my official date." He stares at the table, the candlelight reflecting off of his blond hair. Do I detect discomfort? Shyness even?

"Hmm. That might be okay." There is a circus of flips and fireworks shooting off in my abdomen. This must be what it feels like to stand at the top of a mountain you've climbed. You don't take some girl you're casually seeing to a party where your picture will be taken. Boyfriend status. It's a'comin' round the mountain.

"I'd love to be your date."

He grins up at me and we work on our desserts. We laugh and giggle and he spoons some mousse into my mouth, dotting some of the whipped cream on my nose. Are we a commercial or what? And nothing gets me worked up like desserts. Nope. I start to eat faster than I should so that we can get to the real dessert.

When we're finished, he leans across the table and grabs my hand. "So are you up for a trip to the hotel?"

Not the most romantic line ever used, but what the hell? Of course I'm up.

"Yes," I say while casually tracing circles on the back of his hand. "That would be fine."

He pulls out my chair for me, walks to the coat check, and helps me into my coat. A cab pulls up to the curb almost as soon as we step outside of the restaurant, and I think that God must be our personal stage manager tonight, because everything is perfect. We snuggle in the back of the yellow taxi and laugh at the "Things to Do in New York City" minifilm playing on the television monitor. Usually these things really get on my nerves, but with Jasper's arms entwined around me I am learning to love it. Soon enough Jasper is kissing behind my ear. Before you can say *Taxi Cab Confessions,* I am on top of his lap and his hands are on my behind and the top of the yellow dress is caught between his teeth. So inappropriate! The last time I got busy in a public place….oh, um. Well I doubt I can remember the last time, but not because it was that long ago. Because of the quantity of chocolate martinis imbibed just prior to the Great Mauling of Stella in the Back Room of Hell's Bar by Ned the Soon-to-be Naked Man.

"Hel–loh? Hel–loh?" An Indian accent stops us in the middle of our groping session.

"Yeah?" Jasper says, pulling his face out of my chest. Lipstick is smeared all over his chin.

"Where yoo goh?"

"Aw, right here, actually. This corner is perfect."

We pull over, Jasper pays, thanks the driver and hustles me through the hotel lobby. We can barely keep our hands off each other in the elevator and by the time we're at the door, my dress has already been unzipped.

Later, when we're in his bed and his hands are all over me, and he is whispering my name into my ear, I'm the happiest girl in the entire world. He pushes himself up on his elbow and stares at me.

"You're beautiful." What's with this blushing thing?

"*You're* beautiful." I say. This is all so perfect. It's like a movie scene. And seriously, who wouldn't want Jasper Hodge to be playing the part of the romantic lead? But then, our mood is shattered. The cell phone. Again.

He jumps out of bed and runs over to his pants, which are spread out on the floor by the door, where they were ripped off of him by some lusty girl. Okay. By me.

Now I prop myself on my elbow, to hear what he is saying. And I check the clock. It's almost midnight. Maybe it's his assistant. Or somebody from California is calling. When he says, "I told you not to worry about that," I want to know what is going on with whoever it is on the other end immediately. I don't mind having my dinner interrupted. But afterglow? Call me old-fashioned, but it is *not* all right to have afterglow interrupted. He turns his back on me and then walks into the bathroom. Hmm…secretive, secretive. Where have I observed this behavior before? I shoot up into a sitting position. Joshua. When his wife would call.

Okay, okay. Stella. You're being silly. There is no wife. Right? No wife. No wife. Chant it like a mantra. No wife. But then some sort of survival instinct takes over and I get out of the bed and run for my clothes. No wife. No wife. I am going straight home to Google this bastard. Where the hell is my underwear? I find them hanging off the side of a table lamp. By the time they're on my body, Jasper has come out of the bathroom and does a double take when he sees that I'm dressing.

"What are you doing?"

"Yeah, I've gotta go." The cool, collected tone of my voice shocks me. I am so in control. "I have a big day tomorrow."

He leans against an overstuffed chair and folds his arms. "Really?" Do I detect disbelief? I wander over to him, fully aware that all I have on is a thong.

His expression changes and he is no longer looking at my face. "A very, very big day tomorrow," I whisper as I uncross his arms and place his hands on my hips. I kiss him and I hear his breath catch in his throat. Pretty sure that he has forgotten whoever it was who called him, because he leaps into a standing position, picks me up, brings me over to the bed and removes my thong before I have a chance to object.

But I stick to my guns and leave an hour later. It seems like a good idea to keep some boundaries. I am shocked at my reaction, really. Usually I trust people every which way, but I guess that Joshua experience left me with more than a red suede coat. I got me some trust issues!

Chapter 13

I discuss the mystery of the anonymous cell phone caller with Michaela the next day after we've plowed through IMDB and a handful of Jasper Hodge fan pages looking for mention of a wife, which, of course, there is none. Michaela sits on my bed loading film into her camera while I ransack my closet, looking for good tops for our photo shoot.

"So what do you think? Permanent damage?" I shout over the din of Avril Lavigne, blasting from the Top 40 station on the radio, and the *plunk-plunk-plunk* of Christian's typewriter keys.

"I don't know, sweetie. It's probably smart to be cautious." She flips the lid on the camera shut. "Jesus, that is *so* loud."

I throw her a shoe. "Just hit the ceiling with that." She does, and Christian responds with his typical three boot kicks to the floor. Michaela starts to giggle.

"What do you think of this?" I hold up a pink-and-white striped halter top that has blue and green bowties adorning the top edge.

"I think that's awful. Thrift?"

"Yeah, yeah." I turn back into the bowels of the closet, take a step and hear a screech. Miss Bubbles claws at my leg. "Ow!" She runs away and disappears around the corner.

I limp back to the bed to see if I'm bleeding. Michaela hasn't even moved. "Did she scratch you?"

"I don't understand what's going on with her! She's been so touchy lately." My leg is scratched up pretty good but not bleeding. The bed feels nice, though, so I lie back and snuggle with Mic. "I have nothing to wear." I whine into her shoulder.

"Sure you do sweetie, let's see." She gets up and bounds for my closet. "Don't you worry, darlin'. We are going to do you up right!"

After Michaela has picked out three shirts (one black sleeveless with a v-neck, one red with sequins sewn in a swirly design and one pale pink) and has custom designed the jewelry to be worn with each top, and after I have downed another sip of mimosa and put on all my makeup, touched up my beauty mark and spritzed my hair, we pack up all our gear and head out to the back patio. It's a perfect day—the sun is out, it's about ten degrees warmer than it should be for late February, there are birds chirping and the air is fresh and clean-smelling.

Michaela turns the stereo in the main room on full blast, and opens the windows. Outkast's "Hey Ya" attacks the outdoors, and I actually see two birds fly away. "It's just hip-hop!" I shout at them. Then I head over to the corner of the deck to push the table and chairs out of the way. We haven't been out here since last fall, and there is a pool of mucky water sitting atop the table. "Bring me some paper towels," I shout at full voice to make sure Michaela hears me. But it's Steve who brings them out to me, with a smirk on his face.

"What are you doing home?"

"Girl, there is no *way* I'm missing *this* debacle." He takes a chair and places it facing me, like an audience member. Then his boyfriend, polite Peter, strolls outside holding a pitcher of sangria and five plastic cups. I look at Steve in shock, because he almost never drinks during the day. He just raises his shoulders as if to say, "What the hell?" and pours five glasses full.

Michaela finally comes outside, followed by Carlo, whose brown hair falls past his shoulders like the hem of an oversized dress. "Fun! A party!" Michaela shouts as she and Carlo each take a cup and clink Peter and Steve.

"Whoa, whoa, whoa—" this is not how I envisioned my photo shoot at all "—Carlo, when did you get here? Steve take Carlo inside with Peter, and watch TV and don't come out until we're done."

Michaela clutches onto Carlo's arm and Steve simply says, "No way in hell."

Carlo smiles at me. "You won't even know we're here."

"You'll know I'm here." Steve chortles into his drink then reaches for the pitcher and pours himself some more.

Before I can launch another protest, Michaela starts ordering me around. She positions me against the wall of the building and tells me to put a leg up. "You know, casual, right Steve?"

"Right, Mic!" He nearly shouts as he wipes his mouth with the back of his hand, smirking the whole while.

"Hey," I say, pointing at him. "Hostile onlookers will be evicted."

"Aww, look who has an attitude?"

By this time, we've heard Nelly and Kelly, Beyoncé and Eminem, and now they're launching into a little Justin Timberlake, which, I might add, doesn't bother me as much as it should. Pete is getting lit, while Steve is shouting, "Work it to the Right! Work it to the Left!" Michaela snaps away, telling me to flip my hair this way, to look over my shoulder that way, and to "make love to the camera." As soon as this phrase leaves her lips, Steve and Carlo start laughing so hard, I think they might choke. Michaela punches Steve in the arm and tells him he isn't helping. Carlo tells her she's doing a great job, and doesn't say a thing about how good I'm doing. So I just lean against the building and say a silent prayer that at least one of these pictures is going to look okay for Ezra.

Michaela tells me to go and change into the red shirt, and to change my lipstick and to put my hair into barrettes. I follow her directions dutifully, and when I come back out onto the deck, the pitcher of sangria is full again and Polite Peter and Carlo are chopping up apples on a cutting board. Steve and Michaela are peering upward and talking to Christian, who is leaning over the railing of his deck and smiling. He is wearing a loose-fitting cotton button-down shirt and telling Steve about some movie that he should see.

"Go inside and leave us alone," I say as Polite Peter refills my plastic cup.

"Well, gee, I'd love to, but the blasting music is making the walls shake."

"Really? Welcome to my world, noisy neighbor." I hear Steve say, "good one" under his breath before he grabs my waist and picks me up.

"Be polite!" he whispers in my ear and places me down against the wall. "Chris, do you want some sangria?"

"No!" I say. "No!"

"I'll be right down." What the hell is going on here? Why are all these people congregated to watch my folly? And then the phone rings, and I just know it is my mother, because she is the only one missing from this little party.

I run in and grab the phone just as Christian is letting himself in. He eyes me up and down then shakes his head. I stick my tongue out at him while he goes into the kitchen and helps himself to a cranberry peach muffin. I should start charging him.

"Hello?" My mother is screeching into the phone, because I clicked it on and forgot to say hello. "Hello? Little Star? Oh my goodness, are you there?"

"Mom?" I shout over a Maroon 5 song. "Is that you?"

"What are you, having a *party?* It isn't even three o'clock yet!"

"No, no, no, Mom," I turn down the volume and then run to my room. Just as I get over to my bed, Steve comes in and turns the volume right back up. I shove myself under the pillows, to create a sound barrier.

"Sorry, Mom, Steve has some people over."

"Stella Aurora, you'd better not be drinking this afternoon, and *partying* when you have such a big week coming up."

"I know, I know."

"Have you picked out your outfits for the dress rehearsal? And the opening night party? Appearances are so important, you know."

"I know."

"Of course you know, Star Baby. Well, even though you didn't call me back to talk about taking Frances to lunch, I've come to a decision. I'm sending you a little bit of money to help with the costs of everything."

I feel like I've been punched. "You are?" My mother hasn't given me money since I was sixteen years old. "Really?"

"Well, honey, it was Sal's idea. He had a little windfall here and we know you need pictures."

"Wow, I don't know what to say."

"Well, Star Baby, you and I still have to watch out for each other, don't we? I know you're trying real hard. Well, that is, I think you're trying hard. Hopefully you're not just drinking your afternoons away."

"No, Mom, no I'm not."

"Good girl. Now the check will be in the mail. It won't be much, but I know every little bit helps. Knock 'em dead. And don't wear purple to the party. You look like a big fat grape in purple."

"Yes, Mom I know. I love you."

"I love you, too."

I hang up in a daze and have to go fix my makeup again. Michaela finds me at the bathroom sink as I'm retouching the beauty mark.

"What's the matter?"

"Oh, nothing. My mom called, that's all."

She picks up my lip gloss and grasps my chin. Her touch is so light, I feel like I'm a little girl again. I tell her about the money.

"Well that's good, isn't it?"

"But even with the money she sends, I didn't have enough for a new outfit tonight. And all the people at the final dress will probably have designer outfits with designer hair and designer dates and my mom thinks that I'm going to be one of them."

She puts the lip gloss down and leans against the counter. "Stella. It's gonna be great. After the shoot, we'll pick out the perfect thing to wear, and if you have to come raid my closet, that's what we'll do." Then Steve thrusts his head in the doorway.

"The boys are getting restless. We need the women out there." I can hear Madonna telling me to vogue from the living room.

"I'll be right there." Michaela follows Steve out the door, and the mirror stares out at me. What's up with me anyway? Is today the day where all my insecurities parade around on my skin? It's the damn underwear commercial! My nudity has shaken my confidence. And the phone calls on Jasper's cell. Something doesn't feel right. And the fact that my mother is sending me money when she probably doesn't have it. All I need now is for Ezra to call and yell at me.

"Hey."

I look up and Christian is in the doorway. "What do you want? Can't a girl get any privacy in her own bathroom?"

"Michaela told me to come in and get you."

"She did, huh?"

"Come on." He gestures with his arm out the door, intimating that he'll follow me. "You're the life of the party." I don't move.

"You look good, if that's what you're worried about."

"I know I look good."

"Then come on. For crying out loud, Peter won't make more sangria until you're out there. Come on."

"Okay." I take a quick last-minute glance in the mirror and see Christian appear behind me. He's almost a full head taller than me, and his cheeks are flushed from all the drinks.

"Look at you. Nothing to worry about." His voice is very quiet and I decide that there's no way I'm going to fall so low that *Christian* has to talk me out of a funk. I make to leave and he steps back.

He looks at me and lifts his arm, bending his elbow. Oh, man, is he drunk. "After you, madam."

Maybe it's all the sangria I've had to drink, but for some reason this doesn't annoy me all that much and I take his arm. "Why thank you, sir," I reply as he ushers me out to the rest of my photo shoot.

Chapter 14

Michaela was true to her word. After the photo shoot, she stayed with me until we were both content with my appearance. It's not normal for me to be so worried about how I look. I mean, I'm always concerned, but with the mood I've been in even simple decisions are stressing me out.

But at least the photo shoot went well. Michaela shot three rolls of film and the boys got fairly drunk. They were having such a good time that they kept right on partying after Michaela and I left, commemorating the warm night with tequila shots. Christian was too drunk to notice that Miss Bubbles and I were being picked up by a limo. Well, just a car. But still. Being picked up by a car service at your home to go to a theater to go to work. These are things that Bernadette Peters gets to do.... I should be happier.

Miss Bubbles is in my red bag. It matches my outfit, thank God, because it's the only bag she'll allow herself to be transported in. Usually she's antsy in the car, but today she doesn't even seem nervous. If I was her, I'd be worried about my lack of rehearsal. I've asked Jasper why they didn't want her there earlier, but he says it'll be fine. They sure do seem to have a lot of confidence in her ability to whistle on cue. I don't know how she'll do under the pressure though. What if she runs and hides? What if she scratches Jasper the way she scratched my leg? What if she leaves the stage area and walks past the audience straight to the exits, and makes her way home? *Why didn't they rehearse her?* We're not prepared!

"Can I roll the window down?" I gasp this question to the smelly man driving the car.

"Yes, yes, roll down." He checks me out from his rearview mirror and pretends I don't notice.

When he pulls up to the street in front of the Cherry Lane Theater, it takes thirty seconds before I realize he isn't going to open my door for me. We're not in the big leagues yet, but he does croak out to meet him right here after the show. I collect my bag, open the door and make my exit. The big red stage entrance door is waiting for us, but before we go inside, I rub Bubbles's neck and whisper some reassurances.

"It's going to be fine, Miss Bubbles, don't worry. It's just a dress rehearsal. There'll probably be lots of stops and starts. And I don't think anybody will get mad at you for needing a few takes under your belt."

Her cold purple eyes blink at me and then she yawns, exposing her fine white kitty teeth. I say a quick prayer that she doesn't bite anybody.

When I knock on the door, the attendant opens up.

"You the cat?"

"Um. Yes. I'm the cat." This teamster is the same one who opened the door the last time. He motions for me to step inside and wait. I take in the scene while he puts a call into a walkie-talkie. Members of the stage crew are bustling back and forth—two guys with a ladder and one with a coil of electric wire—and the costume lady swishes by with a cup of coffee in her hand and a needle in her mouth. Kevin the stage manager is leaning against the far left wall, talking to somebody on a red phone, and the lights are coming up and down in focused locations on the stage. It's been a long time since I was in a theater during a dress rehearsal. I reach down and murmur to Miss Bubbles, "Isn't this exciting?" She turns her body away from me.

Kevin hangs up and ambles over to me.

"Stella, right?"

"Hi!" I gasp and thrust out my hand to shake. Kevin looks utterly confused. I don't think his parents taught him basic social conventions, but he eventually grabs my hand and gives a limp shake. "This is so exciting," I say to his deadpan face.

"Yeah, yeah. Well, let me introduce you to Shirley." He looks over his shoulder and shouts to the air, "Has anyone seen Shirley?"

The meaty teamster from the doorway shouts back, "Yeah. I'll buzz for her." He speaks into his walkie-talkie and then says, "She'll be up in two, three seconds."

"Who's Shirley?" I ask.

"She's the cat handler. You'll love her. She's a real professional."

"Yeah, about that," I start, fully aware that this should've been taken care of well before now. "I was thinking that it might be best for *me* to be with Miss Bubbles during the shows. She doesn't take too well to strangers." Just then a five-foot-tall woman I'm guessing is in her fifties and whose hair looks like she dyes it with a mixture of ketchup and paint thinner walks up to us. She has no makeup on and is wearing what can only be described as a lime-green housedress. It actually looks a bit like the outfit my mother used to wear when she was cleaning hotel rooms.

"Is this the kitty-witty?" She gurgles this question in a mocking tone. Oh, man. Miss Bubbles is going to eat her alive.

I instinctively shift my bag to the shoulder farthest from Ketchup Head Shirley. "Yeah, hi, I'm Stella." I extend my hand and she just looks at it. What's with these nonshakers?

Kevin starts in, "Well, Stella, the contract you signed clearly said that we were choosing to use a handler. You did sign it, didn't you?"

"Well, yes, but…"

"And you did see the list of Shirley's qualifications, didn't you?" This is the first I've heard of them, but I say, "Yes, but…" Miss Bubbles starts squirming around in my bag, clearly agitated by this confrontation. She pulls her torso out and starts trying to climb my arm.

"You see, we can't have you backstage during the whole show because of liability issues," Kevin explains this to me as Bubbles makes her way out of the bag and proceeds to walk a tightrope behind my neck. She precariously balances herself on my right shoulder while I plead our case.

"But Kevin, she's my cat and she doesn't even know her lines yet! I mean, she's never really been in this situation, and I'm the only one who can get her to whistle, and sometimes she can be temperame—"

"*Ow!*" Miss Bubbles claws me as she bends her knees and leaps from my shoulders into Shirley's arms. Shirley looks only slightly shocked as Miss Bubbles situates herself in her arms, mews like a baby and starts licking her face. "Aren't you a *beauty!*" Shirley coos. "Aren't you a *princess!*" Miss Bubbles starts purring like an idling motorcycle, and then Shirley begins stroking her under her chin, "I heard that you're quite a talented little girl! Can you whistle for me? Can you whistle for Auntie Shirley?"

I am aghast. Miss Bubbles stops cleaning Shirley's face long enough to let out the clearest, most beautiful whistle you've ever heard. This delights Shirley, who squinches up her nose and rubs it back and forth with Miss Bubbles's. "We're going to have such a *good* time, you and me! Yes sir!" And then she looks at me. "She's such a love!"

"Yeah, yeah, a love," I say, feeling what you must feel if you find your husband cheating on you with your best friend. Miss Bubbles is such a…a…a *cheat*. I am betrayed. By my own cat.

"It looks like they're going to get along just fine, don't you think?" Kevin is desperately trying to get me to agree, but I am too stunned to speak. Shirley assures me that everything will be fine and then she swoops the cat onto the stage, presumably to show her around the set, before I have a chance to say anything else.

Kevin and I watch her go. He turns to me, places a hand on my shoulder, which totally freaks me out, and tells me that everything is "going to be totally cool, 'kay?" He ushers me out through the stage and into the audience seats. When I ask if I can go and speak with Jasper, he looks a little surprised at the request and just shakes his head. "I don't think you want to do that."

"Why not?"

Kevin stops walking and turns to me. "Between you and me, the guy's a real asshole."

I blink twice and shake my head. "Huh?"

"He's an asshole. He's real serious and he won't talk to anybody."

"Maybe he's just committed."

"He *should* be committed." And he points me toward the house seats.

Final dress rehearsals usually have a "by invitation only" policy. But there are a lot of people here, more than I would have thought. Judging from how the house is filling up, everyone remotely associated with the play is attending tonight, probably second cousins of the crew are here.

There's a cluster of seats open about eight rows back in the center section and I run for them, nearly tripping down the stairs in my almost-too-tight faux leather pants that make a squeaky noise if I don't walk in them just the right way. The desk setup that was here when Bubbles auditioned is still in place. The director sits there, talking to who I guess is the lighting designer. There are computer monitors and a big operating board with switches and lights atop it. Two people in black jeans, black teamster shirts, and with grimy-looking hands run up to say something that clearly disappoints all the others. I really want to know what they're talking about, and when the teamsters rush past me, I squelch the urge to ask.

I take a seat and look at the set. They have constructed a perfect replica of a New York City apartment. The front part of the stage has a desk with a typewriter on it to the left, and a leather couch to the right. There is a door leading to the "outside" on the far left, and through its windows you can see fake sunlight streaming into the fake apartment. The back half of the stage has a little kitchen to the left and a long island running the rest of the length of the stage to the right. On this mantel is a large, comfy looking cat-bed. I can only assume that this is meant for my cat, who is currently perched on the mantel and sniffing the inside of the cushioning, batting at it like it's a mouse. Shirley is perched beside her, crouching and whispering into her ear. Miss Bubbles turns to her and whistles. The entire audience stops what they're doing and turns their attention to the stage. Just then, the curtain, a big, velvet, blue number begins to slowly close, blocking off my view.

The lights dim to half and the audience starts clapping. Frances and Frederick Paine make their way down the side staircase and walk back toward the house. They stop at my row, and smooth out their clothes before sitting. Frances takes the chair right next to mine! I can smell her perfume, it's like flowers drenched in alcohol. Must cost a fortune. No match for the vanilla body spritz from Bath and Body Works that *I'm* wearing. I hope my cheap scent doesn't offend her. My body goes stiff and blood pounds in my temples. Should I say something to her? Will she remember me? What would Mom do?

I decide to take no prisoners. "Frances! You look darling!"

She whips her head around like Gloria Swanson in *Sunset Boulevard* and does a little double take. "Do I *know* you?"

Wow. She *is* Gloria Swanson. I wish I could dissolve into my seat, but I can't very well abandon my mission. Nope. Gotta fake it until I make it. *"Stella,"* I say in a totally exaggerated tone. "Stella *Monroe."* I place my hand on her knee. Why do I do these things?

Must press onward. "So *good* to *see* you again. I am just *dying* to see how this thing runs!" And I jerk my hand from her lap and gesture with my thumb toward the stage.

"I'm sorry?" She looks horrified. Her hair is perfectly coiffed against her head, which completely adds to my vision of a Swansonesque turban. She's wearing a matching navy blue pin-striped skirt and jacket, in the style of Jackie O. Elegance, cool-ness, sophistication. I'm wearing very tight, very brown, very fake leather pants and a red vertically-striped, almost sheer top from Joyce Leslie that cost Michaela maybe fifteen bucks. No wonder Frances looks so pained. Pardon the pun.

Just then Frederick leans over her petite lap and clasps my hand. His palm is warm and almost wet, and the black hairs cov-ering his wrist are evident to me even in this dim light. My stomach reacts the way it did last time I saw him.

Attraction.

Not good.

"Ms. Monroe, we are very excited! Your cat is going to steal the show!" He squeezes my hand, which sends a little electric cha-cha down into my pants. I squirm and cross my legs, hop-ing Frances doesn't notice that her husband is lighting my fire.

She doesn't. She just curls her lip and lets out an "Ooohhh. The cat. Right. The cat." Then she pries Frederick's hand from mine and places it on her own thigh, which I might add, is creamy and quite attractive for a lady of her age.

Thankfully I am spared from having to make any more con-versation because the lights dim completely (this doesn't stop me from catching Frederick nuzzling Frances's ear as the lights come down) and a follow-spot lights on the director as he walks onto the stage with a microphone in hand.

"Welcome, welcome," he says. "I'm so happy to see all of you here tonight. Tonight will be our last run-through before pre-views, so there may be a few stops and starts. But this is very exciting for me and for all of us, because *you're the first audience we've had!*" He says this last part with the same inflection one

would use to say, *"You've won a brand-new car!"* The audience
bursts into spontaneous applause, and I twist around in my seat
to see exactly how full the house is. The upper balcony is
empty but the front mezzanine and most of the orchestra are
full of people, and judging from the outfits, they're mostly just
wives and sisters of the crew. I feel like I'm an extra in *Goodfellas,* actually.

The director continues, "So because it's just a rehearsal, there
will be no programs. I think you'll follow along just fine,
though. Let me set the scene—New York, present-day, the
apartment of a writer who can't seem to unstick his writer's
block or his lover's block, if you know what I mean." This joke
kills and all the teamster wives giggle appropriately.

"So without further ado, I give you *The Happy Ending!*" The
lights go out, the director walks off the stage, and the sound of
typewriter-typing pipes into the house. My own lips curl as I
realize that I may be about to witness an artistic account of
Christian's life. Heebie-jeebies.

The spotlight comes up and with it goes my breath, because
there, in front of the closed curtain, standing in the center like
the sun, is Jasper. He stands for a minute, removes a pair of prop
glasses from his face, rubs his eyes, looks to the audience, takes
in his surroundings and then launches into a monologue.

The audience is transfixed, and my worst fears are con-
firmed. He's great.

Even though I'm still worried about the phantom phone
caller, I know I'm in trouble here.

When the curtains open, Miss Bubbles is contentedly nap-
ping in her new bed, and my breath again catches. I'm nervous.
She looks comfy but could snap at any minute. Those lights
are hot, and she doesn't take well to extreme temperatures. I
am also aghast because there is a half-dressed blond woman
reclining on the couch. She looks familiar, and it takes me only
a minute to realize she was Jasper's date at the New Jersey
party. Jealous. Jealous and pissed. Did I mention that she's half-

dressed up there? I make a mental note to grill Jasper about the nature of their relationship. He walks to her and kisses the inside of her wrist. Not liking this play so much. She pulls her hand away coyly and starts petting Miss Bubbles. Hey! That wasn't part of the deal!

Why am I annoyed by this? I don't know. I don't know at all. The dialogue is some flirty fluff—the chippy is saying that she bets the cat would do its trick for her and Jasper says that the cat only does the trick for *him*. This leads to a comic bit where Miss Bubbles looks back and forth between them, then lets out a loud, clear whistle for Jasper. When the hell did Shirley have the time to teach her this? Bubbles then bolts from her bed and curls up in his lap, to the immediate enjoyment of the whole audience. Clapping ensues, even Frances and Frederick are pleased, but I want them all to stop. I lean forward in my chair, trying to get everyone to be quiet. The noise could disturb her and then we'll all be in trouble.

But she looks happy as can be, and proceeds to command attention during the whole show. Now, I can't say that I don't think that Jasper is the best, hottest, most awesome actor of all time. Because he is. He times all his jokes perfectly, he commands the stage, he has great chemistry with all the actors (much to my chagrin), Miss Bubbles included. But more than once, I find myself uncomfortable in my seat and skeptical of the proceedings. Why?

I'll tell you why. This play stinks! That's why. It's a self-indulgent piece of malarkey! The playwright obviously sees himself as the great lover of the world, a man whose artistic talents are only diminished by his ability to charm the pants off of women and animals alike. There is scene after scene of Jasper flirting with the blonde and a redhead, interspersed with scenes of him talking to his friends about how he can't write if he's in a committed relationship.

And I'm annoyed because Miss Bubbles is *really* good. It's like she's professionally trained. She never upstages anyone unless it's her moment, and the audience seems to be in on all her jokes. My cat has laugh lines. It's like she and Jasper are a modern-day Abbott and Costello. Or that fat guy and the skinny one. What are their names? Laurel and Hardy? Or the Marx brothers. They have the ease and chemistry of an old vaudeville act. I realize that I don't even know my own cat anymore. She has a secret life. All this time, I thought of her as my pet. As part of the furniture. But no. No. She could, quite possibly, be the biggest thing to hit the animal acting world since Eddie the dog on *Frasier.*

I descend into misery. Act one ends, finally, with Jasper and the redheaded girl falling into bed while the cat whistles in mock arousal. Awful. This playwright should be shot.

But then I hear Frances say to me, "This is just amazing!" so of course I agree with her.

"I have *never,* and I really mean it, *never* seen something this fantastic!" I gush as soon as the lights are completely up.

"Isn't he fabulous!?" She turns to Frederick, who rubs the back of his neck and tells her he'll be right back.

She turns to me. "And the cat! What a find!"

"Yes, yes, unbelievable, isn't it?" I return her enthusiasm with a smile that could squeeze half of my facial muscles into paralysis.

She exhales like she's just climaxed and sits back in her seat. "*What* a relief!"

"Oh, I *bet,*" I reply in a conspiratorial tone. "It must be such a worry, you know, to have a play in the works." Hobnob, Stella, hobnob like there's no tomorrow!!

"Well," she turns to me, "once Jasper Hodge agreed to do it, I just knew this play would be a big hit. Isn't he wonderful?"

I nod, knowing how wonderful he really, truly is. But then she starts to go on and on, extolling his virtues as both an actor and a human being, and I start to get a little territorial. It seems that Mrs. Paine has a thing for the leading man. I shift my shirt slightly and wrap a finger around a lock of hair while staring at this vision of middle-aged loveliness. I guess it's okay. I mean, I have the hots for her husband, so we're even. Right?

"So," she turns in her seat to face me. "A little birdie told me that you and Jasper have become *friends.*" She smiles, the fakest, scariest smile I have ever seen this close to my face. For a second I wonder if maybe I *am* in *Goodfellas* and am about to be whacked. I do a quick survey of the crowd and see that all the teamster wives and girlfriends are chatting away in their seats.

"Well, I don't know exactly what you've heard, but," I swallow, determined to choose my words carefully, which isn't always an easy task for me, "I would say that we are *acquaintances.*"

Frances Paine throws back her head and emits what can only be described as a delicious, malevolent cackle. "Oh, Stella!" She places her hand on my knee (that's my move!) and squeezes the fake brown leather, which makes a very disturbing noise. "That's a good one."

"It's the truth," I reply and try to move to the other side of my confining theater seat.

"I can't see who wouldn't want to be Jasper's *acquaintance.* He's handsome, talented, and definitely going places."

"Is he?" In moments of discomfort, I find that stupidity works very nicely as a distraction technique. "I guess he is!" Her gaze is intense, but her smile perfect. She's like the baroness in *The Sound Of Music* when she questions poor Julie Andrews about Captain Von Trapp. I am *really* not comfortable playing Maria the singing nun and want desperately to get away from Frances, who I think, in the right set of circumstances, wouldn't think twice about stabbing me to death with her fingernails, carving up my dead body and serving me to her help.

And so, I am extremely relieved when Frederick comes bounding back down the aisle. But goddamn it! So many conflicting emotions! My loins get all heated up. His suit has to be worth more than all my year's living expenses combined, and that collar! Why doesn't he button that thing all the way? Why must he taunt all the single, poor ladies? And right in front of Frances, who, by the way, still has her hand on my knee. I don't move an inch.

"Darling!" He plunks into the seat and kisses up and down her neck.

Fear.

Turned on.

Fear.

Turned on.

"Things are going swimmingly!" His geeky choice of words helps ease my lust.

"Stella," he reaches over Frances, and places his hand on her hand which, *hello?* Still on the knee! "That cat has made my night!" Frederick removes both his *and* Frances's hands from my cheap imitation leather pants. How did this night turn into a horror movie?

"Well, we're all very proud of her!" Then the lights dim and I let out my breath. During the second act, while Jasper proposes to both girls, walks out on both weddings and gets his book published, I plot my escape the whole time. I hope Jasper realizes the shortcomings of this play.

He does a nice job with the last scene, though. His character, Max, finally has his catharsis, learns what life is all about, finds love *and* writes a bestseller, and somehow Jasper makes it all seem believable. He's a good actor. There's no question. The show ends with a touching moment—him sitting on the couch, rubbing Miss Bubbles's head. The curtain descends and the lights come up. I am spared any more Paine conversation by Frederick, who lifts Frances to her feet and leads her out of the row. He leans down to me, though, and I have to stop my vision from roaming to the crotch of his silk pants. "Great work, Stella. You're a real find." And he pats my cheek and exits. Not a moment too soon.

After the audience mills about and finally leaves, I go outside and walk to the stage door. The air does me some good and I lean against the side of the building, staring at the back of a Mexican restaurant. The big red stage door swings open and shut over and over again, and happy family members hug stagehands and the costumer and the director and the other people associated with the show. Then both the blonde and the redhead come out to a smattering of applause. My heart stills and I start to feel really, really jealous. I kick the wall. I should be one of them, coming out of the stage door to meet my adoring public. It's good my mother isn't here. I hang my head and turn my foot's wrath on the ground, when I hear the door open and shut and another round of applause. I look up to see Ketchup Head Shirley holding Miss Bubbles, who is relaxed, composed and displaying a very polite, humble gaze.

A chorus of oohs and aahs floods the air as people surround the two of them, petting Miss Bubbles and complimenting Shirley on the cat's performance. This is supposed to be my big moment. And Shirley's hogging all the spotlight. My eyes roll to the heavens despite myself. If I were holding Miss Bubbles, she'd totally snap and hiss. But Shirley has worked some sort of ketchup-toned voodoo and turned her into a cat puppet.

"Unreal, huh?" Kevin sidles up alongside me and lights a cigarette. "You want one?"

"Nah." I shake my head. "But have you got any whiskey on you?"

He chuckles and says no. He's the thinnest person I have ever met. He can't weigh more than one hundred and forty pounds. All my money is riding on vegan.

"Oh! I got something for you." He reaches into his back pocket and pulls out a folded-up, slightly sweaty paycheck and a small piece of notepaper. "Here."

The check makes all the annoyance worth it. I glance over to Miss Bubbles, who is still earning this piece of paper with perfect dignity and patience, letting people paw at her like she's the main attraction at a petting zoo.

I open the note, expecting to find a cut and pasted death threat signed, "Love, Frances." Instead I read,

Lovely Stella,
Knowing you were out there made things real easy tonight. Meet me at the hotel. Wear something invisible.
Jasper

I smirk. Kevin exhales to my left and shocks me with, "So I have some things to take care of, but maybe later we can meet up for a cheeseburger or something?"

A cheeseburger? I have absolutely no ability to read people at all.

"Um, uh, that sounds fun, but I think I have to get the star home." And I jerk my head toward Miss Bubbles.

"Well, some other time then."

"Okay! Some other time!" I run to Shirley, push my way through the crowd of cat-worshippers, grab my charge and head toward the smelly car-service guy. I think I'll head over to Hell's before trotting off to Jasper's. Yep. I definitely need a drink.

Chapter 15

Even though I can't see that well through my veil, I can tell the church is packed.

"Mom?" My mother looks over to me and adjusts the tiara on top of my head. She's glowing, and cushioned in bright pink tulle. "Who are all these people?" I whisper through the gauze. She pats my hand in response.

"These are the people I've met on my adventures."

I can see tears in her eyes. Maybe it's just the veil playing tricks on my vision.

The organ begins to play the church march, the "Here Comes the Bride" song. My mother leans in and tells me I look so much like Julia Roberts in my wedding dress, it's breaking her heart. But in a good way.

"It's my proudest moment."

She takes my hand and leads me down the aisle. I can't make out the faces, and I can't remember which side Michaela said she'd be on. I hope she's not mad at me for getting married before she does.

My mother takes long strides, the kind you take when you walk down the aisle. First her left leg, then her right, then her left. It isn't *difficult, but still I can't seem to get it. I keep stepping left when she steps right, and right when she steps left. She grabs my hand and holds it tight. "You're out of sync." She pronounces her consonants crisply.*

"I know, just hold on. I'll catch up." But before I do, we reach the front of the church, and the priest is standing there. Christian is the priest. He's holding a Bible in one hand and a yellow plastic cup full of sangria in the other. He closes the book one-handedly, sips his drink and looks toward my mother. She lifts my veil, and gives me a hug. "I'm so proud of you, my little star. You're just like that girl in the Steve Martin movie." She leans back and wipes away a tear. But it's Frances, not my mother, and I turn to the pews of people and search for Miss Bubbles. She isn't there. Miss Bubbles isn't coming. I stand there, at the front of the church and stare at everyone. It's just me up here. Christian the priest takes my elbow and spins me around. "Are you ready?" he asks me.

"No!" I shake my head and pull the tiara out of my hair. I can't get married without Miss Bubbles. "No!" and I run back down the aisle.

I should know when I round the corner of 23rd Street, find building #256, see that it's just a plain old apartment complex and read a handwritten, paper sign Scotch-taped to the front door that says "Audition. Ring buzzer #3," that this is a bad idea. Ezra promised me this is legit, that this is a great role for me in what is sure to be an edgy and groundbreaking new independent full-length feature film. In my experience, auditions at people's homes in the middle of a Monday morning never amount to much.

But I'm brave. I have to take all the chances I can, so that someday the blonde coming out the stage door of the Cherry Lane Theater to a round of applause is me. My efforts have to be unbounded. I cannot turn down any auditions. In my apartment right now, between me, Steve and Miss Bubbles, I am definitely the one whose career is in the worst shape. I really don't think this is how it's supposed to be. I mean, Steve, yes, okay, he works very hard for what he is accomplishing. But what about Miss Bubbles? All she does now is lounge around the apartment all day, lick her paws and meow at me when I displease her. She didn't even study acting in school, and I *did*. I should be further along than her. I really have to kick it up a notch here.

That is why I let Ezra talk me into this audition, even though there is no audition material, even though the director/ writer/producer/auditioner happen to be all the same guy. Even though I am expecting a middle-aged loser with no visible income who thought he'd take a screenwriting course at the Learning Annex and become a filmmaker.

When did I become such a pessimist? I catch my reflection in the glass window running alongside the front door, grab my cloverleaf pendant and repeat my mantra. "My career comes first. My career comes first. My career comes first."

This is not an original mantra, that's true. I lifted it from my mother, who called this morning in a fit of frenzy:

"Little Star! Why haven't you *called* me? The final dress rehearsal was on Friday night and I haven't heard a peep!" I didn't have the heart to tell her I've been too busy with Jasper to call. His schedule is pretty tough—he doesn't get out of the theater until around 11:30 or midnight, and I've been meeting him for late cocktails, late dinners and even later sex.

So I went with this: "Sorry Mom, I was catering all weekend." Not a total lie.

"Uh-huh."

"And I joined a gym." This one was a total lie.

But my mother ate it up like caviar, "A *gym!* I am so proud of you."

"Well, I gotta stay in shape. That's what Ezra says." If only I could get paid to lie, I'd be rich.

"Well, Little Star, he's absolutely right. I knew I liked that Ezra. J-Lo goes to the gym all the time, you know. And so do Reese Witherspoon, and Pamela Anderson, and Halle Berry. I read all about it in *People.* And *Entertainment Weekly,* too. Some of these women do yoga, Madonna, and Charlize Theron, and Courtney Thorne-Smith—"

"Courtney Thorne-Smith? From *Melrose Place?* And the Jim Belushi show?"

"Yes. Courtney Thorne-Smith."

"But all she does is television shows."

My mother sniffed rather loudly. "All she does is *television* shows? My, my, look who thinks she's somebody! I know I've never been on a television show. Have *you* ever been on a TV show?"

"No."

"Well, until you have, Courtney Thorne-Smith should be a role model. Television is where it's at these days. Look at Jennifer Aniston! TV. And that Sarah Jessica Parker. TV. And Heather Locklear! Are you going to look down your nose at Heather Locklear? I don't think so. I'll tell you one thing. Heather Locklear's mother isn't worried about who'll pay for her nursing home. If you were paying attention to your career options, you'd know that television is the shit."

My mother said "the shit."

And then kept right on spouting at me.

"I'd be *thrilled* if you had the career of Courtney Thorne-Smith. She consistently gets work and has a very nice home. I saw pictures of it in *InStyle.*" She stopped her tirade long enough to take a sip of what I assumed was a Diet Coke, and let out a snort. "But we're getting ahead of ourselves. I'd be happy if you'd get your act together enough to land even a non-speaking role in a commercial. Or a reality show. You could be on *Survivor.* Oh! I know! You could be one of those Golden Globe girls."

"Mom, you only get to be a Golden Globe girl if you have a famous parent!" I regretted saying this almost as soon as it left my mouth.

Silence for a good three seconds. Oh, man. I knew it was

gonna be good. And she didn't disappoint: "So it's *my* fault that you have no career?"

I sat down on the couch to cushion the emotional blows about to rain down all around me. "Of course not, Mom. I'm just saying that being a Golden Globe girl has nothing to do with how your career is coming along."

"Oh, I see. You know all about whose career is how far along now. The girl who thinks that Courtney Thorne-Smith is a nobody! The girl who can barely get an audition together!"

"Mom." This is where I began to pretend I *was* a yogi, and breathed peacefully into my toes to avoid crying. "I've been auditioning. I've been trying. You know that."

"Oh, Stella," she exhaled dramatically, "I know you have. I can't help but worry, though, that's what mothers do." Then she inhaled, sipped and exhaled again. "You know, sweetheart, that just because it didn't work out for *me,* doesn't mean that you can't have everything we ever dreamed of."

"I know, Mom."

"I never intended to live my life in Michigan. Of course I didn't. But I don't complain, because I got a beautiful baby girl out of it, didn't I?"

"Yes, Mom."

"And when you were born and the nurses put you in my arms, I knew that you were the absolute best thing I had ever done. Didn't I?"

"Yes, Mom."

"And you're still the light of my life. You're my shining star. My Stella Aurora. You were born to have the things I couldn't, Stella. I know you know that."

"I know that Mom." A lump sat in my throat, an immovable lump.

"So we need to make sure that you are putting your career first. Are you putting your career first? Because if you're not, well, I can just take this pile of clippings of hairstyles and

dresses and health regimens and spas and send them to some
other girl who wants them."

"Mom! I'm putting my career first. I promise!"

"Okay. Now tell me about the final dress rehearsal."

A horn's honk behind me dislodges the memory of this
morning's conversation, and I remember that I am still outside
on 23rd Street. A huge orchestra of car alarms, horns and angry
voices bounces off the buildings, reverberating all over me. I
shake my head to stop the thoughts of my mother, and oh, yeah,
the guilt, from swallowing me up. I must have a clear head. A
clear, poised head with which to attack my career, as well as the
guy about to audition me. I reach out my hand for buzzer #3.

A voice crystallizes from thin air and tells me to "come on
up."

When I get to apartment #3, I am welcomed inside by a
shabby-looking gray cat. No match for Miss Bubbles, I tell you
what. This cat looks up at me and runs away and I think how
lucky I am to have a pet with special skills. A male voice from
behind a closed door to my right screams for me to wait just
where I am.

I look around for a place to sit but there is nothing. This room
is just a vestibule, really, a hallway with about a hundred coats of
white paint on it. There are places where the paint bubbles and
juts out from the wall, so typical of New York City apartments.
An expandable set of hooks is suspended from the wall, and laden
down with Yankees baseball caps and winter scarves of every
color plaid you could imagine. A pile of mail order catalogs rises
a foot off the floor, L.L. Bean on top of J. Crew on top of Banana Republic, and an occasional table adorned with pictures of
who I assume is the owner of this establishment. He's in an array
of different sporty, action shots. I walk over to get a good look.
There he is on the slopes of a wintry mountain. Lounging by a
pool with three overweight women, his sisters no doubt. Standing proudly with half a dozen guys on the streets of Vegas. The
guy has money for vacations, obviously.

Overall, this apartment isn't so bad. I can see through to the bedroom, decorated in Pottery Barn shades of brown and neutrals. His room looks nice, clean and well kept. There are pots of dried hyacinths lining the wall underneath a huge picture window, which unfortunately, looks out on a brick building. But even though there is no view, sunlight streams in and plays with the light in the room.

I shouldn't judge this guy before I've met him. Who knows? Maybe he's the next Ed Burns. Or Paul Thomas Anderson. Or Steven Spielberg. Yes! Who knows what's about to happen? I have to remember that I've been really lucky lately. Maybe I'm about to fall into a pot of gold. Then, when I'm famous and publicizing my new movie on *Letterman,* I can tell the story about how my manager insisted that I audition for *name of movie here,* and I was skeptical, but went anyway and the rest is history. And Dave will laugh and lean his head in close to mine, make a joke that I respond to by placing my hand on his arm, and voila! A media darling will be born!

Yep. This audition is going to be great.

Muffled voices float over to the vestibule from behind the closed door to the right. A man is saying something and then a woman responds with a long giggle. Footsteps shuffle over to the door. It looks like I'm up.

The door opens and a man, bearded and about five foot two, and wearing a tweed jacket over a brown turtleneck, the man from the pictures, ushers out a tall, statuesque blonde. She actually looks a bit like Michaela, and for a moment I wonder if we are reading for the same role. We can't be. We look nothing alike.

The short man shakes her hand. "That was really great." He places his left hand over their shaking hands and drives the point home. "Really great." The blonde giggles, pulls out her hand, shoots me a "there's-no-way-you-can-get-this-role" look and heads for the door. Before she leaves, she says, "So maybe I'll run into you at the ranch."

Shorty chuckles and replies, "I'm sure we'll see each other before that." Then he turns his attention to me. "Stella?"

"Yes, I'm Stella Monroe." I extend my hand, and again, he pulls his two-hand move. His palms are sweaty, and the scent of patchouli oil fills the air. I look down at him, into his brown eyes, stubby beard and pasty skin.

"Enchanted," he raises my hand to his lips and kisses. "Shall we?" He shows me the way through the door and into his living room.

Another nice room, with exposed brick walls and unlit candles everywhere, potted plants and pillows and framed opera posters on the wall that lead me to believe that his sisters helped him decorate. I turn to him as he closes the door and makes his way toward a camera that is balanced on a tripod, waiting patiently in the middle of the room.

"So," I look around for the audition material but can't find it. "What am I auditioning for?"

He looks up from the camera, and says, "An excellent question!"

I raise my shoulders as if to say, "That's me! An excellent question-asker!"

He leans against the camera, "Stella. I want to make a film. A *film*. Something of meaning." Then he stops talking, stares into my eyes. I think he's waiting for me to say something.

So I say, "Neat!"

He still stares, almost thoughtfully. "I've always wanted to move people with my art. Do you find as a creative person that you want to move people?" I feel like I'm missing something in the translation. Like I don't speak this guy's language.

"Sure." I nod. "That'd be great. To move people. I mean, while I was acting and stuff." *Babble, babble, babble.* The blood rushes away from my head, and I sink down onto the navy futon couch behind my knees.

"Well, Stella. What I'm looking for are people who are as interested in art as I am."

"I like art."

"So let's make a movie together, Stella. Let's rock the world."

"Um, okay." I am still pretty unsure about what he wants me to do, and keep folding and unfolding my hands like a nervous child.

"I'm just going to let the camera run, and I want you to tell me a little bit about what you love in this life."

"Huh?" Now he's got me stumped. What I love in this life? I don't know. Does chocolate count? And Michaela? And my KICK IT sweats?

Apparently my confusion shows on my face. "Your passions. I want to know your passions."

"Oooh. Okay." He fiddles with the camera a bit, and a red light goes on. "Do you want me to slate my name?"

"That's okay," he says from behind the camera. "Just tell me about what turns you on."

And so I start, still not entirely sure of what to say, "Um, hi. My name is Stella, and I like chocolate. And Miss Bubbles, my cat. I like martinis, too. And granola." He motions with his hand for me to keep talking. "And, um, I like the smell of croissants baking."

"What else?" He steps around the tripod and stands next to it, casually draping an arm over the top of the camera. "Keep going."

"Umm, okay," I shift uncomfortably in my seat. "Well, I like when you get just the right amount of glaze on the top of a baking ham. With brown sugar. Brown sugar is the best, which most people mix with water and egg, but it's better if you use a mixture of pineapple juice with a dash of lemon and peach."

"Uh-huh." He rolls his wrist to let me to know that I should keep rambling on and on about my likes. But then I have a brainstorm, because I remember what it is that I truly love.

"*Meringue.* I *love* when you can get meringue to form perfect, erect peaks. And then when it browns, it looks like spires on top of a Russian building. There is nothing as beautiful in the whole world as perfect meringue." I could go on and on about this topic, but the bearded one interrupts.

"Stella, can you tell me something that turns you on, besides food?"

"Oh, um okay." What the hell else am I supposed to say? I love orgasms? Actually, I'd probably definitely get this job if I said that.

"Well, let's see." I blow air out of my lips and make that funny raspberry sound. "I like the look on my neighbor's face when I leave him a plate of apple pie. Oh, I guess that's food again. Huh. Well. I like *Oprah*. Yes, Oprah is good. And *Animal Planet*. I like *Animal Planet*. And of course the Food Network."

"Good, that's good Stella." And he walks toward me, and sits next to me on the couch. "Keep talking," he advises as he scooches me out of the shot.

I look at him out of the corner of my eye and try to push him back over so that I'm centered in the camera shot. "What are you doing?"

"Keep talking, hon." He places his fingers on my chin and pushes my head back so I face the camera. "I just want to capture us together. To see how we look." And he drapes his arm around my shoulders, places his hand on my thigh and kisses me right on the mouth.

I jump off of the futon. "What are you doing?!" And in my zeal to put distance between myself and the short bearded one, I knock the camera down.

"Oh my God! My baby!" He leaps toward the fallen camera, but I get there first and bend down to pick it up. The delicate art of balancing the tripod on its legs eludes me, though, and it goes crashing down again.

"You idiot!" Name-calling? Okay, this really gets my goat!

"Hey shorty!" I assume my full height so that he knows that, in the event of a rumble, I'd win. "I'm not an idiot. A klutz, but not an idiot."

"Well whatever, you can go. Your audition is over." He says

this with finality and confidence, and for a moment I just want to smack his smug face. Or step on his foot. Or hurt his feelings.

But I don't. Because I remember that as soon as I leave, this short, bearded, horny, son of a bitch scam artist is going to call Ezra. And tell him that I didn't get the role.

As I slam the door to the apartment, run down the stairs and reenter the busy world of 23rd Street, anger overwhelms me and tears sting my eyes. I quickly run toward the street and hail a cab. I give the driver Ezra's address and work up my tirade in the back seat as Ahmet Souradi the taxi driver weaves and bobs his way through the traffic of Gramercy Park.

I run into the Park Avenue building of Greenblatt and Associates and don't even stop to catch my breath. I get to the second floor, throw open the glass door to his office and rush up to Nancy behind the front desk, who is puffing away on a one hundred-length cigarette.

"Stell!" She croaks out the side of her mouth. Her helmet of blond hair stands four inches high. "Good to see you, hon, let me ge—"

"Stel-La!! Stel-La!!" the booming foghorn voice of Ezra Greenblatt interrupts Nancy, and I look to see the hulking, suspendered girth of my agent taking up all the space in the doorway to his office.

I point at him and shout, much louder than I intended. "We have to talk!"

Spit flies out of the corner of his mouth as he says, "You're damn right we do."

I rush into his office, which hasn't changed at all in the two years since I've been here (still brown and smoky and crowded with piles and piles of headshots, old newspapers and videotapes) and can barely hear him tell me that it's lucky for me that I'm sexy when I'm angry. He closes the door and I whirl on him, thrilled that I haven't lost any of my anger during the length of the cab ride.

But before I can speak, he lets loose with, "What the hell

happened? Russell called me and said you broke his camera?" He rubs his sweaty forehead with a handkerchief that he takes from his pocket. "I said to myself, I said, 'that doesn't sound like my Stella.' So? What the hell happened?" he extends his hands in the air, a suppliant, begging gesture. "Toots?"

"Ezra! The guy made a move!"

Ezra picks an already lit cigar up out of an ashtray on top of his desk. "And?"

"And?" I slump into the red velour chair across from him. "It surprised me!"

Ezra leans back in his chair and purses his lips. "Boy, did you just hop off a bus or what?"

"Ezra—" But his gaze silences me. So I stare out the dingy window and focus on a pigeon who is clucking around on his fire escape.

Ezra takes out his handkerchief again and alternates dabbing his forehead and talking right into it, "I gotta tell ya kiddo, I don't like what I'm hearing from ya. I thought you were serious about coming back to this."

"I am! I'm serious!"

"Then why are you reacting like such a woman after these auditions? Do you know how hard it is to get you in?"

"Ezra! I'm not acting like a woman!" I slide back in my chair, cross my arms and feel a pout coming on. "The guy just wanted to videotape himself with cute girls!"

He slams his hand on the desk. "Stella. What is wrong with you? What do you think this business is about? Guys only do this to meet hot chicks. That's the best part of the business!"

"That's why *you're* doing it," I say in a moping tone, and am greeted by Ezra's rumbling chuckle. I stare at the fading *Odd Couple* poster hanging on the fake wood paneling behind his head.

"That's why *any* of us are doing it! You think Joe Pesci got girls before *Raging Bull?* He's a freakin' midget for chris' sake!"

"Ezra! That's not true!"

"Wake up kiddo. I don't know about this naive thing you're

trying on me. You know what you're doing, dressing in your tight pants and halter tops! That's why I rep you, cause you know how to play the game."

"I'm not playing any games!"

"Yeah, right."

"I'm just trying to get some roles here so that I can buy my mom a house!"

"Okay, sweetheart, and when you're famous, you won't date any hot movie stars, right?"

He totally gets me and it pisses me off. "Oh, shut up, you sleazy, girl-getting, jerk!"

"Huh-hoh, little girl. You're lucky I don't get insulted easily."

"Ezra, you're lucky *I* don't get insulted easily."

"Ha-ha! Right you are honey pie. Well, at any rate, ya got spunk." His shout makes me jump in my chair. "I *love* it! Now don't sweat it. So you ruined his equipment. That role wasn't for you. Next time, kid. Next time." He claps and hits a button on his phone. "Nance, hold my calls. Now break out the shots, doll cakes."

This conversation is not over to me, and I want to tell him how angry it makes me when a guy puts a move on me while I'm trying to be serious about getting a job, or how dumb I feel when I have to take my clothes off for no reason, or how hard it is to drum up enthusiasm for these calls when I consistently audition for things I don't get. But his flabby, expectant face tells me he will no longer be listening to my concerns. So I reach over to my bag and pull out the pictures. They are in three paper folders, and right away I feel Ezra's expectant stare turn into a menacing, laserlike grimace.

"What the hell are those?"

I freeze and look intently at the red-and-blue design on the flap of the envelope. "My pictures." My voice squeaks out entirely too timidly.

"Where the hell is the contact sheet?" Usually, when a real photographer takes your headshots, you get a sheet with miniature pictures all on one page and can pick the best ones to blow up into eight-by-tens. But since I did this on the small end of the scale, I have just regular old Duane Reade paper folders full of overexposed three-by-fives. I was hoping Ezra wouldn't make an issue of this.

"This photographer didn't give me a contact sheet." I hand them to him over his desk, and place my bag on my lap as a protective barrier in case he throws something at me.

He shuffles through the photos while furiously puffing away on that cigar, creating clouds of blue smoke around his head, which is turning both purple *and* red. "Unbelievable," he thunders, throws the pictures down and yanks the cigar out his mouth. "What the hell *is* this Stella? I told you to get real pictures taken, and you said you were doing it!"

My foot taps furiously and the brown-paneled walls seem to be closing in on me.

He picks up the pictures again, thumbing through them as fast as his chubby fingers will let him. "What, did that friend of yours take them? The blonde?"

"No. No. No." I can't think of anything else to say.

"Well explain yourself!" But he doesn't give me a chance to. "Stella, didn't I tell you that I wasn't going to represent you unless you could get new pictures? *These* are not *pictures!* What the hell? Are you deliberately trying to play me here, sweets?" He ashes his cigar.

"Play you? Aren't you being a little dramatic?"

"Stella. I don't have time for this." He replaces the cigar in his mouth and tilts his head back toward the ceiling. Then he rocks forward and points at me. "I don't have time to deal with you if you aren't serious about this. First the bullshit about the underwear commercial. Then claiming you don't want guys to be attracted to you at auditions—"

"The guy made a move!"

Ezra holds up his hand to silence me. "And now this! Pharmacy pictures! I don't have the time!"

"But—" The jig is up. I can feel it. I have to come clean. "I didn't have the money, Ezra." For the briefest of moments, he looks like he might give me a break.

"Find the money. And until you do, don't come back here. I have plenty of hot girls with good-looking headshots to send out in the meanwhile."

Then we stare at each other for a bit. "It's too bad, Stell. You're not getting any younger, ya know?"

I collect my bag, make to collect my pictures, think better of it and rush out the door. My head feels like it's going to pop off of my neck. I want to run back in there and tell him that I don't even want to go to the stupid auditions that he sends me on, that only a fool would want to get a job where a short bearded man makes passes at you, and that he's a sucky agent anyhow. But I don't. Why don't I? Because when I get onto the street, I see a bus waiting for a traffic light to turn green. And on the side of the bus is one of those ads for TNT or TBS or one of those dumb cables stations that has movies on at night. And the ad says, "The Movies You Love." And the ad pictures Steve Martin in a tux, standing with his daughter in *Father of the Bride.* And then I, for some reason, think of my mother, and my stomach drops into my feet, and I realize that I have to come up with something good to tell her about Ezra and my pictures. And then I have to put together a chunk of change to get real pictures taken.

So I step out onto the curb and hail my second cab of the day. And I go to Hell's Bar and wipe my eyes on the red velvet entryway curtain before going in. I see Michaela sitting with Steve, grinning and laughing and doing a shot.

And as I approach them, I hear Michaela screeching, "You're gonna be *rich!* And you might get to kiss Susan Lucci!"

I stand in front of the two of them, my mouth is hanging open but I don't have the strength to close it. They turn to me, like in slow motion. Michaela jumps up, shouts my name and asks me what I want for my celebratory shot. Steve leaps from his chair, picks me up, twirls me around, shouting, "I got it! I got it! I'm the new Rocco Ramone on *All My Children!*"

I bury my head in his neck and start to tear up. I hope he thinks it's because I'm happy for him.

Chapter 16

"Steve!" I shout this over the din of show tunes and the pounding of Christian's godforsaken keys.

"What?" he replies from behind the closed door of his bedroom.

"We have to leave *now!*" I whine back and stretch my legs out on the couch, keeping my head firmly tilted toward the television.

"Oh, for Christ's sake. Keep your panties on!"

"Well, I don't want you shirking your duties! You promised to be my slave today!"

"Easy there, missy."

I sit up long enough to empty the bottle of Bud Lite. Since Ezra dumped me last week, I've been revisiting my former career of daytime drinker.

"Just hurry up!" I slouch back down into the cushions of the couch and adjust the pillow behind my head with a few well-placed punches. Miss Bubbles's shadow curls in front of the TV and snakes its way toward the lump I form on the couch. When Miss Bubbles stops and purrs three times, I tense in preparation for the onslaught. She leaps and lands with her claws firmly clenched into my stomach. "Ow!"

She stares at me.

"I'm not so into our new routine, cat."

She sits on her hind legs and continues to unblinkingly stare. My cat. Perched on my tummy like a predator on top of dinner. Not two weeks into her theater career and she's already a diva. She's started this little game of staring at me until I give up the couch to her. Then, she stretches her four little cat paws out in all directions and has a good nap.

Not that I can do anything about this. If it weren't for Miss Bubbles, I'd have no visible means of income. Not only did Ezra give me the boot, not only have there been no good open call auditions this week, not only did my mother's "help money" card arrive in the mail with a good-for-nothing thirty-two dollar check crammed inside, but Debra has succeeded in blackballing me from the catering industry. That little troll put her evil troll head together with all her catering cronies and ousted me. The nerve!

But back to my point, which is this. I am no longer on equal footing with my pet. And Miss Bubbles knows it. She's been acting uppity ever since the day of the first preview. Coincidentally, the same day the little actress was awarded her own dressing room—which is fully loaded with every amenity a cat could ever possibly want. And now, she's peering down at me as if to say, "Get off of my couch, you good for nothing human taxicab." Because that's what I am now—her personal, private taxicab. My new sole purpose in life is to take her to the theater and pick her up from the theater. But if I'm a good little girl, I get to wait in her dressing room until Shirley's done giving her a massage. I'm not kidding. Daily massages—for a cat! While I wait, I'm allowed to drink from *one* of the individual bottles of Evian that line the back wall of Miss Bubble's makeup table. But no catnip. Kevin actually told me not to touch the catnip plant they've put in there. He should tell that to Shirley.

Miss Bubbles is getting impatient with my belligerence, because she whistles at me. Long and clear and now worth three hundred and fifty dollars a week. We have a stare-down. She makes to claw my thigh, threatens to scratch a hole in the KICK IT sweats. She wins.

I leap up, not caring that she goes sprawling. She hisses, but is soon licking her paws contentedly. I turn off the television and stare into the kitchen. God, life is boring. It's like I'm back to my old life, pre-Ned the naked man. My mother would kill me if she knew what was going on. I don't work during the day, and I see Jasper at night. Just like it used to be. All I've done the past week and a half is sit in my apartment, work on Michaela's wedding cake, try decorating techniques I learn from the Food Network, watch *General Hospital* and *Oprah,* and make up raps to the steady beat of Christian's typing. Then at night, it's taxi duty, fancy dinners and sex. After Jasper's show gets out of course. And after his cool-down time. Actually, we've not had any dinners lately, now that I think about it. We usually have breakfast the next morning, though, before I go home.

Thank God for Michaela's wedding feast. Though it's put a serious dent in the last of my catering money, Christian's sure had it good—he's my unwitting guinea pig. On Monday I left him a prosciutto and melon quiche. Tuesday was goat cheese, walnut and shaved pepper salad. Wednesday he got a steak sandwich with homemade steak sauce. Thursday was crabcakes, using fake vegetarian crab that tastes the same but costs a third of the price. Friday I just made him homemade macaroni and cheese and sweet potato fries. We're back to normal, too. He hasn't been down to the apartment since the photo shoot and I've been leaving his meals on his doorstep.

Today I have to whip up all the food so Carlo and Michaela can taste-test it. And, as soon as Steve hurries up and gets dressed, I get to do something I've never done before in my whole life.

Go into the kitchen of Hell's Bar.

It's funny to me that I'll be cooking in Hell's kitchen, which is located in Hell's Kitchen. If I can get all my stuff over there. Hence the need for Steve.

"Steve!"

"One more second, for chris'sake!"

The click of his door gets both my and Miss Bubbles's attention, and we turn in time to see him strut out, wearing brand-new leather pants and an Izod shirt.

"Your wardrobe's really benefitting from the new job." The snide tone of my voice isn't on purpose.

He arches an eyebrow, "You're not wearing those gross sweatpants, are you?" He looks disgusted. The past week has been quite a whirlwind for him. He got to go to *All My Children* for measurements and hair consultations, got loads of tapes from the producers and has had to watch hours and hours of back shows to catch up on his character. I keep telling him that he should watch at home and not at Polite Peter's, but apparently he "can't concentrate" with me around. Now that the initial shock has worn off, I have to say the idea of Steve making out with girls and becoming the fantasy of housewives and college kids all over America cracks me up.

I head for the kitchen and bark an order at him for good measure. "Grab a bag." He grabs three, that show-off, and follows me out the door.

"What's in here? Bars of gold?" Steve shouts to me as we waddle down 10th Avenue, burdened with bags of groceries.

"Just shut yer trap back there. A few bags won't kill you. Besides, you need to keep in shape now that you're going to be a matinee idol."

"Uh-huh. Keep the comments coming, Mistress Kitchen."

I shake my head. "I don't even get your insults. Make sure your wisecracks actually make sense, Dreamboat," I shout over my shoulder.

When we get to Hell's, Michaela, Carlo, Carlo's brother,

whom I've never met before, Rod, Polite Peter and Christian are standing around, chatting and sipping glasses of wine.

"Didn't you get enough free food out of me this week?" I hiss like Miss Bubbles.

"Well, I can't miss the feast, can I?" Christian finishes off his wine. I sneer at him and turn to Michaela, "Where do these groceries go?"

Carlo answers, "Rod'll take you." Ugh. Not even married and he's already taking away her ability to answer for herself. Steve and I follow Rod, whose hulking frame completely blocks my view of where we're headed, and silently curse the institution of marriage the whole way.

I am not prepared for the sight of the kitchen. Let me preface by saying that when I think of a kitchen in New York City, I imagine grime and rats. And immigrants sweating over open pots of food. I know that's not very PC of me, but there you have it. But the kitchen of Hell's Bar is like the kitchen of a society wife on the Upper East Side. My brow weaves itself into a confused knit, and I spin around to Rod.

"This is fucking beautiful!" The appliances look brand-new and are gleaming. It's like a showroom in here, but peppered with the scent of rosemary and thyme. I drop my bags and run around, touching the pots and pans, which hang from the ceiling, running my fingers alongside the countertops, basking in the sunlight glow of the industrial refrigerators, testing the burners, lovingly grabbing at the wooden spoons. "Fucking A, Rod!"

"You're such a lady, Stella, really." Steve sneers while he bends down to gather all the items I unceremoniously threw to the floor.

"You like?" Rod replies and his smile is almost as bright as the reflection of the neon lights bouncing off of the chrome.

"I love!" I thrust my arms over my head and squeal and launch myself into Rod's burly arms. He catches me and lifts me into the air.

"Will you go out with me now?"

"Stella, get a hold of yourself." Steve is pissed at me.

"I can't help it—this is my version of heaven! It's so clean in here! Steve! You could eat off the floor! Can we, Rod, can we eat off the floor?" I am purring into his big beefy face because he still is holding me a few inches off of the ground.

"Let's hope your food is as good as my kitchen." He puts me down and I twirl à la Julie Andrews in *The Sound of Music.*

"This is going to be the best meal New York City has ever seen!"

"Yes, Stella, the best meal that the entire city of New York will ever have seen. You're a fucking lunatic." Steve rips open a bag of raisins and shoves a handful in his mouth. Even watching him eat my ingredients, I feel happy.

I push the swinging doors open ceremoniously and announce, "Let the tasting begin!" I wipe my brow with my left forearm so that Carlo and Michaela and Polite Peter and Carlo's brother and Rod know just how hard I've been working. "Steve?" I call over my shoulder, "It is time!"

And he follows me out balancing a tray laden with goodies: plates with individual, bite-sized portions of lemon-soaked salmon; pepper-crusted filet; a small, rosemary-and-caper-stuffed cornish hen; asparagus drizzled with truffle oil and feta cheese, fresh-baked onion and fennel foccaccia topped with goat cheese and hazelnuts, garlic mashed potatoes, baby carrots and haricots verts sautéed with crème fraîche and a small, but gorgeous, apple, raisin and pork tartlet. I realize, as I look at the tray, that I probably spent as much on this food as real headshots would have cost.

But the expectant faces gathered around the bar, some of which look a little boozed up (I did take a bit longer in the kitchen than I intended), save me from slipping into a melancholy fit. "Let the tasting…commence," I intone before bowing and passing out forks. Michaela claps and jumps up and down. "Everything looks so good!"

"I know."

"You're so conceited," Steve says this through a mouthful of mashed potatoes.

"Aren't those potatoes going to show up on screen, Steve?" I stretch my fingers out in front of me and take the seltzer water that Rod slides in my direction. Everyone is crowded around the bar, heads bent over their plates and shoving food into their mouths. It's kind of gross, really. Michaela looks over at me and covers her chewing mouth with a dainty, manicured hand. My own fingers begin tapping the rhythm to "Meet the Flintstones" on the cool sleek surface of the bar and I take an ice cube from my glass and crack down on it.

Carlo grins at me and says something in Spanish to his brother. Rod chimes in with rapid-fire Spanish, and Michaela nods and says, "Si, si." God bless her. I don't think she knows what the hell they're talking about. Neither do I and all of a sudden the "test" tastes I had in the kitchen don't feel so good in my tummy, and for a split second I hope that everything is okay. I don't want to disappoint them all, or, Jesus, give them food poisoning or, why isn't anybody saying anything in English?

I tug on Steve's five hundred dollar sleeve and whisper in his ear, "Does everything taste okay?"

Christian answers, "Don't worry, they're just talking things over."

I smack the tartlet out of his hand. "That's not for you!"

"Ow!" He rubs his hand, which looks kind of red. "What's the matter with you?"

"You weren't invited! Don't eat the food!"

"What is your problem? Why are you so bitchy lately?"

"Christian, I'm always bitchy to you. Where have you been?"

"I invited him, Stella."

I look at Steve, then slap the tartlet out of his hand, too.

Christian laughs now. "I think someone's cranky because someone's boyfriend doesn't care enough to taste her cooking." The sing-song of his voice makes me want to stab him.

Instead, I sit in silence. Steve turns to Peter and they start talking about some character on *All My Children*. Christian pokes my rib.

"Hey. Don't be nervous. Okay?"

"I'm not nervous." I purse my lips and watch him shovel forkfuls of filet into his mouth. "You like it, right?"

He lifts his head up. "It's great. There's more garlic in the steak sauce than last week."

"You can tell the difference?"

"Oh, yeah. It's more flavorful this way. It was good before, too, but it's better now." He continues to eat.

Then the Spanish gets heated. "Spanish, Spanish, Spanish," says Carlo.

"Non, Spanish, Spanish, Spanish," responds Carlo's brother.

"Sí, sí!" Michaela.

"La Cucaracha!" shouts Steve. I must look green because Michaela screeches out (in English) "*Stell!* Don't worry! It's all great! We just don't know what to do now."

"There's no way to choose. It's all *muy delicioso.*" Carlo slips into some Spanish that I actually understand.

The smile I've been holding on deck behind my eyes slips into place, and I say, "Wait until you taste the cakes!"

Two hours later I'm sitting on the counter in my bathroom while Steve applies my makeup. The dress he has purchased for me in honor of the official debut of our cat is hanging from the back door of the closet, next to his new silk suit. He has his hand firmly clamped on my jaw and even though he's pinching me, this is the calmest, happiest I've felt all week.

"I'm glad they liked the food." I try to say through my squished lips.

"Mmm-hmm." He lets me go and looks into his tool box-size bin of makeup. He begins weeding through several different shades of eye shadows.

"I guess I was pretty nervous about it." He opens a lid on a small jar and dabs his pinkie finger into the shimmery pink powder. "That's pretty." I say.

"Yeah. It's pretty, but it—" he sprinkles a little on the inside of my wrist "—isn't right."

He keeps digging until he finds another tube. As he brushes this one onto the white of my arm, he says, "You know Stell, you were nervous today because you care about doing a good job."

"I know that."

He tilts his head up and brushes my hair behind my ear. "You're a really talented cook." This is the first compliment he's ever given me. His fancy new job must be making him appreciate the little people. I feel tears come into my eyes. "And I know it's tough on you right now, Stella. With *All My Children* and Michaela getting married and Joshua and everything." A tear slips down my cheek. "What are you doing!" Steve jumps to his feet and the moment is ruined. "Don't cry on the foundation! Jesus Stell!" He stabs at my face with his bony fingers.

I giggle and snot flies out of my nose. "Aw Jesus." Steve reaches for some toilet paper and cleans me up. "This is just like old times, you cleaning me up!"

"Yes, the good old days when you needed me to hold your hair back while you puked up your night's adventures." He resumes his makeup application squat and finds the tube of foundation to touch me up. "Now don't ruin it this time!"

"Well, don't say sweet things to me this time!"

He grunts and while I'm sitting there it occurs to me that Steve needs some correcting. "Steve, you know that I'm totally over Joshua, right?"

Steve grunts again.

"I have Jasper now."

He peers up at me with one eyebrow raised.

"Oh, what do you know! Well don't act all surprised when I become Mrs. Jasper Hodge."

He stops brushing on the blush long enough to look into

my eyes. "I hope so, Stella. I hope you do find what it is that will make you happy."

"It's not a matter of finding it, it's a matter of timing. I just have to wait it out, and then I'll get a great job like yours and maybe Jasper will come through and be the 'one' and then I'll live happily ever after!"

"I think you will live happily ever after."

"I think I will, too. Don't forget my beauty mark."

He sighs. "You know. I think it's time you got rid of that thing."

"I know what you think. Just don't forget it, okay?"

"Don't worry, when I'm through with you, nobody will be able to take their eyes off you. Even when the play starts." And he kisses the top of my head.

Chapter 17

Steve and I make our way to Miss Bubbles's dressing room after the play, a feng shui'd space complete with miniature water fountains, bowls of pennies and soothing ocean sounds being piped in from a sound machine in the corner. It's a jungle in here. There are all kinds of floral arrangements: plants, orchids, lilies, bushels of pink and yellow roses. But there's more than just wildlife. Did I mention the catered spread? I didn't? Well. Miss Bubbles has a catered spread. From Balducci's. Life isn't fair. And also, this room is a cat's wet dream. There are two huge wicker baskets full of Fancy Feast and other assorted cat foods. Both are wrapped in pink cellophane, one is sitting on the floor and rises three feet from the ground. There's also a planter full of fresh catnip, and dozens of little kitty toys littering the floor and countertops.

"This is something else," Steve says as a wayward fern frond tickles his ear. "This cat has it better than we do." Allow me to point out the difference between me and Steve. Steve finds all of this mildly amusing in an ironic, life-affirming kind of way. I, on the other hand, am having a hard time keeping perspective, keeping my heart rate down. Every time I see the gold star colored in on Miss B's doorway, I hear my mother shrieking and having a conniption fit. *"This is supposed to be yours, Little Star!"*

I don't think I'll tell Mom about the flowers. I don't think she could take it.

I try to distract my plummeting mood by encouraging Steve to make fun of the play. "So what did you think?"

"I think," he says, plucking a piece of caviar and toast off a tray, "that this was the worst play I ever saw."

"I told you it was bad." Why is it that dissing somebody else's hard work always makes you feel better?

"They should have this playwright drawn and quartered in the town square. The only saving grace is Miss Bubbles's comedic timing and Jasper's hot ass." He washes down his hors d'oeuvre with a swig of Evian water.

"Don't talk about my boyfriend's ass."

"Why not? If Peter's ass was that cute, I'd let you talk about it."

"I would never talk about Peter's ass!"

"Well you could, if you wanted to."

Just then a peal of hysterical laughter leaks out of the bathroom doorway, where Shirley is bathing the star. Miss Bubbles has her own bathroom. With an endless supply of one hundred percent Egyptian, no doubt one thousand thread count cotton towels. With a monogram "THE" on them for *The Happy Ending*.

"That woman—" and Steve points at the door "—is crazy as a loon."

"Shhh…" I swat at his knee. "She'll hear you!"

"Aw relax, she's floating on a happy Zoloft cloud. She can't hear anything. Except the animals talking to her." And he makes the crazy sign by rolling his finger at the side of his head. "Koo-koo!"

I can't help myself and start to giggle. It's been a long time since I've had such a good day with Steve. He was an excellent sous chef, then he did my makeup and now we're bonding over the success of our cat. This almost makes me forget how shitty my life is right now. And as soon as Jasper gets in here and sweeps me off of my feet to that party, I'll really feel good.

"Are we ready to see Mommy and Daddy now? *Are we ready to see Mommy and Daddy now?*" Shirley's baby voice reverberates off of the bathroom tile and announces their entrance into the dressing room. She sweeps the door open and shouts, "Ta-Da! The greatest cat ever!" And there the greatest cat ever sits, hair newly dried, pink bow sitting perfectly atop her head, and her faux-diamond col—

"Shirley, is that collar new?"

"Oh, yes." Shirley tries to hand Miss Bubbles off to Steve, but she leaps out of his arms and jumps up onto the countertop. "Mr. and Mrs. Paine gave her a present for the run." She leans toward me and whispers in a stage voice, "They're *real*. I checked."

I have no idea how she could check to see if they're real, but when Steve lets out a three-toned whistle and says, "They sure look real!" I believe him.

Shirley thanks us, grabs her bag, walks to the cat, who is daintily lapping up water from a dish, kisses her head and walks out the door.

"Bye, Sybil," Steve says under his breath as he walks toward the cat and grabs at her neck, "Let's see this gift."

Miss Bubbles just stares at him and turns back to her water. He tries to get a close-up one more time, but she shakes him off and sashays over to the catnip. She casually bites off a stalk and proceeds to chew and swallow the whole thing down in one gulp.

"Good lord. Her opening night and already she's a drug-addled leading lady."

"She can hear you, Steve."

"Oh, right! The cat can hear me."

"Hey, favorite girl." I turn to the doorway, and there stands Jasper, cleaned, shaven, totally refreshed-looking. You'd never be able to tell that he just finished a play. His eyes are twinkling and the crinkles in the corners dance at me. I run over and jump into his outstretched arms.

"You were so, so good!" I kiss all over his face despite his laughter. His grin warms my lips and I feel like a starving person just getting a taste of food.

"Hey, man, you were really great tonight." Steve goes to shake his hand.

"Thanks so much, and congrats on the new job. That's really something!" They shake furiously while I cling to Jasper's neck like a necklace.

"So are you ready for the big shindig?"

"Yup!" I take my fuschia iridescent wrap from Steve and thank him for assuming cat-taxi duty tonight.

"No problem. I can give her some performance notes on the ride home."

I feel like a princess making her entrance at the ball. Jasper's hand is melded to the small of my back, and the flash of bulbs steals my vision and my breath. The doors to Tavern on the Green are held open, and Jasper whispers a soft breeze against my ear, "Go ahead, sweetie, go first."

I step through the doors into a magic land of string lights and rosebuds. Waiters line the side of the great hall. I look at their tuxedos, then down to the magenta satin top that hugs my chest. Jasper steps alongside of me and takes in the scene before a petite Hispanic woman rushes into his face—it's the same reporter from the night Jasper and I met. She shoves a microphone under his nose and asks, "This is Jennifer from Channel 11. How's it feel to be the toast of New York?" Another blasting, disarming light blinds me, but I never feel Jasper's hand leave my back as he answers her, "Well, I feel so very lucky, so very lucky to be working on this amazing play with these amazing people." Then Jennifer from Channel 11 turns to me and says, "You must be so proud." I flash my most sincere smile and hope silently that the camera gets a clean shot of me.

"Yes, yes. I'm as proud as can be." And Jasper kisses my head. I hope Channel 11 sends a feed to the local news in Michigan.

Jennifer finishes her interview with Jasper and then jumps into the path of Frances and Frederick, who are dressed to the nines. Frances is wearing another navy suit, but the material looks like it cost a million dollars a yard. It glows, and the shell she wears underneath her tailored jacket is the creamiest color white I have ever seen. She has a huge diamond on her finger that looks like it weighs more than Miss Bubbles. And Frederick looks just as expensive, in a dark gray, double-breasted suit. His tie is sky-blue, and his eyes match. He looks like a big, silky, happy teddy bear.

"Sweetheart, come here," Jasper pulls on my hand, leading me to the candy store of life that is this ballroom. I can hardly feel anything anymore but a tingly sensation, the taffy-pull of perfection saturating my senses, violin music lulling me to my dreamworld. There are sparkles in my hair and I'm sure they're twinkling in the soft glow of this room. Couples are dancing everywhere. Groups of hip young theatergoers are huddled in corners, discussing the play. And crowded among the tables, hovering near the buffets, and lining the room, holding us up like a dozen rows of matchstick soldiers, are the tuxedoed waitstaff. Jasper touches the inside of my palm lightly and says for me to follow him.

I'd follow him to the ends of the earth.

He leads me to the terrace. It's a remarkably warm night for early March, and knotted pine trees stand guard like scarecrows, but covered in hundreds of tiny white and blue and green string lights. Lanterns are descending from the branches and a second set of string players is gathered in the corner, plucking their strings with gentle caresses. Jasper swings me into his arms and we start to dance in a slow, languorous circle. He growls into my ear and I melt into him, all the while wishing that cameras were taping me. I want this moment to be the movie of my life, to be played for all eternity, to be preserved and polished and trotted out in my most dire of moments.

He lifts his head off of my shoulder as we circle and holds me out at arm's length.

"You look really pretty right now."

I look to my toes, suddenly shy and overcome. "Thanks." My whisper fills my thickening throat.

His hands find my face and his lips touch mine and we're dancing and circling and his hand is on my back again and I don't want this moment to ever end. This is what I always dreamed it could be. Fancy parties on the arm of someone important. Interviews and dancing, string lights and perfect weather.

"There they are!" A swoosh of navy silk cuts me from my moment. "You! You have *made* our *night!*" Frances air kisses all around Jasper's head and he makes a funny face at me.

"Goddamn was that a fine piece of acting tonight. Yep, yep, you're gonna make us back our money." Frederick links his arm around my shoulder. "I'm a happy man. A happy man." He collars a passing waiter and passes out champagnes to all of us. "A toast. A toast. To happy endings!"

Frances sips and starts to tell Jasper something about his line in act two and how it made her "dizzy with delight." I stare at Frederick's neck and try to forget that it looks nice enough to sink my teeth into. People keep interrupting our conversation, congratulating Jasper and Frances and Frederick and looking at me, peppering their praise with conspiratorial comments directed at me. "Aren't they just amazing?" And I agree.

"I'm the cat's owner," I say to a white-haired poodle of a woman, whose cologne is perfuming the air all around us. Jasper takes the hand I've extended and pulls me toward him, cutting me off with a hug. I turn around and he keeps his arm around me. "We're a talented, happy family," he gushes. I could eat him up, and so, despite the proximity of the Paines, I turn back into his chest and nuzzle his ear, and tell him how happy he makes me. He glows down at me and for a second we are the only two people on this planet.

And this lightning bolt hits me. I think it's happened. The gaze of his eyes is showering my face in love, his teeth are pulsing and so much warmth, so much is penetrating my very being. This is it. This started as a game to me, a game, a chance for me to have all my problems solved, but here it is. He is the beginning of the end of my problems. Because I've fallen in love with him. I always wanted to know what that felt like, and this is it.

"You've made me a princess." I gasp this and he kisses my forehead.

"Now you two, stop acting like a couple of teenagers." Absolute venom is what Frances spits at me. "Besides we want to introduce you to someone very important, Jasper."

"Jasper, Stella, come meet the man who keeps my nose clean." I turn at the sound of Frederick's warm bellow.

The man Frederick refers to stands between Frederick and a gorgeous blonde. I get that she's blond and tan and tall, but I can't take my eyes off the man long enough to see what she really looks like. He's taller than she is and broad-shouldered, and his laugh lines make his face look loving. His brown eyes are almost too far apart, and his nose is crooked but in a sexy way. His bottom lip is fuller than his top lip, both of them looking pink and delicious. I can smell him from six feet away. Musk. My heart speeds up and my breath comes short.

"This is Jasper." Frederick is making introductions and the lights are fading away, like in the scene in the gym in *West Side Story* when Maria and Tony see each other across the sea of gangland dancers. The lights are dimming all around the man and I can't focus on Jasper or Frances or even Frederick's voice as he says to us, "Meet my lawyer. This is Joshua Davis."

As soon as Frederick speaks Joshua's name my heart starts to pound thunderously in my ears. Joshua stares from Jasper to me to Jasper again and reaches out his hand to shake an introduction. I want to slap his hand away from Jasper's, but I can't. My arms won't move. They feel like they've been wrapped in hot, wet towels.

Jasper the gentleman says, "This is my girlfriend, Stella."

For the sixteenth time tonight I want to start bawling because Jasper just called me his girlfriend and I don't even have the space to rejoice. Because this goddamned devil-man is here to ruin it.

"Your girlfriend, Stella," Joshua says and fixes that look onto me, that *look* that used to be able to hypnotize me into going along with anything he said. I don't respond. My blood feels like it's freezing and boiling all at once and I wish I could press the pause button on this moment so that I could study Joshua's face and remind myself why I don't love it anymore. He must be able to tell that I'm over him, because he flashes a lopsided grin and picks up my leaden hand and kisses it. I look quickly at Jasper to see if he's aware of what's going on, but Jasper's grinning and apparently thinking nothing of the fact that a perfect stranger is kissing his girlfriend's hand.

"I'm glad you could make it, old boy!" Frederick points a finger at Jasper but continues to speak to Joshua. "The kid's got something, doesn't he?"

"Oh, yes, yes. He's got something all right." Joshua is still just looking straight at me and I wish more than anything that Jasper and I could leave. Then the blond Amazon starts tugging on Josh's sleeve. "Honey, aren't you going to introduce me?" Honey? It's right about now that it registers in my brain that this blond giantess is certainly *not* Joshua's wife. My teeth gnash against each other and my jaw clenches.

Josh looks at her and says, "How could I forget. Ivy—" *Ivy?* "—this is Frances Paine, and of course you know Frederick, and Jasper Hodge and his girlfriend, Stella." He says this last part and again he looks me dead in the eye, sporting that mischievous grin. Why won't my heart rate slow down? I'm over him. I'm totally over him.

Ivy the Amazon comes over and kisses Jasper on the cheek. I grab a glass of champagne off a passing tray, down the whole thing, and put it back before the waiter even knows what's happening. Ivy inserts herself between me and Jasper and starts to tell him how handsome he looks onstage. I turn my attention back to Joshua, who's telling Frederick and Frances how much he loves coming to openings. Frances stands with her arms resting on Joshua's shoulders, and stares at him like he's Jesus. Then Josh turns to me and says, "So Stella. Have you had a chance to go to many openings?"

I want to shout that he knows very well that I have never been to an opening before because he would never *take* me to one. But instead I step past Ivy and whisper up into Jasper's ear that I'll be right back.

"Are you okay?" he says gently into my ashen face.

"I'm fine." I manage a giggle. "Too much champagne on an empty stomach. If you'll excuse me," I apologize to the rest of the crowd, avoiding Joshua's demon eyes.

The bathroom is inside and across the foyer. Throngs of people are blocking my route, but disappearing into a black hole of designer bodies suits me just fine. Just before the ladies' room is a bank of telephone booths. I dash into a small and claustrophobic stall and dig through my handbag. *Michaela's* handbag. No change. Fuck. Can I call Hell's collect? Can you do such things? Should I call the operator? I pick up the phone and dial 0.

"AT&T." A mechanical voice asks me, "What number, please?" I start rambling into the empty space. "Hi this is Stella Monroe and it's an emergency but I don't have any money so I was wondering if you could connect me to Hell's Bar—oh, wait, right 212-555-4937—and maybe ask if they'll pay for it? Or if you guys give freebies I really need one now…."

Miracle of miracles the other line starts ringing.

"Hell's"

"Is Michaela there?"

"Nope. She's not working tonight. Can I take a message?"

"What? She's not there? Umm…no, no message thanks."

I slam the phone down in frustration at wasting my free phone call, slip out of the booth, and run to the ladies' room. Cool water on the face always makes one feel good. That's all I need. Some cool water and another cocktail. I push open the brown door and walk to the sinks and stare in the mirror.

"Stell. Calm down. Calm down. Calm down." I stare myself down, play chicken with the old me, the me that would run out there and punch out that pretty blonde with one slug and yell *"Mine."* "Wait a minute! Just wait one minute." My reflection listens. "You don't even want him back, do you?" My reflection tells me no. *No, I don't want him back. I am so over him. Right? Of course right.* Maybe it's just because this is the first time I've seen him since we broke up. But it's been almost three months. Surely I should be reactionless? Maybe I should march back out there and ask, right in front of everyone, how Joshua's wife is doing. That'll teach him to show up and ruin my perfect moment.

A fat Spanish attendant with a huge gap between her teeth offers me a paper towel. "Ju can let go of the sink now." Then I notice that my knuckles are white from gripping the linoleum. "Right."

"Boy trouble?"

"Huh?"

"I see lots of pretty young girls in my line of work, and whenever they no smile, it's because of jerky louse somewhere. Ju got louse? I tell girls to deflea."

I let out my first exhale since seeing Joshua. "I did deflea. I just saw the louse with a new girl. A new girl that's not the pregnant wife I broke up with him over."

"Honey, ju no worry abow heemmm…ju just look at jourself, okay?" She tilts my face toward the mirror. "Ju are gorgeous." Her rolling *r*s beat out the rhythm of my distress. "Gorgeous, no? Say it. Gorgeous."

"Gorgeous."

"Ju go out there and forget about heem. Forget."

This bathroom pep talk fortifies me and I make to leave. What is Joshua anyway? Just an *ex*. An *ex* I broke up with! What do I care? I wipe up the tears on my face and fix my lipstick. The Spanish woman clicks her tongue to the roof of her mouth and says, "Pink! I like! Makes ju more gorgeous." I dig through my purse, hoping to find a stray dollar or anything to leave her with, but I have nothing to give. I lift my head up sheepishly and find her waiting expectantly for her tip. I hold up my hand full of pink sparkly rings and tell her to choose one. I mean, I can't very well leave my Fairy Godmother without a tip, can I? That would be major bad luck and my luck cannot get any worse tonight without it meaning bodily harm to myself. A pink ring for good advice is more than a fair trade.

When I make it back out to the terrace, I decide to just ignore Joshua and act like I don't care. Because I don't care. So he's here with someone who isn't his wife. So what? That just confirms what a bad guy he is. And I have Jasper now. Except, at the moment, there is no sign of Jasper—Frederick and Frances are talking in a corner, but Josh and Jasper aren't with them. I wander back inside and turn down a hall that is lined with glass cases full of I ♥ NY snowglobes, ceramic taxicab models and, inexplicably, Hello Kitty! T-shirts. The hall lasts forever, and empties out into a series of rooms, none of which Jasper is in. So I head back to the main room and do a quick look, before heading outside again. I hang back near the wall, keeping an eye out for Joshua and the Amazon and skimming the crowd for signs of Jasper's blond hair. There's a set of glass doors that lead from the terrace to yet another room, where a thousand sweaty bodies are getting down to the sounds of Lionel Richie. Not for me. If Jasper's in there, I don't want to know. So I go to the little upstairs bar, since that's the only place I haven't checked yet.

I order a chocolate martini, silently praying it's an open bar and cursing myself for not being able to even afford a drown-in-your-panic drink. A hand finds my shoulder followed by lips. Fingers trail my back. A shiver racks my body and I turn and melt into Jasper's body, so happy to have found him.

But the wrong voice whispers, "Fancy my pretty little girl here with a hotshot actor." I jump out of his arms, with a shocked inhale.

Joshua just grins and wedges his body in between a column and me and touches the skin of my shoulder with his pointer finger.

"Where's your date?" I manage oh-so-weakly as I back as far away as I possibly can and chant in my head, "I'm over him. I'm over him. I'm over him."

"She's in the bathroom. A scotch and soda please." The bartender sets my drink down and nods to Joshua.

"She's pretty." I say this to the bottom of my martini glass. "And tall as a basketball player."

"I know." His drink is placed in front of him and we both stare straight ahead. "How have you been?"

"Great. Actually, the best I've ever been," I lie.

"Good." He finishes his drink and nods another order. One for me, too. "Anything this lady wants all night is on my tab."

"No it isn't," I shout after the waiter. "Jasper is taking care of my drinks, thanks," I snap like a turtle.

He chuckles and tries to pat my hand. "Jasper Hodge, your new boyfriend. I see you turned me in and traded up. Just what you always wanted. I have to say, I'm impressed."

"What is that supposed to mean?"

"Nothing. Nothing at all. Just that you always wanted somebody who could show you this lifestyle and now you went and hitched your wagon to an up-and-comer. Very shrewd. You know that there's no bigger turn-on than a woman who knows what she wants."

I am getting so furious, partly because of what he's saying

and partly because of the joking tone in which he is saying it. And, because a devil sits on my shoulder and prods me at all hours of the day, I say the dumbest thing possible. "Well you never once brought me to anything like this!" I hear a slight shake to my voice but tell myself it's imperceptible to anyone but me.

Joshua grins into his glass and says with a wink. "My point exactly. I wouldn't bring you so you found someone who would. Very enterprising."

My head is spinning and I can't help but slip into my old pattern of wanting to yell at him. Even though I'm totally over him. "All I ever wanted was to come to these things, why couldn't you have done that for me?"

He sips and turns to me, adopting a casual, warm tone, "Stella! How could I bring you to these events? Look at you?" He's smiling like he's sharing a joke with me and lifts my pressed cloverleaf pendant in his hand. "You wear homemade jewelry and sparkles on your face! For crying out loud. That's okay for a bohemian actor-type to trot around. But how could I be taken seriously if I brought a girl like you to business functions?"

It wouldn't sting this much if he'd slapped me across the face. But he doesn't stop there. "We were fun. But what was going to happen with us Stella? Nothing. Because you're a fantastical kid who knows nothing about the real world."

"And so now you found someone who knows about the real world? Does this girl even know about your wife?" I talk loudly, hoping she'll hear.

"Stella," he leans in to shush me. "I left my wife."

All I feel is my own spastic blinking. "What?"

"I left my wife. And I'm marrying Ivy."

Again, he could've slapped me and I'd feel better than I do now.

"You're getting married." I repeat it out loud, to buy myself time to think of what I want to say after this sinks in. "But when? When did you meet her?"

"Last October."

"Last October?"

He sips his drink and doesn't look me in the eye.

"But you were seeing me in October. And you were married in October. And you were having a baby in October."

"Stella. Try not to overreact." No matter what I say now, he is winning. I wanted to be able to dance all over him the next time I saw him, but I can't. He's winning.

"I don't understand this." But I know. I know in my heart that I am totally over him.

"Stella. Let me tell you something." He puts his drink down, takes mine from my hand and looks me in the eye. "You're a great girl. But you're not the type to leave your wife for." He chuckles, as if amused by the very thought. "You're no wife."

It's good my drink is on the bar, because if it wasn't it would be on Josh's face.

"Glad to see you're getting to know each other." The boom of Frederick's voice claps us at the same time as his meaty hands descend onto our backs. "Josh, did you know that Stella is the owner of the cat who was in the play?"

Joshua gets a surprised look on his face. "You have a cat? Since when?"

Frederick buys another round for us all but Josh mercifully leaves. I watch him go, truly dumbstruck, full of rage and yet knowing how lucky I am that he is no longer in my life. I drown myself in the drone of Frederick's voice, and muster up as much enthusiasm for what he is telling me as possible. I keep drinking until my glass is empty. He orders *another* for me and puts his arm around my shoulder. I try to start the "I don't care" chant up in my head again, but it's no use. Josh is gone and I do care that I didn't get in more parting shots.

"Do you know why I love the theater?" Frederick purrs at me and I shake my head "no."

"People always say to me, 'Freddie! Why not give up the theater! Go to Hollywood and make a fortune.'" He squeezes my shoulder and I nod vigorously. "Can you believe that? Hollywood. *Bah!*" Then he belches up some of his cocktail. The hand leaves my shoulder to cover his mouth. I eyeball the crowd, looking for Jasper.

Frederick replaces his arm around my neck. "I'll tell you, Stella. I'll never leave the theater, because being involved in a play is like being in a big family. And you can never leave your family. Can you?" He waits for me to say "no" and then goes on. "Like Jasper. Jasper could be my son. And you could be my daughter." He hugs me and kisses my cheek, downs his drink and orders two more. Once more I scan the crowd and once more come up with no Jasper. Frederick scoops the fresh drinks up and gives me one, taking the half-full glass I'm sipping out of my hand. He stops midmotion and looks at me. "Actually, Stella, you remind me of someone."

I find my voice. "I do?" My tone sounds thick with alcohol and emotion, even to my own ears.

He stares at me, swaying just a bit, squinting and humming to himself. "God, I can't place it. Have you ever auditioned for me? You're not a dancer, are you?"

"No, I'm not. But my mom was, back in the day—Sue Miller."

His eyes go wide and he snaps. "Sue Miller! God, I haven't thought of that name in years, but that's it!"

"You know her?"

"Gosh, everyone knew Sue. She was a real talent." He sounds truly surprised. "Well how about that! See? One big happy family!!"

"She never mentioned knowing you—"

"Oh, she wouldn't have known me. I was just starting out when she was around. But I saw her on Broadway in *A Chorus Line* and *Annie*—one of those chorus girls who really stood out. And I monitored an audition she was at, once, for this tour of *Bye, Bye, Birdie*. She was great." He shakes his head. "What happened to her, anyway?"

"Well. Me. I happened. She had to leave that *Birdie* tour because I was, uh, you know, on the way."

He turns to me and rests his hand on the bar. "That's too bad. She had a lot of buzz for a while. She could have been huge."

"Well, she had me instead." I swig the whole rest of my chocolate martini down. I'm starting to not be able to feel my feet or my face.

A man in a silk suit approaches us and grabs Frederick's shoulders, congratulating him for about five minutes straight. I use this excuse to leave and find Jasper. I want to bury myself in him and forget all about Joshua and me not being wife material and ruining my mom's life and having no money to even pay for my own drunkenness.

But I still can't find him. Instead I turn to my left and see Joshua nibbling away at his new fiancée's earlobes.

I run out onto the terrace and start weaving and bobbing through the crowd looking for Jasper. I think I see him a couple of times but I'm wrong. So I go out to the bathrooms again and wait to see if he's in the men's room. After a few seconds, I head out to the circular driveway at the front of Tavern on the Green to see if he's out there. Maybe he's sneaking a cigarette. Even though he doesn't smoke. I turn to my left and walk toward Sheep's Meadow. A hansom cab pulled by two dark horses trots in front of me and when it pulls away, a glint of light catches my eye. I walk toward the Green, and hear a couple making out in the woods. As I step out into the trees, I can see a man's body lazily leaning against a tree, being pinned there by a woman in a knee-length suit. The lights from the front of the Tavern are just barely lighting this part of the rough, but I recognize the outfit. And the mellifluous, emerald-sounding laugh bubbling from deep in the lady's throat.

It's Frances Paine. I freeze and wonder if I'm seeing things. I just left Frederick at the bar. I turn to tiptoe back without her seeing me and then I freeze again. Oh God. Frederick's at the bar. Frederick isn't with Frances. And then, if a frozen girl can possibly freeze anymore that's what I do. Because all of a sudden I know who she's there with. I spin around and walk back.

And because I'm in no mood to be cheated on twice in one night, I clear my throat really, really loudly and say, "Frances Paine, get the hell off of my boyfriend, you home-wrecking bitch!"

Chapter 18

As soon as the words are out of my mouth, all my courage seeps away. I spin on my pinpoint high heels and run, past the Tavern on the Green, up the paved hill past the jungle gym, through the stone entryway out of Central Park, down 68th Street and head for home.

Jasper doesn't even try to follow me.

I go to Hell's first, hoping that Michaela has shown up since my desperate phone call, but no dice. I push through the sweating night bodies and sloshing drinks to the bar, and the only person I recognize is Juan the busboy who is transferring beer bottles from a box to the little fridge behind the bar.

"Juan, Juan! Did Michaela show up yet?"

"No, no here tonight, missus. I tole you."

"Um, okay. How 'bout Rod? Is Rod here?"

"No, no. No Rod tonight, missus. Ees good night!"

"Yeah, yeah." My fingertips find the bar and tap a murderous beat. What to do. What to do. In the olden days, when something in my life blew up and I was crying like I am right now, Michaela would absolutely, positively be available for commiseration drinking. "Gimme the phone," I command Juan, "and pour me a shot of whiskey." He looks at me and only complies with my order after I say, "In honor of Rod's night off." I furiously dial Michaela's home number, and throw the shot back while the phone rings.

"*Sí?*" Carlo's voice cuts off the sound of the ringing phone, and the whiskey threatens to come back up.

"Carlo, is Michaela there?" In the background, Spanish music and giggles create an atmosphere of intimacy, and I know I've interrupted something.

"*Sí, sí,* Stella beauty. Hold on—"

"Forget it, Carlo. Just tell her I'll see her in the morning." I click the phone off, throw it down to the bar, and push a stray piece of hair off my head and try not to notice the stares I'm getting from all the other underdressed people. I briefly contemplate begging for another shot of whiskey but can't take another minute in the stuffy, stale atmosphere.

The door to Hell's feels really heavy but I heave it open and start for home. I stare at my feet as I walk and count the tears that actually hit my toes, my perfectly pinked toes. What the hell was that? Jasper and *Frances?* Is there no decency anymore? Has this whole situation between us been a front? No. It can't possibly have been that. Maybe I missed something tonight, maybe Frances got really plastered and nailed my boyfriend to a tree where she had her way with him. And Jasper is so sweet and sincere, he didn't have the heart to turn her down.

I get to my front door and stare up at the stone angel. "That's not it, is it?" Her face is angular and silent and melancholy. Her hands extend themselves in a conductor's pose, as if she's orchestrating all the tragedies of my life, and I know, without question, that it's *not* it. I lean my head on my folded hands at the angel's feet and start to moan. And wail a little bit. Jasper was probably seeing Frances this whole time. I'm such an idiot.

My keys are at the bottom of my handbag so it takes forty-five seconds for me to find them, during which time I buzz for Steve to just come and open the door. But of course he isn't home. Because why would my friends be home on a night like this?

The apartment is empty, except for Miss Bubbles and two flower arrangements that Steve swiped from her dressing room. The couch says a dirty hello as I stand in the doorway and start to strip off my night. I take each of my shoes off and throw them one by one at the couch, making sure that I yell a curse with each one. One of them narrowly misses Miss Bubbles. She runs up to my feet and sits on her hind legs, her open white face showing concern. I lean down to scoop her up, but as I'm lifting her, she hisses and scratches my arm.

"Son of a bitch!" She's gone, taking off for the comfort of my closet.

My arm is bleeding. Not much, but just enough to amplify how shitty this evening has been. I stick my arm underneath the faucet in the kitchen and watch as the rushing water mixes with my tears and washes rusty brown streaks of blood into the drain. I press some paper towels to the cut and start opening cupboards until I find something to help the pain.

Two bottles of red wine are shoved behind the cleaning supplies under the sink. Steve must've stashed them there, figuring I'd never go near any cleaning supplies. Well, the joke's on him. I grab a pint of Phish Food from the freezer, open the first bottle of wine and get a spoon. I won't be needing a bowl. Or a glass.

The outdoor air is cool on the patio and laps at my toes while I arrange a pink plastic lawn chair and situate myself. I run back inside and put on a Billie Holliday CD that Steve gave me one year for my birthday. The mood is complete.

Let the wallowing begin. The night is not quite pitch-black. I can make out the branches of a tree overhead, its arms scratching the sky and covering the stars. The sound of cars going by barely infiltrates my den of despair and after a good hearty swig of red wine, I crumple over on myself. First Joshua. Then Jasper. Maybe I should promise myself to never date anyone whose name begins with a *J*.

The phone rings inside and I perk up, anxiety doing a square dance with hope. This has to be Jasper calling to apologize and explain. Calling to tell me what I didn't know that will make it all better. I stand in the doorway, straining forward, preparing to dash for the phone.

"Little Star." My mother's melodic tone tells me she's expecting great things from tonight. "I just can't wait to hear all the details. Did anyone take your picture tonight? I hope you remembered to only let your left profile be photographed, but I'm sure you did just fine. I can't wait! Call me right away!"

The excitement in her voice makes me want to vomit. I brace myself against the doorway, and all of a sudden, the whole night just comes pouring out of my eyes and I start sobbing. I struggle over to my chair and wail away, bent over, sitting up only to sip, cursing my mother and Jasper and Ezra and Michaela and Steve and Joshua.

"What the hell's going on down there?"

My head lifts up but my body stays crouched in the fetal position. Christian is leaning over his railing, looking annoyed.

"I'm having a private moment."

"Actually, you're having a very public moment. You want to keep it down?"

"Can you just leave me alone?"

I must look awful because his eyes go wide and he kind of stammers. Typical guy. Doesn't know how to deal with tears.

"Hey, are you okay?"

"Yes, I'm fine. Now just go back inside and leave me be, okay?" The wobble in my voice is unmistakable and so I cover my embarrassment by taking a big swig from the bottle.

But instead of the sound of his door closing, I hear the fire escape ladder make a rusty whooshing sound and before I know it, Christian is climbing down to me and then I am looking down at his feet. He crouches in front of me.

"What happened to you?" He tenderly takes the paper towels away from my bloody arm and walks into my kitchen.

"Help yourself, why don't ya?" I mutter under my breath. He returns with wet napkins and resumes the crouch. He swabs at my red-stained arm until I'm all cleaned up, then he takes a second napkin and dabs at my face.

"What are you doing?" I try to avoid his cleaning attempts but he catches my chin in his hand.

"Just keep still. You're a mess!"

"I want to be a mess!" I bat his arm away and he sits back on his heels. His glasses are on so I can't make out his eyes, but the rest of him looks pretty good. He's wearing a white T-shirt and gray sweatpants and all of a sudden I'm really glad not to be alone.

"Listen, I promise to be nice to you if you'll just sit here with me and keep me company."

He smiles, kind of funnylike and says, "That's fine, but we're using glasses."

He goes back into my kitchen and comes out with two plastic cups. Once he's settled into the other chair, he starts firing away. "So what happened?"

"What happened?" I belch out after a sip of wine, "I'll tell you what happened. Men are unfaithful assholes. That's what happened."

"Aaahh." He sits quietly, at my side, only the small side table between us. We sip for a bit, and I undo my hair so that it plops down around my neck and shoulders. Then I start crying and spilling all my secrets to a man who might laugh at me.

"It's just that tonight was supposed to be so perfect. It was supposed to be my night! And then Joshua showed up and told me I wasn't wife material and Frederick told me my mom could've been a superstar if it weren't for me and Jasper started kissing Frances and Bubbles attacked me and my mother is going to be so disappointed." Christian doesn't make one single dig. Instead he reaches out his hand and massages my neck.

"You're gonna be fine. It's just one of those nights." His fingers feel warm and strong, and I lean my head into his hand.

"One of those nights? That's an understatement." I finish off my cup of wine and get up. I walk over to Christian's chair and look down at him. He has a nice face. I never really thought about it before. "Make room," I say before sitting on his lap, curling myself into his arms, and burying my head in his chest.

"Stella." He squirms, and his body tenses, and his voice sounds a tad uncomfortable.

"Oh, shut up."

He shuts up and rubs my back and gradually the tears stop dripping down my cheeks. The building on the other side of the courtyard is all I can see and Billie Holliday is crooning about Vermont in the background and Christian's hand is making lazy circles on my back.

"Christian?"

"Yes?"

I close my eyes before I ask, "Someday, someone will marry me, right?"

He shifts his weight underneath me. "Stella, that guy's an idiot. Don't listen to him."

"You didn't answer the question."

"Stella."

"Just answer the question!" I lift my soggy face to his and look him in the eyes.

"Stella, of course you'll get married someday. You're one of the best people I know."

"I am?" He nods and grabs a paper towel and wipes off what I imagine is drippy mascara. When he's done I burrow back into his chest.

"Really. You're smart and hopeful and you have complete faith in the world. And you try so hard to do the right thing."

"I do?" I lift up again and again he starts cleaning my face. I bat away his hand.

"Stop it, will ya? You have stuff all over your face!"

"Well I like it there." I look at him and he looks at me. Then he holds my cheeks in either of his hands and kisses my forehead.

"You're gonna be fine, kiddo. Just stop dating these losers who don't care about you at all and you'll be fine." I'm sitting up now and leaning my head on his shoulder.

"The problem is that I think these losers do care about me."

"You just have to figure out what caring for somebody really feels like." He sips his wine.

"Christian?"

"Yes."

"Thanks for being here." I stay on his lap for a few more minutes and we sip our wine.

"I know something that'll cheer you up!" He sits upright and points to the building across the way. "Look in the third-floor window."

Two people walk in front of the window. "Oh my God! They're naked!" A man and a woman are standing in their kitchen, chopping vegetables and wearing nothing.

"They're naked all the time. I call them 'The Nudies.'"

"They always run around like this?" I am in disbelief that something so entertaining could be taking place outside my very door without me knowing about it. On *Friends,* sure. On *Sex in the City,* of course. But practically in my backyard. "Steve will love it."

"Yep. Naked from sunup to sundown." I start to giggle. Christian is so funny. It almost makes me forget the hole in my heart.

"Do you need more wine?" It's incredibly important to keep this good time going, or else I will totally melt down. Actually, I'm feeling okay. The wine is doing the trick. I can't even feel from my toes to my ankles anymore and my head is buzzing.

"I'll get it," he says and reaches for the bottle.

"I always have to drink when I'm around you." I giggle this and he says, "Okay."

"Because if I don't drink around you I'd probably kiss you."

I really shock him with this one, not to mention myself. "Oh, really?" he splutters, and shifts uncomfortably.

"Stay still!"

"I think we're done now, Stella."

"We're not done. We're not done. Just sit still!"

He settles down and drinks a whole glassful in one gulp. I never noticed how nice he feels before. Maybe because I've never sat on his lap before.

I wiggle around a bit so that I can look at him. "You probably could really care about a girl and not cheat on her."

"Probably could."

"And you eat all my cooking and tell me how good it is."

"It is good."

"Maybe I should date you then."

"Okay, that's enough wine." He takes my glass from me and I start wailing.

"Hey! That's not fair! I have a broken heart!" Christian shakes his head and stands up, which leaves me scrambling to find my feet. He takes the melting ice cream and the two bottles of wine into the kitchen and I follow him. I'm having a hard time walking.

"Christian, why's the party over?"

"Don't worry Stella, just go and clean up, okay?"

"Okay." I give him the soldier salute and spin around, nearly trip on one of the heels in the middle of the room and try very hard to walk a straight line to the bathroom.

My reflection displays all the red blotchy marks covering my face. I wet the bar of soap by the sink and scrub at my face until every ounce of hurt and makeup is gone. Then I brush my teeth and take off my necklace and bracelets and the pins out of my hair and the rings off my fingers. My face looks okay now, but I feel too good to stay in this bathroom.

I run out and see Christian standing behind the kitchen bar, hands leaning on the countertop. He is staring at a spot on the counter with so much intensity it makes me wonder what he's thinking about. And he is finishing the bottle of wine. The CD starts over, and I run up to him, to the other side of the bar.

"All clean!" I say. "You're right. Jasper is an idiot. And tomorrow I won't care at all."

Christian doesn't say anything, he just pours another glass of wine and drinks the whole thing down.

"Dance with me, Christian. Come dance with me!" I pull him out from behind the bar and yank him to the middle of the room. The music is so good. Billie Holliday sounds as sad as I am, but like she has nobody to share it with. And I have Christian, so I tell him, "I'm so lucky to have you." And I dig my forehead into his shoulder for the second time tonight. His hands are around my waist and I can tell that he's staring straight ahead of himself, not even looking at me. But that's okay. He smells good and I wonder why it is that I've been running around with Jasper when Christian is right here, smelling good and eating my food and caring about what happens in my life. So I lean up and put my arms around his neck and say, "I'm so silly. I could've been with you this whole time." And then I kiss him.

We stop dancing and he pulls away from me. We stare at each other, then I walk toward him. This time he doesn't pull away from me. He just kisses and kisses me and when I break away and try to lead him into my room, he says, "Oh, Stella" and shakes his head a little, so I tell him. "It's okay, Christian, it's okay. You can stay with me." And then I kiss him again and this time he follows without a fight.

Chapter 19

My house smells good enough to eat. My body stretches toward the ceiling, and I lean over and lick the wall. Gingerbread. The yummiest. I take a bite of my spun sugar sheets and luxuriate in the sweet, warm wonder of my bed. Miss Bubbles runs into the middle of the room and screeches to a halt. She rears up and I notice she's wearing her aviator goggles. "Catch me if you can," she growls before bolting out of the room. I watch her run away. I'm never leaving this house, not even to catch up to my cat. I pad into the bathroom, and turn on the faucet. Hot chocolate. My water runs hot chocolate. Happiness swirls inside me like a giant soft-serve ice-cream cone. When I lift my chin from the faucet, where I've taken a sip of the hot-but-just-warm-enough-to-drink chocolate, Christian is standing there with a towel. He dabs my chin, and asks, "Do you like the gingerbread house I made for us? You said you always wanted one."

There's a *throb, throb, throb* in my head, and my thoughts are fuzzy, and my bed is a perfect temperature for sleeping in. There's an arm lying across my chest, my naked chest, and breath warming the side of my neck. I snuggle in, and the arm tightens around me. Maybe I'll just stay here for the rest of my life: warm and cozy and safe. Whatever happens, I'm not going to open my eyes. I'm not going to open my eyes. I'm not going to open my eyes.

So I burrow down into my covers and lean even harder into the body next to me. He smells so good. Jesus. How does he smell good right now? And now he's kissing my cheek and my neck and adjusting his body so that we face each other, his arm still draped over me and I feel so completely peaceful and contented and *warm*. The throbbing drumbeat in my head is fading away, and I open my eyes. Yep. It's Christian all right. I wish I didn't remember anything that happened last night, but every detail seems to be indelibly etched in my memory in lush, vivid Technicolor surround sound. He kisses my forehead and whispers, "Hey." His eyes close and his head drops onto the pillow.

And at that moment every molecule in my body seizes up and scrambles like an egg, and all my hopes and dreams for my entire life backflip into a hodgepodge of panic. *I had sex with Christian. Christian.* Christian is *not* my friend. He's the annoying, snooty, neighbor who calls the cops on me and makes fun of me and has absolutely no connections to Broadway or Hollywood whatsoever. And my boyfriend Jasper, who *can* introduce me to the powerful people of the world and maybe *can* get me some jobs, is probably rolling around on his thousand thread count sheets with Frances Paine *as we speak*. It's all too much for a girl to take. I leap and stand, picking up the first piece of clothing I see—which just happens to be Christian's T-shirt. "What the hell happened?" I demand this of him, before he has a chance to lift his head from the pillow. I inhale his scent from the T-shirt before putting it on and staring at him.

He sits up and rubs his eyes and stares back at me. "I think you seduced me," he croaks out through a dry throat.

I try to form words but nothing comes out except shocked, squelching sounds and so I storm over to the kitchen. I pour two glasses of water and walk back over to him. *"Seduced you? I never!"*

"You did." He looks at me and I slump down to the bed and hold my head in my hands and say, "Oh God oh God oh God."

He finishes a sip of water. "You're kind of hurting my feelings right now."

"Stop talking, stop talking." I moan this to my hands. His stare is penetrating through my protective pose, though, and pretty soon I find myself looking into his eyes. He's sitting up now, with the sheet covering over his middle and just looking so, so good for early in the morning.

"That was fun." He runs his tongue over his lower lip and I can't concentrate.

"Yes, fun."

"Are you okay?"

"Yes, okay."

"You're totally freaked out."

"No I'm not." I lift my head up from my hands. "Aren't you late for your vacuuming appointment?" Just then a blur of white fur whooshes out of my closet and lands on the bed. Miss Bubbles hisses at me and then plops herself in the middle of Christian's lap.

"Fantastic." I grab a pair of clean underwear and a bra off of my dresser and head for the bathroom. Pretty soon, the faucet is gushing cold water onto my hands and the mirror is staring back at me.

"Stop looking at me," I tell myself. But it's too late. I know that this means trouble. This means that a slightly annoying but comfortable relationship I had with my upstairs neighbor has been irrevocably damaged. Now who the hell will I give my leftovers to? A thud interrupts my musings, so I pull up my underwear, hitch up the bra and go see what fell.

Christian is standing in the middle of my room, opening drawers in my bureau and throwing things around.

"What are you doing?"

"Looking for my blazer."

"Oh my God! Get *out!*" Miss Bubbles apparently thinks I am going to attack Christian, because she inserts her little white body in between ours, rears up on her hind legs and then starts batting at my ankles.

"Look, your cat likes me better!" He is smirking, and I'd wipe the smirk off his face with my nails, but the phone interrupts us. Its ring freezes all three of us in motion, like we're ten and playing statue. Christian's hand is wrapped around my wrist and the cat is folded over my foot. We wait out the rings, and then hear my voice message and then…

Beep.

"Stell. It's Jasper. Don't not pick up this phone right now."

Christian whispers "double negative" under his breath and I cover his mouth with my palm.

"I know you're upset and angry but I want to talk to you before the show tonight. Please call me, sweetheart." *Beep.*

Christian splutters out "Sweetheart! What an idiot."

I tell him to stop it and walk out into the living room and replay the message.

"Stella."

I swoosh my arm back and forth behind my back to let him know not to talk while I'm replaying. *"Stella."* His voice is totally commanding and if I wasn't busy trying to analyze every lilt and modulation of Jasper's voice, I'd notice that I'm kind of turned on by it.

"It's time for you to leave." I spin around and face him. He is just inside my room, wearing his sweatpants and no shirt. Miss Bubbles stands between his legs and looks at me earnestly. My heart does the strangest little dance in my rib cage and I can't help but feel that this is a defining moment in my life.

I gulp and tell him. "It's just that he could be my shot, you know? And I can't let it pass by."

Christian just looks at me.

"I've worked really hard so far, and I need to be further along in my career and Jasper can help me with that. I have to at least hear what he has to say."

"It doesn't matter what he has to say! He's a player and he doesn't care about you!" I have never, in the whole time I've known him, heard Christian yell. Tears instantly populate my eyes and my body jumps back.

"What do you care anyway?"

His face goes all red and then purple and then red again and he stomps toward me, so loudly that Miss Bubbles goes running into the closet. "What do I care? Stella, I spent all last night drying tears off your face that this guy put there!"

"But, he's got an explanation and I..." I can't think. Christian wipes his hand over his face and reins in whatever it is that he wants to say. Then very quietly he says, more to his feet than to me, "Stella, don't you think we're good together?"

Alarm bells clang throughout my brain. Good together? Me and Christian? "No."

"No?"

"No, Christian." My body shakes. "I need somebody who can help me with money and my career. And that's not you."

Christian looks up and then walks toward me. My breath stutters in my throat and I pull the edges of his T-shirt down toward the tops of my thighs. He stands right before me and reaches his arms out to me. Before I can protest it, he kisses me and as I melt inside but try to hide it, I hear the key jiggle in the door and then the screeching sound of Steve shouting, *"Oh my God!"*

I leap out of Christian's arms but he just turns to Steve very calmly and says, "Hey. I was just leaving."

Steve nods and tries to catch my gaze, but I'm too busy counting the threads in our rug. Christian whispers in my ear, "Don't worry. We don't have to talk about this again. You can keep the T-shirt."

Then he walks out. And I start to cry. Again. Steve is frozen still in the doorway, his mouth hanging open like a wet noodle. I brush the tears away with the backs of my hands and look up at Steve, begging him silently with my eyes to leave it alone.

"Stella." I contemplate running away and locking myself in the bathroom. But Steve hits the ball out of the park. "Put some pants on and let's go to Hell's."

An hour and a half later, I am metaphorically spilling tears in my beer telling Michaela and Steve about my night. Michaela's face gets rounder and redder with each detail, and she's gone from seltzer water to Diet Coke and I think the next stop is her standard glass of straight scotch. Steve sits on the stool to my right, stroking an imaginary beard and nursing a Bud Lite. Thank God I can still drink with my friends in the middle of a weekday, even if I feel crappy and my cocktail of choice is black coffee and all Steve can say is, "I can't believe you fucked Christian."

Michaela is more concerned with the emotional damage seeing Joshua has caused me. "So think back, did he seem like he gained any weight or lost any hair since you dumped him?" She smiles weakly to convey her attempt at cheering me.

"No, Mic." I start to rip a poor cocktail napkin to shreds. "He looked just like he always did. A million dollars. With a billion dollar beauty on his arm."

"I can't believe you fucked Christian."

"Steve! Stop saying fuck!" Michaela snaps a bar towel at him.

"What? When did your sensibilities get so sensitive?"

"People!" I start dinging my glass with my finger, imagining that I'm making actual sound. "Can we focus on me and my shitty life please?" As if on cue, "Loser" by Beck begins to drone over the sound system. Fantastic.

"So you have to go to the theater tonight?" Michaela tries to get back on course.

"Yes, and I don't know what to say to him. I don't even want to go." I turn to Steve and start to open my mouth but he stops me with a "Don't even think about it."

I hang my head while he lectures me. "Stell—" and he checks his watch "—I have to run to rehearsal, but this is what I am going to say to you. Go to that theater, tell Mr. Hodge where he can shove his cheating hard-on, and then run, don't walk, back to Christian, declare your undying love for him and have a wonderful life. There. Done. Problem solved. And with that I leave you fair ladies to your discourse." He gathers up his bag and zips up his coat. "Mic, make sure Ms. Monroe sticks to coffee."

Michaela gives him the thumbs-up. I can barely lift my head from the bar to say goodbye. I moan at him instead.

When he's gone I lift up a bit and stare into Michaela's cool, knowing eyes. "Mic," I ask, not wanting to know the answer, "what do you do when you know someone is right for you heart-wise, but at the same time, know that it isn't right for you life-wise. And vice versa."

She leans down, fetches two cherries from the fruit case on the bar and hands me one. "Honey. The two aren't separate. One who's good for your heart has to be good for your life."

I suck the cherry off of the stem, chew and contemplate. The heaviness in my heart is weighing me down, so much so that moving from this stool seems like an impossibility. "I think Jasper's my last chance. I'm twenty-five and this is the closest I've ever gotten to this life." Another in the long fucking line of tears I've been shedding slips down my cheek and I think to myself how much like Demi Moore in *Ghost* I must look.

"Stella. This is what you are going to do. Take your cat to the theater and when you see Jasper you'll know what to say. Then, tomorrow morning you are going to any audition you can find."

I stare at my palms, unsure. She continues, her honey voice massaging my heart. "And you are going to become a world-class star all by yourself. No Joshua. No Jasper. No nothing. Just you."

I nod and finish my coffee and slide off the stool, carefully making my way home.

New York smells clean today, and that is a rare occasion. I pick my way alongside the street edge, between the curb and the parked cars, not looking at any of the other people walking in this beautiful afternoon. The sounds of the city fill my stomach and make me feel floaty, like a heavy melancholy balloon.

My thoughts turn from Joshua and Jasper to my mother. My mother, who walked these streets over twenty years ago, looking for the same thing I am. Luck and the chance to have the life she always wanted. And then, as I stare down the row of theaters, whose billboards and lightbulbs are striking even in daylight, I remember that it's my fault she never got to have it. The sun bounces from the windshields of the passing cars and the buildings facing me into my eyes. I don't care. I've been blind this whole time, so what does a little sun-in-the-eyes hurt?

Walking through the hall to my front door, the *thud-thud-thud* of Christian's typewriter keys echoes down the walls, making me feel like I've lost something. Clutching a fistful of his T-shirt—which I'm still wearing—I debate going up there and having it out, but I know I have to see Jasper later and I can't take two confrontations in one day. So I open my door and slip inside quietly.

Kevin is lounging in front of the Cherry Lane Theater, an apple in one hand and a rolled up copy of a used novel in the other. A chain hangs down around his hip, keeping his wallet close by and immune to a stranger's grasp. He looks up when I exit the cab and says hello.

"Hey, Kevin."

"I didn't see you at the party last night." He stuffs the novel into his back pocket.

"Oh, I left early. You know, too much champagne, goes to my head."

"Well, anyway. Shirley's not here yet. But you can wait in the dressing room for her."

"Thanks," I say as I knock on the door. Just as it creaks open,

Kevin says, "And Frances Paine called looking for you. She said to call her right away."

A knot forms in my stomach. Of course she did. That un- believable...she wants *me* to call *her?* Shouldn't *she* be calling *me* and begging me not to tell Frederick what I saw? How un- believably *rich* of her....

A few stage crew guys are huddled up in a corner and sip- ping coffees and I shout over to them to ask if it's okay to walk around on the stage.

"Not today sweetheart," a big man called Joe responds. "There are paint touch-ups drying."

A shrug heaves my shoulders down into place. No putting it off. I shift the red bag and Miss Bubbles over to my other shoulder and head down into the dressing room lair. I wonder if Jasper'll defend himself, if he'll tell me that it was all a mis- understanding. "I wouldn't believe that," I tell Miss Bubbles, who appears to not be able to care less about me or my prob- lems. While she licks her paws, thoughts of Jasper's possible lines of defense cloud my head. Will he go for contrite? A tough love attitude maybe? Will he get down on his knees and beg my forgiveness? I spent the whole cab ride and actually, all af- ternoon, practicing my retaliatory speeches. The thing is, I don't think I know him enough to be able to hurt him with my words. Unless, of course, those words are whispered into *Frederick's* ear.

My first stop is Miss B.'s dressing room. On the counter, in the midst of the play toys and new bouquets of flower arrange- ments, is a big vase full of pink roses. Three dozen pink roses. And a card that says "Stella." I set the bag down on the counter and Miss B. zips herself from the counter to a padded bed un- derneath the makeup station.

I lift the card to my nose and it smells like lavender. When I open the envelope, an image of a little girl in a ballerina out- fit is teetering over the edge of a balance beam. Her cheeks and her skirts are a tinted pink and the rest of her is drenched in sepia tones. The inside of the card says, "It's okay to fall down sometimes." Underneath is scribbled something in Jasper's scratchy hand. He says for me not to worry, that there's an explanation. I wonder if that's true.

It'll be so easy if it's true.

The door to the dressing room glides open and then I am confronted with Jasper, standing in the doorway where he stood almost twenty-four hours ago. He looks at me for a long time before saying anything, and I notice how wrinkled he is. Not just his ratty KISS T-shirt and ripped khakis, the clothes he wears to warm up before a show. Not just his hair that he probably slept on and didn't comb. But his face is wrinkled, curled up in a ball of apology.

"Stella. You ran away so fast." He can do a lot better than that.

"And you didn't follow me or even call until this morning." That's right cowboy, let's take the gloves off!

Jasper enters the room, takes two quick steps over to where I am. His hands come up to my waist and before I can think to stand my ground, he kisses me. Deeply. I give him a little shove and back away, then just look into his eyes and wait for him to say something, anything to make it okay. To make it okay for me to keep seeing him. He runs a thumb over my lip.

"I just want to make sure that you know you can't talk to Frances like that."

Just like that, something snaps in me and I push him away from me, with both hands on his chest, hard. And start yelling.

"I can't talk to Frances like that? Guess what? I can say anything to anybody that I want!"

He apparently decides the gentle approach has run its course, because he comes back at me with both guns blazing. "I wouldn't do that if I were you, Stella. We have a good thing going here, and I'd hate for your cat to lose this job."

This is a quick, clean fight. He KO's me with one sentence. He's right. I have no hand here. But at least I can still be bitchy.

"So you get to screw the boss's wife and I get to be your fucking beard?"

Jasper slumps against the wall and looks at me, his voice grows softer. "Stella, be smart. If you want to make anything of yourself in this business, you can't make enemies."

The truth of this is jarring, but I decide to think about it later and just try to make him feel really, really guilty for two-timing. "Yeah, well, I thought you cared about me and it was all a big lie!"

He doesn't look as guilty as I hoped he'd look. Why can't a person, in moments of extreme drama like this one right here, have a team of writers to supply good, moving lines? Jasper just gets annoyed and rolls his eyes to the ceiling. "You don't have to be like this. It's not like we were really involved with each other."

"It's not?"

"I told you I was looking for some fun!"

At that moment, Miss Bubbles emerges from her bed and walks to the middle of the floor. She lies down between Jasper and me, and all of a sudden I remember that she's bringing home all the money right now. No job. No Ezra. No pride. No nothing. I look at Jasper. "Get out of Miss Bubbles's dressing room, Jasper."

He grudgingly lifts off the wall, pushes toward the door and looks back at me over his shoulder. "It doesn't have to be like this, Stella," he repeats himself. "There's no reason why we shouldn't be able to see each other, just because I'm in this situation."

"Well, jeez Jasper, thanks for the lovely offer!" I call out after him as he walks away. "I'll keep that in mind the next time I'm in the market for a cheating bastard!" I say this more to myself and Muss Bubbles, who looks at the empty doorway, looks back at me, and promptly spits up a hairball.

Chapter 20

The next morning, I wake up on my couch. Christian's T-shirt rides up around my chest, Miss Bubbles curls at my feet, an open bag of baked Lay's beckons from the coffee table, and Emeril Lagasse screams through the television. My answering machine flashes its light—Frances's office called for me, again, but I didn't pick up. My head aches. Propping myself on my elbow, I listen to the vacuum cleaner run over Christian's floor and reach for a chip. Miss Bubbles stretches and finds a more comfortable position.

The remote digs into my sides. After detaching it from my ribs, I start flipping channels until I end up back on the Food Network. Emeril is cooking up a shrimp and steak feast, with this creamy jalapeño sauce and corn bread and hush puppies. God, hush puppies are good. I still use the recipe Thelma taught me. All these years later, and I've never found a better one. One time I left a basket of six hush puppies on Christian's doorstep, and found a note slipped under my door the next day saying that if I couldn't commit to making a dozen, then not to bother. A smile breaks out on my face and I lift his

T-shirt to my nose once again before sadness forces me to change the channel and lose the memory.

As I settle into a good *Three's Company* rerun—the one where Jack and Chrissy handcuff themselves to each other—the whir of Christian's vacuum ceases, and footsteps beat out a rhythm across my ceiling. I could go up there and talk to him. No big deal. Just go up and ask him how he is. Ugh! What has brought me to this place, this place where I want to engage in small talk with Christian? I look up at the ceiling, count the cracks and paint bumps and my mind starts to wander. Christian would be a good boyfriend. That much is clear. Not to me, because of course we don't fit, but to someone who can appreciate his ideas and his sense of humor and his appetite. He'd never cheat. Or lie. I'm pretty sure of that. And he'd probably be one of those guys who turns down the bed at night and leaves little presents lying around and calls just to hear your voice and totally supports anything you want to do. Everybody should have a boyfriend like that.

He's walking around up there, I can hear footsteps carry toward his front door, and my heart revs up. The door slams shut and his footsteps fall onto the stairs. I shoot off the couch and run to the peephole in my front door. Crouching and winking, I see him walk to the bottom of the steps and head straight out of the apartment building, without even looking in my apartment's direction. He *never* just goes out in the middle of the day. This is supposed to be his typing time! My stomach heaves the way it does when I'm told, "Thank you very much," at an audition. I turn around and lean my back against the door, slamming my fists three times.

What am I worried about him for anyway? Do I have time to be daydreaming about him and feeling bad over a situation that shouldn't be? No! All of a sudden, the image of my mother standing on the stage of the Shubert Theater permanently molds itself to my mind. I can't be worrying about Christian now. I have to make things right. I turned Jasper loose, I don't have any pictures and my manager won't return my calls. But Michaela is right. I need to take things into my own hands. This is it! No more depending on Steve or Jasper or Joshua or the next-man-who-turns-the-corner to come and start my career for me. I rip the T-shirt off over my head and run into the bathroom. I stand naked in front of the mirror, take the cloverleaf pendant between my thumb and forefinger and start my new chant: "It's all up to me, it's all up to me, it's all up to me." I go to my wallet and open it. Empty. I hold the empty wallet up to the mirror and repeat, "Filling this is all up to me. It's all up to me. It's all up to me." And I know what I have to do today. I have to make peace with Frances so that Miss Bubbles can keep her job until I get my own. And then I am going to an audition.

In the living room, on the dingy old coffee table, is Steve's rolled up copy of *Backstage*. I plop into the scratchy tweed of the sofa and thumb through until I find the list of auditions for the day. Miss Bubbles emerges from her slumber and slinks over to where I am, whistling the whole way.

"What are you up to?" She looks up at me in response and leaps into my lap, crunching the paper and making me lose my place. "Miss Bubbles!" I shout and jump to my feet, sending her sprawling. She hisses and leaves. We are so not friends anymore.

My life sucks.

I quickly find the right page in the paper and spot an audition.

Wanted. Singers with personal style. 5'5" to 5'9." Standard uptempo, for *South Pacific* tour. Songs from the show. 406 West 46th Street, 9:00 a.m.

Perfect! I know a song from that show! My mother used to sing it to me after school! Screw you, Jasper and Joshua and all men. I am going to get a show, a *tour* and blow this joint! This has to be meant to be.

I run and look at the clock. If I leave right now, there's just enough time to make it to Frances's office before the audition.

After a faster-than-fast shower, clothes change and quick check in the mirror, I grab my sheet music from the shelf by the kitchen and run out the door.

Sprinting down 9th Avenue in heels and a miniskirt is just the sort of activity I need to get my mind in gear. What I'm doing is this: I'm shedding bad behavior. No television and ice cream for me today. No sir. And what have I been thinking all my life? That men could solve my problems? They never solved my mother's. Me and her, it was all we needed. And now I am going to go and stick it to Frances and then nail this audition and take care of myself.

The Paine Group offices are located on 41st Street and Seventh Avenue, right near the Nederlander Theater. Close enough for me to walk and work up a good dose of attitude, because I'm sure I'm going to need it. Now remember, Stella, the goal here is to get the cat a stable slot in the show. This will be a tremendous acting challenge for me, to pretend that I don't care about what she did, but that I'm completely willing to go to Frederick if my desires aren't met.

Can I bargain with her? You bet.

The offices are gorgeous, just as I imagined they would be. The lobby is decorated with dozens of theater posters, all sporting the line "The Paine Group presents" along the top. Raul Julia, Nathan Lane, Kevin Kline, Natasha Richardson, all manner of stars have received paychecks from these people. And in the corner, by the elevator bank, hangs a picture of Jasper, seated, with Miss Bubbles on his lap. It mesmerizes me, Miss Bubbles hanging side by side with all these theater powerhouses. There's no way I am going to let them take her out of the show. I take a deep breath to prepare myself for my mission.

The elevator is bigger than my bedroom and moves faster than your average taxicab. In no time at all, I'm stepping into a penthouse office on the twenty-fifth floor of this luxury building. The walls are white and the ceilings are high, so high that you can't tell what color they are. Huge, industrial-size ceiling fans spin lazily and stark chairs are provided in the lobby area. There is one, huge, nearly six-foot-tall desk sitting in the middle of the whiteness, and a perky blond girl, no more than twenty years old, sits behind it wearing a headset. I step up to her and adopt my most haughty of voices.

"I'm here to see Frances Paine."

"Do you have an appointment?" she squeaks this out. "Because Mrs. Paine doesn't see anybody without an appointment."

"She'll see me. Tell her Stella Monroe is here. I'll wait." She looks at me dubiously before buzzing an intercom and saying that I'm in the lobby. She gives me the "you can wait" nod and I sit in one of the chairs.

Man, does Frances Paine have some grade A nerve! Does she think that because she's a gajillionaire she can screw around behind her husband's back with my meal ticket and then fire my cat? *No way José.* That's all I have to say.

Soon a stick-thin man wearing leather pants and a cashmere sweater enters the lobby from a door on the right. "Ms. Monroe?"

I stand and smooth down my miniskirt. I purposely wore a really short skirt so that Frances will see that even though she has all the money, the men and the power, I still have the better legs. I follow the thin boy down a white hallway on whose walls are hanging a series of photographs of body parts. We pass an ankle, an earlobe and a kneecap before getting to a corner office that is marked, "Mrs. Frances Paine."

The man opens the door for me and motions me inside. I take a deep breath and summon all the false bravado I can. Because no matter how much I want to pretend that this is just a game to me, it's not.

Frances is standing at the back of her office, staring out a window and clutching a necklace in her fingers. Her deep thoughts must be fascinating because she doesn't even turn to look at me when I come in. I clear my throat twice, really loudly, and she doesn't move. This gives me time to notice that she's wearing a turtleneck and a leather skirt, with a chain link belt draped across her middle. She looks fantastic.

Finally, after a good minute and a half, I say, "Frances. You've been calling, what was it that you wanted?"

The barest hint of a smile cracks onto her skillet of a face and she continues to stare out of the window. "I don't love my husband, Ms. Monroe."

I roll my eyes and take a step back. "So divorce him."

She turns to me and laughs that throaty, green laugh of hers. "How profound. Di-*vorce* him." She walks to her desk and sits down, and motions for me to follow suit. "I have no intention of divorcing my husband, and I have no intention of having him divorce me." She fixes me with an icy stare and I look away for a second, rattled by her cool determination.

"Then why did you call me?"

"Stella, let me tell you something." Frances takes two crystal goblets from the side of her desk and pours water from a pitcher. "Have you ever been to Montana?"

I shake my head no and sip the water. She is hopelessly in control of this conversation and all I can do is wait her out until we get to the good stuff.

"Well, there's nothing there but cow shit and mountains that block out the sky."

"Sounds lovely."

"I got out of there, and I hitched my wagon, so to speak, to Frederick, and he has single-handedly given me everything I've ever wanted in life." She's talking so softly, and smiling at me, like we are old friends having a long-overdue conversation.

"No offense, but why are you telling me this?"

She leans forward in her seat and angles her head toward mine, like she's about to give me Tom Hanks's personal phone number or something. I can't help but lean in, too.

She whispers at me, "Stella. I know you. You are what I was thirty years ago. Wanting a better life, and trying to find the man who can give it to you."

I say nothing.

"You can have it, all of it, but you have to deal with certain things that aren't going to be perfect."

"Like what?" Despite myself, I am buying her friendship routine.

"Like love is never going to be as rewarding as sex or power."

"I want all of it wrapped up in one."

She cackles and leans back in her chair. "It'll never happen. You grab whichever piece of happiness falls in your lap. But don't expect the whole kit and kaboodle wrapped up in a big fancy bow."

"Frances." I put the goblet down and stand up. "Thanks for the little pearl of wisdom. But save your breath. I'm nothing like you."

She laughs. "Then why did you come here?"

This is when a negotiating diva takes over my soul and I spit out my demands. "I want a limo to pick up and drop off Miss Bubbles every day. I want her to make fifty more dollars a show. And I want my name in the programs."

"The limo, thirty-five a show and no name."

"I want my name."

"The limo and forty a show and no name."

I take a deep breath and wait for three seconds before speaking very, very slowly. "Frances, I want my name in that program. No name, no deal."

Frances leans back and looks at me. She cocks her eyebrow and smiles. "A regular car service, thirty-five a show and your name in the program."

"Done." I reach out to her, and we shake hands. "You'll send the car tonight."

"And you'll forget all about that little scene in the bushes."

"What scene?"

"See what I mean Stella? You're exactly like me. I bet you've never let marriage get in the way of good sex."

"Frances." My head is shaking and for a second I'm about to spit on the deal we've just hammered out to rip her a new one.

But she interrupts me with, "At least that's what I hear from Sandra Davis's friends."

Sucker-punched right in the gut. My face goes cold and I'm sure very pale, and my fingers curl until my nails have little pieces of desk underneath them. How could Frances know about Joshua and me? I suddenly realize that she is completely playing a game with me, one in which I don't know the rules at all.

Frances sips her water. "It's been a pleasure speaking with you, Stella. Have a nice day." She sits and picks up some papers from her desk, swivels toward the window and leaves me to walk out unobserved.

When the cool air of 7th Avenue slaps me in the face a few minutes later, I am still unsure of what just happened. And despite myself, Frances's words spin around my head, like a tornado, picking up memories and sloshing them around in my brain while I ask myself, "Is that an example of how I'm like Frances?" The time I told Joshua I loved him. Did I mean it? Or when I met Jasper and felt relief and hope. Finding a meal ticket, like Frances did? I start walking really fast, trying to get away from my own thoughts.

Because none of those things that happened in the past matter anymore. I am going to do this on my own. A man? Who needs one? No man has ever brought me happiness, from my nonexistent father to my stepdad to Joshua to Jasper to all the countless nobodies who have shared my bed and not cared a whit about my aspirations.

Well, fuck 'em all. From this moment, here in Times Square, staring at the billboards and theater advertisements and TKTS line, I declare that the rest of my life, all my successes, money and accomplishments, are going to be earned the old-fashioned way. *Work* and *talent*. It's about time I did my mother proud.

When I get to the audition five minutes later, I am filled with determination. This feeling is new to me. It's like I know what is going to happen. I have no choice but to succeed.

The monitor stands, leaning against the wall and looking surreptitiously down the shirt of a girl who is seated to his left.

"Hey are you the monitor? Is it too late to sign up?"

He puts my name down and I see over the edge of the clipboard that I'm up in three girls. This is fate! It's never this unpopulated at these things!

I wait patiently and hum my song under my breath until my name is called.

I slip the headshot into the sweaty hand of the monitor and hear him call my name.

"Stella Monroe."

"Stella," says the fat, bald man behind the table at the far end of the room. "Did you know your name means star?"

A deep breath fills my lungs and with my exhale I feel supreme. A grin creeps across my face and I say, loud and clear and bellowing, "I know. I was named for it and I'm meant to be one."

The man chuckles and turns to the smallish, facial-hair covered man on his right. "A confident singer. I like that. Okay, star-to-be, what are we hearing today?"

"'Cockeyed Optimist' from *South Pacific*." I hand my sheet music to the pianist who looks it over and then says, "No problem." My feet root themselves to the spot. I look at the people behind the table and pin all my hopes on them. The piano trills and the descending arpeggio of the introduction curls its way toward me. I take another deep breath and open my mouth, and start singing about being optimistic despite living through some sad times, and about not caring that I seem naïve. My voice sounds clear and sure, and I know I'm nailing the song. Then the plunk-plunk of the bass notes leads me into the second verse.

"*I ha*—"

"Okay. Thank you." I keep singing.

"Okay! Um, Stella? Thank you, that's enough!"

I stutter and stare at them. "Thank you very much," the bald man says.

I'm supposed to leave now but my feet aren't moving. "But that can't be it," I say, more to the walls than to anybody. "I need this job."

The bald man looks at me and says, "We've seen one hundred and forty-five girls today who need this job. Next."

The pianist hands me my sheet music with nary a word and I walk, numbly, into the hallway and head for home.

My luck has run out. And though it's a short walk and though my trips home have been fraught with tears lately, I decide to throw an all-out temper tantrum on the way to my apartment. Crying, sniffling, wiping my nose, yelling at pedestrians who are walking too slow in front of me, getting angry when pedestrians cut me off. Beautiful. A homeless person on the corner of 9th and 48th actually gives me a Kleenex. That's how awful I look.

When I get to the front of my apartment building, I rail at the stone angel like I am King Lear. And, here's a news flash: slapping stone isn't so easy on the palms. My path of destruction continues when I get inside. I throw my sheet music at my reflection in the television, and the pages scatter like confetti, celebrating my failure. Miss Bubbles goes running for the closet, and she makes quite a racket barricading herself behind all my shoes. I throw myself on my couch and beat my fists into the cushions, really reveling in my despondency.

Then the phone rings. I freeze with a fist midair, just waiting to hear my mother's voice.

And sure enough, my psychic powers don't disappoint.

"Little Stella-star, call your mother!" When she hangs up, I continue my tantrum. After a good half an hour of this, I go to the deli on the corner, get two pints of Ben and Jerry's Phish Food, a six-pack of beer and a bag of Twizzlers. Then I ensconce myself on my couch and watch old movies on AMC, stopping only to deliver Miss Bubbles into the waiting arms of Shirley, who apparently is going to be accompanying the cat on her chauffeured trips to the theater. How nice for them both.

I fall asleep on the couch and wake up the next morning with tangled hair and Phish Food smeared across my chin. I don't call my mother back. Because I don't think she wants to hear what I have to say, which is this.

I'm tired. Of not getting ahead. And I just don't want to do it anymore.

She won't understand wanting to take a break. And so, I am going to avoid her like the plague, like any good daughter would do to their sweet mother who only wants what is best for them.

Chapter 21

I've decided that I am going to die all alone, with a stick of butter in one pocket, my cloverleaf pendant tied around my neck and Miss Bubbles's diamond-studded collar around my ankle. People will find my rotting body three days after I've expired, shake their heads and say, "Her mother will be so disappointed."

Speaking of my mother, when the phone rings I just know it's going to be her. I grab my glass of lemonade from the counter, set my mixing bowl down, pick up the copy of *Backstage* from the coffee table and answer the phone.

"Stella? It's your mother."

"Hi, Mom." I balance the phone between my ear and my shoulder while I thumb through the paper and look for today's auditions.

"Well, my darling, and how are you today?"

"Mom, I'm good. I can't talk now, though, because I just walked in the door." I rapidly leaf through the pages. Skimming, skimming, there! Found one.

"You weren't out drinking were you?"

"No, no, Mom," my thumb follows the edge of an audition ad for *Man of La Mancha.* "I was auditioning for *Man of La Mancha.*"

"Little Star! You were? For the Broadway company?"

"Nope. The tour. It was a singing call. I'm going back to dance at the end of the week." I sit on the couch, stretch my legs out in front of me and stare at the ceiling.

"Little Star, that's fabulous. I'm really proud of you, what is that, the sixth audition this week?"

"Seventh. I've been going once a day. But listen Mom, I've got to go, I need a shower."

"Okay, darling, knock 'em dead."

And that's how easy it is to keep my mother happy. All week, since the *South Pacific* fiasco, I've been picking auditions out of *Backstage* and telling her that I went out on them. She totally believes me, and just to keep all my bases covered, I've made sure that every single call I tell her about is one that has actually been listed in the paper. There is such a thing as the Internet and she could easily go to www.backstage.com and check up on me. My business with her done for the day, I retreat back into the kitchen and try not to think of what a coward I am.

Things have been awfully quiet here since Frances and I struck up our deal. I've only been to the theater once, and that was to see the new program with my name printed on the inside as owner/trainer of the cat. I grabbed a few extra copies to send to my mother. They're still sitting in a neat stack on my kitchen counter. I don't have the money to send them, and truthfully, she might not think they're that special. I mean, *owner/trainer?* Is that what I've spent all these years trying to accomplish? A ten-point font mention at the back of a program to an off-Broadway play?

The day after I lost the *South Pacific* part, I locked myself in my apartment and baked twenty cakes. *Twenty.* I scraped together what little catering money I had left and bought enough

flour, sugar and eggs to feed a small battalion of freedom fight-
ers. You name it, I baked it. Chocolate, peanut butter with
chocolate chunks, vanilla, strawberry, layer cakes, tortes, an up-
side-down pineapple/plum cake, angel's food, devil's food, a
marshmallow contraption with cinnamon and cocoa, I could
go on and on. By the time the car service came to pick up Miss
Bubbles, I couldn't even see through the stacks of cakes into
the rest of the apartment.

And of course I had no one to eat them, since Christian has
kept his distance. A couple of times I thought about leaving
him a cake as a peace offering, but then I'd remember the look
in his eye when he walked out of my apartment that day. I
know I'll have to go up there eventually, even if just to return
his stinking blazer, which I had dry-cleaned in a fit of penance,
and his dumb T-shirt. But that can wait until I've washed the
T-shirt, which can wait until I'm done using it as my night-
gown at night, which will have to wait until I get off my ass
and actually do some laundry. So you can see how dim a possibility he and I ever seeing each other again truly is.

Anyway, the morning after the cake-baking extravaganza, I
started walking around to the delis, cafés and restaurants in my
neighborhood asking if they would take some free cakes off
my hands. It's amazing how acquiescent people will be when
you are standing in front of them with a dripping cake in each
palm. I unloaded fourteen cakes in two hours, and then I
wheeled the rest in a red wagon to Hell's Bar and begged Rod
to take them.

I stayed and had a drink on the house before going home and
starting the whole process over. So it's been a week and I've since
supplied the neighborhood with almost three-dozen cakes.

Right now, it's Friday, Bubbles is gone for the day because
of a benefit matinee performance, and I am whisking some egg
and sugar, creating a meringue topping for a raspberry tart.

This is the happiest I've been all day, even though the thunk
of Christian's typewriter keys is chipping away at my resolve.

The front door's lock clicks and Steve comes walking in, coiffed and tanned to perfection.

"Hey, daytime diva," I say while whisking an egg frenzy.

He throws his bag on the couch and comes bounding over to the breakfast bar. I haven't seen him too much since he started taping this week. He's at work from five in the morning to almost eleven at night. No joke.

"Still baking I see."

I smugly sneer at him. "Leave me alone."

"This is some therapy you've got going here." He sticks his finger into a bowl of buttercream frosting and takes a nice long lick.

"If you do that again, I'm calling the soap opera police."

"Now explain to me why you are holed up in this house baking away and not going to auditions?"

"I'm never auditioning again."

"Uh-huh."

"I'm serious. I'm tired of being cut off and rejected and not discovered."

He smacks his lips together and takes another fingerful of frosting. "Michaela told me that you've been supplying the neighborhood with sweets."

"So what if I am."

"Well," he gets up and goes over to his bag, opens it and starts digging. "I got you something." He pulls out a small stack of what looks to be business cards and hands them to me. I wipe my dusty fingers on a dishtowel before grabbing them. He smiles expectantly, waiting for my reaction. On top of the cards is a cartoon image of a girl in a pink tutu and shimmery top, with a plate in her hand. On top of the plate is an oversized cake decorated in peppermint stripes of white and pink, with gummy fruit and strawberries teeming on top of it. On top of the card these words are printed: STELLA'S SWEET SUPPLIES. Underneath in smaller print is: CAKES TO MAKE YOU FEEL GREAT. I look up at Steve and he is grinning, "Do you like them? Peter made them on his computer but you can't tell, can you? Don't the graphics look professional?"

"But what are they for?" I hand them back to him.

A puzzled look overtakes Steve's smiling face and he waves them away. "They're for you, to give to people when you're giving away your cakes. That way if people want more, they can call you."

I shake my head. "But I don't care about that. I just needed to get rid of them."

"But this way, you can get repeat customers and maybe make a little bit of money."

They feel hot in my hand, and the bright colors of the girl's outfit swirl around in my brain. "Thanks, I guess." I put them in a neat pile on top of the playbills.

"What's wrong?"

"Nothing." I put the meringue in the refrigerator and walk over to my bed, where I collapse in a heap.

Steve follows me and stands in the doorway for a second before picking a hairbrush up off my dresser. "Sit up." He crawls onto my bed and situates himself behind me.

"Don't you have to be at the studio?" My voice is a monotone moan.

"I have the afternoon off."

"Don't you have to be memorizing your dialogue?"

"I can take a half hour to spend with my good friend Stella." He sinks the bristles of the brush into my head and starts stroking my hair until I close my eyes.

"You used to do this all the time in school." He begins to divide my hair into sections. "Gosh, things were simpler then."

He kisses the top of my head. "Things are still pretty simple, you're just not letting them be that way."

I say nothing. He changes the topic. "I was thinking. What are you wearing to the wedding?"

"I don't know."

"It's in two days."

"I'll figure it out in two days, then."

"Are you going to hide out in this apartment for the rest of your life?"

"I was thinking about it."

"Well I'm doing your hair up just right so that we can go have a drink at Hell's."

"I don't really feel like it, Steve."

He throws his hands up in mock frustration. "That's it! I'm calling a doctor."

"I don't need a doctor." This discussion is making me sleepy.

"Well you're coming with me. It's the last chance the three of us will have to be together before Mic becomes a married hag."

A half hour later the three of us are huddled around one of the small circular tables at the back of Hell's. The light is soft around us. We're far enough away from the door that it looks like dusk. People are everywhere, and I see at least three people sinking their forks into my cakes. Michaela is giggling while trying to read Steve's palm.

"Wait, that's the life line, right?" And she consults a miniature volume that is spread open on her lap.

"You don't know what you're doing." Steve guffaws and takes a sip of his cappuccino. My heart feels heavy and I can barely lift my hands from the table to sip my chocolate martini.

Everyone seems so carefree. Steve, of course, because he has a great job and a good relationship. He just looks so, so relaxed. I guess that's what comes of being secure in yourself. And Michaela, who could be happy in any situation. But her skin is glowing. In two days she's marrying an illegal alien in a New York City bar and inheriting a family of Venezuelan refugees. She couldn't look happier.

"Oh, wait, it's the love line. Right." She peers into his hand.

"Yep, success in love and work. See how this line is deeper than the other two? That means that your career is always going to be the most secure thing in your life."

"Read mine," I say, and thrust my hand at her.

She takes my hand gently in hers and looks for a second.

"Do you see anything about her doing the dishes in there?" I shoot Steve a look.

"Nope, just see here how this line splits in two? It means you have an important choice to make in your life."

"An important choice?"

"Yes. You can do what you are meant to do or what you think you want to do."

Steve makes an agreeing gurgle in his throat, fully supporting this crock of bull that Michaela is spouting.

I look into my hand and don't see anything but dried-on flour caked to my wrist. I flake it away with my pinkie nail. "A choice, huh?"

"Yep, it's up to you."

Steve stretches and points to the table next to us. "Is that one of your cakes?"

I look over and see a couple sharing a bite of chocolate mint cake with mint sprinkled across the top. "Yeah, that's mine."

"Oh! This reminds me!" Michaela gets up and runs into the back of the bar. She runs back out and screams, "I'll be right back!" before disappearing behind the thick red curtain that leads to the kitchen.

"There she goes, our little angel." Steve says.

"She sure seems happy, doesn't she?" I manage weakly, feeling far too tired to make conversation but knowing I have to at least try.

"Yes she sure does, and someone I know feels like their life has been flushed down the toilet." He puts his elbows on the table and supports his chin in his hands. "Let's talk, little lamb."

"I don't feel like talking," I mutter, and grab a dinner roll.

Butter and bread and chocolate martinis are the only things that are going to make me feel better.

"Spill it right now or I won't order you another martini."

I throw the knife down on the table and it clatters. After shoving a huge bite of buttered bread into my mouth, I respond to Steve's inquisition. "I've just got a lot on my mind."

"Such as…" He is not going to quit until I talk. I can tell by the quiver of his upper lip.

"Such as Frances Paine told me that I am just like her, looking for a man who can make all my dreams come true."

"So?"

"So?"

"So she's right. You've been saying that as long as I've known you."

"Well, now I'm wondering if that's such a good idea. I mean, I broke up with Joshua because—"

"—because he wasn't helping your career."

"No! Because he was married and because he wasn't ever going to marry me!"

Steve stirs the ice cubes in his water and thoughtfully replies, "So my little girl's getting a conscience, huh?"

"I guess so. It's just that maybe I shouldn't be looking to someone else to make my life more comfortable. Maybe I have to do that on my own."

"Sheesh, a conscience *and* maturity all in one sitting. I don't even know you anymore."

At this I laugh, even though a bottomless pit of insecurity is devouring my insides. I chew another piece of bread slowly.

"Dare I even ask about the great audition crisis?"

"I've given you enough for one day."

"Don't talk with your mouth full." I lean over and kiss his cheek. "Yuck!" He shouts and starts wiping my kiss off. Michaela comes running breathlessly up to our table and plunks herself down. "Here!" She screams with glee and thrusts an envelope into my hand.

"What is it?"

Steve and Michaela are grinning at me.

"This is a thank-you from Carlo and me for being our head chef."

Inside the envelope there's a check made out for one thousand dollars. I look up confusedly.

"What else is in there?" she gently prods me to look again. Behind the check is a little note that says: *Earmarked for nonbackyard headshots.*

"Michaela, this is a lot of money." My voice sounds choked up.

"No it's not, Stell. Do you know how much it costs to have a wedding catered? And you're totally doing it for free when you could be charging a bundle for your time. *And* I know you spent money on all the practice food you made for us."

She reaches across the table and hugs me, so tight that I can't breathe. Steve just sits back, grinning like an idiot. "Look at my girls," he says.

When I get home, later, I place the check on the pile of programs and business cards. Then I take a dish towel from the pantry and cover the whole stack of items, so I don't have to look at them.

Chapter 22

Before I know it, the day I've been dreading is here. Michaela's wedding day. The day I add "best friend" to the list of things I don't have anymore. Along with "pet who depends on me for a living," and "neighbor who eats my food," and "career possibilities," and "boyfriend who is going to help me get ahead."

Not that I'm depressed or anything, but I have noticed that lately I've been talking to my kitchen supplies. If Miss Bubbles is home, she'll listen in and try to give advice, too. Too bad I don't understand "Meow," because I'm sure that she's got my life all figured out.

But for now I am standing in the doorway of the kitchen of Hell's Bar, my back to the ovens and amazing ranges, where all my work has been completed. Though I've been avoiding the reality of Michaela's impending marriage, I will admit that this little food project has kept my mind off the pit of despair that is my life. In times of trial, I've always turned to my kitchen, and I know that I'm hiding out from my mother and auditions, but whatever. I don't know what else to do.

Now the filets are in the oven, and the chicken is done. I made the cakes yesterday. There's nothing left to do, so I stand and survey the scene at the bar. You'd never know this was a place where Michaela and I have gotten drunk and sick at least a hundred times. The bar is draped in gauzy white material that is knotted in sections and gathered up to create a curtained effect. Soft sounds of the *Buena Vista Social Club* fill the room, and the whole mood in here is relaxed and happy. The lights are up, and Michaela, who's wearing a slip, and Rod, who is dressed in a very nice suit—jacket spread out over the back of one of the bar stools—are putting out candles, three each of varying length and color, on the small tables. The tables have been cleared away from the floor, and the chairs too, so that they line the sides of the room. This, I suppose, is to provide a dance space after the vows. Michaela looks lovely, with her hair pinned to her head but hanging down in soft curls. Her green eyes are shining with happiness, and she sets the candles down with such a gentleness, you just know she is going to treat her marriage the same way. She catches me staring at her and grins.

"How's the food coming?" Michaela's voice drifts over to where I stand, and I can't believe how calm she sounds.

"It's all set, except I burned all the chicken."

"What?" She stops what she is doing and turns to me, a look of horror on her face.

"I'm kidding!" I step up to her and wait for her to put the candle down before hugging her as tightly as one girl can ever possibly hug another. "I love you, Mic." I hope she knows that she is the best friend I've ever had.

"Aw, Stell," she whispers into my shoulder. "You're my sister. I'm the luckiest girl in the whole wide world."

"Hello girls." Carlo's Spanish accent greets us and I immediately jump in front of Michaela's body. "Carlo! Go away! You can't see her yet!"

Michaela laughs at me and steps out from my cover. "Stella, you're so superstitious. Nothing is going to go wrong." She peers into his eyes and he touches her face. They kiss while I watch, my hands folded against my waist. Carlo asks me if everything is all set and I tell him not to worry, that he is going to have the best day ever. They hold hands and walk toward the back of the bar. When they get to a stool, Carlo helps Michaela sit down before pulling out a tiny box from his pants pocket. She throws her arms around him before even opening it.

"So cute it's sickening, huh?" Rod steps beside me and watches the cooing couple.

"Yeah, pretty sickening. But in a good way."

"So Stella, you have everything you need back in the kitchen?"

"Oh, yeah, everyone back there has been really helpful. It's all done, actually, I'm just going to go back and change for the ceremony."

"Stella, we missed the cakes yesterday."

"Well I was working on the wedding cake. No time for anything else, you know how it is."

Rod crosses his arms and looks up at the ceiling for a minute. "I was thinking, Stella, that I'd like a standing order from you." I don't understand what he's getting at right away, until he says, "Of the cakes."

"A standing order?"

"Yeah, I'd like to order six cakes every Monday and Friday from you. How much do you charge?"

I know that I'm staring, but I'm trying to process the question. It's never occurred to me to ask for money for my food. "I have no idea Rod, I'll have to ask Steve and get back to you."

Rod smiles and laughs. "Well, just let me know, because my customers love them and I think we could make some money if we had them all the time."

I tell him I'll think about it and he resumes his candle-setting-out activity. I head for the door, and home.

There's so much to think about these days, and every walk, even a short one from the bar to my apartment is filled with thoughts and life-altering moments. In the days since the *South Pacific* audition, something has shifted. I don't know what it is, but now when I look up at the billboards, like I'm doing now, confronting the black-clad legs of *Chicago* dancers, I don't feel envy. Just a feeling like heaviness creeping on top of my shoulders.

One thing I've absolutely decided for sure. I don't want to be like Frances Paine, trolling for actors when I'm fifty. And as much as I love her, I don't want to be like my mother, constantly worrying about something that she has no control over, thinking of a life that has passed her by. And I can't live my whole life feeling guilty about her. And I don't want to depend on fickle, unfaithful characters like Joshua and Jasper for my happiness. The problem is now I don't know what the hell to do with my life.

But when I get to my apartment, I know exactly what I have to do. I kiss the feet of the stone angel, gaze up into her rocky face and ask her to wish me well. Inside my building, my front door looms ahead of me. I walk toward it slowly, like I'm heading to the gallows. I let myself in, go to my room and open my closet. Hanging there is Christian's blazer, its shoulders covered in dry cleaner's paper and wrapped in plastic. I lift the plastic and try to smell Christian on the coat, but it's been sanitized away. I had it cleaned for him, because he'll probably want to wear it to the wedding. It's been sitting in my closet since Thursday, three whole days before I've worked up the courage to bring it upstairs. And now I'm running out of time. I wish Miss Bubbles were here or Steve, anyone to give me an encouraging glance. But Steve's at Peter's and Miss Bubbles is once again at a matinee. That cat goes out more than me.

God there are so many steps leading up to Christian's apartment. Eric Clapton seeps into the hallway, and the sound of Christian walking around behind his door fills my ears. I lean against the door, just like in a scene I'm sure Steve will someday film for *All My Children*. The blazer weighs my arm down, causing my shoulder to cramp, but I'm too scared to knock.

I don't want him to look at me like he did the other day. Like I'm too stupid to know what's good for me. But I can't be a coward, forever, right? I touch my pendant to my lips and knock, three times. The sound of him walking around gets louder and louder until he finally opens the door.

Christian looks surprised to see me standing there, and just stares at me at first, with his arm on the door. He looks so good, in jeans and a button-down shirt, but hardly appropriate for a wedding. He's barefoot and just standing there. So I say, more to his feet than his face, "Hey."

Christian purses his lips and says nothing while I grind my toe into the floor.

"Is that mine?" he asks and gestures toward the blazer. His voice sounds sweet and gentle, like caramel melting over vanilla ice cream.

"Um, yeah." I finally find my voice but not words. He takes the blazer from my hands and our fingers touch briefly. "I thought you might want it for today. I mean, you can't wear jeans, right?"

Christian looks at the coat then back at me. "Thanks Stella," he speaks so softly. "I appreciate it."

"It's not a problem." He looks into his apartment and back at me. There is so much sun streaming into his windows that it makes him look backlit, like a really cool stage effect. Our silence is bottomless, and I want so desperately to say something to him that will make everything between us okay. "Listen, Christian…"

"Thanks a lot, Stella. I'll see you later." He kind of half smiles before closing the door in my face. And really, what else do I deserve but this? I go back down to my apartment, and with each step I think of all the ways I have manipulated Christian for my own purposes, like Frances said I did. I palm off my food on him. I expect him to take care of things for me, like when my doors squeak or the blinds need to be hung, but whenever we've had a social function and he's shown up, I've been incredibly rude to him. And I never enjoy his company without ridiculing him for some reason. By the time I get to my front door, shuffle through my empty living room and start the shower, my brain is flooded with remorse.

I mean, really, just because he isn't an actor and can't bring me to any openings or fancy parties, is that a reason to totally discount somebody?

I sit on the edge of the tub and let the steam of the shower permeate the room. When it's good and hot like a steam bath, I step inside and let the water wash away a tear or two. I haven't felt this awful since the day I found out Josh's wife was pregnant. And here, standing naked with the water running over my body, and a bar of Dove soap in my hand, is when I realize something I should've known all along.

I'm in love with Christian. My skin breaks out in a rash of gooseflesh, and I stare openmouthed at the walls of the shower. I'm in love with Christian. I love him. I love how he looks and that he's smart and how he always has something obnoxious to say to me when I'm being fresh. And I love that he appreciates my cooking. It sounds stupid but that's a big thing. Because cooking is what I love most.

And then another thunderbolt hits me. Cooking is what I love most. What the hell's in this water, anyway? But it's true. If I stop to think about whether I'd like to be in a play or making a lemon tart, there's no contest. I sink down and sit in the tub, and the water runs over my back, cascading down into the drain. Another scene I'm sure that Steve will be filming for *All My Children* soon.

After I finish my shower, I step into the bathroom a new woman. A bit panicked, but a new woman. With the palm of my hand I clear away a circle of clarity on the mirror and stare. No mole, no pendant, no nothing. Just me with no makeup and my hair dripping down to my shoulders, looking clear-eyed and very, very naked. Walking to my room, my legs feel stronger, like my muscles have doubled their size in the past sixty seconds. But I also feel like I'm in a brand-new pair of shoes and am having trouble walking in them. My bed is a sloppy unmade mess and I pull the covers straight and tidy over the mattress. The towel clings to my body until I let it drop to the floor in a puddle, and then I select clothes to wear, a pink dress with rosebud flowers along the hem and neckline that Michaela specifically asked for.

I put minimal makeup on, don't draw in my mole for the first time in over a decade and leave my hair alone, not even bothering to dry it. I bang into my glass coffee table on the way to the kitchen, and then lift the dish towel that covers Mic's check and the business cards like a magician revealing his magic trick. The cards fit neatly in the palm of my hand, and I look at them as you would look at a new baby. An introductory look, a look that says hello and we are together now.

As I'm walking out the door, trying to come up with a speech for Christian that will simultaneously move his heart and drive him to bend me over in a movie-ending kiss, clutching my purse under my left arm, shaking my semidry hair from my nonmoled face, ignoring the sticky feeling of the cloverleaf pendant against the skin of my chest, and wobbling in the shoes I can't afford, the phone rings.

I throw everything down and pick up.

After a five-second silence, the person on the other end clears his throat and says, "Stella? It's Kevin."

"Hi. What's up?" It doesn't occur to me that Kevin should be getting ready for the show he has to run and not calling me.

But I'm way too anxious to get to Hell's and see Christian in his blazer to sit on the phone with this guy, so before he has a chance to make another lame offer to get together, I say, "Kevin, I can't really talk right now. Did Bubbles get there okay?"

"Well, that's the thing, Stella. Miss Bubbles ran away. We were rehearsing a scene and she ran from the stage, and right out the side entrance. Nobody can find her."

Chapter 23

The first thing I do is get on the phone with Shirley, who between sobs and dramatic gasps, tells me that the Paines have called in the ASPCA to help find the cat. I, of course, can do nothing until after Michaela's wedding, and tell Shirley that I'll be there as soon as I can.

Then Kevin gets back on the phone and tells me the matinee has been canceled and that the entire production is in jeopardy if they can't find her. I tell him I don't care about the dumb play and that my cat better be safe and sound or else. Then I slam the phone down, without really meaning to. Kevin sounded appropriately apologetic and it's obviously not his fault, but come on. I mean, what the hell kind of a joke is this? My fists curl toward God or whoever is up there and a scream gurgles up from the pit of my sorrow. *"Ha! Very funny!"* Because, this is just ridiculous! I want to go to my dear friend's wedding and grovel at the sexy feet of the man I love. And I want to *enjoy* these things.

When I get outside I just shake my head at the stone angel and rush past her, trying not to fall off of my heels or rip my dress.

I run into Hell's Bar with about five minutes to spare before they start the vows. More than two dozen people are sitting in the seats, craning their necks and turning to each other,
chatting, preparing, buzzing about. "What do you think her
dress is going to look like?" drifts over to where I stand in the
doorway. Bob Marley asks "Is this Love?" and an official-look-
ing man mills around the bar, holding a Bible against his torso
with a death grip. It looks like everyone's waiting on me, because as soon as he sees me Steve throws up his hands and
rushes toward the back, I assume to let Michaela know we can
begin. I walk through the crowds of people gathered around
the tables. Christian is sitting with Peter at a table off to the
left. He looks at me and betrays nothing. No smile, no blink.
He doesn't even look away. I try to convey everything I feel
for him through my eyes but soon Steve's torso is poking out
from behind the curtain and he's violently gesturing for me
to get back there.

"Where the hell have you been?" He grabs my arm and
walks me into the girls' bathroom, where Michaela is standing
in front of the mirror, staring at herself.

"Mic!" I can't help myself. I rush her like she is a superstar
and hug her so tightly. She is the most beautiful woman I've
ever seen, an angel in the restroom of Hell's Bar.

"You're gonna crush her veil you dolt!" Steve pries my arms
off of Mic and straightens first Michaela's headpiece and then
my dress.

"Are you ready?" he says to Michaela.

She nods once. "I can't wait."

I get teary-eyed, and follow them out into the main room,
where Carlo is standing in front of the tables wearing the
dorkiest grin I've ever seen plastered on a sober person. He's
in a white linen suit with a black tie and his face is completely
clean-shaven. The reverend clears his throat and Steve and I take
our places behind Mic. I'm standing right in front of Christian, and I can sense his presence like a force field, a magnet that

I'm trying to ignore. I hope he likes my dress. I hope he thinks I look pretty. Does he like pink? Oh Jesus, is *this* love? Insecurity and worry?!

So what I learn at Michaela's wedding is that I'm a shitty friend. Because throughout the whole service, I can't concentrate. Thoughts of Christian flicker through my head like a film, alternating with images of Miss Bubbles huddled against a doorway. Like the night I found her wrapped in a coat of mud and papered in a newsprint blanket and mewing desperately against the alley walls of a 34th Street gutter. These thoughts fill my mind while I stare at the reverend. I float in and out of consciousness enough to hear Michaela say "I do," and see Carlo wipe a tear from his face. I hope some nice girl will find Miss Bubbles and bring her to a nice apartment with a view and huge closets and an industrial-sized refrigerator. When the ceremony is over and Mic and Carlo kiss, I look at Christian to see if he's watching me, but no, he's focused on the happy couple as they walk to the crowd of their friends and family. I sidle up to Steve and tell him the news about Miss Bubbles before running into the kitchen and taking care of getting the plates of food out to the masses.

And still, Miss Bubbles's delicate little body is in my mind, and I spill some au jus sauce all over one of the busboys who is helping to serve. "Sorry, Juan! Sorry!" I blurt as I swat at his pudgy middle with a dry towel. I tell all the waiters not to bring a plate to the man in the double-breasted navy blazer. They stare at me, wondering what a double-breasted navy blazer is, I suppose. "The table to the right of the bar! With the two men! Just don't serve him, Jesus!" His plate is already in my hands, teeming with extra helpings of everything. I push my body through the heavy curtain and carry it out to him myself.

My feet are cement slabs and my stomach feels like it's a ship being tossed on the waves of a tsunami. Christian is talking to Peter and they are laughing, having a great time. How can he be laughing at a moment like this? I walk up to him and say, "Excuse me."

They look at me. Christian's wineglass is suspended in mid-air and I see that it is filled with water. Peter all of a sudden becomes very engrossed in examining his fingernails.

"You look really nice in your blazer." I catch a quick peek at Christian's face before staring straight into the pork loin on his plate. I'm shy. Apparently love makes you insecure and shy. Fucking great.

"The food looks really delicious, Stell." Peter is so sweet. But I wish he would go away.

I just don't know what to do. I stand there and Christian looks patiently at me, knowing his dinner is in my hands. Peter makes a popping sound with his lips and I know that I can't do nothing. So I put the plate down and whisper in Christian's ear, "I put extra ginger in the apple tart for you. I think you'll like that." Christian stares at me for a second. I catch the scent of his cologne and fight the urge to curl up in his lap and tell him about Miss Bubbles, but he looks at the plate of food and takes a bite.

He takes a second bite and says, with a semifull mouth might I add, "Are you going to stand there all night and watch me eat?"

I say, "sorry, sorry" over and over again and *back away* from him like an idiot geisha girl or something. What the hell has happened to my spunk?

When I get back to the kitchen, I yell at all the waiters to get going. Nothing like venting one's hurts to innocent bystanders. I spend the rest of the reception hovering around the kitchen curtain, straining to watch Christian and eavesdropping on the tables closest to me to see if they like the dinner.

After the desserts and a few more stolen glances at Christian, and Michaela and Carlo's first dance, and her father's toast, and Steve and Peter's karaoke rendition of "Endless Love," I grab my purse and head for the theater.

When I tell Michaela what happened on the way out the door, she gives me twenty dollars and tells me to take a cab.

Which I do.

"Step on it!" I scream through the plastic partition of the taxi. The car peels through the streets and I thank my lucky stars that my driver could care less about all the city's stupid traffic rules.

The daylight streams into the back seat of the car. Sun is good for Miss Bubbles. How far could she have gone, anyway? I reconstruct the event in my mind, over and over, trying to figure out how she made her escape. And though I come up with some good, daring scenarios in my head, one question remains. Why?

Seriously, why? I stare out the car window at the blur of passing window displays and think about what a good life Miss Bubbles has. Why would she want to throw it all away? She has a great job and an owner who loves her. She gets all the catnip she could ever want. Why would she run?

When my *Dukes of Hazzard*-worthy driver squeals up to the curb, I see two ASPCA cars parked in front of the theater. Kevin is taking a smoke break with one of the officers. He flicks his cigarette to the street when he sees me and shakes his head. I totter over to them in my heels

"Stella, I'm so sorry. We feel awful." I shrug off his attempt at putting his hand on my shoulder. "This is the cat's owner," Kevin says to the officer, who looks like Marge Simpson but with regular-toned skin and gray hair.

"Kevin, show me where she was when she ran away." He wordlessly leads me into the theater, and right away I see how dirty and dusty and dark it is inside. Tools litter the floor, coils of wire and plugs and extension cords create an obstacle course that's nearly impossible to navigate. A headless wig lies across a table, and three pinup pictures of half-naked blond women hang lifelessly from the back wall. All the teamsters look away as I pass.

"They were rehearsing the love scene," Kevin warbles his words. My senses are hyperalert as I search for clues.

"And you're absolutely sure she made it out the door? She's not hiding underneath one of the seats?"

Marge speaks up. "Nope. We checked the seats." Her voice sounds like a braying goat.

Kevin speaks over Marge, "No, we saw her run out the door. Johnny the electrician tried to catch her but she was too quick."

We get to the auditorium and Jasper is sitting on the lip of the stage with his head in his hands. I stop in my tracks and try to squelch the urge to run up and hit him with my purse. I just know this is his fault. He looks up and gives me a bland smile.

"So," Kevin jumps onstage. "Jasper was sitting right here," he moves to the couch set piece, "and he had her in his arms."

"You were holding her?" I ask incredulously. I *knew* this was his fault!

"Yeah. And she scratched the shit out of me when she jumped out of my arms."

"Did she hiss or anything?" I turn from Kevin to Jasper to Kevin again. Finally Jasper answers, "She hissed, she scratched, she leaped, she ran." The tone in his voice does something to my resolve and I storm up to him.

"Well, what did you do to her?" I demand, with my hands on my hips and my purse swinging by my side.

"What did *I* do to her? What did *you train* her to do?!" He jumps up and stares me in the eye, and stands so close to me that I imagine we look like two baseball managers debating a call.

"What?" I shake my head furiously, *"What?!"* I oh-so-intel-ligently ask again. "What the hell did you do to my cat, Jasper?!" At this, Jasper pinches my elbow in his hand, wheels me around, drags me out of the room and pushes me out the stage door. I nearly twist my ankle.

He turns around and, oblivious to the city life coming to a halt around us, says in a voice seething in rage, "Don't play in-nocent with me, Stella. You taught her to scratch me and told her to run away to get back at me!"

"What in the hell are you talking about! She's a cat! They're born knowing how to scratch!"

"So you don't deny that you sabotaged my show?!"

"You pompous idiot!" Name-calling. Gotta love it. "I didn't *sabotage* your freaking show."

Jasper says nothing but purses his lips and turns away.

I am too exasperated with him to give up. "And if you're so upset about your stupid play, why aren't you out here with an open can of tuna fish looking for my cat!"

Jasper takes a good long look at me. "I don't give a rat's ass about your stupid cat."

I slap him. Hard. Right across the face. And it feels good. It stings my hand. But it feels really good.

"If I don't find Miss Bubbles, I'm telling everybody in town about you and Frances. And how bad you are in bed. And that you like to have sex with small animals." I don't even know what I'm saying anymore, but I'm too full of steam to stop.

Until Jasper, who obviously had some sense knocked into him with my smack, takes my shoulders in his hands and says, "Okay, okay, okay. Just stop talking. I'm sorry about your cat. And I'm sorry about Frances. Okay?"

I wriggle out of his hands. "Okay. Now help me find Miss Bubbles."

Jasper, Kevin, Shirley and I look for Miss Bubbles all night. After I borrow some clothes and sneakers from wardrobe, Kevin and I wander east, checking side streets, trash cans, alleys, and stairwells all the way over to Avenue A. We head south down to Houston Street and zigzag back to the theater. When Shirley and Jasper show up, Shirley is still crying and Jasper looks like he's getting ready to commit murder.

He finds me sitting on the onstage sofa and plops down beside me.

"I meant what I said before. I'm sorry about everything."

I let out a bubble of air and pick at my thumbnail. "It's okay Jasper. I'm sorry for slapping you."

"I deserved it."

"You totally deserved it." I sneak a peek at him and a small smile tugs the corner of my lips upward.

"Come on," he says. "I'll buy you a drink. We'll make up." He nudges his nose behind my ear and kisses my lobe.

I turn to him. He is shooting smoldering looks my way, and he's backlit by soft stage lighting. I'm onstage with Jasper Hodge in the darkened Cherry Lane Theater, the hum of the lights my only orchestration and the din of a ladder being dragged across the floor of the wings my only applause. I stand up, take Jasper's hand. "I'm gonna go home. Have a good show tomorrow." And I walk out of the Cherry Lane Theater.

It's past two-thirty in the morning when I get home, and there isn't a light on in my apartment, except for the flashing red beam of the answering machine. I press the message button and sink down onto the couch.

Beep. "Stella, it's your mother. Call me right away."

Beep. "Stell, It's Steve. Call me at Peter's and let me know about Bubbles. You were great today. And two people asked me if you catered only weddings. I gave 'em your card."

Beep. "Stella, it's your mother. Call me right away, Little Star."

Beep. "Little Star. Where *are* you? Call me as soon as you get this."

Beep. "Stella. It's Rod. Sorry to call so soon after the wedding. But I really want to talk to you about those cakes."

Jesus is my dance card full. *Beep.* I bet another one from my mom. But no. Whoever it was hung up.

Thankfully the end of the messages. I get up and go into my bedroom, flick on the light and start to unzip my dress. Before I get it down to the bottom of my back, I start to cry. Hard. One of those good, deep cries that pulls garbage out of your toes and your tummy and throws it up in a fit of tears.

There's just been so much to deal with. I've been so worried about money and pictures and auditioning and getting that big break, waiting so patiently and actively for that moment where everything becomes easy and falls into place according to the plans my mother made for me. And I want it to stop. All of it.

I bend over, touch my toes and breathe in. Is twenty-five supposed to be such a hard age, anyway? Nobody really ever told me that it'd be so tough. Certainly my mother never warned me about any bumps in the road. According to her, I should've been too rich and far too famous by now to have to worry about anything.

I sink to my bed and clutch my pillow between my arms, crying the whole time. And then the phone rings. I glance at the clock—2:57 a.m. This can't be good.

I straighten myself out, kick off the dress and walk in my underwear over to the phone.

"Hul–loh?"

"Little Star! Where in God's creation have you been? Do you know how many times I've called you today?" Perfect.

"Mom, is everything okay? It's almost three in the morning!" My eyes are starting to puff shut.

"Well, I have to talk to you. It's important!"

"Oh, Mom. I've had a really long day."

"Well you sound awful. Is your face puffy?"

I wipe my hand over my face and sit in the dimness of my living room. "Why are you calling me so late?"

"Well, Sal and I had a big fight."

I almost hang up on her, because I can't take the dissolution of any more of my life's circumstances.

The words come tumbling out of her, she sounds like a breathless child rushing to get it all out of her system. "He says that I push you too hard. And, of course, I told him that he knows nothing about trying to be a performer, and that it's my duty as a mother to push you hard. Then he said if being a performer is so important to me, I should just go do it myself and leave you alone. And so I packed Stewart up in the car and headed for you and New York."

"Mom—"

"But I started to think about it, and instead of leaving town I went straight to the Saginaw Community Theater and guess what? I talked to some people and they let me sing and do a dance combination and now I'm going to be Auntie Mame in their summer production! Can you believe it?" She guffaws in my ear.

Just a little background here. In all the years I've known my mother, through all the auditions I've been to and all the magazines she's mutilated to send me clippings through the mail, my mother has never once, never *once,* gone on an audition or done any type of dancing or acting.

I'm so shocked I forget to be tired. "What? You what?" I sit up in the dusky light and feel my forehead crinkle.

"It's all thanks to Sal. And you. You inspired me with all your hard work."

I choke like an overfed baby. "Mom, I, Mom, I don't understand." Then I recover myself. "I mean, that's great. Jeez. That's great!"

"Now there will be two stars in the family."

And then, probably because I didn't plan on it, and probably because it's almost three in the morning and there is no sanity at nighttime, and probably because if I don't do it now I'll never do it, I say to my mother, "Actually, Mom? I don't think I want to do this anymore. Acting I mean. I think I want to be a cook instead."

My comment is met with complete and utterly nerve-racking silence.

"Mom?"

Her response is a bit more silence before this gem: "Are you high?"

"Mom! I'm not high!"

"Well, then, what are you talking about? Are you drunk?"

I swallow hard. "Actually, Mom, I'm totally sober. And I love you, Mom, but I don't think I want this anymore. I'm quitting."

I bite my lower lip so hard it can only be a matter of time before it starts to bleed.

"Mom?"

"Stella Aurora Monroe. I'm calling you in the morning when your head is screwed on straight. And I thank you very much for trying to ruin my good news!" And then she hangs up on me.

I stare at the phone and say, "Well that went well," to nobody at all.

What a day. I trudge over to the kitchen to see if there's anything going on. Nothing—all my supplies are sleeping soundly in the cupboards. I open each cabinet, each drawer and look at all my utensils, pots and pans. I open the fridge and take stock of my ingredients. How many eggs would it take to make a batch of cakes every week? How much flour? And what about flavors? I'll have to ask Rod if I can pick the kinds of cakes I get to bake. I finger the remaining business cards that are sitting on the counter and smile.

Even if my mother hates me, I feel pretty good.

If only Miss Bubbles would come home. And if only Christian would forgive me. Life could maybe look up.

Chapter 24

I jam a pillow over my head to block out the sound of the ringing phone. It's before 9:00 a.m., and the sunlight is bothering my eyes. And the ringing. Good lord, the ringing. I start to get annoyed before remembering that it could be Kevin reporting on Miss Bubbles. I leap out of bed, pull Christian's T-shirt down to my knees and stumble over to the phone.

"Hullo?"

"Stella." It's my mother. I'm not awake enough for this.

"Mom." Coffee. A pot of good, strong coffee will help me better deal with the onslaught of guilt about to head my way. I run into the kitchen and trip over one of Miss Bubbles's toys.

"I've been thinking, Little Star." Here it comes.

"Mom, I love you, but I can't change my mind about this." My eyes can barely open to the morning and here I am working on major issues with my mother.

"Well, if you would let me finish!" Her voice sounds chalky and reserved. "What I was going to say, is that I was thinking about your little pronouncement last night and I don't think all is lost."

"You don't?" My hand pauses midtask, my thumb resting on the red perk button.

"No, I don't. There are plenty of chefs who have their own television shows and do quite nicely for themselves. I'm particularly fond of that Nigella Lawson. She's quite lovely."

No, no, no, no, no, no, no. Red alert. She's not getting the point. "No, Mom, that's very sweet of you, but I—" I press down on the coffee button and hear the churn of the machine kick into life.

"Now, now, Little Star. What could possibly be wrong with having your own cooking show? It can't be that difficult, can it? There *is* a whole network devoted to it, you know."

The coffeepot fills up, and I take out a mug to prepare. "Mom. Listen to me, please." I stop what I'm doing. "Mom, I don't want to be famous. Or on television. I just want to bake my cakes and have a nice, quiet life."

Silence again.

"Mom?"

"Maybe you could be Oprah's chef. Or Matt Damon's?"

"Mom," now I'm talking to her like she's a six-year-old. "I want to do this my way. Okay?"

Silence.

"Mom?"

"This isn't the life I planned for you Stella. I wanted you to have no worries."

"Mom. This is the first morning I've woken up feeling like I know what to do in a long time."

I hear her breathe into the phone.

"Besides, the world can't handle the two of us on the stage."

"Stella."

"Mom—"

"Will you come see me in *Mame?*"

"Of course I will."

She sighs into the phone, takes a deep breath. And then she says, "Okay."

"Okay? That's it? Really?"

She doesn't answer me right away. "Yes. Really. I just… I want you to be happy."

"I think I'm gonna be, Mom. I really do."

"Okay, Stella. I love you. Knock 'em dead."

After she hangs up, I hold the phone in my hands for about five minutes and walk over to the mirror in the bathroom. I don't look any different, but boy do I feel it. Taller. And braver. More honest. I walk into my pink bedroom and look at the sequined ostrich feather above my bed. I pull a plastic binful of theater programs from under the mattress and lift the lid.

There are several old pictures of my mom in various productions throughout the years. *A Chorus Line. Little Me. The Fantasticks. The Music Man. West Side Story.* Who knows what would have happened to her if I hadn't come along. But who's to say that I ruined everything? Maybe I improved her life. I have to think I did.

Then I pick up a program from the production of *The King and I* I did when I was seventeen. God I hated that show. There's a picture of me in the back, painted up to look like an Asian princess. I look like my mom. But it's clearly me. I pack everything back up and slide it back beneath the bed. I reach out for the feather and stroke the plume.

I head back into the kitchen and drink my coffee. Two sips before dialing Kevin's cell phone number to ask him if they've found Miss Bubbles.

He picks up the phone sounding groggy and disoriented, and I realize it's so early in the morning he probably hasn't even gotten to the theater yet. "So you haven't heard anything?"

"Sorry, Stella. No sign. And the Paines have made the decision to recast."

I go crazy. "Recast? How can they recast? Miss Bubbles is out there, maybe wounded and scared for her life, and they're recasting?"

"Stella, Stella." He sounds desperate to quiet me. "It wasn't my decision. Frances told me to tell you that they'll be sending some money to cover the damages and that they'll keep the ASPCA on the case."

"I don't want money! I want my cat back!"

"Stella, it's the best I could do for you. I told her you'd probably sue."

His words sink in and my voice recedes into my throat. "You talked to her?"

"Yeah, yeah. Me and Jasper." Well, will wonders never cease? But it doesn't matter. Because I have no cat. And Miss Bubbles is probably scared out of her wits. If she's survived this long.

"So the check's going to be for five grand."

"Huh? You're joking."

"Five thousand dollars. But you'll have to sign papers saying you won't sue. But, I mean, five grand. It's a lot of money. Nothing to them, of course, but a lot of money."

You know those moments where you feel like Dorothy stuck in the funnel of the tornado, and all the details of your life whirl past your eyes in a deluge of smudged color?

That's how I feel right now. Dizzy.

Five grand. More money than I've ever seen in my life. This makes me so angry, and in any other situation, I'd be jumping for joy. Five grand—enough to start a whole new life. Or a new career as a cook. Or to set up shop in a town where strangers don't yell at you in foreign languages and the bars close at a decent hour. But how can I get excited about money when Miss Bubbles is gone?

"That makes me even sadder, Kevin."

He agrees with me. "Well, I'll miss her, too. Now I have to deal with a Chihuahua named Phil who can do a back flip. Shirley threw a fit."

By this point in the conversation, my stomach is completely in knots. It's all I can do to not start crying. I tell Kevin as much and hang up. I finish my coffee, get into the shower and moan while I wash. I want Miss Bubbles to come home. I don't want Frances's dumb hush money.

When I've dressed and dried my hair and not put on my mole, and when I've looked in the mirror and realized I have nothing to ask for, I go into the kitchen and start cooking.

Eggs with spinach and onion. Lemon pancakes with strawberry topping—made from my wedding fruit leftovers—bacon and home fries. While I cook, so obviously for two, I pretend to not notice that there has been no vacuum sound upstairs. No walking around, either. And no typing.

When all the food is cooked and the table has been set for two and the food evenly distributed between two table settings, I go outside to my patio and look up at Christian's apartment to see if he's even home. No lights on. I go back inside and look at all the food. I grab one of the plates. Pancakes and powdered sugar, eggs and bacon and strawberries topped with a sprig of mint and dollop of whipped cream. I grab my keys and am about to run for the door, when someone knocks.

"Steve?"

And then I hear it. The voice that now has the power to make me faint.

"Just open the door, will you?" Christian kicks the door with his foot and I start to turn every which way, momentarily robbed of the ability to place a simple plate on the counter and open a door. I turn myself around at least three times before I figure out what to do; Christian is sighing and knocking and shuffling. And I'm an idiot on the other side of the door.

Finally my sense returns. I put the food plate back on the table and rip the door open. And get attacked by a flying, ten-pound, white furball.

"Miss Bubbles!" She lands square on my chest with her paws around my neck and starts licking my face like crazy and making these sweet gurgling sounds in her throat.

"Miss Bubbles! You sweet little thing!" I can't believe it! I look at Christian in the doorway and he's grinning at us. Miss

Bubbles lets out a long whistle and I dance her around in a circle until she's whistling up a storm and I'm crying like a little baby. "Oh, Miss Bubbles! Miss Bubbles! Miss Bubbles!" I say. And I do one more rotation of my jubilation dance. "You're such a brave girl! Were you scared?" I am petting her furiously, and she's meowing like a, well, like a very happy pussycat who just found her mama. "Well you never have to go to that stupid old theater again, okay? Okay sweetheart?"

I kiss her head furiously and she licks my neck before settling her head on my shoulder. We stand. Woman and cat, hugging in front of my door. And then I walk to Christian and throw my arms around him, trapping Miss Bubbles in between us. "You found her for me. I don't, I don't know what I can do—"

He shifts his weight and steps away from us. His voice so quietly says, "Stell, I didn't do anything. She just came home, is all." He shuffles his feet a bit. "She was standing in the backyard last night and meowing her head off at your back door, but you weren't home. So I went down the fire escape and got her." He scratches Miss Bubbles behind her left ear. "She found you."

Miss Bubbles curls up in my arms and lifts her right ear up to Christian's hand. We stare at her like she's a new baby. "Are you hungry sweetheart? 'Cause I've got lots of food for you."

"Don't worry, I gave her a can of tuna."

Miss Bubbles picks up her head and meows at him. "I think she's inviting you in," I say in a really soft, not-at-all-like-me voice. Christian takes a small step into my apartment and we face each other. Then Miss Bubbles leaps out of my arms and runs into my room.

"Thank you, Christian."

"I didn't do anything, Stella."

I take a deep breath. "Yes, you did." I run my tongue over my teeth and nibble at my lower lip. Words aren't coming. There's so much to say and no words. Thank God Christian knows how to make conversation.

"So no more theater for Miss Bubbles?"

"Yeah, no more. They replaced her." Christian does a double take when I say this.

"I'm sorry, Stella. I know how important that show was to you."

I retreat into my apartment and lean against the breakfast bar. "Actually, I don't think she liked it very much, so it's okay."

He continues to stand near the door. "What about you, though?"

"Well, actually, I wanted to show you something." I grab a business card and thrust it in his face.

He takes it from my hand and inspects it, looks up at me and then back at the card. "Stella's Sweet Supplies. What is this?"

"My new life," I reply, studying his features. How come I never noticed how nice he looks? He's holding my business card and rubbing his thumb across the top.

"A cook, huh?" He takes one step toward me.

"A cook." I stay right where I am and try to slow my heart rate down by breathing steadily through my nose.

"And the acting thing?"

I smile and gain the courage to take a step of my own toward him. I take his hand in mine and look at him. "Christian, do you want to have breakfast with me? I made all your favorites."

"Breakfast? With you? Here?" Christian looks at the plates of food and then back at me, complete puzzlement on his face.

"Breakfast. And, now that we're talking about it, I was thinking that since you seem to like my cooking and all, and since you've been my unofficial taste-tester for almost as long I've lived here, that, well, maybe, well, I was thinking that maybe we could make it official, you know, like you could be my official person from now on." I have never been so tongue-tied in my life. I check to see if he understands what I'm trying to tell him.

Christian takes a step back and crosses his arms. He looks me up and down and scratches the side of his head. Then he laughs, takes a half step toward me and puts his arm tentatively around my waist. His other hand goes to my cheek and he says, "I'll have to think about this."

"Really?" This comes out of my mouth sounding all breathy and sexy, and I can't concentrate anyway because Christian starts rubbing his finger up and down my cheek.

He continues this as he says, "Maybe I could do it, but I don't know. We should negotiate." I wrinkle up my brow. This whole scene is just getting to be too much for me. The doublespeak! My God, the doublespeak. I jump out of his arms and run back three whole steps.

"Christian, do you love me?" I shout this at him and I can see the confusion descend upon him.

"Whuh?" he squints at me.

"Okay, because I just realized yesterday that I am crazy mad in love with you, and I want to cook your every meal, and listen to every detail about your day and have you be my guy."

Christian just looks at me, quizzically, like I'm a sideshow freak. "Okay. Okay."

"Did you hear the part where I said I was in love with you?"

"I heard it. I heard it."

"Well?"

He walks over to me. Six whole steps. He places both hands on my waist and pulls me into his body. He smells so good, I can't help myself. I launch myself at him and wrap my arms around his neck. "I'm really sorry, Christian. I've been a bigger than big jerk to you." He touches the back of my head.

"You have," he whispers into my hair. "But I love you anyway."

I pull back to look at him. "Well, kiss me quick before the food gets cold."

And he does. And Miss Bubbles comes running out of her hiding place and curls up around our feet while I get my own happy ending.

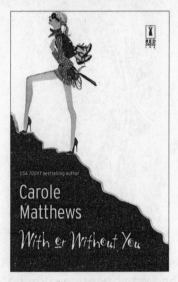

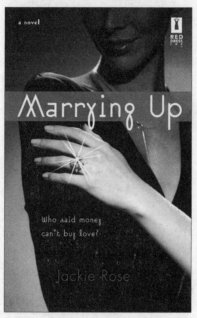

Are you getting it at least twice a month?

Here's how: Try RED DRESS INK books on for size & receive two FREE gifts!

Bombshell
by Lynda Curnyn

As Seen on TV
by Sarah Mlynowski

YES! Send my two FREE books.
There's no risk and no purchase required—ever!

Please send me my two FREE books and bill me just 99¢ for shipping and handling. I may keep the books and return the shipping statement marked "cancel." If I do not cancel, about a month later I will receive 2 additional books at the low price of just $11.00 each in the U.S. or $13.56 each in Canada, a savings of over 15% off the cover price (plus 50¢ shipping and handling per book*). I understand that accepting the two free books places me under no obligation ever to buy any books. I can always return a shipment and cancel at any time. Even if I never buy another book from Red Dress Ink, the free books are mine to keep forever.

- -

160 HDN D34M 360 HDN D34N

_____
Name (PLEASE PRINT)

_____
Address   Apt. #

_____
City   State/Prov.   Zip/Postal Code

***Want to try another series? Call 1-800-873-8635
or order online at www.TryRDI.com/free.***

**In the U.S. mail to: 3010 Walden Ave., P.O. Box 1867, Buffalo, NY 14240-1867
In Canada mail to: P.O. Box 609, Fort Erie, ON L2A 5X3**

*Terms and prices subject to change without notice. Sales tax applicable in N.Y.
**Canadian residents will be charged applicable provincial taxes and GST.

All orders subject to approval. Offer limited to one per household.
® and ™ are trademarks owned and used by the trademark owner and/or its licensee.

© 2004 Harlequin Enterprises Ltd.

RED DRESS INK™

RDI04-TR